*Those who dare to touch the gods
suffer both heaven and hell . . .*

All my pent-up worries and attraction boiled up in an instant, spilling over. "You're playing me like a freaking violin, just like every other god has done when they got involved with a mortal!" My voice rose in pitch and decibel level. "And who's the one that always ends up getting turned into a toad or a tree stump or dying some horrible death in the end? Not the eternal goddamned god, that's for sure!

I stopped, hyperventilating.

His copper eyes bore through me. "If I were any kind of man at all I would get up, come over there and kiss the hell out of you right now until all this stupidity faded away to nothing."

My eyes widened and my knees threatened to buckle.

"But that would simply be one more example of my terrible influence over you and proof positive that all your accusations of psychological and sexual manipulation are true."

We stared at each other for a very long time.

Impasse.

◇◇◇◇◇◇◇◇◇

**Also by Cate Montana**
Non-fiction:
*Unearthing Venus: My Search for the Woman Within*
*The E Word: Ego, Enlightenment & Other Essentials*

Co-author:
*The Heart of the Matter: A Guide to Discovering Gifts in Strange Wrapping Paper*
*Ghetto Physics*

ISBN 978-0-9998354-3-2

Copyright © 2019 by Cate Montana

Rampant Feline Media 2019
www.rampantfelinemedia.com

Cover art by Suzette Mafi

*To the Divine Feminine within us all.*

# Apollo & Me

# CHAPTER ONE

The bookstore was quaint, in a peeling paint kind of way, and empty of customers—a grim situation for an author at a book signing. I'd been told the place had a huge following, which is why I'd passed up the Barnes & Noble at the mall in Braintree, Massachusetts, opting for this vintage venue. And the name had grabbed me: Adams Family Books & Sundries.

There was a maroon leather book in a storage unit back in Washington State with *Adams Family* engraved in gold on the cover, and my name, Kathryn Adams, was one of the last entries in the genealogy charts. When I'd told the proprietor that Sam Adams, the firebrand cousin of President John Quincy Adams, had been my great-something grandfather, he'd crowed, "I can guarantee a local crowd with that on the flyer."

*So much for my genetic advantage.* Pulling my sweater more tightly around my shoulders, I turned to watch the snow drifting past the old-fashioned gas lamps lighting Main Street. It was a dreamy scene and I could easily imagine one of my ancestors trotting past on a horse, tricorn hat dusted with white, headed somewhere on an important nighttime mission.

"Shame about the weather."

Startled out of my reverie, I looked around to find the lanky owner standing behind me, rheumy eyes unexpectedly kind. "No kidding," I replied, glancing at the wall clock. "But it's not eight o'clock quite yet."

I watched him shuffle toward the back of the store, wondering yet again if he were a distant, twenty-times-removed cousin by marriage. But getting information out of New Englanders was like trying to pry a pearl out of a fresh oyster. Undoubtedly, I would never know.

The unexpected sound of the small iron bell over the door and a sudden blast of frigid air announced a last-moment visitor. Whipping around, I saw a heavyset man in an expensive-looking black wool coat and hat coming into the store. He slid inside, hurriedly closing the door behind him, stamping his feet, knocking off the snow.

Unconsciously reaching for my gold "now I'm a famous author and deserve this" autograph pen, I sat up smartly as he clumped over to my table. "You Miz Adams?" he asked in clipped New England tones.

"Yes, I am," I replied. "And you are . . . ?"

"Michael Williams."

I recalled the name and sagged back in my chair, dismayed. *I told Lisa not hook me up again!*

"I'm your driver."

*Yeah, right*, I thought, glum mood deepening.

He peeled back a black leather glove and glanced at his wristwatch. "Lisa Hagan said you'd be wrapping up at eight?"

"Wow, I'm sorry Michael, I told her not to have you bother."

"It's no trouble at all, ma'am."

I looked out the window at the veritable tsunami of snow and smiled at the lie. But really, "Ma'am?" Who called a woman that anymore? *Unless you're in the military or she's like a million years old.* Jesus, did I look as tired as I suddenly felt?

Shrugging at the inevitability of enduring one more date set by my match-making literary agent, I mustered a smile and shook hands. "Might as well pack it in, I guess. You're the only one who's showed up all evening."

It didn't take long. The store owner, grateful to close early, promised to keep a few signed copies on hand and ship the rest of the books back to the distributor. Before I knew it I'd been bundled into my "driver's" luxuriously overheated black Lexus sedan and was slowly heading out of the historical district of old Braintree toward my Airbnb digs.

"Are you hungry?"

Aside from "Where's your hotel?" and "Is the car too hot for you?" it was the first thing he'd said. Even for a New Englander, Michael was taciturn. Eyeing his paunchy form in the semi-dark, I weighed my options. I was famished and tired and wanted some red wine, a steak, and a long soak in a hot tub of water. And after the lonely evening spent in the bookshop some company was deeply welcome. I just didn't want to do a lot of heavy conversational lifting.

"I know a good steak place near here."

That clinched it. "God, yes! That sounds great!"

The restaurant was warm and cozy and a bottle of Merlot helped Michael find his tongue. After that, it was tough getting a word in edgewise. By the time we'd finished eating and I'd been safely deposited outside the entrance to my rented room, I was zoned out and ready for bed. Thanking him for rescuing me from the blizzard and for dinner, I wished him a safe journey home and that was that. I didn't even give him my card.

⊙⊙⊙⊙⊙⊙⊙⊙⊙

"So, how'd it go?" Lisa's voice over my cellphone speaker competed with the sounds of bathwater running in the background.

"Awful," I said, wiping away my eye makeup with a cream-smeared tissue.

"'Awful'?"

"Worse than awful." Gobs of lotion stuck to my lashes, turning my world opaque. "Nobody Lisa. Nobody showed up. It snowed all day. A freaking blizzard demolished the last day of my book tour."

She sighed. "What did you think of Michael?"

Eyes stinging, I groped for another tissue. "You mean the blind date I explicitly told you not to find me?"

"That's the one."

"Quiet and self-absorbed, but a nice guy. Better than most of them these last three months." I tossed the tissues into the wastebasket. "Good thing you're my agent and not my pimp. I'd have fired you ages ago."

"Two for the price of one, such a deal you're getting." She hesitated. "You sound exhausted," she said, flatly.

"I am," I replied. "Who would've thought that living the dream could be so undreamy?"

"So now what?"

I stared at my image in the mirror. Despite the winter tan from the two-week Florida section of my book tour and the exuberantly short, platinum-blonde haircut, for once I looked my age. Every single one of my 60 years was clearly visible under the unflattering bathroom lights' glare, from the dark bags under my hazel eyes to the tired sag of my not-quite-full-enough mouth.

My furniture was in storage, I had no home and no sense of where to settle next. *And no one to go home to* came the unwelcome thought. The silence turned awkward, speaking volumes. I sighed heavily. "I'm back in Olympia for five months house-sitting while my friend Pat is in Hong Kong. After that . . . " I let the words die.

Lisa knew my situation every bit as well as I did. *God bless agents*. The good ones were not just good, they were fans and then, with any luck, they became friends. Lisa had been down the road with me through two book launches now. What was it, four years? Five?

"Here's an idea," she chirped as if she'd just

come up with it. "Why don't you take yourself off to that little Greek island you're so damned fond of? Use what's left of your advance and go hook up with a handsome foreign lover and have some fun for a change."

"Right. Like I'm ever going to do something like that."

"You never know."

"Lisa, I was raised in Virginia." I stressed the *virgin* part of the word. "That's the South, remember? The sixties didn't happen there—or the seventies. Maybe not even the eighties. The lover odds are stacked against me."

"Stranger things have happened."

She was surely right about that.

"The change will do you good."

She was surely right about that, too.

❀❀❀❀❀❀❀❀❀

# CHAPTER TWO

Which is how, five months later, I ended up sitting on a hill above the temple of Apollo outside the archaeological site boundary fences in Delphi, enjoying an unobstructed view of the stadium and the tourist-packed precinct below.

Spring breezes wafted through wild oats, purple anemones and tiny daisies, setting the flower heads bobbing, providing relief from the intense heat of the Mediterranean sun. Somewhere close by a cuckoo was doing its famous song. When all of sudden the general peace erupted as a boldly athletic man bounded over the rocks and brush out of seeming nowhere. Wearing stylishly torn jeans, Nikes, an "Apollo Rocks" t-shirt stretched across ripped biceps and an earth-shattering smile, he walked right up to me and sat down.

Reaching into a pocket (how he could get a hand into those jeans is beyond me) he pulled out a pack of Trident gum. "Ne?" (yes) he offered.

I couldn't believe it. Shaking my head, I gave him my best "go away" glare. Unabashed, he took a piece and started chewing, companionably silent, well-muscled arms wrapped around his bent knees, staring out across the temples and the Pleistos river valley below.

I'd done the crowd thing at the temples yesterday, enduring packs of school children, herds of Japanese and throngs of cellphone-brandishing tourists taking selfies in front of every ancient crumbling column and wall. Hell, I'd been one of them.

But today was getaway day. I hadn't clambered up the rocky, dusty, satisfyingly empty E4 trail above the village of Delphi in search of company. If I'd known enough Greek I would have haughtily delivered Garbo's famous "I want to be alone" line. Instead, I nodded pleasantly, said, "Kalimera," put my hiking sandals back on and started to get up. Lightly he touched my arm.

"Parakalo. Diamoni. Please. Stay."

Alarmed, I faced him square on. He was devastatingly handsome in a classic Greek sense, somewhere in his thirties, with full chiseled lips, straight nose and dark, curly, reddish-brown hair playing over and around his broad intelligent forehead.

None of this was reassuring.

But it was his eyes . . . large, luminous, copper-colored eyes, thickly fringed with long lashes, deep as two wells full of . . . what? Laughter? Sadness? Wisdom? Hope? Despair? I sank as I read the mixed messages, plummeting helplessly into their depths, drinking him in, knowing in one heartbeat I could never drink enough.

Abruptly I sat back amongst the flowers, inexplicably feeling comfortable in his presence, happy even. It was as if . . . *weird* . . . it was as if I knew him. Actually, it felt as if I had *always* known him. Which was, of course, impossible. How would I know a young Greek guy from Delphi? I hadn't traveled the mainland portion of the country since I was 19, and I had no Greek friends aside from the ones I'd cultivated two years previously on the island of Paros where I'd lived for three months while finishing my last book. Pushing a stray lock of sweat-streaked platinum hair out of my eyes, I studied him, confused. Surely, if I'd met this guy before I would remember?

He bobbed his head graciously and looked away over the jagged cliffs rising above the ruins across from us and sighed. "Efkaristo. Thank you." After a timeless time he nodded towards the valley. "It is beautiful, yes?

A neutral statement. A safe statement . . . as if anything about this man could possibly be labeled "safe." I inhaled, only then realizing I'd been holding my breath, and followed his gaze. It was beautiful—although the overworked word failed to capture the essence of the place. *What words could possibly fit?* I wondered, momentarily distracted. *Alive. Vibrant. Ancient. The rocky bosom of the Great Mother jutting towards heaven, sweet springs gushing like milk from the rocky clefts offering refreshment to her human children who came seeking nourishment and succor, relief from sorrow, desiring hope and understanding, giving their worship and awe in return for a little divine direction.*

"Yes," he said softly. "And more. So much more."

I jerked around. His eyes locked on mine and

before I could gasp or react they pulled me in a second time and I moved—body and soul—into and through those eyes as if they were twin bronzed gates. The sun blotted out as I left the meadow and wild flowers behind, senses dissolving into a rush of sudden blackness. And yet there still was a "me." Pure consciousness moving through the deep. The remnants of long-dead star brushed past, a silent ghost beyond memory. Then came its bright birth and a whole galaxy of other stars aborning.

What was happening? Everything was here in the void . . . the stars, the Earth, the flowers, the meadow, the temple, the tourists below, my births and deaths, too numerous and fleeting to catch—all danced here in the black light of this forever place, real and not real, waiting to be born and at the same time existing full-blown in the light of Earth's day and at the same time long faded to nothing . . . all possible potentials drifting in and out of space and time like breath.

It lasted but a moment? An aeon? A heartbeat? And then I was back, sitting in the sun, the winds of Parnassus in my hair, staring into pools of liquid copper.

*What the hell?* I was no stranger to altered states of consciousness. In the 30 years I'd spent studying and writing about psychology, human consciousness and spirituality, I'd had plenty of strange experiences, from visions to full-on out-of-body experiences. I'd also explored more than my fair share of plant medicines working with shamans in the jungles of Peru and Ecuador, drinking ayahuasca and huachuma. I'd even participated in Native American ceremonies with mescaline and smoked DMT, the crystallized poison milked from the sweat of the Sonoran desert toad. But never in my life had I been psychically pulled out of my body by another human being and catapulted into the multiverse. On five minutes acquaintance no less!

I shot to my feet. "What the hell did you do to me?" I cried, panicked all over again, ready to run. "Who are you?"

"Would you like the answers in any particular order?" he replied mildly.

I just stared at him, breathing hard.

"No? Well. First, I did not do anything to you. I simply cut through the awkward introductions by showing you some additional dimensions of information within what you call 'you' that are, by the way, quite available any time you care to open your mind to see them."

He snapped his gum. "However, I suggest you relax more the next time I take you inside me. The multiverse is quite the place. And I," he performed a seated bow, one golden-brown hand splayed across his broad chest, "am an excellent guide."

My mind splintered in a thousand directions. "Who . . . who . . . who . . ." *Jesus, I sound like an owl.*

"Really?" he laughed, interrupting my stutters. "You have to ask?" He pointed to his t-shirt. "Apollo Rocks." There it was—white ink on black cotton shouting the impossible.

*No no no!* It was beyond impossible! Heart pounding, my knees started to shake uncontrollably. *This is insane!* Legs giving way beneath me, I collapsed on the grass, mind whirling.

And yet . . .

Beneath the mental and emotional turmoil, there was something else happening inside me. I could feel a strange undercurrent of some other emotion . . . was it . . . joy? *You came back!* I could swear I heard a woman's exultant cry echoing in the distance, bouncing off the indifferent cliff face of Parnassus. And then the impression vanished.

I took a few ragged breaths, steadying myself. And as I did I saw that, despite my panic and rejection and required modern incredulity, somehow I believed him. Had somehow known who he was the instant I saw him bounding over the rocks towards me.

My companion nodded in satisfaction. "Yes, please. Do yourself the honor of believing what you already know. So many people spend so much time playing games in their heads." He shook his own head, longish curls bobbing, and sighed. "Such a waste."

My mind raced so fast it went blank. My heart continued to pound. Far below us tourists chattered and laughed, jostling for position to snap pictures of the stadium. And for a while, perforce, we just sat, Apollo and me, as my mouth opened and shut several times on the multitude of thoughts and questions stampeding through my brain. *The gods are just myths, don't you know that? Why show yourself to me? Come here often?* Finally, "What's it like?" managed to escape my lips.

"Being a forgotten god?" He shrugged. "Humbling, I suppose."

He didn't look humble. I took a deep breath, doing my best to relax, and really *looked* at him. And I realized he looked . . . present. Powerful. Imposing. Quiet. And yet real. Very real. And normal even. A fabulous-looking guy in t-shirt and blue jeans, fairly brimming over with life like a person should be.

"You got it," he said.

"What?"

"What I really am."

"And that is?"

"What people should be."

"Meaning?"

"There are a lot of words describing what I am."

"Such as?"

He thought for a moment and shrugged a very Greek shrug. "Etheric blueprint comes closest in your language."

*Huh?* It took a few moments for his response to make any sense to my over-heated brain. "A thought-form pattern?" I murmured. "For what?"

He cocked an eyebrow at me, silently commanding me to think. "Us?" I whispered tremulously. "Human beings?"

"Yes," he said, nodding approval. "Etheric template is another term. Or archetype. That is what all of us are."

By "us" I assumed he was referring to the rest of the Olympian gods and goddesses who once took center stage in people's minds and hearts 2,500 years ago.

"Ne," he affirmed. "Personally, I was created to be the archetype of masculine beauty, knowledge and wisdom . . . among others things."

"But," I reached out a tentative hand and touched his arm. "You're physical."

"What kind of template for mortality would I be if I could not take mortal form?"

"But ..."

"We are getting ahead of ourselves," he interrupted. "Why don't you ask me one of the simpler human questions you are aching to ask, such as 'Gee, Apollo, why are you talking to me'?"

Apollo. I couldn't get my lips to even form the name. And yet I supposed I must call him something.

"There are many names I have been called by humanity to choose from." Again, he read my mind with ease. "Pythios, Phoibos, Delphinian, Loxias, Lukeios, Daphnephoros." He thought for a moment. "How about Iatros?"

"What does that mean?" I asked.

"Physician."

I eyed him warily. "Is that how you see yourself nowadays?"

He sighed. "I am so thin on the ground I can barely see myself at all. But yes, I suppose that is the best way to describe my role in the current situation."

Physician. Healer. It had been one of Apollo's

most important jobs back in the day. Then his words sank in. *Current situation.* I connected the dots and definitely didn't care for the implications. "You think I need healing?" I asked, ego pricked.

"Who among you does not?" He jerked his chiseled chin in the direction of the teeming throngs in the temple below.

Of course, he was right. Humanity, as a whole, was wildly screwed up. But his words only made my sudden irritation deepen. All I could hear was that I was just one more cow in the herd. Just one more obviously inadequate, bumbling, screwed-up human for him to have to deal with compared to his equally obvious divine and glorious perfection.

"No," he said, abruptly. "You are not one of the herd and I am not perfect. At least, not in the way you mean it. I am what I am. Although . . ." his swift smile was back, "you could say I am perfectly what I am."

*Damn!* I couldn't have a single thought that was my own around this guy.

"Sorry," he blurted, not sounding sorry at all. "Thought is as clear as words spoken once you get the hang of it." Idly he plucked a flower and twirled it between his fingers.

I was so overwhelmed by the sheer magnitude of *him* and what was happening, I'd already lost track of what we were talking about.

"We were talking about perfection."

"Oh. Yeah. What about it?"

"It is a total limitation."

"What?"

"Everything and everyone is perfect right now, Ekateríni, just as they are . . . simply because they exist," he explained, earnestly.

Intellectually I knew what he'd just said was true. But suddenly it didn't seem to matter. As fascinating as the conversation was, I found myself suddenly derailed—staring at that full, Cupid's bow mouth as if nothing else mattered in the entire universe, longing to hear him repeat my given name, Kathryn, in Greek one more time, caressing the syllables with his lips.

What the hell was wrong with me?

I shook my head to clear it of the fog of sudden, acute longing and failed. It was as if . . . what? Again a faint whisper called from a distance and then faded, leaving me groping for an explanation for the powerful attraction to this man . . . er . . . being, that seemed so natural and familiar. I was so befuddled I didn't even stop to wonder how he knew my name.

To cover my confusion, I pretended to study the temple compound below. No wonder this guy had had such a following! The very model of beauty, intelligence and charisma, to this day thousands worshipped at his shrines, bowing down to him with cameras and videos, euros, dollars and yen. People worldwide studied him in classrooms and read and wrote books about him. And here we sat. *Wow.* Apollo and me. *Dear God, all the statues don't do him justice.*

A sudden wave of self-consciousness washed

over me and I found myself vehemently  wishing I were 30 years old once more.

"Ekateríni? Hello?"

I shook myself and came back down to earth. "Sure. Yes. I got it." I waved my hand to include the mountains and everything else. "All this is perfect just as it is, and so are human beings."

"Ne," he nodded. "Exactly." Then, studying me, he frowned,

And before my eyes the stunning viral male sitting next to me slowly began to morph into a crumpled old man with sagging jowls, withered, age-spotted hands, rotting teeth and greasy, thinning, grey hair. "Stho," the word took on a whistling lisp through several pink-gummed gaps. "Would you have thtayed to lithen to me if I had thown up like thith? Would you be tho enthralled by my prethenth?"

????!!!!!

"Do you think thith, too, ith perfect?" He waved his hands indicating his decrepit body.

I sat, mute and trembling, as his rheumy eyes probed deep to the core of my soul. Then, before my shocked mind could even begin to absorb what was happening, he morphed back into his gorgeous youthful self, shaking his head, sternly. "I know you do not. And if you tell me you do I will call you a liar."

Shaking like a leaf, heart galloping—the only thing keeping me upright and conscious were his eyes boring relentlessly through me. Before I could think a coherent thought, he reached out his hand

and drew his index finger down the skin of my left bicep. My flesh crinkled dryly at the passage of his touch. I watched the tracing and a great weeping rose in me.

"You hate getting old." Eyes fierce and challenging, he leaned into me. "So . . ." sibilant threat replaced his former lisp. "What would you give to have your youth given back to you, Ekateríni?"

I recoiled in shock, but his eyes held mine. He wasn't kidding. My tears vanished in a heartbeat and hope shot through me like wildfire. *Is it possible?*

"Of course, it is possible. I am a god am I not?"

His voice was silky now, his eyes intense. And as I looked, the same finger that had drawn attention to the aging of my flesh traced back up my left arm. And with his touch came spring.

I could feel the tingling.

I saw my fingers, which had only recently begun to sport a few slightly enlarged knuckles, smooth, straighten and lengthen. "Your hands . . . you use them to make music on the God's own instrument. *My* instrument."

*My instrument?*

Of course. Apollo was the god of music. His instrument was the lyre and I played the harp. "They should be strong and true," he whispered, "to sing my praises." I watched in fascination as the skin of my hand and wrist turned rosy, soft and pliable.

*I remember this hand!*

Up my forearm, past my elbow, youth's flush rose. Past my bicep, now firm and strong.

*I remember this arm!*

"Shall I continue?"

His finger stopped its tracing. I couldn't tear my eyes away from the miracle unfolding beneath his hands, unfolding within me. It was as if an IV were dripping vigor back into limbs that hadn't even known life was slowly fading. My lower back suddenly held no stiffness. My heart raced and skipped with joy.

*Yes!*

I wanted this. I wanted it like nothing else. Had wanted it for years. Age was no friend and I despised it. I who had once been so strong and athletic—so lithe of limb and intoxicatingly juicy with life—had begun to feel old. And I hated it. Every bit of it. Even the word itself.

"More?" His eyes recaptured mine. "Yes?"

I quivered on the brink, my yearning total, the word already formed in my heart, racing on wings to reach my lips before he changed his mind.

"And in return," his warm hand was on my left breast, his face hovering inches from mine, copper eyes blazing, holding me transfixed. The nipple beneath his fingers rose quickly at his touch and electricity shot through my womb. My longing grew violent, taking on a new and different form.

"And in return will you worship me?"

God help me, I already did. Desire searing my body, unthinkingly I surrendered to his touch. Little Miss Virginia who wouldn't even *consider* kissing a man on the first date—Ms. Lonely Hearts who hadn't been with a man in years and didn't think she ever would be again—was instantly, shockingly, out of control. *It has been so long! This feeling . . . this fire! Oh, God!*

His hand pulled away and he rocked backwards. I cried out, bereft, leaning into him, seeking his power, his body, his touch. Blindly reaching out, my hands struck his chest, one old, one renewed, and snake-like they wound their way upwards, locking behind his neck, pulling him back towards me until his eyes were inches from mine. Cold, calculating, hungry eyes. His lips softly parted, brushing mine, his breath as sweet as honey, and my tongue flicked out for a taste.

I wanted him! More than anything I'd ever wanted in my life. But even as my lips parted to admit his tongue, I heard a thin, far distant inner cry: *What are you doing?*

I pushed the thought away. I knew what I was doing. My body remembered the joy of it and I gladly surrendered to his probing tongue. But the nagging whisper was coming nearer, pursuing me: *This isn't right. There's something wrong here.*

*Shut up!*
*You know this isn't right.*
*Shut up! I'm doing this!*
*No, you're not.*
*I want this!!*

In response to my desperate inner battle, Apollo deepened his kiss, one arm encircling my waist, pulling me closer as his other hand explored my breast. My body shuddered under the mix of desire and denial.

*NO!!*

I jerked my lips away from his and drew a ragged breath. It was like tearing myself in half. The air beyond his mouth tasted stale and wearisome.

"Let go," he whispered, lips against my throat, trailing fire.

The entirety of my being groaned. Trembling, I drew another deep breath and slowly unclasped his neck. An agonized wail sounded through me. *Noooooo!!*

Slowly, I drew my hands across his shoulders and down his powerful chest, savoring his heat, admiring every square centimeter of male flesh beneath the taut cotton . . . still aching with need but knowing my terrible weakness—and thus his immediate power over me—was finished.

And I didn't want it to be.

*Goddammit.*

I pushed him away.

*Goddammit!!* Every electrified cell of my body, every atom of my being shouted my name, demanding attention, commanding me to give in and to let go . . . to have what I so desperately wanted and longed for.

Him.

And my youth.

My beautiful beautiful lost youth.

Tortured by my choice, my mind still arguing, my body singing its sorrow, I closed my eyes to savor, for just one moment more the possibility . . .

*No!*

*Alright, alright!* I sighed heavily, opened my eyes and patted his chest as I pulled completely away. "Nice try handsome."

Part of me—most of me—couldn't believe it. I was really doing this? I was really accepting age and endings?! I was honestly accepting my mortality when I had a choice? When I had a freaking *Olympic god* giving me the opportunity for eternal youth?

*Are you out of your mind?* the voice inside me shrieked.

Perhaps.

Probably.

I sighed as I searched inwards for the answer to this astounding choice. I wasn't accepting my mortality exactly. It was more like . . . like . . . *oh hell.* Resolution flowed faster through my veins as I was filled with a sudden felt sense of the rightness of what I was doing. There were no words or reasons for my choice, just a feeling that seeing life through the way it was supposed to be lived and letting it flow along its natural course, just like everyone else was destined to do, was the right path for me.

"You are sure?" He tipped my chin up with his fingertips, forcing me to meet green-flecked copper eyes.

I nodded.

Too tired, suddenly, to even speak, I let my hands drop from his arms.

With a slow movement, Apollo passed the palms

of his hands in front of my body, and the process of reversal began. Mournfully, I noted the retreating tide, the loss of sap, the sudden return of the slight sags and stiffness, the aches and twinges, all of which had magically vanished at his touch.

It was not a thing that brought gladness.

But it did return me to me.

∞∞∞∞∞∞∞

We'd moved out of the sun and into the shade of a bay laurel tree.

I lay on my back amidst the wildflowers and grasses, eyes closed. Tears still dripped down my temples and into my hair as my companion plucked a haunting tune on an authentic Hellenic lyre—a golden one no less. But I was too tapped out to care. Too sad to be amazed. Too filled with . . .

What?

I had no idea how I felt. Diminished? Expanded? Exalted? Empty?

"Does it have to be one thing or another?" he asked quietly, still plucking chords that danced into the breeze to mix with bird song and the distant bleating of goats.

"No." I said, sighing. "But human emotions are rarely simple." He shifted the tune to a spritely air and, despite myself, my heart lifted. "No wonder life is so confusing."

He stopped playing.

I lay there listening to the wind pluck its own tune through the leaves. And suddenly I realized he wasn't there any longer. I didn't even have to open my eyes to check. I could feel his absence—like a tiny piece of the sun itself had disappeared.

"Helios . . ." was that his voice, echoing as from a great distance? *Of course*, I thought. Helios, Bringer of Light . . . another name of his after the sun itself.

I sat up and looked around. He was gone. Had he ever been here? Apparently he had, for there was a flattened spot on the grass a few feet away. In the near distance the cuckoo called and I started, remembering there was such a thing as time and that I had—of all things—a bus to catch back to Athens.

I got to my feet stifling a groan, remembering Jane Fonda's advice to women about not giving voice to the aches and pains of age lest we announce the passing of our years to others around us.

*No pain, no gain.*

Her famous 1980s work-out advice rattled in my brain and I tasted the bitter irony of the words. Grimly, I shouldered my backpack and headed back down the mountain.

❀❀❀❀❀❀❀❀

## CHAPTER THREE

I spent the three-hour trip on the bus back to Athens and the rest of that night in my Airbnb room rehashing my experience on the mountain.

Was I crazy? Had it really happened? How could something like that have happened? But then why not? The Apollo cult at Delphi had been built around visions. For over a thousand years the prophecies of the Pythia, the priestess mouthpiece of Apollo, had been sought by kings and queens, pharaohs and generals. Was what happened to me so different?

*It's the 21ˢᵗ century. It was broad daylight. You weren't in a cave inhaling hallucinogenic gases and you aren't a priestess. You're a supposedly sane writer taking a well-deserved holiday.*

Yes, well, minor details.

Again my thoughts traveled back to my strange attraction for the man, or whatever the hell he was, and my even more wildly strange choice. *Why, oh why, if what happened really happened, did I do what I did?*

How could I possibly have turned him down? How could I have been that stupid? And yet how could I have done anything different?

Around and around my mind spun in an exhausting circle until the birds and the church bells announced a new dawn and light spilled over the white-tiled terrace of my room overlooking the narrow streets of the Plaka district crowded around the rocky marble base of the Acropolis.

Somewhere in the middle of my sleepless night I remembered I had a one o'clock lunch date with an old school friend from America who was living in Athens—a woman I hadn't seen in 20 years who was running a cultural exchange program for students and adults. As I lay there, fretting, I couldn't help but wonder what she would say if at some point during our planned lunch I leaned over my Greek salad and casually said, "Guess who I ran into on Mt. Parnassus the other day?"

*Yeah, good luck with that.*

I got up, bleary-eyed, wondering if maybe some exercise would clear my head. I took a shower in the cramped tiled bathroom that had obviously once been a closet, dressed in whatever came to hand, walked down the three flights of twisting stairs and stepped out onto the cobbled street.

The corner coffee shop was just opening and I grabbed a latte before heading towards the vast botanical gardens that stretched between the Plaka and Mets districts. Crossing one of Athens' major streets at dawn wasn't nearly as death-defying as later in the day, and I managed to walk and enjoy my coffee without spilling it like I had the last time I'd approached Hadrian's Arch in a mad dash across multiple lanes.

I entered the botanical park, which was relatively deserted at that hour, and ambled along, enjoying the

Mediterranean flora and fauna. An exquisite path through a tunnel of white wisteria loomed before me and I was just about to enter it when a man dodged in front of two young women pushing baby carriages and fell into step beside me.

I jumped sideways, spilling coffee over my hand. *Apollo!*

"Kalimera, Ekateríni!" he said. "What a beautiful morning!"

I stopped and gaped at him. He was just as gorgeous and filled with life as yesterday, hair, eyes and skin glowing in the morning light. After all my doubts of the night before I couldn't help myself. I reached out a trembling hand—the one not soaked with coffee—and touched his arm.

"It is I."

He was real! As real as anything else in this strange world I lived in.

"Glad to see me?"

Was I?

"I'm not sure glad is the right word," I said, drinking in his leather-jacketed, blue-jeaned form. *Blown away? Ecstatic? Freaked out?*

His eyes sparkled. "I would think you would be very glad to have the question of your sanity answered so quickly."

I tore my eyes away from him, the blood frantically pounding through my veins. With nothing else better to do, I walked into the arbor. I'd seen the movie *A Beautiful Mind*. Schizophrenics had these kinds of conversations all the time—at least the ones off their meds. Just because I thought he was walking beside me didn't mean he really was.

"Oh, come on," he said, reprovingly. "You know in your heart I am real. And I know you are glad to see me. Besides, you have longed to talk with beings from other dimensions for ages. Why the big surprise that I am here?"

"You're from another dimension?"

"Absolutely."

I cocked an eyebrow at him, mind spinning in all sorts of directions, crazy gladness mixing with shocked doubt, overlapped with growing curiosity and excitement.

A sudden breeze ruffled the trees and bushes around us, admitting a few shafts of golden morning sun which scattered across his face, setting his hair aglow. Instantly my emotions whipsawed from confused doubt to awe and then to amusement. If this was all a hallucination at least it was a pleasant one.

"I am so glad you find my presence pleasing."

A little boy ran our way through the flowered tunnel followed by his watchful mother. "Jeez. Why do I even bother opening my mouth if you can read my thoughts?"

"Because if I am the one doing all the talking," he opened his arms and did a quick spinning circle beside me, "people will think I am just one more handsome, self-centered Greek guy hitting on an older tourista for my own devious purposes."

I mustered a smile, pretending his barb about

my age hadn't hit home, knowing he knew it had. "And you're not?"

He laughed. "Ahhh, Ekateríni, there is indeed a purpose for our meeting. As for the age difference between us, it is indeed stunning. Just not in the way that worries you!" He winked and threw a casual arm around my shoulder, pulling me close to his shining warmth.

*God, he feels real!* I tried to pull away in mock outrage even as I felt myself melt at his touch. And suddenly the whole situation overwhelmed me. My sleepless night, my exhaustion, the feel of his body, his incandescent smile and cheerful words, the sheer craziness of his apparent presence—something in me surrendered to the odd ridiculousness of it all.

I laughed.

"That is better!" he enthused, pulling me tighter into a long-striding lock-step. "Ekateríni, I cannot tell you how glad I am to see you again! How glad I am we got all those disturbing preliminaries over with so quickly!"

I jerked away from his arm, laughter dying. "Preliminaries? What do you mean, preliminaries?" I stopped, hands on my hips, eyeing him suspiciously. "Preliminaries to what?"

Apollo stopped as well, nonplussed, saying nothing.

"Do you have any idea what you put me through yesterday? What I'm still going through? The anguish and confusion and . . ."

"That was yesterday, Ekateríni. That was

yesterday! Today," he threw his head back, arms
wide, encompassing the trees, the city, the traffic,
deeply inhaling the scent of exhaust fumes, jasmine
and wisteria, "is today! And we have much to discuss!
Come!" he grabbed my arm above the elbow. "Let
us go walk in my father's temple."

I shook free again, simultaneously intoxicated
by his enthusiasm and pissed at my responsiveness.
"Look," I said, practically shouting. "You can't just
come zooming in and grab me all helter-skelter.
I have plans. I'm headed somewhere. I'm . . ."
*completely wacko, shouting at thin air.* I glanced around.
The two women pushing prams caught up to us and
walked past, unconcerned.

"Ekateríni, why so angry with me?" He was all
Greek now, copper eyes concerned, sweetly coaxing,
bending close. "I must make it up to you, I think."

Making love to me with his voice.

I stood there exasperated and amused, vulnerable
and angry at what had happened the day before, still
agonizing over the missed opportunity. *Eternal youth
for God's sake!! What was I thinking???* Knowing there
had been no other choice.

I was also upset because he was right about
one thing. All my life I'd wished to be one of those
obviously special people that angels and aliens
showed up to talk to. And now that it had apparently
happened to me, what did I get? An archangel? An
inter-dimensional alien from an advanced race? An
ascended master? The immortal German alchemist
Compte de Saint Germain? Jesus? No. I got a self-

absorbed, mythological has-been with enough sex appeal to heat Chicago through a bad winter.

"I heard that, you know."

Embarrassed, I looked down at my hands and realized I was holding a cold cup of coffee in sticky fingers. Looking around for a trashcan, I dumped the cup and started walking again. Bird song and children's laughter grew louder and the traffic noise faded as we got deeper into the park.

I glanced sideways at my suddenly silent companion. He might not be real. But if he were an illusion he was certainly an earnest one. His happiness seeing me was obviously genuine. I had no idea why, but excitement fairly radiated from him. Why was I so intent on putting a damper on things? Why the sour grapes? Why couldn't I just accept the gift and enjoy the magic of what was happening?

I mean, why not?

At a certain point, doubt is a useless habit and a block to progress. For some reason this was happening to me. For some reason it was *him*. For some reason it was happening now, at a point in my life when I genuinely no longer cared about something like this happening at all. Well, almost didn't care.

I snorted at a sudden ironic thought. *You can have anything you want as long as you don't actually want it.*

At my side, Apollo chuckled appreciatively.

I stopped short and looked at him—really looked at him. And as the warm sense of odd familiarity washed through me yet again, the darkness of doubt let go its grip. Feeling a tangible surge of relief, heart and mind suddenly at peace, I sighed and smiled. "I'm having lunch with a friend but we're not meeting until one o'clock." I hooked my arm through his. "I have plenty of time to walk with you through your father's temple."

◌◌◌◌◌◌◌◌

Daddy, of course, was Zeus himself.

"Really?" I muttered, rummaging through my purse for the requisite number of euros to gain entrance to the temple grounds. "Couldn't you rustle up a few coins for yourself?"

The bored cashier waited. A few tourists approached the kiosk, flipping through their guidebooks and pamphlets. A little boy wiggled and whined for a treat while his father pulled out his wallet. Hands jammed in the pockets of his leather jacket, Apollo leaned against the kiosk, looking pleased. "Can't spoil the gigolo image," he whispered, bending close, jerking his chin towards my right. I glanced in the direction indicated and there stood a tall, gorgeous Nordic blonde waiting in line with her *husband? lover?* zeroing in on Apollo, pupils dilating, jaw sagging in unconscious admiration.

Aha!

Chills swept over my body. *Well well well*. That answered the "Is he real?" question. Thank God! Happiness and excitement flooded my body. On impulse I slipped my arm around Apollo's waist as I collected our tickets—a move that plainly said *mine*. Walking away, I glanced back, delighted to see the blonde watching us, eyes hungrily consuming my companion with open desire.

"The game that never grows old," Apollo commented dryly.

"What game?" I asked, feigning innocence.

"Assessing worth by the beauty of your mate."

I bridled, indignantly. "Me? Hardly!"

"Think again, my dear."

I withdrew my arm in a huff then had to laugh at my reaction. He was right, of course. Sexual one-upmanship was indeed a game of self-worth. Oh, but at my age to make that insufferably young blonde jealous. To beat her at her own game—how delicious!

"I guess you're used to having that kind of an effect on women," I said. We were approaching the low-slung marble entry to the sunny field in which the gigantic temple was situated. I slipped off the light sweater I was wearing, knotting it around my waist.

He shrugged. "It was great for the first few thousand years. After that," he sighed in mock heaviness, "it grew tiresome. I have found myself hiding in the bushes more than once."

Now there was a picture! "Poor baby," I crooned. "But you bring it on yourself, you know." I nodded up and down his glorious form. "You don't always have to look like that, you know."

"Like what?"

He was playing innocent and I wasn't going to let him off the hook. But suddenly we were in the temple precinct and another view took my breath away. "Wow," I said, looking past him. It was the third time I'd been to the temple in less than ten days, and still I wasn't prepared for the impact.

Fifteen gigantic fluted columns stood intact. The connecting roof blocks were equally impressive, stained black in places from time and carbon monoxide from exhaust fumes. Swallows darted through the columns searching for insects to take back to their nests tucked into crannies in the marble plinths. Dry wisps of grass grew in the cracks. Most of the original steps and paving were missing and the surrounding buildings were long gone.

Yet the place still reeked of power.

Sacred sites were sacred because they were deliberately located on spots where the vast telluric energies emanated by the planet were strongest. The temple had obviously been situated on a powerful intersection of ley lines, uplifting and strengthening the energies of all who came here.

The meadow was almost empty of people and there was little distraction as we walked around the roped-off temple. Apollo was completely disinterested. But he humored me as I slowly walked the full circuit, touched and awed.

At the south end of the temple complex I stopped, glancing back and forth between the massive ruins beside me and the equally impressive ruins less than a mile away on top of the Acropolis, trying to imagine the place as it had been 2300 years ago.

"Let me help," Apollo said.

"Hm?"

I turned to him and before I could even think he lightly laid his right palm against my forehead. With a splintering internal *Crack!* modern Athens disappeared and I was awash in the sights and sounds of yesteryear.

The light glancing off the white columns of Zeus's temple was achingly bright. The steps were filled with men in togas and women in longer attire entering and leaving the temple. Barefoot slaves walked behind them, carrying their masters' offerings—sheaths of wheat, amphorae of oil and sweet wine. A young boy led a pure white kid bound by a silver rope across its tiny sharp horns up the stairs. The precinct itself was packed, overwhelming with noise and bustle.

On my left, a man on horseback jogged past. Behind him the shop-lined avenue was filled with haggling merchants and shouting, gesticulating patrons. Geese ran noisily through the manure-pocked street, followed by a pack of laughing, half-naked boys in hot pursuit. The city I knew was gone. In its place stood forests and fields dotted with roads and buildings of white marble. The Parthenon, no longer a blasted shell of columns wrapped in metal scaffolding filled with archaeologists and workers, was breathtaking in its majesty atop the Acropolis. Most shocking of all was the immense statue of the goddess Athena facing away from me towards the sea. She dwarfed the Parthenon and her golden helm and spear-tip glistened in the sun.

Then I was back, staggering in shock.

"Whoa ..." Apollo's hand dropped to my shoulder, steadying me. "Let us sit for a while."

Without waiting for a reply, he steered me towards a bench near the edge of the temple grounds across what I now knew had been a bustling road lined with shops filled with food and wine, offerings and other items of worship . . . even temple souvenirs for sale. Now all that remained was the occasional shard of white marble sticking out of the compacted dirt beneath my feet.

The bench was in temporary shade, green paint peeling from sun and heavy use. Gratefully, I sat down, still shocked and woozy from the vision. And yet it had been more than that. *I was there!* I'd felt the sun blazing on my skin. I'd smelled the dust and spices, incense and manure. How was that possible?

"There is only now, Ekateríni," Apollo said softly. "I simply took you to a now that once was and still is."

His explanation for my direct experience into the nature of the space-time continuum was not helping me reorient. Idly Apollo watched the tourists as I collected myself, shocked mind replaying the snapshot I'd just been given—the dark-haired woman tightening her sandal on the temple steps, the young goat-herd leading the kid and the flash of the metal bit in the chestnut horse's mouth as his rider trotted past—a scene stolen from time and now frozen in my mind.

It seemed impossible that such a powerful center of worship could ever dim and die. Dazed and saddened by the vision of this place throbbing with exuberance and vitality, need and hope, greed, worship, and calculation, I gazed around the temple grounds, now reduced to rubble worth nothing more than the indifferent admiration of picture-snapping tourists willing to pay the small price of admission.

"It was a time of deep communion between God and man," Apollo breathed.

A young Japanese couple stopped in front of us to pose, clutching their selfie stick, turning this way and that, trying to catch the best view of themselves with the temple as background color. A portly woman, her nose buried in a guidebook, stumped past, trailed by her husband.

"What's this one called again?" the man asked.

"The Olympiad," replied his wife. "Or Olympeion. Something like that."

"I thought the Olympic Games were held outside of town."

"They were. But all the gods were called the Olympic Gods 'cause they lived in the Olympic mountains or something. This is the temple of Zeus."

"Oh, yeah," the man said. "The guy who threw lightning bolts." He raised his camera. With an obligatory click they walked on.

I squirmed on the bench, embarrassed by the obvious indifference of my modern American compatriots and the cheap, touristy flavor of the current now.

"Do not worry on my account," my companion said, lightly. "I have had a long time to get used to it."

⊗⊗⊗⊗⊗⊗⊗⊗

"So, what did you mean when you said, 'It was a time of deep communion between the gods and man'?" I asked.

Apollo scraped crumbs of apple cake and cream off his plate with his fork, savoring the last mouthful before answering. "I did not say that."

"Yes, you did," I insisted. "Right before that Japanese couple stopped in front of us."

He pushed his plate away. "I said, 'It was a time of deep communion between *God* and man'."

We'd left the temple grounds behind and had wandered up the busy street of Leoforos Vasilisis Amalias, stopping for coffee at a shady café bordering the botanical gardens.

Apollo eyed his empty plate. "Another, I think."
*Really?*

"Obscurity is a hungry business, Ekateríni."

Obligingly, I caught the waiter's eye and ordered another round of coffee and another apple cake.

"Do not worry," he winked. "This one is, as you say, on me." A glint of gold spun between his fingers. I looked closely and gasped. "You can't use that!"

"Why not?"

"It's an *Athenian* coin," I snapped. He stopped the twirling and I could plainly see the off-centered imprint of an ancient seal stamped on the imperfectly rounded form. "You can be thrown in jail for picking up a rock in this place let alone showing off something like that!

He sighed mournfully. "There is much about your modern world I do not like, especially its cheap and ugly excuse for money." A hundred euro note fluttered in his fingers where the gold had just been. He tucked it under the unused ashtray so it wouldn't blow away.

"Paper," he snorted. "You only exchange the *idea* of value nowadays."

Totally disconcerted I tried to remember what we'd been talking about. My last thought before he'd produced the gold coin from thin air was that he could probably eat apple cake with cream twenty times a day and never gain an ounce and how very unfair that was.

"The communion between God and man," he prompted.

Ah, right. "That's a funny thing for a member of the pantheon of gods to say."

He toyed with the spoon beside his empty coffee cup. "There is only one God, Ekateríni. All the gods and goddesses of Olympus are simply unique expressions of the one Source . . . as are you."

Well, *that* was interesting.

"Ah." His face lit up and he smacked his lips

as the waiter arrived with more coffee and another apple desert.

"Efkaristo."

The waiter left and Apollo picked up a fresh fork and dug in, dabbing the first piece in the powdered sugar decorating his plate. "You really should have one of these," he said, chewing happily.

I sipped coffee, waiting for my strange new friend to get back to business. The first round of cake had taught me the futility of trying to get Apollo to talk about anything serious while eating. Food, it seemed, was something to be honored by paying close attention to it.

As I watched him polish off the last few bites I suddenly realized that stopping at the café had definitely reinforced the unlikely truth that Apollo was real. Surely the food wasn't disappearing by itself. And the waiter had been attentive to both of us.

"Wonderful!" He wiped his mouth with his napkin then examined the piece of white paper. "How amazed the scroll makers would be to see this. So thin and pure and white! And how shocked they would be to see something like this used to wipe food off one's lips!"

"And other things and places," I added dryly.

He shook his head in wonder, dropped the napkin then sighed, stretching his long legs under the table, arching his back, stretching his arms in the air. Then he belched loudly. "Ah, good. Where were we?"

I suppressed laughter, marveling at the mundane nature of the situation. "There's only one God," I prompted.

He nodded casually, confirming my guess that he was checking to see if I'd been paying attention. "Very few people over the centuries have grasped the true nature of the divine Ekateríni. And for the very good reason that one has to enter into the nature of the divine mind itself in order to understand the nature of the divine.

"Of course, once you do that, you realize there is actually nothing to understand at all and that trying to intellectually grasp the nature of the divine is what stands in the way of *being* divine in the first place."

"Huh?" I was beyond confused.

He shrugged. "What is there to understand? Divinity is a matter of pure *being*, not thinking. Truth is subtler than the finest-spun gauze. It is invisible. And yet once you have inhaled its fragrance, it is as obvious as a mighty bull of Corinth snorting in front of you, pawing the earth like thunder."

"Only those with the eyes to see and the ears to hear will know it," I muttered, butchering the Bible verse I was trying to quote from the book I'd never actually read.

"Ezekiel," offered Apollo. "And Mathew. And Deuteronomy. It is a popular truism."

"You know the Bible?" I asked, profoundly shocked.

The corners of his mouth quirked. "You think

I am a complete pagan spending my retirement years in a vacuum drinking wine?" He chuckled. "Unlike my Olympian cohorts, I have a profound and ongoing interest in the progress of humanity in general," he raised an ironic eyebrow "and some individuals in particular."

My cheeks flamed and I felt a sudden rush of heat on my neck. *Me?* Was he referring to me? Why?

"Actually, if you ask me," he went on smoothly, ignoring my discomfort, "science is the first religion of man that has actually grasped the truth of the essential nature of the divine."

"S-science?" I stuttered, surprised yet again by his point of view.

"Come Ekateríni, you and I both know that religion, as a whole, is mostly a collection of rubbish—childish psychological projections and anthropomorphic interpretations of what the visionaries and true prophets experienced and what your scientists have now discovered. Everything is one thing. The intelligence of Source, what you call God, is seamless and whole."

"That's exactly what quantum physics has been showing us for over a hundred years!" I interjected, excitedly. "There's actually no difference between this table," I slapped the surface, startling several nearby customers, "and you and me and those trees over there. It's all just a matter of energy *appearing* as different forms—what the Austrian physicist Erwin Schröndinger called schaumkommen."

"Precisely." Apollo airily waved his hand

indicating the world. "None of this is actually physical. It is simply information presenting, as you say, the *appearance* of physicality." He sat back, looking pleased.

"Yeah, but what good does it do knowing that?" I asked.

Apollo looked puzzled.

"I mean, we can sit here and talk about it. But that doesn't mean we," I paused, "I mean *I,* have any real understanding of the nature of reality. I can say it's all energy and feel smug about knowing about quantum foam and quarks and all. But that doesn't give me the *experience* of oneness."

He smiled proudly. "Now there you have hit the head of the nail."

"Hit the nail on the head," I corrected.

"That is what I said."

"Well, yes. But not properly. The expression is, 'That's hitting the nail on the head'."

He shrugged a deeply Greek shrug. "Until a human being directly experiences the oneness of life—what your scientists call zero-point energy— you are left with just the *concept* of oneness. You are still stuck, like the priests and scribes were stuck thousands of years ago, making up stories to explain what the mystic directly experiences."

We were back at square one, using words that made sense on the surface and all the while the truth beneath them remained hidden.

He nodded. "A closed mind that thinks it knows the truth—and I am referring here to what you would call Truth with a capital 'T'—without ever experiencing Truth is the most dangerous thing in this world. Always has been and always will be."

It seemed as if a cloud had passed over the brilliance of the sun and I shivered. Wordlessly Apollo leaned closer, pulling my sweater from the back of my chair, placing it gently around my shoulders.

"So, how do we get there?" I asked. "As a collective, I mean. How do we ever know the truth about life and who we really are?"

"That is indeed the trick," he acknowledged. Then he shrugged. "This will perhaps sound trite, Ekateríni. But humanity comes to the truth slowly, one person at a time. It may take a million years or a million lifetimes. But ultimately the most reliable path to Truth is the desire for Truth beyond the comfort of any belief systems. That and a life well and fully lived following your heart no matter what."

Copper eyes as impenetrable as the metal itself, Apollo waited for his words to sink in.

*A life well and fully lived.*

What a concept! Most of the spiritual teachers I'd followed talked about life as a distraction. And the heavily promoted ideal of most religions was to turn one's back on the world and become desireless—to become pure and high-minded and ignore the pull of all things earthy and sensuous. The goal wasn't money and sex and fast, red cars. To get to God and know the Truth I was supposed to somehow be above all that.

"To be one with life you have to embrace *all* of it," Apollo said in soft remonstrance.

A long silence fell between us. As if on cue, the waiter swooped in with the check.

"Shall we?" Apollo rose.

I glanced at the bill as I stood up. It was thirty-nine euros and some change. I looked at the hundred euro note, still fluttering beneath the ashtray on the table. Our waiter was going to be extremely pleased with his customer's generosity.

*Oh my . . . if he only knew!*

∞∞∞∞∞∞∞

# CHAPTER FOUR

We ambled slowly along the broad avenue past the exhibition building in the center of the park, heading towards the stadium and the Mets district.

It was getting hotter as the sun rose in the sky and Apollo shucked his leather jacket. Unlike me, walking with my sweater knotted around my waist, his coat simply vanished. I quickly looked around to see if anybody had noticed this little feat.

"Do not worry," Apollo assured me. "I know when someone is looking our way."

*Of course.*

"It is all part of that oneness thing we have been talking about." He snorted. "Gods above, Ekateríni, even a dog knows when you are looking at it."

"Well, you know what they say," I retorted. "Dog is just god spelled backward."

He laughed at that and hugged me to him. His body was warm from the sun, strong and, um . . . divine. Suddenly self-conscious, I eased away while he pretended not to notice.

"So, more questions?" he asked.

"A million of them," I gushed gratefully.

"Fire away."

Feeling like a bloodhound on the scent, I circled back to my original query in the café and for the third time asked Apollo to explain his comment about the deep communion between God and man during Hellenistic times.

"I do so enjoy being right," he murmured.

"Huh?"

"Your tenacity is one of the reasons I . . . um, picked you."

Before I could ask him what exactly he'd picked me for, he went on. "Equally impressive is the fact that you haven't yet asked, 'Why me, Apollo'?"

I blushed. "I've thought it plenty of times in the last 24 hours," I admitted.

"Yes, I know. But you have not directly asked me."

It was my turn to shrug. "There just seem to be so many other more interesting questions to ask and things to talk about."

"Exactly my point. Very unusual in a human—especially in a woman. And extraordinary for a woman who is sexually attracted to me."

A wave of heat scalded my face. *Dear God!* "Oh, come on . . ." I rushed to cover my embarrassment. "What woman still breathing wouldn't be attracted to you?"

"True," he said. "But still I am impressed."

I had to laugh at his lack of humbleness. "You know one of the things I like best about you?" I asked in a sudden moment of relaxed candor.

"Hm?"

"That despite our short acquaintance and despite who and what you are and despite your ruthless manipulation of my weaknesses and emotions, you make me laugh. In a good way," I hastened to add.

He thought about it for a second then smiled warmly in response. "I am very glad I bring a lightness to your heart, Ekateríni."

"You're not the 'Bringer of Light' for nothing," I quipped.

He stopped short, catching me off guard, and I turned towards him questioningly. Reaching out, he gently grasped my chin, tilting my face upwards so I was gazing directly into his disconcerting eyes.

"You have yet to realize it, but you and I go way back, my dear." Briefly he caressed my cheek with his thumb then turned and started walking again, leaving me gasping like a fish out of water in his wake.

∞∞∞∞∞∞∞∞

The walk to the Athens Cultural Institute was far too short. And as we stood outside the gates, Apollo bid me leave.

"This has been enough for one day," he said.

Part of me agreed and a larger part violently disagreed. I didn't want our time together to end. *Why, oh, why did I agree to have lunch with Emily?*

My wild early morning questions and fearful uncertainty had been answered. Apollo was real and very much in my life. Maybe I could get out of it? Surely, she had better things to do than take an old

acquaintance to lunch? I was far too full of Apollo
to even think about rejoining the real world. Besides,
I'd just had breakfast. Well, at least coffee.

"Another time, Ekateríni." With a wicked smile,
he lifted my hand and bowed over it, brushing it
with his lips. A shock sparked through my body at
the touch.

*You are going to be the end of me,* I groaned internally.

"Far from the end, I promise you that," he said.

In a heartbeat, he was gone.

∞∞∞∞∞∞∞∞

I drifted inattentively through lunch. Several times
Emily asked if I were okay. "You seem incredibly
distracted," she said, sounding mildly irritated.

"Oh," I started. "Sorry. I'm fine. Just worried
about an article I'm writing."

"Really? What's it about?"

It may have been years, but I knew Emily well
enough to know she was being polite. Little past
the third century AD interested her. Getting into a
discussion about my journalism career and the most
recent story I was researching—electromagnetic
pulsed frequencies and their potential healing
applications for cancer—were about as far out of
her attention range as politics was for me.

All in all, it was a perfunctory get together and
both of us were relieved when the last remains of
lunch had been whisked away.

"Let me know when you get back from Paros," she said as we stood on the street outside the restaurant.

"Thanks, I will," I said, equally insincere. We did the European kiss-kiss cheek thing, then she walked away, leaving me to my undoubtedly unhealthily obsessive thoughts about Apollo.

✧✧✧✧✧✧✧✧

Two days dragged past exploring Plato's Academy and Hephaestus' temple in the Agora, the Cyclades Museum and the surprisingly decrepit National Archaeological Museum—a massive sprawling complex of buildings that took me forever to find on foot downtown. Once there, I moved from room to room looking for one and only one face.

In the process, I viewed dozens of statues of unidentified male and female Kouros (free-standing Greek statues), two statues of Artemis, one of Hera, an impressively large statue of Zeus, left arm outstretched, right hand about to hurl a lightning bolt, and finally one small bust of Apollo.

It looked nothing like him.

Frustrated, I tried to get him out of my mind by walking miles through the city. I sweated up the sharply inclined cone of Lycobettus Hill, then ransacked the flea market, finally hitting the stores around Syntagma Square looking for some light cotton t-shirts. Living in the cool damp of the Pacific

Northwest had not prepared me clothes-wise for the scorching heat of the Mediterranean sun.

Finally, compelled by ulterior motives, I visited the Christian and Byzantine Museum. If ever there was a place that might trigger a visit from Apollo and a vehement discussion about religion, this was it. But I entered the shaded courtyard of the museum alone and walked down the stairs into the subterranean chambers of the labyrinthine collection unaccompanied.

Despite my preoccupation, I found the museum fascinating. Christianity had indeed been built upon Greco-Roman foundations. Exhibits showed how the ancient temples had been restructured and redecorated to Christian tastes and beliefs. Exquisite marble statues of the old gods and goddesses were "exorcised" by carving off their noses, replacing them with the sign of the cross.

I cringed, imagining Apollo's beautiful features defaced and branded with the totem of the latest religion, walking fascinated and appalled through the exhibits detailing Christianity's bloodthirsty early history.

From its beginnings as an upstart cult to its official acceptance by Emperor Constantine as Rome's official religion in AD 334, all the way through the Dark and Middle Ages and into the Renaissance, the march of Christianity was littered with battles and martyrdoms, genocides and torture, crusades and political intrigue, power plays, misery and mayhem.

Panel after gilded panel showed the Fathers of the Church, the saints and martyrs, John the Baptist, the angels and archangels and, of course, the ever-suffering Jesus nailed to the cross. Mary, also long-suffering except in her depictions as the Mother tenderly cradling her infant son, and Saint Catherine, my namesake looking pious and pure, were the only women depicted in the whole museum.

By the time I got to the end of the exhibit I'd contracted a bad case of psychological and emotional indigestion and gladly escaped back into the light and air above ground.

Apollo was not waiting for me.

Depressed, I made my way through the busy streets to the Plaka district and had an early dinner at a famous restaurant Hillary Clinton had once visited, ordering a traditional Moussaka and a full bottle of excellent retsina. Glumly hunched over my wine glass at my courtyard table, I watched early patrons slowly trickle in—all couples, all tourists on the trip of a lifetime, cozily sharing stories and laughing about their day's experiences over drinks and dinner.

My wretched mood deepened.

I was sick of traveling alone. Sick of eating alone. Sick of being the solitary writer exploring new countries and cultures by herself, writing books, blogging and reporting her journeys and insights. I was bored watching other couples be couples. It had been six years since my last partner and I split up, and with all my heart I longed to be a couple again.

But where would I find a mate to match my heart, mind and soul? *Apollo* my mind whispered and I almost wept on the spot. *Of all the ridiculous, unrealistic, weak, stupid, egotistical things to think . . .*

Despite his wicked flirting, whatever reasons the god of wisdom had for seeking me out, love and coupledom were surely not part of the picture. But that didn't stop me fantasizing about it. Didn't stop me wanting something I could never have.

I slugged down the retsina.

*Damn.* After only two—granted highly intense— encounters, I was bewitched and totally besotted with Apollo, obsessing about all of the long-term couple things most women, old and young, dream of.

*I am well and truly screwed,* I thought grimly. *And not in a good way.* Not waiting for my waiter to do the honors, I poured myself another glass of wine.

Several acquaintances had met wonderful partners online, and I'd tried a few Internet dating sites. But all the winks and nods and "He's interested!" notifications came from fat, tired-looking old men whose last major dive into life had been the purchase of a larger flat-screen TV at Costco.

Where was the challenging mind, the romantic heart, the fearless spiritual explorer, the tender lover of life I was looking for?

Across the patio an older white-haired man bent attentively towards his companion, eyes caressing her in the candlelight, and my heart ached with loneliness.

I was in good shape, had the energy levels of a

thirty-something and an intense curiosity about life and how it works that got my nose into all sorts of things. I was fulfilling my life-long dream of being a published author and traveling the world. In many ways it felt like my life was just starting. Before Apollo showed up, this trip had been the start of a wonderful new chapter in a busy, full life.

Now? Now the entire Greek continent was mere background noise as I moved through empty days awaiting Apollo's return.

Surely, he would return?

I swished the golden wine around the bottom of my glass, thoughts morose. The couple across from me was holding hands across the table now. Abruptly I signaled my waiter for the check.

It was all Apollo's fault. My brief, outrageous moments with him had ripped through the barricades of my pretend indifference to being alone. And now he'd upped the ante on love to impossible heights. What mortal man could ever possibly compete?

I sighed. *What a freaking disaster.*

⊗⊗⊗⊗⊗⊗⊗⊗

## CHAPTER FIVE

The taxi arrived at the cool pre-dawn hour of six to take me to the port of Piraeus to catch the car ferry to the island of Paros. Traffic was light and we made it to the busy port with plenty of time to spare before its 7:30 departure.

Forgetting there were baggage areas where I could safely dump my stuff, I wrestled my two heavy bags and laptop backpack up to the 8th story deck overlooking the stern. An old Greek woman chain smoking at the table next to me agreed through sign language to watch my bags, and I grabbed a cup of coffee and settled back at my table for the four-hour trip across the Aegean Sea.

I tried writing, but kept getting distracted. Cigarette smoke from multiple sources wafted my way. Every two minutes a chime would sound and the captain would start droning in Greek over the ship's intercom about the weather, the seas, the passing islands, our estimated time of arrival, the menu from the restaurant which was now open, and, for all I knew, an explicit accounting of his wife's last operation.

After working as a reporter in a busy newsroom, I could write sitting in Times Square. It wasn't the noise, smoke, diesel fumes and bustle bothering me.

Nope. It was pure glum Apollo distraction.

Putting my computer away I grabbed the science fiction novel I was lugging around and tried reading. But within a few minutes I put it back. Hopeless!

The grizzled, black-clad woman nodded her availability for a second round of bag-guarding, waving me away with nicotine-stained fingers. Relieved, I headed to the wind-swept rail. The water was clean, clear, and bluer-than-blue, the mountainous islands in the Cycladic chain passing by—Kea, Kynthos and Serifos—looking like grey-blue meringues floating on top of the waves.

"My mother Leto was cursed by Hera and couldn't give birth on solid land or water. So, Zeus created a floating island for her and that is where my sister Artemis and I were born. Or so the story goes."

"Apollo!"

"Miss me?"

He leaned against the rail to my right, the wind of our passage combing the red-brown curls off his forehead, plastering his t-shirt and black windbreaker to his chest. His eyes were focused across the water towards the nearest island.

Heart pounding, throat suddenly dry, I wanted to simultaneously hit him and hug him.

He looked at me and grinned. "I will take that as a 'Yes'."

"You know damn well I missed you," I scolded. "Greek gods are hard to come by these days. And once you've spent time in their company it's impossible to be interested in ordinary people."

His brows knitted in sudden concern and I realized this might not be the first time he'd heard a complaint like that from a mortal woman's mouth. *What a dent in the female population he must have made over the last few thousand years!* I could see them now, millions of women far and wide, hooked on Olympic love heroin, scattered weeping and destitute in his wake.

"It is not quite that bad," he responded dryly. "At most five or six-hundred thousand. And I have tried to keep the weeping to a minimum."

I blushed. "You Olympians have quite the reputation, you know."

"Please," Apollo retorted sourly, "Do not lump me in with the rest of the Olympians."

"Why not? Family issues?"

"Are you kidding? Father is a short-tempered, narcissistic sex addict who would as soon kill you as talk to you. Mother is an incorrigible flirt needing constant protection from Euboean giants. Hera is an insecure, sharp-tongued harridan with a jealousy streak as wide as Mount Olympus. Hephaestus is a bore and a boor. Artemis," his jaw clenched and he fell silent.

"In other words, with you I get the best of a bad lot?"

"Pretty much."

We stood silently, me basking in his company, so glad to see him I could hardly think. Until I suddenly realized how silly my excitement must look to him. How very boring and naïve and predictable.

My heart sank. *No fool like an old fool,* I sighed.

Abruptly he moved away from the rail and looked at me. "Stop it," he said sternly.

"What?"

"Do not pretend you do not understand. It does you no credit to think about yourself in such ridiculous terms."

"Huh?"

"You are all upset because you are not 25 anymore," he snapped. "But did you ever stop to consider how old *I* am?" His eyes flashed and there was true frustration and anger in their depths. "Twenty-five-year-olds wearied me after the first thousand years. Wake up and get present with me and stop playing head games with yourself."

Shocked into stillness, embarrassed and flustered, I didn't know what to say.

He gave me a searching look as if to make sure his words had hit home, then nodded. "Come," he said. "Let us go somewhere we can talk privately."

Uncertainly I followed him back to my seat to collect my bags. The elderly Greek woman's eyes widened when she saw Apollo, then abruptly narrowed. Dropping her cigarette, she hissed at him in disapproval. Holding the index and middle fingers of her right hand stiffly, like prongs, she made sudden darting gestures towards his eyes as he bent down to grab my suitcases.

Apollo ignored her.

"What was that all about?" I asked curiously, as we moved towards the doors to the interior of the ship.

He chuckled grimly. "That, my dear, is the gesture of a good Orthodox woman warding off the devil and the Evil Eye."

Somehow he managed to open the door for me while balancing the suitcases, then led the way across the saloon crammed with travelers, smoking, drinking coffee, eating, reading, and playing backgammon.

*The Evil Eye?*

I turned around, craning my neck, and caught sight of the black form hunched on the other side of the glass glaring at Apollo's retreating figure, fingers still forked and ready. *Weird.*

We walked through several sets of double doors. Suddenly the flooring changed from slick linoleum to plush burgundy carpeting, the walls from metal to wood paneling. It was quieter here, the pulsing throb of the diesel engines seemed far away. Most of the well-appointed, obviously-expensive seating spaces with comfortable dark green couches facing each other across a table were empty

Apollo dumped my suitcases and we sat opposite one another. Stretching his long legs underneath the table, he slouched into his seat, hands jammed in the pockets of his windbreaker, looking, oddly enough, uncertain.

After my earlier gaffe outside and the weirdness with the old woman, I was in no hurry to start the conversation. I fussed with my backpack, hauled out my water bottle, took off my jacket, kicked off my sandals and folded my legs cross-legged on the couch, getting comfortable.

At some point in my journalism career I'd learned that the quality of an interview is very much based upon the knowledge of the interviewer and their ability to ask intelligent, leading questions. Since my knowledge base in this case was nonexistent and I had no idea where Apollo was headed, why he was with me or what he wanted to say, there was nothing I could do to prime the pump.

I'd also learned the advantage of silence. Most people love talking about themselves. They love telling their story—it's just human nature. If you're quiet and open they just come out with it. The fact that Apollo wasn't human made my tactic questionable. But what other choice did I have?

Eventually, he grunted and pulled his hands out of his pockets, clasping them in front of him on the table. "We have already established that what I am is a template—a template of the masculine expression and the model for beauty, wisdom and knowledge."

I nodded.

"All of us are templates. I think I mentioned that?"

I nodded again.

"We have also established that everything is energy and information and that unified energy is the foundation of all creation. Right?"

"Yes."

"So here is the next point I want to get across," he said. "Nothing can take form without an idea coming first. It is what Plato was talking about all those centuries ago when he rightly intuited that there is a level of consciousness—a level of intangible ideals—that precedes matter." He paused, thinking.

"Do you know what a hologram is?" he finally asked.

"Of course," I said, smiling. "I'm surprised you do though."

"Describe it please."

I thought for a moment then began. "You take a powerfully coherent light source, such as a laser, and split it into two beams. One beam is bounced off an object that then becomes the information source— let's say an apple. The original reference beam is bounced off a mirror. The beam that bounces off the apple "carries" the information of the apple. When the reference beam bounced off the mirror is recombined with the information-carrying beam, a three-dimensional holographic projection of the apple is then formed."

He nodded. "There is a peculiar characteristic specific to holograms. Do you know what it is?"

"Yes," I said, warming to the topic. "One pixel taken from the projected image of the apple contains the whole 3-D image. A hologram is an excellent representation of oneness. There is the *appearance* of discrete physical objects in space-time—apples and oranges, motor bikes and mountains and people— but the whole of creation is contained in everything. Everything *is* the whole. Holograms reflect that."

He sat back, relaxing a bit. "Remember I said God is everything?"

"Yep. I get it."

He raised an eyebrow. "And what is it exactly that you 'get'?"

"What you're trying to tell me is that God, for lack of a better word, is the original coherent Light that split Itself and, forming a pattern of Ideals from which to build creation, shone Its Light through those patterns, projecting life into this hologram of existence we're living in."

I was on a roll. "You and the other Olympian gods and goddesses are all part of the original pattern of Ideals put into motion at the beginning of Creation. You are the *ideas* of man and woman, the ideas of beauty and fertility, the ideas of art and agriculture, wisdom and evolution that the Light or intelligence of God shines through, spinning creation into existence." I hesitated then forged ahead, "The ideas of jealousy and war and . . ."

He held up a quick finger, stopping me midsentence. "The jealousy and war stuff came later. It was not part of the original template for creation." He shook his head wonderingly. "I am almost speechless."

I felt a warm glow inside at his obvious admiration. And yet why was he so surprised?

Apollo smiled, amused. "I am not surprised that you know about such things, Ekateríni. My wonderment is at how far humans have progressed in terms of grasping the true nature of existence."

His eyes were alight with enthusiasm. "You have all the pieces in the palms of your hands!" He slapped his own hands on the table, rocking my water bottle. "If you could but get beyond your superstitious beliefs about God . . . if you would just understand your own science and apply your incredible knowledge, your world would be so very different. So very much better."

He slumped again. "Of course, it is not your fault."

"What's not our fault?" I asked.

He sighed. "Humanity did not come by its superstitions all on its own. I am afraid we helped the whole worship thing along." He averted his eyes, hands balling into fists on the table. "Indeed, we commanded it."

There was another long pause. Finally, he looked up, face bleak. "Creation is a funny thing, Ekateríni. It is not what people think. It is not a fixed picture. It is alive, intelligent, and fluid like a river. Once set into motion, creation takes multiple paths, constantly taking new directions and finding new forms, discovering what works and what does not. The nature of creation is change and growth— unlimited, uninhibited, lawless change and growth."

"Can you give me an example?" I asked.

He thought for a moment. "Let us say all of creation is an apple tree."

I nodded, amused. *Amazing how the apple keeps showing up in creation stories.*

"Creation is not just the apple tree. Creation is also all the potentials of the apple tree—what the apple tree can become—all the different shapes and colors and flavors and textures of the fruit plus the different forms and branching and sizes of the trees. Maybe an apple bush comes into form." He looked at me for the first time with a slight twinkle in his eyes. "Maybe an apple cake tree is brought to life by some geneticist down the road."

"So, what you're saying is once a pattern is set into motion, part of the pattern itself is the potential of the pattern to become whatever it can?"

"Yes. It is utterly unlimited."

*Like a juggernaut set into motion it gathers speed and momentum, creating itself as it rolls along.*

"Very much so," he agreed. "And there is no judgment by Source upon any of those courses, no matter how ill-favored and destructive some might turn out to be."

The ferry's horn suddenly sounded and the ship rocked infinitesimally, reminding me there was a world outside this tiny, intense space between us. "Do you have any idea how big creation is Ekateríni?" he asked suddenly. "How much potential it holds?"

"Infinite," I said.

"Yes. Infinite." He sighed. "For you it is just a word. But for me it is a word that gives great hope."

"How so?"

"It means," he said, "that creation is big enough to allow not just the problems and suffering that arise within a pattern. But also big enough to allow the potentials for the solutions to those problems to take form and unfold as well."

He leaned back on the couch, spreading his arms along the top of the cushions, crossing one leg casually over his other knee. I didn't have a clue where he was going with all this, so I kept my mouth shut and waited.

He eyed me speculatively. "Which brings me, my dear, to you."

ↂↂↂↂↂↂↂↂↂ

## CHAPTER SIX

With a jolt and a thunderous shuddering the ferry changed gears. Simultaneously the horn sounded several longs blasts. Then the captain, who by some miracle had managed to stay quiet the last hour of the trip, announced our arrival at the port of Paraikia. Time for drivers to get to their cars and foot passengers to fetch their luggage and prepare for docking.

"Saved by the bell," he murmured, standing up.

"Just as things were getting interesting," I said, standing as well.

"Perhaps," he said, "we will see."

"Is that a threat or a promise?" I joked.

"As I said, we will see." He picked up my bags and headed towards the passageway, leaving me nothing else to do but grab my water bottle and backpack and tag along.

The lines headed to the stairs and elevators leading below decks were the same unmoving jam of people and bags, dogs, children and excited voices I remembered. Eventually we made it down the now unmoving escalators to the car deck where we waited with the hundreds of others ready to disembark.

"Is somebody meeting you?" he asked politely, although he probably already knew my exact plans down to the square footage of the house I'd rented.

"Sorry," he said. "I am not that nosy."

"Or interested I'm sure."

"Let us say the interesting things about you interest me. The rest . . ." he shrugged.

"A friend is meeting me at the windmill."

He nodded. "Good."

The crowd pressed forward and I was suddenly overcome by the strangeness of my situation. Just three days ago I'd been excited to see my author friend Chris, an ex-pat from Alabama. But now I wondered how in the world I was going to explain Apollo's presence to her. And what to call him? Was Apollo still a legitimate name for a man in modern Greece?

"So how should I . . ." my voice trailed off as I looked around. Apollo had melted into the crowd and was nowhere to be seen.

◊◊◊◊◊◊◊◊

Chris's short brown hair whipped in the wind and her dark eyes sparkled with excitement behind her glasses. "I can't believe you're finally back here!" she enthused as we hugged our greeting.

With a lot of pushing and shoving we managed to get my bags crammed into her little Honda, and soon we were out of the main town of Paraikia, zipping along the winding road that led across the island east to the smaller port town of Naoussa.

"How was Athens?" she asked.

"Hot and noisy." I answered. "Typical Athens."

"How's the book doing? Hey, watch it!" She hit the horn, narrowly avoiding a fat sunburned tourist on a rented Vespa. "Christ, the traffic gets worse on this island every year."

I clutched the doorframe, recalling the narrow misses I'd witnessed last time I'd been in a car with Chris. Knowing the trip to Naoussa was short and that it was probably not my day to die, I ignored the road and answered her question about my latest book.

"Sales have been okay." I sighed. "But not what we hoped. My agent keeps saying nobody's buying books right now. That everybody's freaked out by the presidential election and just wait awhile. But it's hard putting in so damn much time and effort . . ."

"And blood and sweat and tears," Chris interjected.

I laughed. "And that." I shook my head. "The tour was exhausting and frankly I just couldn't face doing any more marketing if it wasn't going to pay off. So I used the last bit of my advance to buy my plane ticket and rent the house for three months."

"I'm so glad I don't have to deal with much of that." Chris downshifted too late in the next sharp turn and the car wobbled unsteadily as we cornered.

"What?"

"Marketing." She floored it going into a long straight stretch. "The romance industry takes care of its own."

"Speaking of which, how's the latest one coming along?"

"*The Blood's Passion*?" she said. "Almost finished. My publisher didn't think there was one more possible angle to be milked out of the vampire genre. But I found one!" she crowed.

"Really? What?" I asked.

"A schizophrenic girl, or at least she *appears* to be schizophrenic, is in a mental institution. She tells her doctor that she's being visited by a vampire lover. She explains how he manipulates her mind, pretending to be interested in everything she says, making her fall in love with him, flattering her, fulfilling all her wildest desires. The doctor doesn't believe a word of it, of course—until he catches the guy bending over her hospital bed one night, sucking on her neck. Of course, it blows his mind and he falls in love with his patient and wants to save her. But the vampire gives the doctor a great run for his money!

"Derik's sooooo evil and sooooo handsome. He's positively delicious! The very incarnation of seduction." Ignoring the road, she turned and winked broadly at me. "I like him better than my doctor hero."

Delicious, handsome, mind manipulation, seduction, *evil*. My mind flashed to the black-clad woman warding off Apollo with her forked-fingered hand gestures and despite the hot air blasting through the car the hairs rose on the back of my neck. *Holy crap!* What was I getting myself into?

I stared at the road whipping past, my mind racing as I remembered Apollo's cold, hungry eyes that morning on the mountain above Delphi.

I recalled how he manipulated me and took me into the dark void. How he tried to seduce me into worshipping him.

Most definitely, Apollo preyed upon my weaknesses and desires. And he wasn't even sorry. Surely, that wasn't the sign of a man who could be trusted? *And he's not even human. He admitted it himself!* And my God, was he a charmer. After only two visits he had me going crazy, fantasizing about a love affair, tossing and turning in bed at night, filled with longing and turmoil.

*It isn't healthy.*

I shivered again. Was Chris sent as some sort of divine messenger, warning me? Waking me up to the fact that I was dabbling with forces I shouldn't be messing with?

"What do *you* think?"

I started. "What?" I didn't have a clue what Chris was saying.

"What do you think about me getting into the horror genre?"

"I'm not much of a fan." I shook my head, panicked by the unwelcome thought that I might be entering into a real-life horror story of my own. Surely not!? Oh! How easy it was to start doubting when Apollo wasn't around!

And why was that anyway?

*If he can read my mind and change my body, he can change my mind as well.* The thought came, unbidden and frightening. Was it possible the whole thing was a manipulation from start to finish? Had any of my thoughts when I was around Apollo even been my own? And why was the attraction so compelling? I'd known him—whatever he was—maybe a total of twelve hours over the space of four days. And what did I really know, anyway? That I was obsessed with a mythic Greek god who resurrected himself from obscurity in order to talk quantum physics and mysticism with a 60-year-old author from America. That was the sum total of what I knew.

Looked at that baldly, I couldn't help seeing what an implausible storyline it was. *It wouldn't even make a good plot for a novel.* My God, what was I thinking—aside from the fact that he was everything a woman could ever dream of?

And I was taking this whole scene at face value?

Yeah, he was real. Waiters and blondes and old women saw him. But who or what was he really? A vampire? *Of course not.* That was ridiculous. But what about a psychotic hypnotist? Some weirdo mind-reading magician who preyed upon older women's lonely fantasies and insecurity, fooling them into thinking he was a god by "magically" producing a gold coin or a 100 euro note.

Was he plucking images and ideas from my brain, feeding them back to me, leading me on with the promise of their fulfillment? "Do yourself the honor of believing what you already know." His words from the first five minutes of our acquaintance came rushing back. And instead of seeming practical and wise as they had in the moment, they suddenly seemed nothing more than ego manipulation.

My stomach did an unpleasant flip-flop. What could his game possibly be? I wasn't young and beautiful. I wasn't wealthy. *What does he want from me?* And how could I possibly know what was true even if I asked him? How could I accurately assess the reality of the situation?

"Kathryn?"

I jerked back to the present. "Are you okay?" Chris asked, brown eyes concerned behind her rimless glasses.

*Emily asked me the same thing.*

I jerked my mind away from the looming snake pit of fear and looked at her wildly, stammering, "Y-yes, I'm fine."

"Do you want me to take you to the house first or straight to Dimitri's to pick up the car?" She was obviously repeating the question.

"Dimitri's, please. I'm picking up the house keys there anyway."

Chris nodded, turning onto the left-hand fork that would take us skirting above Naoussa's harbor and then down into the main part of town. As we approached the bridge over the little creek and the wide, cobbled, shop-lined marketplace she slowed, looking for a place to pull over—never an easy task in this tourist-driven town.

"Dinner tonight?" she asked hopefully as she nosed her car into a place beside a tree.

Did I want company? Not really. More than anything I just wanted to be alone to sort out my crazed thoughts. Half an hour ago, I'd been praying to see Apollo as soon as I was alone again. An hour ago, I'd been happily absorbed in conversation—ecstatic to be in the same room with him. But now?

Maybe a down-to-earth dinner of fresh island seafood and a few drinks with a friend was the ticket back to sanity. At the very least it would be a distraction from my frightening thoughts. "Sure," I said. "How about Mario's at seven-thirty?"

"So late?" she joked, popping the trunk.

I'd never gotten used to the Greek custom of dining late and Chris knew it. She and most of my other acquaintances on the island didn't eat until at least nine o'clock, sometimes much later than that. "Ha ha," I said, "very funny."

I pried my bags out of the trunk and we kissed European style. "It's so good having you back!" she enthused, hugging me. Her soft, corpulent body felt safe, warm and homelike, and I was suddenly glad I'd made the choice to join her for dinner.

With a quick wave she drove off and I lugged my bags across the plaza to Dimitri's door where the ritual of car rental awaited me.

⊙⊗⊙⊗⊙⊗⊙⊗

"Kalispera!" cried the short dark-haired man, dumping his ubiquitous cigarette in the ashtray, bustling around the edge of his paper-piled desk to greet me. "Kalispera!" he pumped my right hand enthusiastically, placing his left hand on my forearm—a warmer greeting than the standard handshake. "Good to see you've come back!"

"Doesn't everybody come back Dimitri?"

His face and mustache drooped. "Not everyone." He shook his head sadly at this puzzlement, ushering me to the wooden chair opposite his at the desk. "Please, please, sit down. Coffee?"

Not accepting coffee and hospitality is a crime in Greece. Yes, I was here on business. Yes, he would rent me a car. But those were simply the formalities. The important part was social. We were two human beings getting reacquainted after a space of years, and it didn't matter how casually we'd met before. Common civility commanded conversation— an acknowledgement of a fellow human's living presence and importance in the world.

We chatted as I drank the thick, heavily sweetened coffee brewed in his back-office supply closet. I learned his mother on Cyprus had finally passed away, God rest her soul. He learned the book I'd written last time I was on the island was out in the bookstores. I learned his oldest daughter in Athens had just had her second baby. And he learned that renting the house outside Apollonias (of all names!) was purely for pleasure.

Eventually, after the second cup of coffee had been drunk, the Medjool dates had been eaten and sufficient conversation had been exchanged, his assistant lightly dropped a piece of paper in front of me to sign. No address, no passport number, no insurance forms and waiver boxes to tick. Just my name and Greek cell phone number.

Dimitri waved the signed paper away, looking pained by its very existence. Car keys, house keys, cash, another warm handshake and promises to "see you soon" were exchanged and then his assistant wafted me out the door to introduce me to the little silver-blue Fiat station wagon waiting for me on the road just beyond the plaza.

Stopping at the grocery store, I bought wine, coffee, cream, a chicken, Greek yogurt and honey. Then I stopped at the farmer's stand to buy some veggies and fruit. Leaving the village, the drive to Apollonias was just as I remembered—narrow winding roads lined with hand-built stone walls, tall grasses and spring wildflowers. The last couple miles the road was dirt, the fine golden sand rutted with potholes.

I passed the concrete shell of the abandoned hotel that had been condemned before it was ever completed twenty years ago. I passed the rocky fields where . . . yes, the two donkeys and brown and white paint horse still grazed there, chomping on the rapidly-drying grasses. Past the overflowing trash bins, past the goat farm with the vicious yellow dog that raged at every passing car behind his tall wire fence, and there it was on the left . . . the narrow driveway snaking across the fields towards the coastline.

Slowly navigating the last stretch, I passed a high-walled villa surrounded by trees and drove across another hay field to the sea, turning left on what was now just a dirt track running along the coast. The house I'd rented sat back from the steep sea cliffs behind a blue-painted gate and creamy cement walls lined with gigantic purple and pink oleanders.

The tree across from the gate under which I'd often sat on my long walks two years before was still there. I stopped the car and went to stand beneath its shade for a moment, peering down into the crystal depths of the water below. Then, eager to see the house, I unlocked the gate, pushing it wide, inhaling the scent of sea and salt and the perfume of jasmine overhanging the porch stretching across the south face of the simple two-story, white-washed cement house.

This would be my home for the next three months and I was thrilled to be back. What would happen here in the ensuing weeks was shrouded in mystery. Charmed, excited, filled with trepidation and overflowing with fears and doubt, I hauled my bags out of the back of the car and dragged them up the flagstone walk to the front door.

∞∞∞∞∞∞∞

The house was everything I'd hoped for. The living room was decorated in Mediterranean blues with contrasting orange cushions and drapery, rustic furniture, a comfy sofa and several woven rugs over the dark slate floors. The kitchen was spacious and opened onto a small back garden. The dining area featured French doors that opened out onto the porch and patio  and a wonderful view of the sea.

Both bedrooms upstairs were small but comfortable with double beds covered in white eiderdown duvets. The rooms were connected by a white marble bathroom, which, as exotic as it seemed to my American eyes, was the cheapest building material available on the island. Both rooms—one of which I would turn into my writing space—opened out onto the second-floor balcony facing the water.

My fears and sudden doubts about Apollo accompanied me as I explored the house and yard, unpacked the groceries and unpacked my bags. Figuring out the Internet situation and checking my emails provided a brief relief. And then it was time to get dressed for dinner.

Hanging out with Chris turned out to be the right choice. I enjoyed an enormous plate of fresh-caught calamari, a bottle of retsina and an after-dinner digestif from Crete called Masthika—all while Chris regaled me with the plot of *The Blood's Passion*.

As she got into the gory details, I found myself relaxing. Parallels between the handsome vampire Derik and Apollo were few. Like most vampires he was a creature who thrived on blood and death, fear and darkness. He had none of Apollo's warmth or enthusiasm for life, and zero sense of humor.

By the time I'd gotten back to the house, opening the gate in the windswept dark, I'd managed to quiet most of my earlier concerns. The house was cheerful even at night. A fire had been laid in the curved white-plaster fireplace in the corner and, strangely untroubled by the thought of visitations from either vampires or Greek gods, I lit the fire and settled down with my sci-fi novel in front of the soothing flames. By the time I tottered off to bed, my heart was at ease, my mind a comfortable blank.

ᘒᘒᘒᘒᘒᘒᘒᘒ

## CHAPTER SEVEN

I slept like the dead and awakened late, vastly refreshed. Surely everything would sort itself out in its own time and its own way? Sunny skies and piles of red geraniums against whitewashed walls outside my windows definitely had a way of tilting my mood towards the positive. And the sparkling wine-dark waters of the Aegean called to me.

Granted, it was only April and far too early in the season for most people to be swimming. As I drank my morning brew, I made use of the binoculars thoughtfully supplied by the owners of the house, watching in amusement as a young man drove his moped to the sandy shore of the bay some distance away. Stripping down to his bathing trunks, he confidently waded thigh-deep into the water—only to immediately turn around and reverse the process, hurriedly leaving the water, putting his jacket and pants back on, getting on his bike and motoring away.

But for me and my nothern-climed blood it was already hot enough to swim. I ate a light breakfast, finished unpacking and handled my emails. By noon I couldn't resist the call of the sea any longer. Shoving a towel and some water in my backpack, I walked the short distance from the gate to the path I knew and followed it to my left along the cliffs.

Within ten minutes, I'd arrived at the gully where I could descend to the beach. It was little more than a washed-out goat track, and I slowly picked my way down the crumbling hardpan cliff face leading to the isolated beach where I could sunbathe and swim nude—if I managed to not kill myself falling the two-hundred feet to the rocks below getting there.

Scrambling down the last bit, I jumped to the sand and headed up the beach. As usual, the pebbles along the shore sparkled enticingly, flaunting their colors and patterns in greens and blues, reds and golds. Paros is one of the most ancient and prolific sources of marble in the world, and the beaches around Apollonias contained a fabulous mix of marble and other stones. I could spend hours ransacking the shores here. Last time I'd visited, before I could pack up and head home I'd had to lug at least ten pounds of rock I'd collected back to the beach.

Ignoring the siren call of the stones, I walked the few yards to my favorite sunning spot, plopped my pack onto some rocks, spread my towel, stripped off and lay down with a contented groan.

For a long time, I soaked up the warmth from the sun above and the sand beneath my towel, listening to the waves gently lapping the stony shore. Not wanting to overdo it my first day, I rolled over, face down, ruminating on my first evening back on the island and, of course, my stupid, ever-recycling concerns about Apollo.

Sufficiently baked, I got up and crunched my way

over the pebbles and thick layer of dried seaweed to the water. The shore shelved steeply and the water was cold, but I quickly dived. No agonizing inch-by-inch immersion for me! The first few seconds were a shock, but I warmed up quickly swimming fast out to sea. Finally, out of breath, I flipped over and floated.

The Aegean has a higher salt content than the Pacific and I rocked effortlessly on top of the water, bright red-painted toes sticking out. Ears submerged, I could hear the crackling of shellfish and other sea creatures on the seabed below. Overhead seagulls circled, their cries inaudible. The high golden cliffs touched the blue above, a carved bulwark between sea and sky.

Finally, thoroughly chilled, I made my way back to shore, blessing the perfect swimming conditions. No tides to speak of, no currents, no sharks or barracudas, almost no waves when the wind was from the south . . . and crystal clear. I could have read a book cover on the seafloor fifty feet below.

Stumbling up the steep pebbly incline, I scrabbled for footing and failed, falling back into the water with a hearty *splash*. Laughing at my clumsiness, I used both hands and feet the next attempt and made it back ashore. Then I dried myself off, dressed and reluctantly packed up. No sense risking sunburn day one.

Climbing back up the cliffs was easier than coming down, but by the time I was at the top I was hot again and out of breath. The narrow footpath through the scotch broom and wild roses clinging to the cliff brought me back to my favorite tree and the gate. And . . . there he was. Even before I undid the latch, I saw Apollo waiting on the covered patio wearing his usual jeans with a white linen shirt unbuttoned to his navel, bare feet on the teak coffee table, watching me.

*Oh dear.*

My heart did the usual jumping up and down thing, but this time there was more than an edge of fear to my excitement seeing him. With no escape possible, quickly I crossed the yard. "Hi," I said, casually dropping my pack on a chair like it was an everyday occurrence having a Greek god waiting for me on my porch—*or a psychopathic hypnotist who somehow knows where to find me all the time.*

I ran my hands over my hair, hoping to smooth out what I knew was a mess of salty drying tangles. The silence stretched. For the life of me I couldn't think of anything to say. "How are you?" seemed silly. And "nice day" was self-evident and dull.

"Nice day," he said, eyes unwavering.

"I've just been swimming." *Duh.* "Would you like something to drink?"

"No, thank you."

I stood there fidgeting, for all the world feeling like a naughty child confronted by its parent. And his next words confirmed there was good reason for my defensiveness.

"I am not accustomed to taking refreshment from someone who considers me a blood-sucking, mind-twisting, psychopathic hypnotist."

*Oh-oh.*

"Yes, oh-oh. What in the world have I done to make you suddenly so afraid of me?"

In that moment, in the light, pumped from my swim and rock-climbing daring-do, hormones triggered by all the sunshiny vitamin D I'd absorbed, excruciatingly aware of my body's reaction to the sight of his well-muscled form under the casually opened shirt, I was definitely not afraid.

I was pissed.

All my pent-up worries and frustrations and attraction boiled up in an instant, spilling over. "What have you done? You gotta be kidding me! What *haven't* you done?" I glared at him, hands on hips. "You show up out of freaking nowhere. You read my mind, zap me into some sort of infinite black hole and presto! change my body back 30 years like . . . like something out of *The Picture of Dorian Grey*. Then you ask me to worship you. Then you take the offer of eternal youth away. Then you leave. Then you come back. Then you leave. What the hell am I supposed to think?"

I was on a roll, waving my arms and stamping around the patio.

"I can't even *think* when I'm around you. I get all hormonal like a teenager with cotton candy for a brain. And all the while you're playing me like a violin just like every other god has done when they got involved with a mortal." My voice rose in pitch and decibel level. "And who's the one that always ends up getting turned into a toad or a tree stump or dying some horrible death in the end? Not the eternal goddamned god, that's for sure!

"And you have the unmitigated gall to waltz in here and ask me why I'm afraid of you? Gee, uh . . . duh . . . let me think!" I stopped, hyperventilating.

There was a long pause.

A part of me wanted to laugh. I always get the urge to laugh at the most critically serious moments of my life—like there's something way down deep inside me that knows better than to take any of this human drama stuff seriously. And I could see the answering flicker of the truth of this in his eyes. But he didn't laugh.

Instead he said, "If I were any kind of man at all I would get up, come over there and kiss the hell out of you right now until all of this stupidity faded away to nothing."

My eyes widened and my knees threatened to buckle.

"But that would simply be one more example of my terrible influence over you and proof positive that all your accusations of psychological and sexual manipulation are true."

We stared at each other for a very long time.

Impasse.

I picked up my pack, muttering, "I'm going to take a shower," and stalked off with as much dignity as my Jell-O knees could muster.

∞∞∞∞∞∞∞∞

*What to wear what to wear?* Savagely I rummaged through the closet. Sundress? Wrinkled. Pants? Too hot. Shorts? They made my waist and hips look thick.

*Who cares what you wear, you silly twit! You don't even know if he's still down there! And what do you care anyway?*

*But he said he wanted to kiss me!*

*And you just told him to piss off because he's dangerous and you need him in your life like a . . . like a . . .*

Hole in the head.

That was it. I had a hole in my head and my brains were leaking out. That must be what was wrong with me. In defiance of my own need to look my best, I grabbed a faded pair of cotton yoga pants, yanked on a rumpled t-shirt and refused to blow dry my hair, running a brush through it instead.

Barefoot and breathless, I rushed back down the stairs, refusing to peek around the corner of the dining room to see if he was still there. Pretending indifference, I sauntered into the kitchen and poured myself a glass of water at the sink, casually, oh, so casually turning around to see if . . .

He was still there.

My hand started to shake and I set the glass on the grey concrete countertop with enough of a *crack!* it was a wonder it didn't break. And in that moment I knew it was over.

He'd already won and we both knew it. Had known it from the start. All my bluster was just show—the little human standing up for her small self in the face of something ever so much larger—

like a flea jumping up and down thinking its actions will move the dog off its course.

Who was I kidding? I might irritate him. But I wouldn't change what he was and what he was about. And I didn't want to.

I wanted mystery. I wanted answers. I desperately yearned for a larger conversation with somebody *larger* than me Most people were so boring. Society was so lost. The day-to-day grind of making money to survive was degrading and soul killing. Where was there any light? Where was genuine guidance without ulterior motives? Where was wisdom? Where could man and womankind find hope? Not the desperate hope born out of pain and despair—but the hope that comes from knowing there is a path out of the darkness?

My body began to shake and tears started in my eyes.

I wanted this—wanted what was happening with this . . . man? God? Thought form? Illusion? I wanted more from life. I had asked for more, loudly and often, and here it was . . . everything I'd ever wanted and oh, so much more being handed to me on a plate. And what had I done? Had I been equal to the opportunity? No! I'd sunk beneath the waves of my own fears and doubts and smallness.

My fist clenched on the countertop beside my forgotten glass of water. What did the spiritual teacher Marianne Williamson once say? *It's not our darkness that frightens us but our Light.* I dashed the tears from my eyes and looked out the French doors.

Apollo had every reason to be angry with me. He was the god of Light for heaven's sake—the template for intelligence and higher consciousness. And I'd let a bunch of stupid talk about vampires and some old Greek woman's superstitions get the better of me, running roughshod over what, in the deepest places in my heart, I knew was the truth: that Apollo was who he said he was, that my own desires and dreams had manifested squarely into my life, and that it was up to me to put my big girl pants on in order to be equal to whatever the task at hand actually was.

I squared my shoulders and took a few deep breaths.

*Nothing like a good, self-administered bitch slap to put things in perspective.* And with that thought, I picked up my glass and walked outdoors to join Apollo.

❖❖❖❖❖❖❖❖

He eyed me warily as I sat down. Which surprised me. I figured he'd remotely tracked the whole emotional storm in the bedroom and kitchen and would be up to speed by now.

He shook his head. "Your thoughts when we are not together should be your own. I should never have pried yesterday. I am . . . sorry."

Apology didn't come easily for him and I was touched by the effort. "No, I'm the one who's sorry," I said earnestly. "I was being incredibly stupid."

"No, no, you were right. We are an entitled lot and it is really not a fair contest . . ." he stopped himself.

"Between the gods and human beings?" I finished his sentence for him, laughing. "Hey, we play along swallowing the whole unworthiness thing." I shook my head. "It's easier thinking you're nothing. That way you're never disappointed in yourself."

We were silent, not looking at each other.

Two raucous crows flipped past overhead, black wings beating the air. I still couldn't get used to Greek crows with their buff-colored bodies and strange calls. A third crow joined the pair and all three circled the house before dropping down to settle on the lawn in front of us, heads cocking back and forth, watching us, beady-eyes curious.

"λίγο αγγελιοφόροι," Apollo whispered, smiling.

"What?

"Little messengers."

Of course. The crow was one of Apollo's sacred birds, along with the hawk, the raven and the swan.

"When I was a little girl there were always lots of crows around. They'd sit in a row up on the telephone lines and hang around in the trees of our yard. I used to try to talk to them and thought they had very important things to tell me if only I could speak their language." I laughed, remembering my mother's worried expression as she watched me sitting patiently in the yard mimicking the cawing noises I heard, hoping for a reply. "Everybody said they were pests. But I didn't believe them. I thought crows were grand and wise."

The three on the lawn hopped closer, clucking softly.

"They were my first connection to you," said Apollo.

I turned to him questioningly.

He cleared his throat. "It was a way to be close without arousing any suspicions."

"What?"

"I could not just show up in your yard," he explained. "Your family would have rightly called the police."

My mouth sagged open.

"You have a thing for hawks too, don't you? You see them everywhere."

"I almost took up falconry," I whispered.

"And you think it is a coincidence that your mother gave birth a month early so you were born under the protection of the lion?"

*Apollo's sacred animal.*

"And it is another coincidence that you play and compose on the harp and are attracted to medical subjects and mysticism, I suppose?" He shook his head, smiling. "And Delphi was the first place you traveled in the world when you were what, nineteen?"

I was shocked. *He knows so much about me!*

Apollo's temple was a place I'd dreamed of ever since I first read about it in grade school. Greek mythology had captured my mind so completely I ended up with a double major in college between English and archaeology. My parent's gift of a three-week trip through Greece at age nineteen, although I had been accompanied by my mother, had been the highlight of my young life.

Apollo chuckled softly. "You were so curious and filled with life. One of the hardest things I've ever done was not talk with you then." His eyes held a distant look. "I remember you walking around my temple barefoot the whole time so you could connect more deeply with the energies of the past. I think that is how you explained it to your mother?"

"And I smoked cigarettes the whole time and had to keep asking her to 'Step on that would you please, mom?' every time I dropped a butt on the ground."

"Never once stopping to think you were desecrating my holy precinct with your trash."

*Ooops.* I thought. *Filthy habit.*

"Hmmmm," he agreed.

"Back in those days you could walk through the amphitheater," I said wistfully. "I remember sitting on the top row one evening at sunset, waiting for all the tourists to leave so I could have the place to myself."

"And you did the same thing this time," he said.

"What?"

"You came and sat just outside the ropes almost exactly where you sat forty-one years ago. And the guards had to fetch you at closing—just like before."

"Oh, my God. That's right," I murmured, awed at how patterns repeat themselves. "So, why didn't you approach me the first time?" *Back when I was young.* I couldn't keep the thought from taking form even though it was silly and I already knew the answer.

He sighed. "You were not ready. You were so

naïve . . . so willing to take the world at face value. So programmed by the world itself. So . . ."

"Ignorant." I supplied. "And pliable."

"Yes." He nodded.

"You would have blown me away," I said bleakly.

"I would have destroyed you," he replied bluntly.

What could I say to that? He was right. But then I suddenly realized he was only partially right. "We destroy ourselves, Apollo," I said, mildly. "Sometimes we just have help."

It was the first time I'd spoken his name.

He looked at me squarely. "That we do, Ekateríni. That we do."

There was more to his agreement than just words. A veritable avalanche of meaning lay behind them and for a little while Apollo just sat there, hands folded across his flat belly, looking out to sea. Then he heaved a great sigh. "You have no idea how convoluted the path to destruction can be."

His words lay heavy upon the air. Finally, he threw his hands up in resignation. "Where to begin?" He looked at me wretchedly. "How do I tell you this?"

"Tell me what?" I asked, growing alarmed.

He sat there, clearly at a loss as to what to say. The crows, feeling our distraction, croaked their goodbyes and flew away.

"Some people start at the beginning when they write a story," I prompted, softly. "Some start in the middle. Some skip around writing whatever parts come to mind and then glue it all together." I pulled my chair closer to the coffee table and Apollo. "Me? I'm boringly methodical. I start with chapter one and plod on through to the end, one step at a time."

He nodded abstractedly, then shrugged and started talking. "Since we began our conversation, have you not wondered how an Ideal—a pure idea such as myself—came to take human form?"

I was confused. "You told me at Delphi." I cast my mind back to that conversation in the sun on the slopes of Mount Parnassus—a conversation that seemed like a million years ago. "I was surprised you were physical and you said something like, 'What kind of template for mortality would I be if I could not take mortal form?' . . . or something like that."

"That is what I said." He paused. "I lied."

"You what?"

"I dodged the truth because in that moment you were not ready to hear it."

"What . . . and now I am?" I asked, sarcastically.

He nodded. "We have touched upon it already."

"We have?"

He made a sweeping motion with his hands indicating his body. "I am a perfect example of how the most pristine precise creation, once put into motion, can run away with itself and produce unexpected forms and derivative creations."

???

"And you . . . you . . ." he jumped out of his chair and started to pace the patio. "You say how easy it is for you as a human to feel worthless. To feel as if you are nothing. Nothing!" He groaned, hands clenched.

"What a foul joke! And by the gods who made you feel that way? Eh? *We* did." He thumped his chest angrily. "And you know why?" He stopped in front of me, glaring down. "Because we were jealous of humanity and ultimately feared you."

"What? B-but that doesn't make any sense," I said.

"No? Ekateríni, I was created to be the ideal of the perfection of masculine beauty and the functioning of the masculine principle through the intelligence of higher mind. But I am a mere blueprint . . . whereas *you*. Good God, woman, don't you see? *You*—man and woman—are the house all the blueprints were created for . . . the temple through which the divine Source can shine in bright fullness."

He stopped, distraught at my confounded look, running a hand through his heat-dampened curls.

"Humans are designed to be creators just as Source itself is creative. Yes, everything ever created evolves and, in a sense, everything creates because it is one with Source. Even rocks dream and have consciousness. But humans were intended to be more than just animals. You were designed to learn and evolve and eventually understand who you are so you could become a conscious creator and take a full part in creation itself."

He shook his head wonderingly. "Even when you dream at night you spin new forms into life. You cannot help creating any more than I can help being beautiful. It is what you are. And just as humans write characters in books and create songs and paintings and civilizations . . . just as your scientists and computer people are now experimenting with what you call artificial intelligence, which will, by the way, be the next derivative intelligence created in this part of your galaxy," he bowed his head and I could no longer see his eyes. "So you created me."

"Excuse me?" I was sure I hadn't heard him correctly.

"Humanity created all the gods and goddesses—the whole pantheon and more besides."

I leaned back in my chair. "I don't get it." I said flatly. "How?"

"You are spirit, Ekateríni. Consciousness. God, if you will. And once God comes into form that form starts its own creative processes. But you got lost in the overwhelming sensory overload of physical existence. You did not know who and what you really are. You still do not."

Abruptly he started to pace the patio. "You got lost and became frightened and confused. And in your confusion you unconsciously invested all your considerable psychic power—all your thoughts and emotion—into worshipping and placating forces outside you.

"You turned around and made gods out of the very Ideals that helped birth you. You invested *us* with independent life and eventually, over eons of time, gave us the power to take form. You made the gods you believed in real by worshipping and fearing them." He stopped once again in front of my chair and looked down at me, copper eyes bleak. "And you are still doing it."

I stared back at him, eyes wide. *Holy shit!!* My mind spun, grasping for something solid and rational and all I could find was wheels within wheels within wheels.

"Ezekiel's vision was an excellent visual representation of what he realized about the nature of reality," Apollo said, visibly trying to calm down. Taking a long breath, he exhaled slowly. And as the tension left his body, his eyes softened. "You look like you are drowning."

"I feel like I'm drowning," I admitted, looking up at him helplessly. "I don't know what to say. I don't know where to even begin to go with this."

"Perhaps some food would help?" he asked hopefully.

*Food?* I laughed semi-hysterically. "You tell me we created the gods that have been lording it over us for thousands of years and ask me if I want to eat?"

He shrugged, looking miserable. "Ekateríni, what can I say? This is one of the things I came back to explain. It is time the conspiracy of silence and the gods' power over you is broken. I have risked much to do this. And I did not know how to tell you except to prepare you as best I could and then . . . tell you."

"Uh . . . a little late aren't you?"

"How do you mean?"

I laughed humorlessly. "I hate to be the one to break it to you, Apollo. But you guys have been out of power here for quite some time."

He shook his head dismissively. "There are other gods, Ekateríni. And they are very real and their influence over humanity today is extremely powerful and completely self-serving."

Shivers ran up my arms and neck. Mutely I looked up at him standing before me, arms dangling at his sides, face naked, as honest and vulnerable as could possibly be. And it was that, more than anything else, that allowed me to accept what he'd just told me. Not understand it. But accept it.

The bombshell he'd just dropped was too big, too otherworldly, too overwhelming to be immediately absorbed. Nor could I connect to it on a personal level. I was, truth be told, numb. Plus, I had the feeling I'd only been allowed to see the tip of the iceberg.

I shivered again.

"Come. Let me cook you something." He reached out a hand. I took it gratefully and he hauled me to my feet. The contact was warm, his touch comforting rather than electric.

"You cook?" I asked, dazed, letting go of his hand. *Of all the silly things to ask at this point.*

He bowed, hand on his smooth tanned chest. "I am a blueprint of many talents," he replied.

"Better watch it or I'll start believing you really are the ideal man," I laughed shakily, then led the way back into the house to the kitchen.

◊◊◊◊◊◊◊◊◊

## CHAPTER EIGHT

Apollo rummaged through the shelves, frowning. I'd only picked up the bare essentials the night before and the cupboards were sparse on supplies.

The tension was easing now that we were dealing with the mundanities of food, and I realized a lot of time and action had passed since breakfast. "Do you have to cook?" I asked plaintively, stomach growling. "Can't you just . . ." I snapped my fingers, "zap a meal out of the ethers?"

"Of course, I can," he replied absently. "But where is the fun in that?" He opened the fridge, peered inside, shook his head and closed the door. "Eating is one of life's great pleasures, Ekateríni. Like the seduction of a woman, it should be approached deliberately, with great attention to detail and no effort spared."

Oh, my God. Would this guy ever cease unnerving me? *Probably not.*

"How about a snack?" I said, trying to ignore the sensual reaction I'd had to his words. I pulled a package of homemade breadsticks from the local bakery out of the breadbox and a tub of Hellman's spicy cheese spread out of the refrigerator—a taste treat unavailable in the States and something I'd been looking forward to for weeks.

"Packaged food?" said Apollo, looking revolted.

"Don't knock it till you try it." I wrestled with the packaging, shoved a breadstick in the cheese and, resisting the desire to eat it myself, raised it to Apollo's lips. "Open wide."

Rolling his eyes, he complied.

Not waiting to see his reaction, I grabbed my own breadstick, dipped it and ate.

He chewed deliberately then smiled despite himself. "Not bad." He reached for another breadstick.

"Ha!" I crowed, vindicated.

A half-pack of breadsticks and a tub of cheese later we were sated sufficiently to consider shopping for food. "What do we need? I asked.

"I think Saganaki cheese, red peppers, capers, tomatoes and whatever is fresh at the docks," he said. Clearly the dinner menu had been decided.

The drive to town was swift with Apollo clearly enjoying the ride. By silent mutual agreement we avoided heavy topics and any reference to our earlier conversation. After a brief stop at the grocery story we found ourselves on the wharf in Naoussa. Traditional Greek kaikis—brightly colored fishing boats—lay at anchor, bobbing with the tide. In the town itself, shops displayed the ever-more-expensive offerings of European clothing and Greek specialty items the tourists expected. But out on the docks, business hadn't changed in thousands of years.

After much sniffing, poking and haggling in Greek by Apollo, I dutifully paid for the large mackerel he selected, placing it, well-wrapped, in my environmentally-friendly hemp shopping bag. Walking back along the narrow, winding streets, I window-shopped, laughing at Apollo's pithy comments about the products on display and how very much better things had been made three thousand years ago.

I linked my arm through his. "Come on old man. Let's hit the wine shop and find something to go with this monster fish you made me buy."

We entered the shop, laughing about something or other. It was cool and dark inside after the late afternoon brightness of the cobbled streets—so much so I practically ran over Chris and another woman standing beside the cash register getting ready to leave.

"Kathryn!" she squealed, pulling me into the usual kiss-kiss greeting. "Angela and I were about to go back to my place and . . ." she stopped mid-sentence as she realized I wasn't alone. "And . . ." her voice trailed off as she examined the man standing next to me.

*Ack!* Introductions! What to say?

The four of us stood there frozen—Apollo grinning fiendishly at me while Chris and Angela stared at him. *Name name name! My kingdom for a name!* my mind shrieked. The silence lengthened uncomfortably.

There was no getting out of it, so I took a deep breath and said, "Chris, Angela this is . . ."

"Apollo Aureleous Tavoularis at your service ladies," supplied Apollo, slightly stressing the word *service.* He shook hands cordially, first with Chris then Angela.

Chris managed a strangled "Hi." Angela just stood there.

I couldn't believe his sexually over-toned introduction. *Not funny Apollo!* I hurled the thought at him with all the force I could muster.

He didn't even flinch. "We were just looking for some white wine to go with an excellent fish I am cooking Ekateríni for dinner," Apollo supplied, not yielding in the slightest. "Might you ladies have any suggestions?"

"I already know what I want," I snapped, stalking into the back room leaving the three of them standing there transfixed. Well, two of them at least. Totally ignoring the sign saying: "Do not touch bottles. Please ask for assistance," I grabbed two bottles of white wine I recognized off the shelves and headed back to the cash register.

*Two can play at this game,* I thought. "Darling," I drawled, smiling sweetly at Apollo. "Would you mind?" I nodded to the shop assistant ringing up my selections.

"Of course, my dear," he said, not missing a beat, fishing in his ever-tight jeans for the wallet he must have just conjured. "How about a digestif for *afterwards?*"

"We'll need a digestif?" I batted my eyelashes at him.

"Of course," he said, ignoring my small riposte.

"Well, then." I edged past Chris and grabbed

the largest, most expensive bottle of Masthika I could find on the shelves and brought it back to the register. Apollo paid for it all with a flourish.

"Nice meeting you both," he said, taking the bag in one hand and my arm in the other. "Perhaps we can all get together sometime?"

Angela babbled something and Chris glared questions at me as I made my goodbyes and accompanied him out the door. I could feel their eyes boring holes through us as we walked across the plaza headed for my car. No way was I going to turn around!

"Well, that was fun," I said, sarcastically.

"Indeed, it was," agreed Apollo. "I think we should have them both over for dinner sometime."

He sounded like the wolf in Little Red Riding Hood. Despite still being in observation range, I stopped, pulling my arm from Apollo's grip, turning to confront him. "How dare you do that to me in front of my friends!"

"Do what?" he replied innocently.

"Act like you're my boyfriend or something. And all those sly sexual innuendos!"

"I never have never understood the modern expression 'boyfriend'," he ruminated. "Boys are worthless when it comes to satisfying a woman, in bed or out. And women do not want male *friends*." He shrugged.

"Wha . . ." I could hardly believe what I'd just heard. "I have lots of male friends," I said, outraged.

"Do you now?" he drawled, eyebrows lifting.

"Several."

"And just how satisfying are those friendships?" he queried.

"Very!" I had to force myself to keep my voice level. "David and I are very close. We've even traveled together and it's been great."

"Of course," he said, implying the opposite. "I am sure it was all wonderfully fulfilling and that it would not have been anywhere near as much fun closing your evenings together with ecstatic lovemaking." He pretended a yawn.

I almost laughed. Doggone it, he was right. And I *so* did not want to admit it.

"Come, Ekateríni, your friends will be thinking we are having a lover's spat if you persist."

Willing myself not to turn around, I stalked off up the road, Apollo trailing behind, laughing softly in my wake.

∞∞∞∞∞∞∞

My anger vanished as I drove. Who was I kidding? I'd love it if Apollo were my boyfr. . . um, lover. I also knew that at a visceral female level I'd thoroughly enjoyed being seen in the shop with him. That part of me had lapped up his public comments like a cat does cream.

*Oh, to be a fly in Chris's car right now!* Idly I speculated on how long she'd wait the next morning before she called me, pressing for an explanation.

"Drachma for your thoughts," Apollo prompted.

"Ha ha," I shot back. "Like you don't know?"

He smiled happily, watching the scenery whip past. "I like how you drive. Very much how you used to handle a double-team chariot."

I took the bait. "And when was that?" *And where?*

"You already know the answer to both questions."

*Hm.* Dodging the issue I said, "I didn't know women drove chariots. I thought it was a guy thing."

"Depends on the woman," he replied. "We all have patterns, Ekateríni. All beings develop their own unique way of operating in the world—a signature frequency that in the East is called karma—impacting what you call the personality over the course of lifetimes." He glanced at me. "Yours is quick and dramatically dynamic."

"Calling me a drama queen?" I joked, far too interested in the topic to pretend otherwise.

"Hardly." He clammed up.

I waited impatiently. The last buildings on the outskirts of town were left behind and I hung an angled left onto the road to Ambalas. Finally, I couldn't stand it any longer and prompted him. "Anything else?"

"Cannot resist your favorite subject, eh?" he asked, drily.

"Everybody is their own favorite subject, Apollo," I replied. "Come on."

"Remember that you asked for it," he said. And when I didn't respond he continued. "You know damn well you are smart, aggressive, and not easily dissuaded from accomplishing your goals. You are a deep and logical thinker, Ekateríni. You come at things from all sides and contemplate what you learn and then apply it. You are egotistical about the depth of your esoteric knowledge. But when you find your information is incomplete or just plain wrong, you don't hold on. To your credit you can shift rapidly, change your position and enlarge your view. You do not make snap decisions unless you already *know* what the situation demands, which you frequently do because you are extremely psychic."

He paused, then chuckled.

"You are also extraordinarily sensitive, easily hurt, and care far too much about what others think of you. You yearn for peace and success—which are mutually exclusive goals, and you want love yet you are a loner. Both of these conflicts bring you much pain. You have tremendous strength and resilience but refuse to admit weakness, physical or otherwise. You lick your wounds in private out of pride which does not serve you. You are insecure in your sexuality, vain about your body, and thus the whole aging process is traumatic for you. Enough?"

I downshifted in a racing change and hung a sharp right at the long wall of golden-colored rock and then, after series of low hills, hung a sharp left, paying close attention to the round road mirror erected by the locals to reveal oncoming cars.

Fishing for compliments, his brutal honesty had been unexpected. But I had to admit it was a ruthlessly fair assessment. And, after all, I had indeed asked for it. *Okay then,* I thought. *Since we're being honest with each other, enough tease and thrust and parry already.*

"What are we doing together, Apollo?" I asked. "Seriously, what are you doing in my life?"

He didn't respond immediately and I was too busy driving the narrow curves to look his way. The donkeys and paint horse grazed placidly as we whipped passed, golden dust rising in the air behind us. Finally, he spoke. "There has to be a certain groundwork of understanding laid before I can tell you that." He tapped his fingers on his left knee. "We are almost to the place where you will know everything."

I turned in the long narrow driveway and my spirits rose as my little house by the sea appeared ahead. Apollo's energy shifted as well, but downwards into a much darker place.

"There are things in this world that need correcting, Ekateríni. Things I am responsible for. Things my fellow Olympians are responsible for. Terrible things," he finally added, voice flat.

We'd left the gate to the house open and I drove straight in and stopped the car. Apollo turned towards me in his seat. "I have come to you because you are my best hope of making amends."

What could I say to that?

Silently we unloaded the car and I unpacked the groceries, placing the bottles of white wine in the freezer for a quick chill. Apollo set about preparing the fish, cracking open the new spice bottles, sniffing and tasting while I took a cold bottle of already-opened  wine from the fridge. Without asking, I poured two glasses. He absently nodded his thanks and I left the kitchen to go upstairs and change.

It cooled off quickly once the sun started its last leg of descent. I washed my face, eyeing the deep bathtub beneath the west-facing windows with longing. I was tired and, despite my recent shower, a long soak would feel good.

"How long before dinner?" I shouted down the stairs.

"Leave the chef to his work," came the reply. "Take your time and relax."

Relax? Like I could relax after his earlier comments. But at least he seemed in a better mood.

As the tub poured, I stood on the balcony, watching a kaiki slowly troll across the bay, its engines throbbing in the deep put-put sound distinct to the craft, making gradual headway north towards home and safe harbor. In the passage between Paros and her sister island, Naxos, a massive blue and orange car ferry motored swiftly along the channel headed towards Santorini. To the south across the bay, the abandoned monastery on top of the high cone-shaped hill shone gold in the last rays of the sun.

It all looked so peaceful. But I knew it was a superficial peace. Sure, left to her own devices, Mother Nature would spin along in perfect harmony. Unfortuantely, it wasn't part of human nature to leave the natural order of things alone—our egos wouldn't let us. Thinking we knew best, thinking we had creation all figured out, we had to meddle in everything. I laughed sourly. *I thought I knew the order of things.* I sighed. *Just this morning I had life all figured out.*

Apparently not.

Mood heavy, I went indoors. The tub was full and, setting my wine glass on the edge, I climbed in with a groan of sensory bliss. *Bodies do have their moments.* I took a sip of wine and relaxed more deeply in the water, letting the heat soak in. *Ahhhh . . .* so much pleasure and joy came through the senses. And yet the body was also the root of so much pain and suffering. And not just physical pain either.

I examined my body floating in the water. Clearly there was a difference between "me" and the water surrounding me. I had a skin boundary. A border that declared "this is me" and "that is not me." And it was this message of separation coming into my brain 24/7 from my eyes, ears, skin and other senses that told me I was alone in the world, that I was separate from everybody and everything else around me.

And it hadn't taken long as a little kid to learn that "not me" things like the kitchen stove, the cat, the paring knife, and even other people around me, could hurt me. The message that I was alone in a scary, hurt-filled world was loud and clear.

No wonder the world was in such bad shape. Most people probably felt just as alone as I did at three in the morning—just as scared, just as vulnerable, just as hard pressed to figures things out. Maybe a lot of people didn't show it. Hell, I put on a good face with others. Hadn't Apollo just pointed out in the car how insecure and prideful I was?

I put on a good show because that was part of the survival game of not displaying weakness to "others" because "they" might take advantage and hurt me. *So much for the nice spiritual idea that all is One,* I thought, chagrined.

But how to genuinely get beyond the illusion of being separate? How to recognize that my neighbor really *is* me—not just because the Bible and quantum physics say so but because somehow I have seen and grasped the truth of it?

A faint rhythmic sound caught my attention. Apollo was chopping something in the kitchen, and I smiled. Of all the mundane things for a god to be doing.

*A god that humanity created.*

I twirled the remaining wine in my glass and took a swallow. Talk about turning the order of things on its head. Holy crap. I hadn't had enough time to even begin to digest what Apollo had told me. And what about the other gods he had alluded to? The more modern ones that apparently didn't have humanity's best interests at heart? That had sounded ominous indeed.

Was that why Apollo was hanging around on Earth? But what could that possibly have to do with me?

No answers forthcoming, my mind slid to the delicious banter in the liquor store. Both Chris and Angie had looked like they were going to explode from curiosity and hormones. Dear God, no woman alive could resist Apollo when he turned on the charm. *Except old Greek women on ferry boats.*

I could still see her face, black eyes glittering, fingers forked, hissing at him to go away. Of all the strange things that had happened since Apollo showed up, that was the weirdest.

My mind dodged uneasily away from the memory and, with nothing else to do, I began to brood on all the other things women brood about when they're hopelessly attracted to a man that's not good for them. Finally, wine gone and pungent aromas wafting up the stairs, I got out of the tub, dried off, and contemplated what to wear.

The fish was smothered in herbs, the cheese was marinating in a bowl, the wine was on ice in a bucket, and the chef was wiping down the countertop as I made my entrance. "Very nice," Apollo said appreciatively, eying the neckline of my low-cut black dress. Or maybe it was the long slit up the side of the skirt exposing a grand amount of leg he was looking at? To my combined relief and disappointment, he'd finally buttoned up his shirt.

We bantered easily for a few minutes, avoiding more serious subjects. Then he put the fish on to grill. "I'll set the table," I said, and commenced poking though drawers and shelves, totally getting in his way as I looked for placemats and napkins and all the other accoutrements to fine dining. And there was no doubt the dining would indeed be fine this night.

By the time I'd gotten to the point of lighting

candles, the fish was resting and Apollo was carrying the first course to the table: marinated Saganaki cheese atop a seasoned and grilled green pepper along with tomato and olives.

I poured more wine and sat down.

"Bon appetite," he said, raising his glass.

"Yamas." We clinked glasses and dug in.

Fried cheese, if not done right, can be tough, tasteless and chewy. His somehow melted in my mouth without losing its firmness and texture, the marinade flavors blending perfectly with the grilled veggies. "Yum!" I said, enthusiastically.

"I knew you would like it."

"Really," I said, taking another hearty forkful. "Okay. What was my favorite food when I was a little girl?"

He was eating gracefully and yet with gusto. He waited to finish a bite before answering. "That is too easy."

"If it's so easy, then what's the answer?

"Grilled cheese sandwiches, of course. Your mother despaired of getting you to ever eat anything else. Especially spinach."

He was right.

"I thought you said you only knew the interesting things about me."

"If I am planning a meal I take great interest in knowing the likes and dislikes of the person I am cooking for," he said, haughtily. "You, fortunately, are easy."

"How so?"

"You have said in the past that you are on the seafood diet?" he asked casually, eyes twinkling.

The see food and eat it diet. *Very funny, Apollo.*

By the time we finished the first course in respectful silence, the mackerel was ready. Considered a bait fish in America, mackerel is a delicacy in Greece. This one was delicately seasoned and grilled, flesh almost falling off the bones yet not overcooked. The accompanying salad of mixed greens with orange and poppy seeds matched it perfectly. A hearty Greek peasant bread sat waiting on the side.

I watched as Apollo sopped up fish juice with a hunk torn off the loaf. "The Greeks have a thing about bread, don't they?" I ventured.

He looked up. "How do you mean?"

"It's on every table at every meal. You can't avoid it. Which plays hell on your diet if you're trying to go gluten-free."

He popped the last morsel in his mouth and chewed appreciatively. "Bread is a sacrament," he finally said. "It is rude not to partake of at least a small piece when people are eating together."

"Really? I didn't know that."

"Obviously," he said, indicating the breadless remains on my plate.

Dutifully I reached out, broke off a small chunk, emulated his plate cleaning and ate.

"We will make a Greek out of you again yet," he said, approvingly.

"Again?"

"Really, Ekateríni. Have you not sensed that you

have lived here before? I have alluded to it several times."

*Delphi.*

"Of course," he snorted.

"And the 'we'?"

"I was speaking rhetorically." He poured the last of the wine into my glass.

"Well, speaking unrhetorically, that was simply amazing. Thank you for cooking. I'm impressed."

"It was my pleasure."

I got up and cleared the table, rinsing the dishes and leaving them in the sink while Apollo disappeared with our wine glasses into the living room. "Shall we open the next bottle?" I called.

"What do you think?" came the answering reply.

I opened the wine, set out some fruit for dessert and walked into the living room. Our glasses were side by side on the coffee table in front of the comfortable sofa. The windowpanes were dark. And Apollo was nowhere to be seen.

No! My heart sank. He couldn't have! Not after such a great dinner! *Not when we're having such a lovely evening.*

The front door banged open and in he walked carrying a large armload of wood. Kicking the door shut behind him he crossed the room, dumping the wood onto the curved hearth, little pieces of bark falling to the slate floor below. Dusting his hands and shirtsleeves he piled kindling into the grate, then turned to me.

"I am practicing being human and doing things

the hard way," he grinned. Then he picked up on my panicked thoughts of abandonment and his face turned serious. "Ekateríni . . ." He closed the small distance between us until we were bare inches apart. "I promise I will not leave you like that ever again," he said softly.

I stood still, feet riveted to the floor, looking up into his strange eyes and my breath caught. They had flecks of green in them . . . and gold. Tenderly he reached out a hand and stroked my face then grasped my chin to make sure I didn't look away. "We have a long road to travel together, my dear—if, that is, by the time you fully understand why I am in your life again, you decide of your own free will to travel it with me."

His thumb caressed my cheek and I had to will my eyes to stay open and not just blindly sink into the sweetness of his touch. And, in that moment, I realized I had nothing to fear from Apollo—only myself.

It had never been a matter of him exerting his godly powers over me, kindling a sexual fire. My body's natural inclinations and my own heart would do all the work for him.

*Dammit.*

I tried to pull away but he wouldn't let me. Strong hands were on my shoulders, fingers softly caressing and I closed my eyes. A wave of desire rose swiftly and with it came a sense of shame and despair. If this were another test, I was failing horribly. Why couldn't I remain cool and logical and detached?

Why couldn't I stand on my own? Why did I still feel such a yearning for love and such a violent physical need?

*Biochemicals* came the internal answer. *I'm being seduced by my hormones . . . cortisol and dopamine and oxytocin and vasopressin. All my cuddle hormones are kicking in and I . . .*

His grip tightened. "Ekateríni, what the devil?"

I opened my eyes to see his face filled with dismay and suddenly I wanted to weep. Here, in this sweetest of moments, I'd ruined everything with my judgment about my body's needs and my personal longing for love. And all the while the real issue lay locked and growling behind closed doors deep down inside . . . the thought I'd held at bay for days . . . the thought that was tearing me apart inside: *He's so young and I'm so old and he can't possibly want me like this!*

Freed from its cage, my mind wailed its wretched, pent-up truth.

"Shush-sh-sh." Gently he pulled me to him until his face was against my hair, lips close to my ear. "Shush." He crooned. "These are crazy thoughts, Ekateríni. There is no test. What you feel is normal. How can you think such things?"

His arms cradled me and slowly I relaxed against his chest. And then my mind stepped in again. *But I am old! Old enough to know that sexual attraction offers false promise and no safety whatsoever!*

Apollo stiffened in response to my thought and pulled away, eyes boring into mine. "Old is relative. But you are right. There is no safety in the flesh,

Ekateríni. Only in the spirit. But that does not mean
the flesh should be despised or feared.

"Περπατήστε τους θεούς!" he cried suddenly,
pulling me back to his broad chest, arms tight around
me. "That this should happen to you of all beings."
He rocked me in his arms like a child and suddenly I
felt his body, so tightly glued to mine, lightly shudder
with . . . *weeping?*

How could this be? What was happening?

I could feel the tears dropping into my hair
as he rested his cheek against the top of my head.
And in that moment of astonished wonder I let him
in—opened my mind and unguarded my heart—
and suddenly there was a bright *flash!* and I heard
laughter . . . a woman's laughter, uninhibited and
free and an answering baritone call.

Through the meadow of anemones and daisies
on the mountainside ran a red-haired woman, naked
to the waist, skirts bunched in one hand, flowers in
the other, laughing, quickly dodging around a bay
laurel tree to escape Apollo who was in hot pursuit,
naked body gleaming in the sun.

Quicker than the eye could follow he darted
around the tree and grabbed her by the waist and
they twirled, locked, spinning, her body arched
backwards, long red hair sweeping the ground,
flowers dropping from her hand. And he kissed
her merrily upon her breast and then her mouth.
And together, laughing, they fell into the sea of
wild grasses and flowers, surrendering themselves
to the sunshine and heat of their passion. And for

one exultant moment I merged with the red-haired woman and I was her and she was me and Apollo was inside us, possessing us both, body, mind and soul.

"This is how I remember you."

The voice was faint and far away.

"Unfettered by rules and silly ideas."

The voice was close, next to my ear, carried on Apollo's warm, sweet breath. "This is the beautiful being you were created to be, not the tortured woman filled guilt and self-loathing I see before me."

Apollo's words slapped me abruptly back into my body, the bright vision and echoes of laughter cut short as if a door had slammed shut upon them. I gasped, shocked and confused, mourning the passing of that all-too-quick moment of shared ecstasy with the unknown woman.

Apollo hugged me tight for a moment longer, then let me go. Instantly, my body was taken with sudden cold and I shivered. "Come," he gently eased me onto the sofa, then went to the dining room where I'd left my shawl. He put it around my trembling body and then shoved something hot into my hand.

"Drink," he commanded. And I did. Whatever it was, it was potent and very good. "Mulled honey wine," he said. With a sweeping gesture towards the fireplace, he set the kindling in the hearth ablaze. Then he sat beside me.

As I drank, a semblance of warmth and sanity stole back through me. Looking at the steaming mug in my hand I realized he'd morphed my cold wine glass into something more suitable for the moment and laughed shakily. "I th-hought you were practicing being more human."

He didn't answer, just put his arm around me. Between the heat of his body where it touched mine and the growing warmth in my belly, I stopped trembling and took another sip of the hot wine. "Who was she?" I whispered.

He sighed. "Her name—your name—was Polymnia," he said softly. "She came from the northern isles from a high house of the Druids. She had the Sight and much more besides. Her family sent her to my temple for additional training with the Pythia, although the Pythia of that time was growing old and she hardly needed it."

He shook his head, remembering. "It was a time of upheaval and change. Political power was shifting from Athens and religious power from Delphi to Macedonia. Intrigue and political maneuvering were the rule of the day. Polymnia came into the temple like spring after a long hard winter."

"What does . . . did her name mean?"

"She was named for the muse of sacred song and dance, but I swear she was the muse herself . . . the way she moved! Απίστευτος! It was a wonder to behold. And her voice! Like the ringing of a crystal bell. And her talents with the lyre were spellbinding. She enchanted everyone . . . including me. And because of this she made many enemies, starting with the Pythia who feared she would lose power to this 'upstart from a tribe of savages'."

He sighed. "Envy is an ugly thing amongst humans . . . and gods."

"What happened to her?"

He picked up his wine glass and drank. "You were poisoned," he said, flatly.

I gasped involuntarily.

"Tanis—the Pythia—moved more swiftly than I thought she would. And she had help from one I never believed would betray me." His jaw and eyes were hard, and he swallowed with obvious effort. "Before I could get you out of range of her priests, those mewling sycophants, and my sister . . . Ρωποπερπερηθρασ!" The air flamed with the curse and I inhaled sharply, shocked and not a little frightened.

It took him a moment to calm down, and I was moved at the effort it took. For myself, I felt very little. Interest surely. Who doesn't love hearing about past lives? And there was a felt sense of connection because of the moment I'd just shared with Apollo and my former self. But the feelings weren't urgent. Certainly I felt no anger. *Amazing that we can forget entire lifetimes and such powerful events!*

"It is a blessing that you cannot remember. And most assuredly a curse that I can." He sighed and continued.

"You were headed to a small town in Phocis near the Corinthian Sea. One of your own priestesses played you false—though she didn't mean to. Artemis appeared to her on the road and told the woman that in the bustle of packing at the temple you had been dosed with a slow-acting poison. She told her she brought the antidote which I had sent, and that she should pour it into your wineskin and give it to you.

"It was a potent dose of a very rare poison. And, trusting the message and the messenger, you drank the entire potion. Within minutes the poison had started eating away at your internal organs."

Abruptly he stood up and started pacing. "I found you dying next to the road, in agony, your attendants frantic. They'd done what they could. But they could not find a healer because all the best were under Tanis' control and forbidden to come to your aid."

"Did I die?" I whispered.

"Worse," he said. "You lived."

He turned away to stare into the fire. "More than my healing skills, it was your love for me that kept you alive. But the damage was terrible." His eyes were bleak, remembering. He ran a hand through his hair. "After that, I could not risk having you stay in Greece. Artemis vowed your death would be on my head if you did. So, I put you on the fastest ship back to the Misty Isles, never to return. And, although you eventually regained your health and vitality, you never bore children."

"But I don't understand," I cried, incredulously. "I thought you were all powerful . . . that you can do anything you want. Look what you did to me! For God's sake, you made me young again! Why couldn't you heal her . . . I mean me?"

Apollo laughed sourly. "Just one more thing I have not gotten around to telling you." He sighed and came back to the sofa. Sitting down he took one of my hands in his. "Ekateríni, I am not all powerful. And every individual human has free will. What happened at Delphi only happened because it was something you wanted."

"I don't understand!" I cried. "What are you saying?"

His grip on my fingers tightened. "I offered you your youth again. But unless you were capable of consciously operating at the frequency of cellular youth from that point on," he shook his head, "the change would have lasted only a short time. A few days at most."

"What?" I cried, pulling my hand away.

Apollo rushed on. "The same was true of Polymnia's healing. The poison she was given affected her systemically down to her very DNA. I could heal the immediate damage and I did. But it was up to her to manage the long-term effects."

My mind was spinning and his explanation about Polymnia barely registered. All I could think of was his betrayal of me on the mountainside, his trickery. "Why did you do it?"?" I whispered. "My God, why put me through that if you knew the effects wouldn't last?"

"I had to test you."

"Test me?!" I repeated blankly.

"Forgive me." He reached for my hand but I snatched it away. He sighed. "I had to make certain of the kind of person you were. I thought I knew. But I had to make sure I could not control you in any way." He shrugged unhappily. "How better to test a person than to offer them their heart's desire?"

I was practically speechless with hurt and indignation. "Why?" I grated.

"It was the only way I could be sure that if you agreed to do what I was going to ask of you that you were doing it with no thought of personal gain."

"And you did this with no concern about my feelings at all?" My voice ratchetted skywards.

"Of course, I cared about your feelings! But there is more at stake here than you know and I could not afford to put your feelings or mine ahead of the goal!"

I stared at him, mind whirling. Would there ever come a time when a conversation between us didn't end with some sort of personal bombshell or metaphysical drama? Would I ever be on any sort of even keel with this being? *Those who dare to touch the gods suffer both heaven and hell.*

No shit.

"So," I sorted through the whirling thoughts in my head, trying to calm down. "What goal are you talking about? What were you going to ask of me?"

"There are many things we need to discuss before we get to that," he said, evasively.

"Oh, I think we can get to it now, don't you?" I snapped, sarcastically. "Surely, we've gotten a mutual feel for the territory? You know you can't tempt me—even though you keep doing your damnedest with your endless flirting. And I know you're a quasi-powerful selfish bastard who only wants his own way and will do anything to get it."

I eyed him. "Does that about sum things up?"

He looked at me sadly. The fire that had been burning so merrily earlier was already dying. The evening that had begun so sweetly was turning into a full-fledged disaster.

"Alright," he sighed. "I will tell you."

For a long moment there was silence.

"I approached you because there are certain misperceptions—outright lies is what they actually were, that I, or rather we, the pantheon of gods, perpetrated on humanity after we had the power of physical manifestation bestowed upon us by *you*. For a very long time we were exactly as you say, scheming, manipulative bastards, with massive egos and outrageous power. And we used it to manipulate human beings into worshipping us and doing our every bidding."

He picked up his wine glass, tossing the contents back in one gulp. Instantly the glass refilled with wine.

He waved impatiently at the glass. "Party tricks. Any being with a true understanding of how life operates can manipulate matter, Ekateríni. It is not even matter. As we have discussed, it is energy waiting to be configured by thought and incredibly simple to do.

"But fill an empty cup in front of a primitive peasant?" He shrugged. "Instant worship. It was like

. . ." he thought for a moment. "What is that saying you have about fish?"

"Like shooting fish in a barrel," I answered automatically.

"Exactly." He set the glass down, stood back up and started pacing again.

"There have been tremendous ramifications to all that we have done with our ill-gained power. As a result of our influence, for example, today on this planet billions of people have highly destructive beliefs about Source Intelligence—God. Beliefs that are, quite frankly, leading you to your doom."

He sighed. "Please understand I am giving you the briefest possible summary and that there is much more involved than I can say right now under these circumstances . . . things you need to know." He stopped pacing, ran an exasperated hand through his hair, and looked at me.

"Basically, I came back to Earth to see if it would be possible to wake people up to their divinity." He rushed on. "I came back to tell people that they worship false gods and to warn them of the consequences. I approached you because you are peculiarly well suited this lifetime to aid me in disseminating my message."

He paused, then came back over to sit down next to me on the sofa again, eye to eye. "In the process of our working together, I hoped there would be a personal healing in it for you."

A personal healing? What the hell did that mean? *I stomped on her heart but then I gave her a healing so it all worked out in the end?* Apollo thought he could just use me to help deliver a message then disappear again, never looking back, thinking I was just happy to have served?

*I'm not that unselfish!*

My face flushed hotly and I looked down at my hands, thoughts and emotions seething. "How could I possibly help you do all that?" I finally mumbled.

Again he reached for my hand, trying to keep a connection going between us, but I moved my hands away. "You are a writer. Your books are published in many countries. You have a tremendous background in spiritual matters and a solid knowledge of modern science, psychology and consciousness. You understand everything I need to say and know how to explain it in modern terms." He paused. "I thought we could write a book together. A book that would set things straight."

*A book?*

Any remaining warmth inside me fled.

"You want to hire my services as a writer," I said numbly.

"Not hire," his fingers clenched on his knees. "I want to collaborate with you. I want us to set things right. To finish what we started so long ago. To help people see the truth about themselves and the gods."

Agitated, throwing off the shawl, it was my turn to leap to my feet. "Why not just show yourself to the world? Christ! All you'd have to do is walk into Syntagma Square and do party tricks! That'd get people's attention. You'd have a YouTube platform and a global following overnight. Everybody would be listening!"

"You know I can't do that," he said calmly.

"Why the hell not?"

"The worship thing."

*Ah yes, the worship thing. Right. Been there, done that, got the t-shirt.*

The silence between us lengthened to an uncomfortable degree. Sensing my rapidly increasing anger and upset, he pounded his knees in frustration.

"There are other reasons I want to do this with you," he rushed on. "You are so passionate, Ekateríni! Like few I have ever known. And you are through the silly stage of needing to project your passion upon an outside source or person. You no longer need to follow another. You know truth can only be found within yourself. And you are exceedingly tuned into your own spirit. If you were not you never could have pushed me away from you at Delphi that day."

So, there it was at last. The real truth behind the song and dance of flirtation and camaraderie Apollo had steadily built up over the past week. It all finally made sense. He needed my services . . . my professional writing skills and marketing contacts and my intellectual passion. Nothing more.

*Why would he want anything else? Silly me.*

I stood in the middle of the room, feeling used and embarrassed. My heart—the heart that had just an hour before felt so full and happy—was now a lead weight in my chest. *What a fool I've been! What a stupid stupid fool.*

Suddenly exhausted, I turned away. The sooner I could get out . . . away from the room, away from him, the better.

"Ekateríni!" he said, jumping to his feet, coming around the coffee table to my side. "You cannot leave! You do not fully understand yet!"

I moved away from him and retrieved my shawl, left in a heap on the sofa. Tossing it around my shoulders I pulled it tight across my bosom like a shield. "As much as it saddens me, Apollo, I really think I do."

"You do not!" he cried. "I love you!"

"Love?" I said, stunned. "How dare you say that! What do you know about love? All you know how to do is manipulate people to your advantage. You don't give a damn about my feelings! All you care about is your own vindication!"

"B-but, if you would only let me explain!"

He reached for my hands clenched at my breast, but I glared at him so fiercely he pulled back. "What else could you possibly have to explain?" I was practically shouting.

He groaned, smacking his hands against both sides of his head, turning away towards the fireplace then stomping back. "That I loved you over two-thousand years ago and never stopped. That I've watched you through incarnation after incarnation, waiting for the right time to come back into your life. That you carry sexual and psychological scars that I desperately want to help you heal. That I want to spend what little time I have left here on Earth with you!"

I faced him, unyielding.

"Gods!" He threw his hands in the air. "I knew I should never have let you talk me into telling you the truth so soon!"

I laughed mirthlessly. "You know, Apollo, maybe if you'd told me the truth from the start, you might have had a chance of this working. In fact, I know it would have worked. But no. You had to go and test me and then make me fall in love with you. You had to make me laugh and feel happy and young again. You had to inspire my mind. You had to stir up my heart with hopes and my body with desires I thought were long gone."

I was shaking again, but not from cold. "After a half-million lovers you'd think you would've learned something about women by now." I shook my head. "Take it from me, Apollo. Honesty really is the best policy."

"My love! Please, believe all I am telling you is true!"

His earnest face and pleading eyes didn't touch me. "Please, get out of my life," I said. And turned and walked away.

∞∞∞∞∞∞∞

## CHAPTER NINE

My cellphone's ringtone across the room was not a welcome sound. *Go away!* But the ringing persisted—a glistening harp arpeggio up and down the scale. Up and down, up and down. Groggily, I got up, staggered across the room to the dresser, grabbed the phone and looked at the caller ID. It was Chris.

*Who did you expect? Apollo?*

The previous night's fight came crashing back, along with its dreadful conclusion. Numbly I dropped the phone and went back to bed, pulling the covers over my head.

I was definitely not ready to face the day.

◎◎◎◎◎◎◎◎

At eleven she called again, and this time I surrendered to the inevitable. "Hello?" I answered thickly.

"Oh. My. Gawd. Is he still there? Can you talk?"

"You woke me up."

"Oh-ho, still in bed are we?"

"Chris, there is no we and yes, I'm still in bed. Or was."

"Up late?" she asked suggestively.

"Yes, I was." *Tossing and turning and crying and . . .*

"Well? You've got to tell me who that gorgeous man is!"

There was no getting out of a major feminine inquisition. "Alright, fine. Forty-five minutes at Christiana's." *I don't want to be alone with my thoughts anyway.*

"You could come to my place," she suggested.

I could. But somehow a public restaurant seemed easier to bear than a more intimate setting. I didn't even want to face my own kitchen, the place where Apollo had been happily cooking and making jokes only a few hours before.

"Kathryn?" she said.

"I'm here." *Sort of.* "Look, I feel like going out. See you there at," I looked at my phone. "Noon?"

"Perfect! Oh, I can't wait to hear!"

*I bet*, I thought sourly.

I took a long shower, got dressed, and fiddled for an uncharacteristically long time with my hair, trying to avoid heading downstairs and facing the scene from the night before. Some of the ashes from the long-since burned out fire had blown all over the living room floor. The strange mug that had once been a wine glass still sat on the coffee table next to the remains of Apollo's wine. I wandered into the kitchen. Dinner dishes still sat in the sink.

Looking around, I sighed. *What did you expect? A note? Flowers?*

Of course, that's exactly what a small part of me had hoped for. That against all odds Apollo would have ignored my command to get out of my life and hunkered down to ride out the storm like a man.

Which, of course, he wasn't.

I refused to cry any more. My eyes were red and swollen enough as it was. Facing Chris was going to include some tough explanations. I grabbed my purse and car keys and headed to the tiny community of Ambalas.

∞∞∞∞∞∞∞

Chris was already waiting for me in the open air dining room at Christiana's, its row of stone and cement arches opening onto an astonishing view of the glistening straits between Paros and Naxos.

"Coffee miss?" asked the waiter as I approached the table.

I loved waiters who called me "miss." *It's the little things as you get older.* "Kalimera. Yes, a latte please."

Chris looked up with eager eyes. "Well?" she said. Then she got a good look at my face. "Jesus, what happened?"

"And a good day to you, too," I said.

"Yes, yes, good morning. What happened? Have you been crying? What the hell's going on?"

I'd spent my time in the shower and the drive to the restaurant thinking about what to tell Chris and whomever else she'd told about Apollo. It was tempting to write him off as a handsome gigolo I'd met on the ferry coming to Paros, a man who'd made inaccurate assumptions about my wealth and status who buggered off as soon as he realized the sad truth over dinner at my sweet but humble rented abode.

But my pride wouldn't quite let me go there. So, I made up a different story.

"He's a film producer I've been talking to about shooting a segment for a documentary here in Greece about the divine feminine and the early goddesses—you know, based on my first book. He's got a house in Faringdon. When he learned I was coming here he rode over on the ferry with me. Then he asked if we could meet yesterday and have dinner and I said 'Yes.' I mean, Jesus, what woman wouldn't say yes. Right?"

I let my face and voice turn mournful. "And we were having such a great time when ..."

"What?"

"His lover called during dinner."

Chris's face drooped with disappointment. "But what about all that flirting you guys were doing? You could have cut the sexual tension between you two with a knife. Angie and I both about fainted just catching the backwash."

I forced a smile. "Since when does a lover keep a man from flirting with another woman?"

The waiter arrived with my much-needed coffee. I thanked him, took a grateful sip, and rushed on. "My God, you should have seen your faces!" I took another hit of coffee. It really was much too easy lying. And I was pointing fingers at Apollo?

"But you've been crying."

"Well, yeah," I said. "I was really pissed. And disappointed. And humiliated. At least I managed to hold it together until he left. Which he didn't want to do. I had to practically throw him out of the house."

"What?"

I snorted. "He kept saying, 'But darling, what difference does it make that I have another lover? I am Greek. And I am here with *you* now!' "

"Men!" cried Chris. "Damn. We were hoping you were . . . well, you know."

"Yeah, me too." Suddenly an impish thought danced into my mind. "Want to know the real pisser?" I asked.

Chris nodded.

"He's gay. Well, mostly gay. Gay with a healthy dose of bi."

"No!" she gasped. "He can't be!"

"Yep," I nodded, trying to look tragic. Which actually wasn't hard. "The lover who called was a guy. And was he ever having a hissy fit!" I heaved a mock sigh. "Why is it always the gorgeous ones?"

Chris allowed that she didn't know and wasn't it a crime. And much to my relief she asked when a mutual acquaintance was coming in from the States and did I want to read the latest draft of her book?

I lied some more and said I'd love to. Then, thankfully, we moved on to other things.

⊗⊗⊗⊗⊗⊗⊗⊗

I did everything possible to occupy my mind the rest of the day. I went shopping with Chris in Naoussa and then hiked to my swimming spot on the bay. But

it was futile. When I wasn't glancing over my
shoulder, hoping to catch a glimpse of red-brown
hair in the sun, my mind was replaying that terrible
scene in the living room, over and over and over—
what I said, what he said, what I should have said
and what I wished he hadn't.

I stared disinterestedly at the water from my
vantage point on the marble-strewn shore, watching
the wind send riffles across the surface. What a vain
fool I'd been letting Apollo's compliments and sexual
innuendos, his looks and touches go straight to my
head. *My God, he knew exactly how to play me!* Making me
laugh. Appealing to my ego, talking about spiritual
topics and ancient mythologies, courting me with
compliments about my knowledge and intelligence.

*Yeah, right . . . some intelligence.*

What had an astrologer once told me about
my love life? Ah yes. That I'd always be attracted to
strange and exotic lovers. Surely a three-thousand-
year old mythic Greek asshole qualified? I sifted sand
between my fingers, ignoring the flash of a piece of
quartz glinting in the sun.

It had been, as Apollo said, like shooting fish in
a barrel. And yet I dared any other woman to resist
him! He was everything my Walt Disney romance-
trained mind had been taught from childhood to
desire: handsome . . . hell, devastatingly gorgeous,
smart, funny, with good prospects and better than
average abilities, like manifesting gold coins from
thin air and catapulting me into psychic journeys to
the past.

I could not fault myself for falling in love with a being so literally divine. But falling into lust over a much younger man? For God's sake, I knew better than that! *And I used to laugh at cougar jokes.*

I couldn't even blame hormones. The time for babies was long past. But chemical habit remained, old powerful chemicals that had a much longer shelf-life than I'd realized. I lay back on my towel, shame-faced, watching a cloud pass overhead. What was that famous guru's comment? "Think you're so evolved? Try spending a week with your parents."

*Ha!* I thought. *Try spending a week with a Greek god.*

My heart sank as I suddenly realized I'd never have another week like it, and in an instant my thoughts did a 180-degree turn, catapulting me from shame to remorse. How could I have been so stupid as to send him away? Would I ever forget his pleas to explain or stop hearing his last anguished "Ekateríni!" as I'd so coldly walked away?

What had come over me?

I was usually a patient soul. Even when I was angry, I always gave people a chance to explain themselves. But not this time. Not with Apollo. And now, almost 24 hours later, I was finally ready to face the reason why: wounded female pride.

No getting around it.

Sure, I was angry at being jerked around, mortified by my gullibility, aghast at Apollo's manipulation and lies, and embarrassed by my cougar tendencies. But honestly? More than anything I was just pissed that my romantic notions had been destroyed. How dare he do what I ask and tell the truth, popping the bubble?!

Then I had to go and make a bad situation worse by flouncing off in a huff. And what had that got me? Ha! A big fat missed opportunity, that's what it got me. A missed opportunity to hang out with a god. *Well, at least a semi-divine blueprint of some sort. If that part of his story is even true.*

But then why wouldn't it be? Apollo might be a scheming, manipulative jerk, but he wasn't cruel. He wasn't playing with me just for kicks. No. He had an agenda and he'd told it to me plainly. And unless I swallowed my pride and took him up on the job he was offering, I'd never know what that full agenda was.

Oh! There was so much I wanted to ask him! So much I wanted to know!

A puff of salt-tanged air caressed my skin and I laughed grimly. *Talk about damned if I do and damned if I don't.* Stick around and take him up on his offer and eat my heart out wanting a relationship I can't have or stay away and regret the loss of knowing the rest of his story for the rest of my life. *Some choice.* What was the ancient Greek myth about being between a rock and a hard place? Ah yes, when Odysseus had to sail between the ship-crushing rocks with the monster named Scylla and the ship-sucking whirlpool called Charybdis.

And then, of course, there was Polymnia.

Holy shit. Talk about unbelievable. I hadn't thought about past lives in a long time. But now that

I knew about her I couldn't stop wondering how did she/I spend the rest of her days? Did she ever see Apollo again? After having been his lover, how could she have lived without him?

"I have caused terrible suffering. Perhaps it is all I will create for you again." Apollo had said something like that to me early on. Was he was referring to Polymnia? There was so much I didn't know!

I got up restlessly and started walking the shoreline. I had to make a decision. A real decision, not a knee-jerk emotional reaction based in wounded pride. Apollo said he wanted to correct ancient beliefs that had bound humanity in darkness for ages. What was a woman's injured vanity to that?

*Nothing.*

And yet how could I bear getting involved with Apollo now that I knew of his duplicity and my own terrible weaknesses?

I reached the point where the rocks fell in a jumble down to the sea, blocking further passage, and then another thought hit me. Detachment was an important spiritual virtue set forth by the Buddha himself. What better way to practice detachment than to go where my heart was most vulnerable? What better way to test my strength?

*Yeah. What better way to torture myself?*

*Well, if I'm tortured, whose fault will that be?*

I turned around and headed back the way I had come, mind churning. And thus it went the rest of my first long day without Apollo.

∞∞∞∞∞∞∞∞

I spent most of that night online researching Apollo's religious cult at Delphi. I'd wanted to do some investigating ever since he showed up. But between bad Internet connections, traveling, the general excitement hanging out with him *and all the time spent in stupid fantasies,* I hadn't gotten around to it.

Apollo was considered the "brightest of the bright" and purest of the gods of Olympus. His temple at Delphi had been one the world's great religious centers. For over a thousand years, wisdom and moral guidance poured from the "shining stones" of the temple at Mount Parnassus, drawing the patronage and support of kings, queens, emperors, generals, and the greatest philosophers, intellects, politicians, writers and artists from across the known world.

Visitors to Apollo's Oracle read like a Who's Who of ancient Western history: Philip of Macedon, Oedipus, King of Thebes, Agamemnon, Alexander the Great, Croesus, King of Lydia, Attalus I of Pergamum, King Nicomedes and Queen Laodice, Mark Antony, and the Roman Emperors Nero, Vespasian, Domitian and Hadrian.

Pythagoras trained one of the Pythia's himself. Plutarch was an Apollonian priest. Herodotus studied the temple's prophesies and recorded many of them for their philosophical and historical value. Socrates and Plato received copious praise and support from the temple and returned the regard. The great Republic of Solon—the world's finest model of political justice and personal freedom upon which much of the Constitution of the United States was based—was to a large degree credited to the laws and wise counsel meted out by Apollo through his temple's voices.

At a time in history when life was cheap and slaves of any color and origin were considered less than human, his Oracle consistently stressed the value of human life. According to Antiphon, the Pythia counseled that even the accidental death of a slave created a stain on the life and hands of the person responsible.

The great philosopher Pindar proclaimed the omniscience of Apollo who "knows the end supreme of all things, and all the ways that lead thereto: the number of the leaves that the earth putteth forth in spring; the number of the sands along the seas . . . and that which is to be, and whence it is to come."

Pindar also praised Apollo's veracity and virtue, proclaiming he "can have nothing to do with falsehood."

I read on.

Apollo's wisdom guided the governments of the Greek city-states, making Greece the birthplace of the highest moral philosophy based in oaths and sacred trust. Historian after historian agreed it was the morality, consistency and honesty characterizing the prophecies and advice that flowed from Apollo's temple that kept its veneration high, inspiring thousands to seek counsel from the 8$^{th}$ century BC when the first official temple to Apollo was erected, to the 5$^{th}$ century AD when the temple was closed after the final pronouncement by the Pythia: "Tell the king to earth is fallen the deft-wrought dwelling, no longer hath Phoebus shelter, or prophetic laurel, or speaking fountain; yea, the speaking water is quenched."

It was after midnight when I disconnected from the web, closed my laptop and went to bed. For a long time, I lay there staring at the ceiling. Then I gave up and went downstairs, poured a glass of wine and went out on the patio.

Honesty, morality, respect and trust had been Apollo's signature for thirteen hundred years—none of which matched my emotional and highly personal condemnation of him as a "lying, manipulative bastard."

I drank my wine, ransacking my memories, recalling every moment we'd spent together, from his first appearance bounding over the rocks towards me at Delphi to his anguished pleas for me to hear him out the night before. Truthfully? I couldn't find a single example of complete dishonesty in our short acquaintance except for the prevarication about how/why he was physical. And he'd admitted the truth as soon as he'd prepared me for it.

Yes, he was guilty of abrupt departures, terrible flirtation, evasion, miscalculation and a total ruthlessness when it came to testing my integrity. But dishonesty?

No.

I went back to the kitchen and started to pour another glass of wine, then grabbed the bottle and took it outside.

And speaking of truth, the whole furor that night had started because he'd told me the truth— that the youthfulness he'd seemed to grant had been a temporary condition and a means of determining my moral fiber. I remembered those cold hungry eyes burning into mine that day on Mount Parnassus as he asked, "And in turn will you worship me?" Even now I shuddered.

When he realized I would not bow down to him, no matter what it cost me, everything had shifted. That had been the start of our relationship, because from that point on Apollo knew he could trust me.

Damn. Looked at from his perspective, how could he *not* have tested me? He'd spent thousands of years with people groveling before him. He knew from experience that he couldn't trust worshippers. He knew they'd lie, cheat, steal and even kill if he told them to. They'd surrender their entire moral fabric as human beings just to win his favor.

I took a long pull on my wine.

When I insisted he reveal the real reason for approaching me, again he told the truth. And what had I done with the information? Taken it as a personal slap in the face.

I groaned.

And then there was that other thing I had yet to face: Apollo's declaration of love. Could it be he'd been telling the truth?

*Christ woman! You've just waltzed through a veritable litany of truth-telling on his part. He's been famous for it for like a zillion years. You think he's going to bother lying to you about something that important just to manipulate you into writing a stupid book?*

Which meant . . .

Frightened of throwing gasoline on a bunch of fantasies whose fire I'd just spent a very long day extinguishing, I peeked back into my memories of our last moments together.

What had he told me at the very end?

"I loved you over two-thousand years ago and never stopped."

The enormity of that one statement threatened to overwhelm me. Tears started in my eyes and I thought I couldn't bear continuing to remember all the other things he'd said that night—things I'd instantly rejected. What were they?

That he'd watched me for lifetimes waiting for the right time to connect. That I had psychological and sexual scars he wanted to help me heal. *Ya think?*

What was the last thing?

I coaxed myself back into the scene. Forced myself to stand there in my mind's eye, shawl clutched at my breast, cold and self-righteous, dismissing everything he said out of hand. "I want to spend what little time I have left here on Earth with you."

Those were precisely his words.

A chill raced over my body. What did he mean? How could he have little time left here? Was he leaving? Why? When?

Was it possible to feel more like an idiot than I did in that moment? Had I ruined everything? Had I convinced Apollo he'd made the wrong choice after all? Or—just as bad—had he taken my last command to heart and honorably removed himself from my life forever?

The wine bottle was empty and my heart was cold. It was going to be another very long night.

∞∞∞∞∞∞∞

## CHAPTER TEN

Apollo's absence dragged on.

I did everything I could think of to bring him back. I talked to him in the kitchen. I meditated on his face and called his name deep in the void at night. I took lonely walks along the ancient Roman roads that crisscrossed the island—windswept empty places that matched my desolation—shouting his name to the skies without even a whisper of a response.

What had started as a wonderful vacation and then turned into a strange and glorious adventure had now become an endless trek of misery. Tempted to get on a plane and go back to the US where I could lick my wounds in private without everything from the kitchen stove to the grocery store reminding me of *him,* only the hope that somehow Apollo would bother to peer into my mind and heart and see that I'd awakened to my silliness kept me on Paros.

Chris called and then Angela, inviting me out. The Sunday hiking group called about the next jaunt. A friend from the States arrived on the ferry and got in touch. But I turned everyone and everything down.

There are many wonderful things about being a writer, including the ability to play the recluse card at will without anybody thinking it odd. But by the end of the second week I could tell by the puzzlement in my friend's voices that "the muse has got me" excuse was wearing thin.

Then, late on a Wednesday night, I had the thought to visit the island of Delos.

As the birthplace of Apollo and an enormous temple and trade complex, the island was second only to Delphi in religious importance when it came to all things related to the Greek god of Light. Perhaps just being there would somehow make the severed connection spark once more?

It was a long shot, but what did I have to lose?

As luck would have it, the tour boat was scheduled to run from Naoussa to Delos the next morning at 8:30. Excited, I got ready for bed, listening to the growing rumble of thunder that had been threatening all evening. By the time I was under the covers the wind was lashing the house in powerful gusts. Somewhere a shutter came loose and started banging against the wall. Lightning flashes illuminated the whitewashed walls of my little room as the storm came at me, straight across the bay.

*FLASH BANG!* A bolt hit right outside the house almost hurling me from the bed. And with the lightning bolt finally came the rain. Not just rain, but hail and a sudden ceaseless outpouring of lightning and thunder the likes of which I'd never experienced. The room was constantly alight now and I could see pink lightning bolts sizzling across the sky, the *CRACK!* of thunder simultaneous.

Quivering in my iron bed I was glad the house was made of sturdy thick concrete walls. The noise was deafening—I couldn't even hear the banging shutter anymore. Maybe it had torn off in the wind? *Maybe Apollo talked to daddy Zeus and the gods are pissed?*

It was a silly thought, but I could see how ancient people could take this kind of display personally. It really did seem like a direct assault . . . a storm so fierce and concentrated the only thing that could have made it worse was if there'd been an earthquake at the same time.

Another *CRACK!* and the sudden sound of shattering glass made me jump. Briefly I considered getting out of bed to close the window that had obviously blown open in the bathroom and decided against it. Standing in a small wet room amidst broken glass, electrical conduits and plumbing during a frenzied lightning storm was not a smart choice.

I wasn't getting out of bed for anything. And then, as suddenly as it hit, the storm passed, the wind dying down and the rain and hail abruptly ceasing.

Wow. That was power—exactly the kind of power that Apollo had, literally, at his fingertips. No wonder he'd been such a Big Cheese. Most mortals running afoul of the gods hadn't lived to tell about it. Briefly I wondered if murder was one of the many acts Apollo had committed that he now regretted.

I got up and turned on the light to check the bathroom and it was a mess. Wind still roared into the room. The walls were soaked and water was pooled an inch deep on the floor—but draining quickly. Glass from a lotion bottle was everywhere, shards glinting in the light, white lotion puddled in disgusting-looking gobs in the water.

I closed the window and picked up the glass as best I could, resisting the urge to wipe the excess lotion on my dry arms and legs—Greece played hell on aging skin. By the time I got back to bed it was two in the morning, the wind and lightning were picking up and another storm was on its way.

The second pass wasn't quite as bad, and by the time the rain, thunder and lightning ceased pounding the rocky peninsula and the house, I was asleep, dreaming of blue lightning in the heavens—violet-blue lighting arcing from a golden nebula, vaulting across the void, striking deep into a horrific black and puss-green shape that writhed and recoiled from the explosive thrust of the nebula's unimaginable energies. Then the revolting dark mass regrouped, roaring, spewing vile projectiles of light back at the golden cloud—bolts of vermilion, green and blood red.

The heavens of my dreamscape erupted in volcanic argument and the greasy stygian mass slowly advanced, overwhelming the golden nebula, snuffing it from sight. I shrieked in despair, my scream jolting me into wakefulness as yet another violent storm rolled in across the bay, igniting the sky and shaking the house. And I lay cowering and trembling in my bed, wondering if this was what the end of the world would look like if the gods ever decided it was time.

◎◎◎◎◎◎◎◎

Despite the night's turmoil, little sleep, and my strange violent dreams, the morning dawned cool and clear. I jumped in the shower, wary of broken glass, got dressed and headed straight to the port of Naoussa to purchase a ticket to Delos from the quartermaster on the quay.

The seas were running high from the storms, but the tour was still on. Before I knew it, I was jammed into a herd of French tourists on the upper deck of the boat, sitting on a narrow wooden bench open to the sun and wind, motoring out of the harbor towards Naxos. Surely this visit would reawaken my link with Apollo? And if it didn't? Well, I'd go back to Delphi and slog up that God-awful trail one more time and stand under the bay laurel tree at the top of the hill shouting his name until he either showed up or the temple guards came to see what was wrong and hauled me away.

The sun grew hot and the open sea was rough, tossing the little boat to and fro. A nice-looking older Frenchman tried to make conversation, but my French was limited and his English even more so. After the first comments, we were reduced to hand gestures and well-meaning smiles. To my relief he gave up and moved away, sidling up to another unaccompanied female nearby to start over.

Watching him go through the same opening spiel with equal enthusiasm for woman #2, I contemplated whether I would ever be interested in another man again. It didn't seem likely. Not only was Apollo . . . well, Apollo, ever since meeting him my cougar genes had apparently been permanently switched to the "on" position. Every male over fifty now seemed positively decrepit. I glanced over at the Frenchman. Woman #2 was laughing at something he said. Encouraged, he edged closer to her on the bench. Amused, I wished him *bon chance* and turned to lean on the rail.

An hour's travel later, the narrow entrance to the harbor at Delos lay dead ahead. Only five kilometers long and about a kilometer wide, Delos is a tiny rugged island much lower in elevation than most in the Cycladic chain. At the height of its glory it was one of the most important cultural and trade centers in the Mediterranean, housing over 35,000 inhabitants plus the priests and priestesses of the various temples, including a large temple to the Egyptian goddess Isis.

The last time I'd been here the sense of familiarity had been overwhelming. Now it seemed even more so. Whether this was because of my link with Apollo or simply the result of having been here two years previous, I couldn't tell.

The aquamarine waters turned brilliant as the bay shallowed out. Slowly the captain began the tricky maneuver of bringing the boat's stern around, backing into the mooring next to several larger tour boats already docked at the ancient stone jetty. By the time the ship had been secured and the gangway

rolled out, everybody was already edging towards
the exit. A tired-looking mustachioed Greek sailor
held up a plastic clock with its red hands fixed at
1:15 indicating our departure time for Mykonos, the
next stop on this excursion combining three hours of
cultural history on Delos with three hours of rabid
tourism on its internationally-popular neighboring
island.

I smiled at the man with the clock, but his eyes
were glazed and he took no notice as he repeated
"departure time" in several different languages.
The confused bustle on the jetty was the same as
I remembered—professional guides hawking their
tours in French, German, Italian, English, Japanese
and Greek, husbands and wives bickering over
whether to spend the extra 12 euros on a tour, kids
running ahead, glad to stretch their legs after the
confines of the boat.

I stepped around the bunched-up throng, got to
the ticket entrance before almost anyone else, bought
my five euro ticket and headed for Apollo's temple
and the famous lions lining the road, guarding its
now non-existent gates.

The palm tree that Apollo's mother, Leto, clung
to while giving birth, first to Artemis then Apollo,
was clearly visible and the only tree on the island.
Obviously, the story was just a myth. And even if
it hadn't been it certainly wouldn't be the same
tree. But somebody in the Greek archaeological
society had seen fit to ensure that a mature palm
was present in the middle of what had once been

a swampy lake, drained in the 1930s because of the danger of malaria.

I slowed my pace as I got to the neglected little park with its scrub and tangled bushes. Most of the people were behind me in the old port city, poking around the extensive ruins. Only a middle-aged woman and a young boy were wandering the sandy paths through the bushes, looking for a way to get to the museum and restaurant on the far side.

Now that I was there, I found myself suddenly uncertain. What was I going to do? Thrash my way to the base of the palm and cling to it like a distraught, aging Medea, wailing for all things lost?

As dramatically appealing as the thought was, I walked to the little round brick well built near the palm instead and, after peering inside and satisfying myself that it was still empty of water and still littered with a few scraps of paper just like the last time, I sat on the rounded bench seat of its circumference and waited.

And waited.

I tried to meditate on Apollo. I contemplated his birth—not Leto clutching the palm in heavy labor— but the weight of thousands of peoples' worship, the carving of statues in his honor, the desperate need of his followers to have a face to pin their prayers upon and how those thoughts had impressed the quantum field, eventually bringing him to life. I conjured his face in my mind's eye, his rakish smiles and easy laughter, his utter self-confidence and frequent unexpected gentleness. All to no avail.

A couple came and sat on a nearby bench, talking and laughing. A few people wandered casually up to the well to peer inside then wandered away. I glanced at my phone: One o'clock. Fifteen minutes to go before the boat left.

Despondent, I got up and retraced my steps to the lion walk and the scarcely-visible remains of Apollo's temple, making my way back towards the harbor. I turned around a few times, hoping to see his bright figure striding to catch up with me, but there was nothing but picture-snapping tourists milling along the wide, pottery shard-strewn pathways.

The thought that possibly, just possibly, he was waiting at the boat made me quicken my steps. It would be just like him to materialize onboard, pleased at dodging the need for a ticket, lounging against the rail, wind ruffling his curls, soaking up the sun and admiring glances of the other passengers. Anxiously I scanned the upper rails of the boat as I approached. I saw nothing, but held onto my sliver of hope as I explored the deck-level cabin, then mounted the stairs to the upper deck.

Nothing.

How could he not be aware of my thoughts and changed feelings? How could he refuse to respond? Was he punishing me? I swiftly banished the thought. That would be beneath him. I was simply punishing myself.

Giving the decks one last sweep I turned and went back down to the saloon. It had been hot and dry on the island and I ordered a beer and took it to a cushioned seat next to the windows and open door to the deck and bridge. Looking around I saw the Frenchman and Woman #2 sitting close together across the saloon, chatting animatedly. Other couples were talking, looking at their phones, going through the images they'd captured. Others were stretched out, intent on catching a quick nap before the next docking at Mykonos.

I was not looking forward to the three-hour forced travel stop. On that teenage trip with my mother we'd visited the island and found it beautiful with its white buildings and windmills silhouetted against the blue sky, the curved stone-rimmed bay with brightly painted kaikis moored close to the tavernas serving fried calamari and fish fresh-caught from the sea. Back then the island had been rustic, romantic and real. But my last trip had shattered those memories. Mykonos was now a hyped-up tourist trap filled with expensive restaurants and exclusive shops—Dior and Brooks Brothers, Tiffany's and Hermés—a Greek village Fifth Avenue.

The winds were picking up and our passage to the island was a crosswind dip and bob affair with the bow going under the waves, throwing up water against the windows. A sailor quickly came and closed the open hatches to the bridge, cutting off light and air but saving me and the other people close to the door a drenching. Bottles and glasses clinked and rattled in the bar and people laughed nervously, calling to one another across the saloon as the ship bucked and rolled, keeping a tight grip on their glasses.

The barman was indifferent. He'd seen it a thousand times before and people took comfort in his casual stance. If it had really been bad he would've closed up shop. So, the sunburned group drank merrily and relaxed, women giving occasional squeals as the boat pitched and wallowed.

Arriving at Mykonos, I navigated the gangplank past the bored sailor holding the plastic clock with its red hands now reading 5 pm. Stepping onto the stone pier I saw that we'd moored next to four of the most gigantic private yachts I'd ever seen. The smallest had a lean, hungry look and dwarfed our little 200-person tour boat.

Everyone stopped to stare and take pictures, trying to grasp the lifestyle these behemoths of the sea represented. Deck crews kitted out in insignia-embossed blazers and white pants went about their business while deck hands polished miles of brass and manicured lackeys stood at attention at the end of each red-carpeted gangplank, politely smiling at gawkers, making it clear we shouldn't get too close lest our tacky tourist vibe contaminate the lofty atmosphere.

It was straight out of *Lifestyles of the Rich and Famous* and I found myself as repulsed by the sight as I had been the first time I saw the palace of Versailles outside Paris with its vast gold-gilt halls, ornate furnishings, fine art and crystal chandeliers, knowing it had all been built on the backs of wretched French peasants.

No wonder there'd been a bloody revolution!

I stalked past the yachts, quickly leaving the crowds behind, heading into the village itself. Making my way past the immaculate fashion shops with gaily painted doors and window trims, I strode uphill towards the non-tourist side of town. Here the paint was long-faded. Laundry hung over rusting iron balustrades, skinny cats slunk from step to stair, and wizened old men spent their days sitting on narrow stoops in rickety cane chairs, cigarette smoke curling in front of their rheumy mistrustful eyes as they watched the world go by.

Finally, I broke out at the top of the hill near the signature Mykonos windmills, vanes fixed in place, no longer filled with white sail, tourists all in a row taking pictures. For a long time I stood there, disconsolately gazing over the wind-tossed waters towards Delos.

Nights of poor sleep, days of emotional upheaval, and now disappointment. *What next?* I wondered, sad and tired from having drunk a beer in the middle of the day. What next indeed?

◎◎◎◎◎◎◎◎◎

It was a quick trip back to Paros. The wind and seas were with us, we didn't have to repeat the trip to Naxos, and three vodka tonics in a little bar on Mykonos had guaranteed me a sound nap.

I awoke as the seas subsided. Half the saloon was filled with sleeping, snoring, sunburned people leaning against one another's shoulders. The customerless barman, quietly wiped glasses, stowing them away. I got up, stretched, and glanced out the starboard windows as we motored past the little lighthouse perched in the hills north of Naoussa's harbor, whitewashed walls casting deep shadows in the gathering evening light.

By the time we approached the docks everybody had wakened from their naps and was gathering their shopping bags and cameras. I leaned against the rail as we chugged into port. There was Mario's restaurant where a bunch of us regularly gathered for coffee and stuffed crepes in the morning. Next door was the family-owned taverna that served an amazing risotto, black with squid ink and filled with chunks of fresh seafood. And there, straight up the quay, was the stone bridge arching over the little creek that ran through town, designed by a Greek architect I knew who had lived on the island his whole life.

Very much the kind of place Mykonos used to be, Paros was friendly and still relatively unpretentious. As the boat backed into its mooring and the captain loudly announced our arrival, I felt the grateful rush every sailor experiences coming back into their home port at dusk. I loved Paros, and it saddened me knowing that if it hadn't been for this whole affair with Apollo I probably would have come here again and again over the remaining years of my life. But now? I couldn't wait to get away and couldn't imagine ever returning.

I grabbed my purse and shuffled into line like a

zombie. The mustachioed crewman was nowhere to be seen, his plastic clock stuck behind a rack of life preservers on the wall next to the gangway. He was headed home. Where was I going? The gangplank rocked and a crewmember reached to steady me as I jumped to the jetty. Turning to say a tired "Efkaristo," I caught a flash of reddish brown hair amidst the jostling French tourists.

*Could it be?*

I jumped up, trying to see over the bobbing heads, jostling several startled people around me. But I didn't care. I jumped up again and *oh!* there he was, casually leaning against a black wrought-iron lamppost on the quay, waiting for me. My mouth went dry with shock and my stomach did somersaults, churning the vodka I'd drunk, and before I knew it I was shoving my way through the crowd, running straight at him, falling breathless into his arms.

◎◎◎◎◎◎◎

Can you die of happiness?

I actually wondered as I hugged him, feeling his arms around me, my head crushed to his chest, right ear smashed so close I could hear the rapid thudding of his heart. And I kissed his bare chest through the opening in his white shirt, deciding I never wanted to go anywhere else ever again.

*Maybe I'll move to Paros,* I thought, happily content.

I heard the deep rumble of laughter in my ear as he caught the thought. And then he was ruffling my wind-tangled hair with his fingers and I looked up and before I could catch the expression in his eyes he bent down and kissed me squarely on the mouth.

My knees gave way and I gasped in surprise, opening my mouth under the insistent press of his lips, and his tongue slipped inside, gently exploring. Fire shot through my body and I instantly responded, pressing against him with a muffled groan.

*So much for maintaining detachment.*

Despite the deliciousness of the moment, I couldn't stop the thought and Apollo lifted his lips from mine, laughing. "Oh, Ekateríni, whatever am I going to do with you?"

My body definitely had a few ideas, but certainly the public quay was not the place for that. Several people were openly staring, and it was about that moment that I realized we were still plastered together and that one of Apollo's large warm hands was splayed across my butt, lightly squeezing.

I tried to extricate myself but Apollo just kept laughing, refusing to let me go, leaning down and kissing me once more, firmly but not languorously. Then he lifted his head and asked, "I gather you missed me?"

"Oh, Apollo!" I cried, all the pain and worry coming back with a rush. Throwing appropriateness to the winds, I pressed myself close, arms tight around his waist. "I was such an idiot! I should have believed you but I didn't and I thought all those stupid wrong things about you and I almost gave up hope of ever seeing you again!"

He disentangled himself, keeping one arm about my waist. "Come," he said. "We have a lot to talk about." We headed up the empty quay towards the main harbor where the French group was being herded onto a bus.

"I thought I'd driven you away," I said, forlornly.

"My dear, I have great faith in your ability to see through your own crap. I grant you, that was an enormous pile of it you deposited the other night. But it was surely nothing that could drive me away."

He gave my waist a squeeze.

"So where were you all this time?" I asked in mock accusation. "If you had such great faith and knew I was over it, why did you let me hang for so long?" It was a valid question and we both knew it. He stopped mid-stride, let me go and turned to look at me.

"It was not done to make you suffer, Ekateríni. And if I could have gotten back to you sooner I would have. Of that you may be certain." Gently he stroked my cheek with the backs of his fingers.

I took a deep breath and nodded. Despite my gigantic insecurities, which apparently had not automatically evaporated at his return, whatever misunderstandings there had been between us and whatever the depth of my former mistrust, my doubts about Apollo were behind me.

I reached out and took his hand, abruptly switching subjects. "I'm starved. Would your exquisite taste buds be offended if we grabbed a gyro before we went home?"

Suddenly realizing the rather large assumption in that statement I added, "if you're coming back to the house with me, that is?"

"That sounds delightful and yes, I would like to come home with you," he replied.

The old teasing suggestiveness was gone. It was a flat statement. And behind it I sensed an urgency I hadn't felt before—an urgency I knew wasn't personal. And I wondered, briefly, what had changed. But I was too intoxicated with joy and relief and far too hungry to do more than notice it.

There was a marvelous gyro stand at the corner of the harbor across a little service road near Mario's. We placed our order and the heavy-faced cook with bushy Scorpio eyebrows immediately started sawing away at the juicy rotating pork quarter turning on the spit. Being American, it'd been a surprise to discover that, in Greece, gyros are made of seasoned pork, not lamb. They're also stuffed with the most delicious French fries on the planet, plus onions and lettuce then doused with a homemade yogurt-based sauce—all of it costing no more than two and a half euros—about three bucks.

We ate with gusto, paid the bill and, hand in hand, headed up the road to where I'd left my rental car that morning. Had a day ever held such disparate energies? Twelve hours ago, I'd been a hopeful wreck. Three hours ago, I'd been half drunk and filled with despair. Now I felt such gladness I didn't think I'd worry about anything ever again.

We didn't say much on the way back to the

house. It was nearing dark when Apollo got out to open the gate, bowing me through with a flourish. And it wasn't until we got inside that I realized I felt like I'd been keelhauled all the way to Delos and back. The long day after a bad night's sleep, the heat and sun, the open sea air, the beer and vodka, the two-week emotional roller coaster, had all taken a toll. Maybe a quick shower would help? I told Apollo to make himself at home while I cleaned up.

In my mind's eye, I ran lightly up the stairs. But in truth I stumbled halfway up, dragging feet that suddenly seemed made of lead. The hot shower removed the sea salt and travel dust. And feeling clean perked me up momentarily. But blow-drying my hair seemed like far too much effort. And figuring out what to wear? Maybe I'd just lie down and mentally peruse my travel wardrobe from my still unmade bed.

I crawled under the duvet and stared at the closet door. I'd read once that women, on average, spend a whole year of their lives deciding what to wear. I giggled groggily. *I guess that means men spend at least a decade thinking about their penises.*

And that was the last thing I knew.

I didn't hear Apollo come softly up the stairs. Didn't see him stand there looking down at my half-exposed naked body. Didn't see his smile as he tenderly covered me up. Didn't feel the kiss upon my forehead. Didn't see him leave. Wherever the soul flies at night, mine took the path straight from daylight into blessed darkness.

∞◈∞◈∞◈∞

But there was light in the dark.

A strange scintillating pulse in the distance, like a semaphore calling my name . . . *Kathryn* . . . *Kathryn* . . . Then a deep roaring sound and a sucking and tugging at my limbs as a golden ocean dragged me, tumbling, tumbling, to another shore. And I opened my eyes to white soaring cliffs and stars in a dark night sky . . . and then suddenly a red curtain came down and a face loomed over mine, blue eyes probing, fair skin shining, soundless lips from a familiar woman's face calling. And then the pounding ocean sucked me back down into darkness once again.

∞◈∞◈∞◈∞

## CHAPTER ELEVEN

I awakened to sunshine, calm winds and a sense of great peace. For a few moments the whisper of a dream tugged at the corners of my mind. But it was too vague to chase and I let it go, stretching luxuriously as only one can after a full and restful night's sleep.

*Apollo!* I shot straight up and out of bed. Surely his return had not been a dream and I really had met him at the harbor and he really had kissed me . . . twice. My body tingled at the memory. How could I have fallen asleep? Was he still here?

Anxiously, I looked in the mirror. My hair was at its normal crazed, punk-rock morning best and I mussed it a little more neatly, brushed my teeth, threw on a caftan I'd bought in South Africa and headed for the stairs.

The place was the same as I'd left it the morning before, except the coffee pot was full and the red light was on. Before I could even wonder if he was still around, a shadow fell across the floor and in he walked through the open French doors, just as normal as you please, wearing a crisp open-collared blue shirt with rolled-up sleeves and, as ever, blue jeans.

"Kalimera."

"Morning," I replied, suddenly shy. "Thanks for making coffee."

"Hmmm." He walked over and casually reached over my head, pulling down two mugs from the open shelf behind me, pinning me neatly against the cabinet next to the sink, body pressed close to mine, my nose practically touching his naked chest. Nervousness shot through me and I blushed. Why did he always have to look so casually sexy and emanate such a charismatic vibe? But he moved away without touching me, setting the mugs down, then reaching for the pot.

I escaped to the refrigerator and pulled out the cream.

"You were sleeping like the dead last night. I heard your snores all the way on Mt. Olympus."

*Oh!* Sudden embarrassment mingled in with the nervousness. I picked up a mug, waiting my turn, not looking at him.

He smiled. "I am joking. Everybody snores, Ekateríni. Especially when they are exhausted." He gently removed the mug from my hand, set it down, and raised my fingers to his lips. "I am sorry I caused you so much pain and worry . . . and for such a long time."

His touch was steadying. Reassured, I smiled in return into those luminous copper eyes. "I'm sorry I was such a mistrusting asshole that you had to leave in the first place," I murmured.

He brushed my hand again with his lips. "Then we are even."

Would there ever come a time when he ceased

making my knees go weak? And if it did would that be a good thing? Taking the mug he offered I slopped in a healthy dollop of cream and headed out onto the patio.

It was a gorgeous day. Cool and clear with not even a hint of a breeze. The bay was quiet as deep blue glass. The scent of jasmine and honeysuckle filled the air, the purple and red bougainvilleas were in bloom along with all the pink oleanders and enormous orange and red geraniums. And the god of Light himself was sipping coffee across from me.

What a wonderment.

"So," I ventured. "If I asked where you were, would the answer make any sense?"

He thought for a second then said, "I was on a planet in another part of this universe where another humanoid race similar to yours has evolved to the stage where art and the first glimmers of scientific knowledge are beginning to develop. These people are at the stage where inspiration breathed into their dreams and thoughts in the right way can take root and advance their civilization."

He smiled. "As the Bringer of Light it is my task to be there at this stage in their evolution to assist and guide," he paused, "as I did here on Earth and as I have for countless other humanoid civilizations over the past several billion years."

My mug froze halfway to my mouth in astonishment. Well, what did I expect as an answer? "Sorry, I ran out for cigarettes and got lost on my way back from the store?"

I cleared my throat, setting my mug back down. Surly, I hadn't heard him correctly? "I-I thought you said we created you about 3,000 years ago," I stuttered. "Which you still haven't explained, of course . . . how that could actually happen. Uh, I've got some ideas about that but . . ." My voice dwindled and died. *Several billion years?*

"To be accurate, I said humanity created us. I did not mention when and I did not say which race of humanity or in which galaxy," he replied calmly. "Or universe, for that matter."

"Right," I muttered. "Um, I think I need a top-up. Do you want more coffee?" He shook his head and I escaped back inside, mind dazed, poured coffee into my almost full cup and headed for the door only to realize I hadn't put in any more cream. *Several billion years?*

"I am curious about your thoughts on the matter of my physical creation," he said as I tottered back outside and sat down.

"You once said there was a stunning age difference between us," I blurted. "But billions of years? Come on!"

"As a Light spark of consciousness you have been around just as long, Ekateríni," he said, amused. "Just not as . . . well, not as conscious the whole time is all. And, if it helps, please understand that I have not been able to manifest in the body all that time either. Physicality has been a relatively new experience for me." He shook his head. "No more than ten million years at most. Trust me, I will get back to this point shortly. But first I would like to hear your thoughts on how it happened at all."

"Gimme a minute, would you?"

He looked at me, compassionately, murmuring "Of course." Then turned his gaze out to sea, giving me space.

I took a deep, calming breath and exhaled slowly, trying to gather my shaken wits. And as I continued to breathe deeply and deliberately, following his gaze out across the placid waters of the bay, I realized it was hopeless. There was no way my limited, linear, intellectual mind was prepared to grasp either the expanses or the implications involved in Apollo's reality. I should have realized long before now that when he talked about his creation as an archangel and an Ideal that we were talking in terms of billions of years. After all, the Big Bang had occurred almost 14 billion years ago. But I hadn't gone there. Instead, I'd stayed skating along on the surface of things, fooled by his appearance into unconsciously associating my human experience with his. And yet, truth be told, his experience and mine were about as far apart on the evolutionary spectrum as my life experience and that of a hamster in a cage.

"It is not that much of a reach," he said, drily, interrupting my thoughts. "Being in a human body has been quite the leveler. As you are about to find out."

I shook my head to clear it, then took a sip from my still-steaming mug. Despite his kind comment, I remained deeply shaken. *Well, at least I no longer have as many illusions about what I'm up against as I did half an hour ago!* I mused.

All I could do was accept what I was hearing, do my best to fathom it and move along with the rapidly changing tide.

I took another deep breath. So what was he asking? *Ah, yes,* he wanted to hear my thoughts on how humanity ended up creating the gods. I cleared my throat again, forcing myself to ground energetically in the present.

"Well, I thought maybe it was the collective consciousness of man and womankind focused on what the gods might look like. You know, needing a visual representation to get a grasp on a being that was, um, originally just an abstract thought like a Light Bringer or music maker or the being responsible for inspiring art or sending the thunder and lighting and rain and, uh, that it was the power of our mental and emotional focus on the physical images we created of you guys plus our worship and fear and all the energy from all the sacrifices that ended up giving you the power to manifest into physical form."

He nodded, looking satisfied. "Yes, that is basically what happened. It was most unexpected really." He shrugged. "But then that is life. If it does not shock the hell out of you occasionally, you are not doing it right."

"So, humans here on Earth didn't create you?"

"That is correct."

"Then who did?"

He settled more deeply in his chair. "It was actually a cumulative effect that built up over eons of time. Some deities, such as Zeus and Hera, took form first for the simple reason that humanoids tend to worship and try to placate the things they fear and love the most: The god of lightning and storms, the goddess of the hearth and home, for example." He chuckled grimly. "Worshipping the light of knowledge and wisdom comes a little later in the scheme of things, unfortunately."

"But how did all these other races end up evolving faster than us?" I asked.

Apollo stretched his legs out into the sun as it angled around the patio roof. "It is not a competition, Ekateríni. The humanoid pattern develops at different times with different variations in different parts of the universe. The primitive beginnings of humanity began here on Earth around four million years ago. But there are many other human civilizations closer to this universe's central sun that evolved much much earlier."

"Oh." I considered the vast ramifications of this new piece of information "So, you're just sort of passing through?" I asked. Was this what he meant about his limited time left on Earth? How long did he have? Was he leaving soon?

"The answer to all of that is complicated. But essentially, yes. We come at the right time in a species' development and then we move on when that group evolves beyond animism and human projections of God, moving into the Christos phase, which is when the divinity within all beings—including humanity—is realized. Then we go where we are needed next. All of the other Olympians left Earth well over a thousand years ago for a planet named Sira in what you call the SO901 galaxy.

He sighed. "I am the only one who has continued to remain tangibly involved with Earth."

"Why?" I asked.

"Things did not follow their usual pattern here. There have been influences we failed to control, problems and unexpected influences that have negatively impacted human evolution—problems we are largely responsible for."

His face was tinged with a deep sadness. "It is a long story, Ekateríni. And not very pleasant." He smiled bleakly. "At last we have come to the point where you are ready to hear all of it. No more secrets."

I nodded nervously. No more secrets.

He stood up suddenly and stretched, then extended his hand to me. "It is not a tale to be told or received on an empty stomach. Do you have any eggs?"

I took his hand and let him pull me to my feet. "Yes," I said. "And cheese and bread."

"Good," he said. "I will fortify us and then let the storytelling begin."

⚬⚬⚬⚬⚬⚬⚬⚬

By the time we'd finished breakfast and I'd piled the

dishes in the sink, I was both impatient and—
considering the bombshells he'd already dropped on
me—uneasy about what I was about to hear. Before
we settled back in our patio chairs, I turned my
phone off, closed the gate, got water and went to the
bathroom. No more interruptions!

Apollo was gazing out to sea, fingering a curious
set of black and white worry beads I'd never seen him
with before. *Click click click!* They glinted and danced,
crystal and onyx. *Click click click!* After a minute or so,
he set them on his knee and began.

"Do you know what a tulpa is?"

"A tulpa?" I repeated, jaw dropping. *Of all things
to ask!* "Wow. Um. Actually I do. It's a human being
deliberately created via a particular meditation
practice given to monks in Tibet that . . . oh!" I
stopped, shocked.

Up until that very moment, the story of how
Apollo and the other gods had taken form had
seemed fantastical to me—like something out of a
science fiction novel—distant and otherworldly. But
his mention of tulpas suddenly brought the whole
thing right into my own sphere of knowledge.

I'd once written a screen adaptation of a novel
based around the subject of tulpas, and I'd learned a
lot about the ancient and obscure mystical practices
surrounding their creation. In Tibet certain monks
were taught to focus on a picture of a man and invest
it with sufficient energy to take physical form—
life-size physical form. Most monks worked at this
practice for a lifetime without success. For the few

who did manage the task, the creation of the physical tulpa turned out to be only the first step in a much larger discipline. Not only was it a test of rigorous mental focus and decades-long spiritual dedication, it was also an important lesson about the human ego. For once the tulpa had been created, the second stage of the test was for the student to dissolve his creation and destroy it.

I squirmed in my chair, rearranging my legs to get more comfortable, imagining what it would be like to actually create a living human being from my mind alone—and then the distress of having to destroy it. *Jesus!* After thousands and thousands of hours and years and years of mental effort, I'd be hugely proud that my tulpa appeared! I'd love it! I'd be enormously attached to it and possessive. And then to have to kill this living, breathing human being I'd created?

I shuddered.

"Do you know the consequences if the tulpa is not destroyed?" Apollo asked quietly.

His voice brought me back to the patio and our conversation. "If the monk didn't dissolve his tulpa, not only would he fail his test of non-attachment, the tulpa would become dangerous and eventually run away. Or it would overthrow its creator and destroy him." My flesh crawled. "Or so the story goes."

"Why were they so dangerous?" he asked, voice oddly controlled.

I thought about it for a moment, at a loss. "I'm not sure. Nothing I've read really says. Maybe it's because tulpas have no life experience? I mean, they come into form fully mature physically, but with no training or life experience to teach them how to be human. So, I guess they'd have no moral compass? No emotional intelligence and no empathy, just uncontrollable impulses and intelligence?"

It was a strange subject to be pursuing. But before I could even ask Apollo about it he interjected.

"For millions of years, primitive humanoid species across this and other universes have worshipped and feared the forces of Nature as well as the ideals of beauty and perfection, power, strength, intelligence, fertility, creation, art and music and so forth, as gods.

"As you have correctly surmised, after a time, the thoughts and energies of human worship and fear, plus the belief that the gods were physical, just like themselves, gained sufficient gravitas—and the gods took form."

It hit me like a ton of bricks.

"Are you trying to tell me you're a . . . a tulpa?" *Holy shit!* My mind was whirling. "I thought you and all the other Olympians were part of Plato's Ideals?" *Which sounds much more . . .*

"Acceptable," Apollo finished the thought for me.

That was exactly the word.

"I am sorry if I mislead you. But I am not the original Ideal of Light, beauty and wisdom, Ekateríni—not any more. The Ideals themselves are incorruptible. We—they—are more than just archetypes. They are living presences—Archangels of the most high and rarefied frequencies. What you see before you," he splayed a hand across his chest, "Is a hybrid."

He saw the puzzlement on my face and forged on. "I am both the original Ideal and the tulpa mankind created—a strange mixture of the Ideal of beauty and proportion, intelligence and the masculine principle, combined with the unlimited power and immortality human beings conferred upon me, all embodied in flesh."

It sounded like a strange amalgamation indeed.

"Problematic is a better word," he said, toying with the beads once again. "All matter comes from consciousness—stars and galaxies, horses and trees, Tibetan tulpas and the gods of Olympus." He exhaled a long sigh. "Once consciousness comes into form, however, things get complicated. The form itself begins to mold and dictate consciousness. In the case of tulpas, they develop a mind of their own and continue to grow in strength and power as long as they continue to be fed energy from the attentive mind, or minds, that created them.

"Which is why the Archangels of the realm of Ideals—myself included—ended up extending part of our consciousness into the tulpas the humans had created."

"Okay, I'm totally lost." I said. "Can you make that any simpler?"

"Of course." He uncrossed his legs and leaned forward, fingers steepled between his knees. "First comes God/Source. God/Source extends itself into creation, and one of the first creations are the Ideals, the blueprints for everything. You are following me so far?

I nodded.

"Humanity was birthed through the lens of multiple Ideals—beauty, proportion, intelligence, masculine, feminine, wisdom, knowledge, clarity, swiftness, Ideals that have their own individual consciousness and their own presence in the intangible 'form,' he made quote marks in the air with his fingers, "of Archangels.

"Then the humans started worshipping various Ideals, making physical gods out of them in their own minds, investing the Ideals with sufficient energy to take form as tulpas."

"Okay. I'm with you. Thanks. But . . ."

"Why did we, the archangels, place part of our consciousness into the tulpas?" Apollo sat back looking grim. "We couldn't risk having immortal, all-powerful tulpas with no moral compass running amok. So, we took the plunge and descended into the tulpas, taking possession of them with the intent of controlling them. And then . . . well . . ."

He paused, shaking his head. "Please understand that on the plane of abstract Ideals, everything is all tidy and perfect. As angels we were unflappably what we were designed to be and nothing more. But when we took the plunge into form . . ." his eyes took on a haunted look and his voice dropped, "Everything we were shattered."

Abruptly he got to his feet and started pacing, worry beads slipping to the ground, unnoticed.

"The instantaneous transition between the angelic kingdom to this place . . . you cannot imagine the shock and horror of it. You . . ." he spread his hands indicating not just me, but humanity in general, "gestate for nine months, floating gently in amniotic fluid, riding the tides from unicellular organism to the complexity of the body you are in today. You grow into it. The consciousness you call "you" develops out of the body . . ."

"Wait a minute," I cried, momentarily sidetracked. "Consciousness is a spiritual thing and not really . . ."

He held up a stern hand, frowning. "I know where you are going with that and you have no idea what you are talking about."

"But . . ."

"The ego is directly created from the sense perceptions of the body. It has nothing to do with your spiritual essence."

"But . . ."

He was firm. "I am not going to get into this right now. As much as you might like to think otherwise, your grounding is physical, Ekateríni. It is your birthplace. Your default awareness as it were. And by the time you are physically born you are immeasurably comfortable with it."

"But us?" He stopped pacing. "Taking form literally tore us apart." His eyes showed me a place I didn't want to go.

"Imagine if something grabbed you right now and ripped you in half and that you remained conscious throughout the whole agonizing process. Imagine being stripped of wholeness, crammed into a confusing space of half-measures and qualifications with no absolutes . . . a reality that is a storm of differences and opposing forces vying for equal attention, where the music of the spheres is unheard and biochemical emotions overwhelm your system in unrelenting waves.

"And the crushing weight of this place! Gods! And that was just the physical experience! The real pain . . . ahhhh, the real pain was in the mind, Ekaterini, knowing what we left behind."

With obvious difficulty, he pulled out of the shattering memory. "But then there were advantages," he said, smiling crookedly. "I could smell the sea for the first time. Could feel the wind in hair I could call 'mine' and run my fingers through the sands on the beaches, roll pebbles in my hand and grasp their hardness and texture, see their colors and know what a stone felt like for the first time.

"You have no idea what sensations are like, Ekaterini! You are born into sensation. But for us it was shocking and intoxicating.

"Imagine dwelling in an abstract reality of ideas and suddenly being able to touch and smell flowers and water, earth and rain, feel warmth and cold and the squish of soft mud and hardness and pain and pleasure." His eyes darkened. "My first woman . . . my body burned at the sight of her and I took her like an animal in the dirt."

I gasped, shocked.

"It was a rape. Hard and fast. No more. And I didn't care. I was a god amongst mortals who had no idea where I really came from or what I knew or what I could do."

He stopped and stared out to sea for a long time then bowed his head. He saw the beads on the flagstones, leaned down and picked them up, looking at them as if he'd never seen them before. "It was new and raw and terrible and wonderful, and we hungered to touch and taste and smell and feel and experience all our new bodies offered. We were arrogant and proud, insecure and possessive, cocksure and filled with glory, immortal and all-powerful—everything the humans had created us to be. And the humans recognized us and fell on their faces to see their statues and paintings come to life."

"But what about what you originally were? Didn't being an Archangel and still connected to the realm of Ideals—didn't that have some influence?" I barely knew how to phrase the question.

"What is a whisper compared to the shriek of a hurricane?" His fist clenched on the beads, knuckles white, his face haggard. "Do you remember who you really are, Ekateríni? No? You embody far more Ideals than I do. And yet look at humanity and the condition of your civilization. Where are those Ideals? How well are they expressed?" He shook his head and sighed.

"The body, as we discovered too late, is all-consuming. Like you, for us the abstract realms of the angelic kingdom became inaccessible. Mere ideas and memories that receded further and further away over time."

Heavily, he sat back down, dropping the beads on the table top. "We thought we would possess the tulpas," his voice was barely a whisper. "But they possessed us."

I sat there, riveted, not knowing whether it was his words or how powerfully the story was affecting him that shocked me more. I waited as he gathered the strength to continue.

"The humans worshipped us in awe and terror and love. They fed us and housed us and built temples, even though we could create anything at will. And indeed, we created our own glorious domain in the highest mountains far from their meager villages where they gave themselves to us for our pleasure.

"Soon we began fighting amongst ourselves to see who could own the most land and women and young boys, who could prove most mighty. We laid waste vast stretches of the world in our constant battles, killing countless thousands of innocent people."

Despite the building heat of the day, my body flooded with chills.

"Living in the rarified strata of the angelic kingdom we had not known what emotion was. Oh, we could see how emotions arising from biochemical exchanges in the body dominated the humans, dictating their thoughts and actions. We understood that emotion is pure raw energy that can be directed. But we did not know what a potent source of fuel they are! Nor did we know how it would feel to receive the worship, awe and fear of millions of beings!

"The *feeling* . . . it makes your heroin seem like cotton candy fit for the consumption of children! It was so easy to inspire fear and worship in humans, so easy to manipulate them and drink the elixir of their emotions! Gods!" His fist pounded one knee.

"Imagine the frustration and temper tantrums of an infant new to the world expressed through the body of an Immortal Titan who can level mountains with a sweep of his or her hand, raise the seas to mountainous heights and crash them down across continents, boil the magma in a planet's depths and unleash it on our enemies."

He rose again to his feet, unable to sit still.

"The more power we wielded the more terrible we became. We destroyed Ger—the planet most of us were birthed upon—wiped every living thing out of existence. And the harvest of energy we reaped as everyone died, kneeling in the ruined temples, weeping and sacrificing what was left, begging for forgiveness and salvation—bloated us with power beyond imagining.

"And then we moved on." He stopped in front of me, face naked.

"The next planet we reduced to rubble. And the next and the next." Looking suddenly exhausted, he stood, head bowed, arms drooping limply at his sides. "We were mad with power.

"Some of us still are," he said flatly, "quite mad."

I sat frozen in my chair. Even if I could've

managed to think of something to say I couldn't have uttered a peep. Shakily I reached for my water and cracked the glass against my teeth trying to drink. The awful silence between us stretched and stretched.

Finally, Apollo raised his head, regarding me with empty eyes. "Not a pretty story."

*Do something!* I thought. *Now!* Squelching the icy apprehension within me, I stood up. If ever there was a moment for doing and not more talking, this was it.

"Come," I said imperiously, taking his hand.

"Enough for now. Let's go for a swim."

⊗⊗⊗⊗⊗⊗⊗⊗

I managed to drive my quivering legs up the stairs to change into a bathing suit and shorts. Then I shoved two beach towels in my daypack and headed out the door into the heat of the day. Apollo silently followed me across the yard towards the narrow cliff path.

The baking sun, the scratching of thistles at my bare legs, the crunch of dirt and gravel under my hiking sandals, the weight of the pack and the glinting water were all happy signs of normalcy. Normalcy! Amazing how the world carries on even as harrowing revelations change your personal landscape forever.

*He raped women, slaughtered millions, and destroyed whole planets! Unbelievable!*

It was like dating a nice guy in college, then

picking up a newspaper one day and discovering he was Ted Bundy. I shook off the creepy thought by focusing on my breathing as I walked, forcing calmness into my body. By the time we got to the cliffs I was a bit more steady and present, but not much. And then the rough scramble down the cliff took my full attention.

I led the way, not stopping and certainly not looking backwards for his help on the climb down. Whatever small scrap of human pride remained, I would try to hold onto it. Or maybe I was just trying to use physical fear to drive away the image of his beautiful face so hard and cruel, reflecting memories that had shriveled my human soul.

I was way out of my depth. And, for the first time, I realized it.

Up until now the relationship had been a big adventure, a whirlwind of paradigm-busting conversations spiced with the thrill of potential sex and romance and . . . okay, a lot of pain, uncertainty and misery. It had been a rollercoaster ride for sure. But the whole time I'd been lulled by his seeming humanity, by his obvious male appearance, his sensitivity and gentleness, his sense of humor, his cooking. Sure, he'd done a few party tricks, as he called them. But aside from that, he'd seemed totally human the whole time.

But now!?

I scrambled the last bit, sliding recklessly and then jumped to the sand at the bottom. I heard him scrabbling for footing behind me and didn't look back, walking the few yards to my favorite spot beside the big boulder, slinging the daypack off my shoulders, setting it down in the sand and dried seaweed.

Apollo walked up and silently helped me lay out the towels side by side. *How pleasant this would appear to anyone watching from above!* I stripped off my shorts, and, without a word, turned and walked to the waves lapping the shore, waded in up to my thighs and dove. The cold smacked me almost breathless. But the water felt cleansing and I stroked out into the bay, catching glimpses of the bottom as it fell away, turning from pebbles and dark seaweed to clear white sand fifty feet below, then sixty, then a hundred.

I swam until I couldn't swim anymore and then swam on, forcing my legs to kick and my arms to reach until I finally rolled and floated, lungs bursting, gasping for breath, staring up at the Mediterranean sky.

What a beautiful world this was. A beautiful planet that Apollo could destroy in a heartbeat just like he had so many others. Inconceivable. And yet there it was. What could I do in the face of such a story? Such power? Such honesty? Such horror?

*Absolutely nothing.*

For a long time, I floated, wrestling with my thoughts and emotions. What he'd done was beyond appalling. But, if I were to be ruthlessly honest, aside from a matter of scale and thoroughness, how were Apollo's deeds and the actions of the other Olympians any different from what humanity had done in the past? Hell, what humanity was doing right now! The one percent elite were ruthlessly destroying the planet, pillaging its resources for personal glory and gain. And unless the general population woke up to their power play in time, the end result would be the same: global annihilation. We didn't need the gods to destroy us. We were well on our way to doing it ourselves.

A large wave washed over me, rocking my body.

The icy detachment emanating from him as he'd told his story had chilled me to the core. But, I reminded myself, that story was also probably a million years old. The Apollo sitting on my patio, the Apollo who'd cooked me dinner and spoken of his love, the Apollo of justice and mercy who'd set Solon's Republic in motion 2500 years ago was not the Apollo of conquest and destruction he'd once been.

*Even megalomaniacal monsters can change given enough time. And eternity contains a boatload.*

Another large wave slapped me and I righted myself, treading water, looking around. Apollo had entered the water as well, easily keeping pace with me, maintaining a safe distance, keeping me company while respecting my obvious need for space.

Without stopping to think, I swam towards him. What a joy it was to have a strong body! I dove briefly as I closed the distance, and his nakedness gleamed whitely against the blues of the sea. Then I broke the surface, catching glimpses of his face as I swam the last few yards.

His curls were flat, his hair dark, touching the top of his shoulders. His eyes were dark as well, watchful, his mouth unsmiling. He didn't move and I swam straight to him and kissed him swiftly on the mouth. Then, before I'd lost momentum, I dove to the right, came up, rolled, backstroked and kicked water in his face.

That was all it took.

Trying to outswim him was impossible and I didn't try. I lollygagged in the water enjoying the feel of it on my skin as he closed on me, snaking an arm around my waist, pulling me under. I struggled, pushing my hands against his shoulders, trying to get away, but his arms were iron bands and if he'd wanted he could have easily dragged me below to meet Uncle Poseidon and a watery death.

But, of course, he didn't. Instead, he gave me my first underwater kiss in forty years and let me go.

I sputtered to the surface, laughing, and Apollo rose beside me. Rolling onto our backs, we bobbed side-by-side on the gentle waves, thinking our own thoughts, watching the sky and birds and cliffs, the cold salty water slowly sapping heat from our bodies. Well, at least my body.

Suddenly, I realized I was freezing.

I turned and breast-stroked to shore, my heart giddy, mind relaxed, soul surprisingly at ease. Whatever Apollo was, wherever this journey was taking me, whatever things I learned, I was in it for the long haul or the short haul or the hard haul, whichever it turned out to be.

Reaching shore, I would have loved to do an elegant Bo Derik exit onto the beach. But the steepness of the loose pebbly bottom ensured my usual crab walk out of the sea, bottom inelegantly sticking in the air as I used both hands and feet to secure a purchase.

"Charming," Apollo observed.

He was already on the beach, glistening in the sun, his naked maleness directly at eye level as he offered a hand. *Uncircumcised* I couldn't help but notice, surprisingly unembarrassed for me. I took his hand and he hauled me ungracefully out of the water.

"Remind me soon that this is something I need to help you correct," he said as we walked the short distance to our towels.

"What?" I threw myself down, grateful for the sudden warmth of the towel and the sand beneath it.

"Embarrassment about these exquisite bodies is a slap in the face to every god I can think of," he observed, lowering himself down next to me.

He was right, of course. But that didn't change the fact that I'd been raised in a straight-laced Christian family in the South in the 1950s. Yes, I'd traveled light years towards sexual liberation since then, and ordinarily I wouldn't hesitate to skinny dip. But no way was I going to be naked and exposed around Apollo at the moment. Not after that saga on the patio. *And not with the sagging belly fat I now carry!*

He sighed next to me. "That is exactly what I mean."

"What?" I asked.

He rolled over, propping himself on his elbow, his penis dipping towards the towel along his sculpted thigh. "You perceive physical aging as ugly. But it is not ugly, Ekateríni. It is simply a part of life and therefore beautiful."

"And would you say that what you did on Ger and those other planets was simply a part of life and therefore beautiful as well?" I retorted.

He thought for a moment before replying. "It was something I had a choice about and therefore should have somehow avoided. You, on the other hand, have no choice in the matter of aging. It is totally different."

I turned to face him. "I beg to differ, sir."

His eyebrows raised and the corner of his mouth quirked. "How so?"

"If you could have done anything differently, you would have. The thing is, you couldn't—which you may see as a weakness and imperfection just as I see sagging skin and extra pounds as an imperfection. But it's not. It's just what had to be in order to bring you to the place of being the beautiful person, um, being that you are now."

"My point exactly," he smirked. "Too bad you refuse to listen to yourself."

For a long, heated moment we stared into one another's eyes and I found myself suddenly breathless, wondering if Apollo was about to make love to me.

He chuckled. "I learned a long time ago that

the beach is a lousy place to make love to a woman, Ekateríni." He lay back down and that was that.

I flopped back on my towel, laughing in relief, and we lay there, soaking up the sun, idly talking of little things. We swam again and then thawed out on the beach until the sun started its slow descent in the sky. Then we shook the sand out of our towels and clothes, got dressed, and headed back to the house.

⊗⊗⊗⊗⊗⊗⊗⊗

Apollo was the first of the Olympians to begin to loosen the hypnotic grip of the body and its emotions, slowly gaining self-control. Which made sense. After all, he was the god of Intelligence—the Light Bearer—for heaven's sake. No surprise he would lead the way amongst the Olympians. I also learned just how accurate some of the ancient myths I'd studied in college actually were.

"We may have arrived as emotional infants," Apollo said, as we sat drinking tea out on the patio, "but we arrived fully grown. Your legends of the birth of Athena, for example, have her rising fully mature and armored out of Zeus' head. And Zeus himself, of course, is the archetype of beginnings. It is why he is always depicted carrying a lightning bolt."

I knew Zeus personified natural law and that he regulated space/time as opposed to his father, the god Cronus, who was the ruler of the absolute NOW called eternity. But I'd always wondered about the lightning bolt. "What has lighting got to do with beginnings?" I asked, curious.

He looked surprised at my ignorance.

"There were scientific experiments done on this world, at least forty years ago now, that proved lightning caused by volcanic conditions igniting through Earth's primordial atmosphere triggered the birth of life on this planet." He waved one hand airily. "Something to do with it creating the amino acids necessary for protein development and more complex molecules necessary for life itself."

*Is there anything this guy doesn't know?* I wondered idly. Then, mulling it over, I made a connection. "Hey! I guess that's what you meant at Zeus's temple that morning when you said people back in your day were in close touch with the nature of God!"

"How so?" he asked.

"Well, they didn't have electron microscopes and know about proteins, but they still came up with the picture of Zeus with his lightning." I shrugged. "Pretty tuned in, don't you think?"

"The archaic mind is fabulously intuitive and uncluttered by facts," he agreed. "People understood the fundamental intelligence of life. They intuited there was not a tree or plant in existence that did not have some beneficial property for healing disease and increasing health in the animal life coexisting on the planet. Thus, the ancients were exceedingly respectful in how they approached the Earth and her creatures. They were also terribly superstitious because they didn't have the scientific understanding to give them any context."

*Hmmmm.* I stretched my legs out on the chaise cushions. I'd slipped into my caftan after a quick shower to rinse off the salt from the sea and it was slit far up both sides exposing legs that were, I was happy to see, getting nicely tanned.

Apollo chuckled. "You have fine legs, my dear. I've admired them for many years and they are about to get me completely off track." He set his mug down on the table, cocking his head at me. "Speaking of which, do you understand how the human body defines space and reality and the implications of that?"

"Huh?" I was still back at the part where my legs were distracting him. "Sorry. What was the question again?"

"Tsk, tsk," he smiled wickedly. "I asked if you understood how the body defines space and what kind of reality that sets up."

I scrambled to organize my thoughts, pleased that Apollo's old teasing ways were back. "Funny you should ask. I was thinking about that in the tub the other day while you were cooking." *The other day?* Dear God, it'd been two weeks. I shook my head, bemused. That night of personal outrage seemed years in the past.

"And?" he prodded politely.

I dragged myself back to the present. "I've realized that having a body is wonderful and all, but it also gives me the disturbing sense that I'm separate from everything . . . and everybody. And that sets up a lot of problems."

"Very good. Exactly the point I wanted to make." He sat for a minute, staring out to sea. "Frankly, as angels we used to scratch our non-existent heads over the trouble humans have seeing that they are connected to everything. We didn't understand—*couldn't* understand—until we took form ourselves.

"You see, in the abstract realms oneness is fundamental and inescapable. But here? The exact opposite holds true. Here everything appears bounded and divided, distinct and separate—that is what the body does. It tells you that you are separate and alone. And there is nothing wrong with that," he said earnestly. "The perception of separation is inevitable and it gives a human being a sense of self. Fortunately, it's not an illusion that lasts forever."

"It doesn't?"

"Being physical and being run completely by physicality is a phase, Ekateríni, a natural stage of evolution all intelligent species go through. And it ends—or at least it begins to end—with the arrival of the Christos stage of consciousness. Yeshua, the one you call Jesus, was one of the first on this planet to understand that separation is an illusion. 'Treat your neighbor as yourself,' he said. And he meant that quite literally, because from both the spiritual and the quantum perspective you are literally both of the same substance and one. Today your scientists, your physicists, are finally seeing the truth that everything is really energy and interconnected."

He sighed. "Religion is the main thing still keeping people stuck on this planet. It enforces the continued belief in separation by posing God as something *out there*, far distant and better than you. And it pits people against one another, clinging to their opposing belief systems, instead of bringing them closer together.

"The gods have used religion to their advantage, keeping you at each other's throats for far too long. Which is why I wanted to come back and have this discussion." He leaned back. "Any questions?"

Any questions? Jesus. A million of them. But at that particular moment it felt like my head would explode if I tried to digest one more massive insight.

He chuckled. "I do not suppose you have any more of those wonderful breadsticks and that spicy cheesy whatever-you-call-it?"

"The disgusting commercial concoction in a tub?" I swung around on the chaise bringing my bare feet to the flagstones with a thump. "Coming right up."

"And perhaps some wine to go with it? And olives?" Apollo waved a hand at the mugs. "Afternoon tea is all very civilized. But exposing one's terrible character flaws is thirsty work."

"Of course." I was ready for some wine myself.

Sliding past him to go to the kitchen, he snagged my right hand and tugged me against his knees. Then he grabbed my other hand and held them tight. "Thank you, my dear," he said, looking deeply into my eyes.

"For what?"

"For not judging me."

"But I called you an egomaniacal monster."

"Not to my face."

"I thought it!"

He chuckled. "Ah, well, that was just calling a spade a spade. There is no judgment in that."

I blushed.

He caressed my fingers. "Don't sell yourself short, my love. It is a terrible habit—one that you and your entire species endlessly indulge in, making it even easier for the gods, myself included, to take ruthless advantage of you."

I couldn't think of a thing to say. But, oh, my, was he ever right!

He let me go and I tottered off to the kitchen, hands tingling. Ransacking the cupboard, all I could come up with was a Merlot, which was a bit heavy for an afternoon wine. But it was the only thing I had on hand, so I uncorked it, tossed breadsticks in a basket, pulled the cheese spread out of the fridge and took them outside. Then I went back in for glasses and olives.

Apollo was already digging into the cheese as I walked back outside. "Little piggy-oink couldn't wait for the wine?" I joked.

"No, I could not," he replied in as dignified a manner as possible with his mouth full.

I poured two glasses and we raised them in a toast. Apollo said nothing, just lifted an eyebrow, waiting for me. I thought for a moment then said,

"To a better world based in greater understanding."

"Amen," he said grinning.

We drank and snacked in companionable silence, watching the breeze stir the waves on the bay and toss the branches of the oleander and geraniums in the yard. Finally, he sat back with a contented smacking of lips. "Ready for more?"

I took a deep breath.

"We can stop if you need more time."

I looked at him. Part of me desperately wanted to just chill for the rest of the evening. But there was something about his energy that said we needed to press on. Despite the wine and his relaxed posture, I sensed an urgency in him. It was as if we were climbing a great mountain together and he now wanted to get me to the top as quickly as possible. Why the rush and what lay on the other side I had no idea. More mountains? There was only one way to find out.

"Lead on, Macduff," I said.

"Now there was a vast and potent mind," Apollo mused.

"What?"

"Shakespeare. And it is actually, 'Lay on, Macduff,' not 'lead on.' "

"Really?"

"Hm."

"Who was Shakespeare anyway?" I asked. "Was it Francis Bacon writing under a pen name like so many people think?"

"I am not an encyclopedia, Ekateríni," he said,

sipping his wine. "But I must say I find it interesting that you automatically assume Shakespeare had to be someone famous and better educated than a simple bailiff's son." He arched his eyebrows. "Cannot a common man or woman achieve brilliance on the weight of their observation of human nature alone?"

"Huh," I cocked my head. "I guess that means that Will Shakespeare was Will Shakespeare?"

"Hm." He set his wine glass down and folded his hands across his stomach, looking contemplative. Finally, he roused. "What is the main question you are wanting to ask at this point?"

I swirled my wine, looking into its ruby depths. "I guess the main thing is, why come out with all this now? I mean, what difference will it make? Done is done."

"Is it really?" He looked at me bleakly. "The vast majority of people on this planet still worship gods outside them even today."

"Sure," I said. "But we're getting past that."

"Are you?"

Were we? The weird political situation, the increasing public rejection of scientific evidence for everything from climate change to evolution, the stunning, inexplicable rise in popularity of fundamentalist Christianity, Judaism and Islam, the increased Christian influence in American government, the stunning increase in hate crimes around ethnicity and religion, walls being built against our neighbors—all of it pointed to a devolution in spiritual thinking and consciousness, not an evolution.

Apollo picked up the worry beads he'd left lying on the table and fingered them. "There are many gods still manipulating events and people to their advantage on this planet, Ekateríni. Always with the end goal of maintaining the source of their power and strength—the human emotions of fear and love directed their way." He paused, toying with the beads. "Their survival depends upon it."

*Click . . . click . . . click.*

"Most of the old gods are fading, yes. But in the West there is one god in particular that is actually growing in power on your planet. And it is the most powerful tulpa ever created."

"What?"

"This particular tulpa is the projection of humanity's ideas about Source itself and has been masquerading as the false representation of what is called the One God for a very long time on many, many planets. Currently it is busy here, manipulating the people of this world, accepting their worship, manipulating their emotions, driving them towards division and hatred and violence, leading them steadily towards creating global annihilation and Doomsday, what your Bible refers to as Armageddon."

He looked at me squarely. "And *that*, my dear, is what I've come back to try to help humanity avoid."

◇◇◇◇◇◇◇◇◇

## CHAPTER TWELVE

Waves of cold chills cascaded through my body at Apollo's words—a sure sign that truth had been spoken.

"But," I searched back through the day's mind-boggling conversation. "I thought you said all the tulpas were taken over by the archangels in order to save people from their destructive potential?"

"We did. All except for this one."

"Why not?"

"Ekateríni . . ." he paused, seemingly at a loss, then smiled a crooked smile. "Stop and think for a moment. We are talking about a mental projection of *Source itself* as a singular human being.

"Myself and all the other human-created gods over the ages, Isis, Ra, Sekmet, Osiris, Mithra, Odin, Ammon, Asherah, Baal, Nuozha, Taiziyeh, to name but a few, were created with specific attributes in mind—tulpa forms reflecting different principles and aspects of creation. But Source itself?" He shook his head.

"Humans took the mighty truth they finally intuited—that there is only one intelligence, one underlying principle, one Creator of all things—and they projected onto their idea of the One God all the terror and awe such a being would inspire. And because they only knew the world of form and flesh they projected the One God as a Big Man. And they gave him the white hair and beard that so often mark the wisdom of the elderly and terrible eyes of flame and a booming voice and immortality and unlimited power and the desire to rule.

"Because would not the One God rule over all things and creatures He had created?"

The hair rose on the back of my neck.

"No individual angel could step into those shoes. There was no matching frequency." He shrugged helplessly. "Source itself is beyond such ludicrous imaginings. Which means there was no guiding intelligence, no archangel available to take this terrible form over and eventually control it."

He stared down into the bottom of his glass, then downed the contents. "We—the Olympians and others—were bad enough. I've already described some of the horrors we perpetrated. But underneath our madness and initial lack of self-control there was always a solid core of sanity available to us. We still had memories of who we really were.

"We could not live up to those Ideals for a time—a very long time as it turns out. But those Ideals led us—at least most of us—back to sanity eventually. But this tulpa?"

He set his glass down and didn't wait for me to pour, picking up the bottle himself. "It is a renegade and law unto itself and has no guiding spirit. As a result, it has evidenced remarkably little evolution over the millions of years of its existence. It simply lives to feed on human worship and fear in order to satisfy its lust for power and fulfill the purpose humans gave it."

"Purpose?" I croaked.

"To rule as it sees fit over its domain and its chosen people . . . planet after planet after planet."

There was very little wine left in the bottle and Apollo emptied it into his glass, drinking morosely. The air was getting cool as the sun dipped below the western horizon behind the house. But it wasn't the dropping temperature making me go cold all over.

"Um, " I already knew the answer but had to ask anyway. "I don't suppose this creature has a name?"

Apollo looked up. "Of course, it does, and you know it well. Its name, my love, is Jehovah."

◇◇◇◇◇◇◇◇

I was emotionally exhausted and Apollo didn't look too hot himself. Neither of us felt up to cooking.

Again I changed clothes, putting on long black pants with an ivory top and long-sleeved black sweater. Running a brush through my tangled hair, I ignored mousse and everything else. The issues were too big, the topics too serious, the revelations too astounding to be dithering over hair and makeup— although I did choose some gold dangly earrings to wear.

Earrings always cheered me up. And boy, did I need cheering.

*Jehovah!* The God of Abraham himself. I'd

known from the outset who Apollo was referring to. But I'd held out hope it was a different being from the ghastly presence I'd tried so fervently to embrace . . . was it only three years ago?

It seemed much longer since my disastrous almost-love affair with a musician who, after a year and a half of passionate yet non-physical courting, had finally revealed his Christian fundamentalist beliefs. He'd kept them secret, talking my language of spirituality, consciousness and quantum physics, leading me to believe he thought about life and God as I did. But when our mutual feelings grew to the point of talking about a deeper, more permanent relationship, the truth had finally come out.

"I can't be with someone physically who doesn't believe exactly as I do," he said.

"And what do you believe?" I'd asked, startled.

Turns out he worshipped the Lord God Jehovah who had, according to his view, taken the form of a man named Jesus Christ in order to come to Earth as a teacher and savior. If we were to have sex, we had to marry, and if we were to marry, I must give up my pagan ways, accept that I was a wretched sinner from birth and beg for Jehovah/Jesus' forgiveness for being created this way and never stray from my worship of Him in order to be saved and allowed into heaven. Entertaining even the slightest doubt of Jehovah/Jesus' supremacy and rule meant I was being tempted by the Devil and I'd be pitchforked into the abyss where I would burn for eternity. No exceptions, no mercy.

Impossible as it seemed now, such was my infatuation with this guy, I actually tried to find a way to embrace Jehovah without betraying myself and my deepest spiritual knowledge. Which meant that one night I went to bed and instead of doing my usual meditation, I tried embracing Jehovah instead.

I forced myself into the mindset that I was born into sin and was disgusting in Jehovah's eyes. I adopted an attitude of cringing supplication and begged forgiveness from Him in His form as Jesus. I lay in bed, bathed in self-loathing, accepting that I deserved damnation and punishment, begging this terrible Creator to forgive me . . . if He saw fit.

Apparently, He didn't, for I lay there for hours, weeping and gnashing my teeth, ripping my soul to shreds until I finally said "Fuck it!" and let the whole thing go . . . including my earnestly fanatical not-quite lover.

Before that encounter, the only thing I knew about Jehovah was that His name was a modern version of the Hebrew God Yahweh in the Bible, and that dark-suited Jehovah's Witnesses were tasked with knocking on my door occasionally to distribute copies of *The Watchtower*, looking for an opportunity to proselytize.

I had no knowledge of the fundamentalist mindset. But after my one-night stand with Jehovah I started reading up. To my dismay, I discovered that fundamentalism—Christian, Jewish and Islamic—was the fastest growing religious movement in the world and that a surprising number of American governmental representatives and senators were fundamentalist believers like my lunatic ex-boyfriend.

Fundamentalist websites hailed Jesus/Jehovah's blood sacrifice as humanity's only salvation, actually promoting the violent destruction of the world in the flames of Armageddon as the precursor to Jesus' return and humanity's only hope—which explained the solid conservative Republican core constantly voting to impede environmental legislation and curtail women's rights to equal pay while denying them the right to deal with their own bodies as they pleased. That and install the Bible as the inerrant word of God in schools and other national institutions. And now that I'd heard Apollo's explanation, I was more disturbed than ever.

If all this were true, a sizable portion of the world's population—including much of the United States government—was under the sway of an egotistical, power-mad tulpa bent on retaining and increasing his power by initiating global destruction while parading itself as Jesus Christ and God Almighty.

Was I in some sort of weird science fiction movie or what?

I recounted my unpleasant encounter with Jehovah to Apollo as we drove to dinner. He listened quietly—indeed he seemed almost subdued—saying he regretted that I'd had such an experience. But, he added, in the long run it was a good thing because at least I was under no illusions.

"Jehovah is ruthless and cruel and exceedingly

clever. He twists people's natural love of goodness and purity into a distorted hatred for all things physical. He pits Heaven against Earth and man against woman. Sex, procreation, and the normal desires for pleasure all humans seek are made into vile temptations they have to resist in order to be worthy of his love and his heaven. And when people don't succeed in rejecting the joys and natural gifts of fleshly existence—and almost no one ever does— then he has them."

He sighed in the growing dark as I sped along the back roads towards Piso Livadi. "Fear, guilt, and shame are the most easily aroused human emotions, Ekateríni. If you can inspire those emotions in people, you own them."

He was so right! My wannabe-lover Rick had been the sweetest man and a true musical genius. Oddly, considering what he believed, he was also one of the most intelligent people I'd ever met. But he'd been raised by strict fundamentalist parents and was tortured by guilt and an ever-growing sense of worthlessness and hatred for his humanity. His only happiness lay in believing his self-hatred and self-denial were pleasing to his god.

*Ugh.*

We motored the last miles in heavy silence and I was glad to reach the outskirts of Piso Livadi—a jolly little town wrapped around a tiny bay with a long line of tavernas and restaurants built down the west side of the quay. I drove slowly past the gaily-lit, open-air restaurants facing the water, each one filled with people, candles, bustling servers and good eats. It was a reality a million miles away from our day's dark conversation. And I realized that was precisely how the whole issue could be so easily swept out of sight.

The subject of religion is horribly fraught with emotion and bitterly contentious. And everything Apollo had told me sounded incredibly far-fetched. Who would take this stuff seriously? How could I share what Apollo had told me and not be laughed out of the room or ripped to shreds on social media?

I finally found a parking space at the end of the quay facing the heaving dark sea. "I have one last question," I said, switching off the ignition and turning towards Apollo.

"Only one?"

I smiled in the dark. "For now," I amended.

He waited quietly.

"I'm confused about the whole Yahweh/Jehovah name thing. The original translation of God's name in the Bible is Yahweh. Then about a thousand years ago the name Jehovah starts popping up. What's the deal with that?"

"That is a very important question." Apollo moved around in his seat to face me. "You have noticed how the god of the Bible is . . . what is the psychological word you are so fond of using to describe him?"

"Schizophrenic?"

"Yes. Exactly. One minute you have God saying *Thou shalt not kill* and twelve verses later in Exodus he says, *Put every man his sword by his side ... and slay every man his brother.* Have you ever wondered about this?"

"Sure. I think most people wonder." I laughed mirthlessly. "I read somewhere that the number of killings God either does himself or orders done in the Bible is upwards to 25 million people. That's a lot of blood on the hands of a god of love." I shook my head. "Never mind the uncounted zillions of people condemned to burn in hell for eternity for not believing in him. If you have an answer, I'd sure like to hear it."

"Then hear this. Physical mass is built upon opposing forces of positive and negative—protons and electrons. Yes?"

I nodded. "Of course."

"Duality and opposition rule the physical kingdom. And when people imagined and worshipped the One God they ended up projecting him in two very different lights." He paused. "Depending on their mindset, some saw the One God as the god of mercy and love. Others saw him as terrible, fearful, and vengeful. The tulpa that resulted contains both sets of qualities. It is a terribly confused, bi-polar creation. And its acts and deeds reflect this dichotomy."

My jaw dropped. It was such a neat explanation I wondered that no one had ever seen it before.

"Unfortunately, it is much easier to inspire fear and dread in humans than it is love." Apollo shook his head. "It didn't take this tulpa long to learn that lesson. Thus, its main focus is always to inspire fear."

There was another one of our long silences as I digested this new information. Outside in the dark I could see waves breaking against the rocks beyond the nose of the car and a fine mist of salt spray gradually covered the windshield.

"But why the sudden name change a thousand years ago?" I asked as my stomach growled emptily.

"That one is easy," he said. "Divide and conquer. Now, time to eat." He reached for the door handle.

"Whoa, whoa, wait a minute. What do you mean divide and conquer?"

"Ekateríni, it could not be simpler. When the emotional power source looks like it may be running out of steam, the tulpa simply creates more factions, more conflict, more confusion, more argument, more names, more controversy, and thus more bloodshed and more pain and suffering to feed on.

"The name the tulpa goes by does not matter. All the fear, love and worship go to the same source." He looked at me. "Get it?"

I nodded. Suddenly I wasn't all that hungry anymore.

∞∞∞∞∞∞∞∞

We strolled arm in arm along the line of open restaurants running together in one long sweep of tables and chairs. Only the changing colors of the canvas canopies, chairs and tablecloths identified which tables belonged to which kitchen housed in the row of buildings across the little cobbled street.

"Kathryn!" I heard my name over the bustle and din. "Over here!"

I looked around and there was Chris and several other friends sitting at a long table by the water. *Great. Company.* Just what I didn't want. But it was too late to turn around and pretend we hadn't seen and heard and too late for Apollo to evaporate.

"Hi!" I said, walking over to their tables, smiling. There was a general scraping of chairs as people rose to make room, and we all kiss-kissed as I introduced Apollo who shook hands with the men while the maître d' brought two more chairs.

Mostly it was the gang from the Sunday hiking group, none of whom I'd connected with since I'd been back on Paros except Chris. Snacking on bread and drinking wine, I fielded questions left and right about where I'd been and why they hadn't seen me and how the book I'd been writing last time I was here was doing, and was I working on anything new? And all the while Chris was eyeing me accusingly as if I'd been withholding state secrets.

Finally, all eyes turned to Apollo—at least the eyes of the males around the table. The women, except for Chris, had never stopped looking at him.

"So, Mr. Tavoularis," began George, an ex-building contractor from Brussels who had built a house on the far side of the island with his German wife, Gita.

Apollo held up a quick hand. "Please," he said, "no formalities. Call me Apollo."

"So, Apollo," George seemed to be struggling

with the name. "Where are you from and how do you know Kathryn?"

I turned and mentally shouted, *You're from Athens and you're a film director and you make art films nobody has seen and we met about a film I'm doing on the divine feminine and you have a lover in Faringdon near Alyki and you're gay!*

He didn't flinch, but I saw his left eyebrow rise ironically. "I am from Athens . . . George, is it?"

George nodded.

"Just to get the basics out of the way for everyone, I am a film director and make art films nobody has ever seen except, perhaps, Ekateríni." He turned, grabbed my hand and kissed it lingeringly, eyes smoldering. "She and I have been discussing a film segment she wants to shoot on the divine feminine here in Greece. That is how we met. And since she was coming to Paros I decided to come as well. I have a house near Faringdon."

I yanked my hand away. The two eligible women at the table, Francine and Doris, sipped their wine, eying him speculatively. I so wanted to kick him in the shins! But since he was sitting next to me it was impossible. Fortunately, at that moment, the waiter arrived and everybody joined in the argument about what to order.

Rarely, in Greece, does a group of people order individually. Depending on what's fresh in the kitchen, they order as a group and share. And although the waiter always does the menu spiel, it's a tradition for someone to go to the kitchen, poke around, sniff, and talk to the cook.

"We'll go see what looks good," said Chris, jumping to her feet. "Come on, Kathryn." I rose reluctantly, knowing what was coming. *It won't be just fish on the grill tonight.* She grabbed my arm as soon as we got to the street and hauled me towards the kitchen door.

"What are you doing with this guy?" she hissed. "And where have you been? Nobody's seen or heard from you since you got here—except for him obviously." She jerked her head back towards the table where Apollo was now holding court, spinning God knows what tales about his life and our relationship.

"I told you already. We're just friends and business associates."

"Friends my ass," she snorted. "I saw the look in his eyes when he kissed your hand."

"I don't know what to say," I said helplessly. "It's nothing."

"Yeah, sure."

The kitchen was busy but one of the cooks took a moment to proudly show off the fresh smelts and red mullet, the octopus seethed in wine sauce, the calamari stuffed with mushrooms, the dolmas and a traditional lamb moussaka. Chris asked questions as I dithered, wishing on the one hand I could confess everything and on the other wishing I could keep it all a secret and Apollo very much to myself.

And yet if he was going to be part of my life, which it seemed he truly was, how could I successfully compartmentalize things? And what would happen when I went back to the States? Would he stick around? How long was this relationship, whatever it was, going to last?

I'd known him for three weeks and my life was a total mess. I was completely obsessed and lived for my moments with him. I was also stunned and horrified by his revelations and clueless about what form a book presenting the information he was giving me could possibly take. And the whole thing about Jehovah! Jeez. How much more complicated could this whole story get?

"And the donkey ears?"

"Sure," I said absently.

"I knew you weren't listening!" Chris crowed, triumphant.

"Huh?" I jerked out of my reverie.

"You haven't heard a thing I've said. You're obsessed with this guy and you can't hide it!"

I looked at her as harried waiters dodged us coming into and out of the busy kitchen. Hands on her hips, head cocked to one side, brown eyes flashing, she definitely wasn't backing down.

"I think the mullet and the calamari look good," I said lamely.

"You're not going to tell me anything, are you?" she asked.

"Chris, I'd love to. Really. But it's complicated, really complicated and I just can't talk about it right now. I would if I could, believe me." My voice dwindled and died, swallowed by the kitchen din.

"Let's get out of their way," she said, heading

out of the building. Then she stopped in the middle of the well-lit cobbled street. "Just tell me one thing," she said.

"If I can," I said reluctantly.

"He's not gay, is he?"

I looked at her, feeling the pressing need to let at least a small piece of information out, mentally sighing in exasperation with myself. "No Chris," I said. "He isn't."

∞∞∞∞∞∞∞

Dinner passed in a blur. I was physically beat and emotionally exhausted, feigning interest in the conversational topics that ranged from how to find a decent contractor on the island to the best way to fight a brush fire, always a hazard in the summer dry season.

Apollo silently ate with a focused hunger I hadn't seen in him before—like he was starving and needed the food. But when it came to wild fires, he spoke with authority about the effectiveness of setting back fires ahead of the main blaze itself to eat the brush the fire would feed on before it arrived. And he spoke about building houses to sacred geometric specifications that would "make a fire less interested in consuming the building."

Nobody seemed to believe that a guy in the film business looking like him would know much about fighting fires or sacred architecture. But they were polite. And Doris stared at him the whole evening, nodding at every point he made. Eventually the conversation drifted to the upcoming Sunday hike on the Roman road to Lefkes. Would I be joining them?

"I think that would be excellent," Apollo said, turning to me. "Of course, that is, if you don't mind me tagging along?"

"We'd love to have you join us," sighed Doris who was recently divorced from a wealthy London barrister. "Absolutely!" Francine chimed in, not to be outdone.

"I guess that settles it," Apollo smiled at me happily.

What could I say? I nodded and then, pleading fatigue, said we needed to leave. Apollo tossed a healthy wad of euros on the table murmuring, "That should cover our share," expressed his pleasure meeting everyone and got up to pull back my chair from the table.

"See you Sunday!" I cried, feigning cheerfulness as we escaped, leaving my friends to their speculations over the last carafes of wine.

"Why didn't you back up my story?" I groused as we strolled to the car.

"You mean telling people I am gay just to get you off the hook of your own embarrassment about being with a younger man?"

I was too tired to argue. "Yes."

"Because while I have certainly made love with my fair share of men over the eons, I am not gay and not embarrassed by being with you. Nor do I care what people think. And I do not believe it is healthy for you to care either."

Well, that told it straight. "And Sunday?" I asked.

"What about Sunday?"

"Are you really going to join us on a hike?"

"Why should I not?"

"Beats me," I said, groping in my purse for the car keys.

"Ekateríni . . ."

"I just don't like sharing my time with you with anybody else," I blurted, staring at him in the darkness of a half-moon night across the roof of the car. The wind had picked up and the waves were pounding the breakwater. Along the quay behind us the lights and colorful lanterns swayed. "Door's unlocked."

We settled into the snug interior and the pounding of the waves became a muffled background roar. I fastened my seat belt and started to key the ignition but Apollo stopped my hand.

"My dear, do not for a moment think I do not cherish every moment with you," he said, quietly. "And I, too, would prefer we be alone. But," he hesitated. "But at the same time I want to share in your life as it is. I want to know you the way your friends know you. I want to feel like a real part of your life. I want to be able to have that. I want both of us to have that."

*After I go away.* He didn't need to say the words for me to hear them clearly, and I flinched at the sharp pain they engendered in my chest. I didn't have the

courage to ask *How soon will that be?* I merely started
the car and headed back through the bustling town
into the night.

⊗⊗⊗⊗⊗⊗⊗⊗⊗

Apollo followed me as I stumbled up the stairs to my
bedroom. *Really? Now? Of all times?* I thought blurrily.
*I hope I can stay awake.*

He laughed as I turned on the side-table lamp
next to the queen-sized bed. "Everything has its
time, love. Now is the time for sleep. I came up to
tuck you in."

*Tuck me in?*

I didn't quibble and went into the bathroom to
wash my face and brush my teeth. Then I slipped
into the only nightgown I'd brought, a simple
brushed cotton scoop-neck gown, and went back to
the bedroom.

Apollo was sitting on the bed, the dim light
catching his hair turning it a dusty red-gold. His
eyes were unfathomable as he watched me open the
windows to let in the fresh night air. Then I turned
back the bedclothes and got into bed, stifling a
groan. Too tired to be shy or question his presence, I
switched off the lamp, plunging the room into semi-
darkness.

As soon as I settled, Apollo moved next to me on
top of the duvet, slipping one strong arm under my
head, pulling me close to snuggle against his chest.
Then he wrapped his other arm around me.

It was intensely sensual feeling his maleness and quiet hard strength beside me. It felt unbelievably safe . . . as if the Great Father himself, or maybe the father I had never really had, was cradling me to sleep.

Was that an incestuous thought, given my attraction to him?

I felt-heard the rumble in his chest as he laughed softly. "My dear, if everything is one thing in the mind of Source, then incest is not the half of it. Go to sleep."

Which conjured up interesting images of God making love to himself over and over in myriad forms. But I couldn't hold onto the thought for long. I was so relaxed, I didn't even care if I snored.

⦿⦿⦿⦿⦿⦿⦿⦿

There was light in the darkness. A strange scintillating pulse in the distance, like a semaphore calling my name. *Kathryn* . . . *Kathryn* . . . Then a deep roaring sound and a sucking and tugging at my limbs as a golden ocean dragged me tumbling to another shore. And I opened my eyes to white soaring cliffs and stars overhead and then suddenly a red curtain came down and a face loomed over mine, pale blue eyes probing, soundless lips moving.

"Have we got her this time?"

"I don't know. She keeps fading in and out. Faster with the drums!

"How can she not see you?"

"She sees me. She just doesn't believe what she sees. They don't journey much in her time."

Someone seemed to be talking about me? To me? Was this a dream? It didn't seem like a dream. But then what were dreams? My body felt like a thousand-pound jellyfish dangling over a cliff, but I made an effort and reached out a bulbous unformed hand, trying to brush away the rippling red curtain impeding my view.

"Who are you?" I managed to croak.

"She's with us! Praise the Goddess!"

A woman, face sternly concentrated, took form in my awareness. She reached out and I felt her surprisingly strong grip on the unformed flesh of my hand—a grip that seemed to get firmer as she pulled me away from the great sucking heaviness that said *sleep . . . just sleep now.*

With a sudden *pop!* I found myself sitting upright, cold sand beneath me, a piercing wind blowing icy damp into my very real body and a woman's hand holding mine. Drums beat rhythmically and vague figures of women and men danced and swayed around us under white cliffs so huge they seemed to merge with the night sky.

I looked around wildly, finally fixing my gaze on the one substantial object in this dreamscape—the woman kneeling in front of me.

"Who are you?" I asked again, then gasped wonderingly, reaching out to touch the dark tresses spilling to the sand. They were red.

"Hello," she said softly. "My name is Polymnia."

∞∞∞∞∞∞∞∞

I'd known a split second before she said her name.
The beating drums and the cries and vague forms of
the dancers faded away until it was just the two of us
sitting on a strange twilight shore with a still black
sea and the wide beach of a crescent bay rimmed by
massive cliffs curving away into forever.

A billion stars glimmered in the half-lit heavens
above and I gasped again as I realized not one,
but three enormous moons hung in the sky, their
reflections glinting on the obsidian waters giving the
whole eerie scene its light.

"Where are we?" I whispered.

The penetrating wind had died completely
and there was absolutely no movement or sound—
not even a lapping of water on the sand. Polymnia
shrugged, looking as if my question and the place
were of no importance. "Clearly we are in the place
where we could meet."

"But . . ."

"Don't waste energy on such things. We have
little enough time as it is." She looked at me, frowning,
as if sizing up a questionable piece of meat in the
marketplace. "Do you know what he's planning?"

"Wha . . . who?" My mind was spinning.

"Apollo," she spat. "Who else? Do you know
what he's planning?"

"Okay," I muttered to myself, "this is just a weird
dream. Just breathe and focus and it will all go away."

"Goddess!" she cried incredulously, slapping me so hard across the face my jaw practically dislocated. "Is that a dream? Don't be stupid. We have to work together. Why else go to all this trouble bringing you here!?"

Hand to my stinging cheek, anger flared. "How dare you . . ."

"I dare plenty to save him. Gods!" she looked at me stunned. "I've come to this? You don't even realize he's sacrificing himself, do you?"

"What?"

"You're so excited with his attentions you haven't even noticed how his energy is waning?"

"Uh, well . . ."

"Of course, you haven't. And, of course, he wouldn't tell you. Stupid male pride."

"Look lady," I shot back. "Instead of wasting time insulting me why don't you tell me what the hell is going on?"

She actually smiled. "That's better." She gave a quick nod. "You know he's left Sira—the planet where the rest of the Olympians are now, right?"

"Y-yes."

"And he's come back to Earth in your time to try to balance the scales and get the truth out about the tulpa Jehovah, yes?"

"How did you . . ." I swallowed. Of course, Polymnia knew. "Yes," I nodded.

"What you don't know is that he's not going back to Sira."

"He's staying?" My heart leapt.

"He's not staying, you stupid cow." She gritted her teeth. "He's dying."

"What?" I cried. "But he's im . . ."

"Immortal?" she interrupted. "Yes and no. Yes, as long as he continues to harvest energy from people's worship. No, if he doesn't. He's come back to Earth on and off for centuries waiting for me . . . or rather you." Her tone made it clear what a poor exchange she thought that was.

"Now, because of you, he's staying on Earth in fully manifested form for longer and longer periods of time." She shook her head. "His last trip back to Sira he didn't stay long enough to fully replenish his energy. Nowhere near."

"He was gone for almost two weeks!"

"Earth time," she snapped. "And he was wild to get back to you the whole time because he knew how distraught you were." She spat on the dark sands in disgust. "Now he's drained so much energy he can no longer get back to Sira. It's only a matter of time before he fades away to nothing." She shook her head until her long hair fell over her face and she rocked for a moment, sitting in the sand, moaning her despair until it became a loud keening cry. *"Eeeeeiiiiiiiiiii!!!"* she screamed into the silence.

I started, shocked at her outburst. "Jesus, lady! Get a grip, would you?"

"Get a grip?" she shrieked. "Get a grip?? Goddess preserve us!" she laughed maniacally. *"Lady,"* she spit back at me, eyes fierce, "that's all you've got. A grip on your emotions and your mind, a grip on your vagina—a grip so tight no juice can flow and nothing can get through."

She shook her head wildly. "You're afraid to laugh too loud or cry too hard or feel too much. All you do is think think think all your dry stupid thoughts about how to look good and make money and how you don't dare upset anyone and all the while you feel *nothing!*"

She leapt to her feet, long hair and skirts swaying, while I watched, stunned and frozen, my sore jaw gaping in shock.

"You're terrified of life, terrified of sex, terrified of doing the wrong thing. And you know what scares you most of all? *Yourself!*"

Hands on hips, she loomed over me threateningly. "Has he told you that *you* and your whole race of dead machine-people are what we were working together trying to avoid? He knew what the downfall of the Goddess would portend. It's why he made women the guardians of his temple even though it flew in the face of all tradition! He knew the impact of worshipping a terrible Sky God filled with judgment and rules. He knew that to kill the Goddess is to kill the Earth and all hope. He knew we had to bring the idea of the Great Marriage of masculine and feminine as equals into the minds and hearts of the people. But we were too late! Too late, too late . . ."

Moaning, she reared back, ripping her bodice in anger and remorse, exposing the white flesh of her breasts.

Profoundly unsettled at her words and even

more so at the display, I looked away . . . which was a mistake. Seeing the very proof of what she despised sitting right in front of her, she pounced on my discomfort. Darting closer, she grabbed both breasts, shoved them together forming creamy mounds, nipples protruding, bent and shoved them in my face.

"Does this shock you little prune? My little shriveled grape of a woman?" She let her breasts go and roared bitter laughter at the twilight sky. "Goddess! What am I to do with *this?*"

I sat frozen and quivering in an alien landscape, a bare-breasted temple goddess screaming in my face. I desperately wanted to *do* something! Be angry or defend myself or, better yet, run away. But I couldn't. Plus, she was right. She was right about it all.

"Teach me," I said quietly.

"I don't have *time* to teach you," she snarled.

"Well, then you're just going to have to make do with what you've got. So, stop bitching and let's get on with it!"

We stared at each other, ancient flame-haired goddess-woman breathing hard, nostrils flared, and modern peroxide-blonde . . . what? New Age goddess wannabe? I shook my head impatiently. *Irrelevant.*

"What do we need to do?" I asked.

She glared at me a moment longer then abruptly sat down, skirts billowing. "We need to get him back to Sira."

"What about the other Olympians?" I asked. "Can they help?"

She shook her head. "They made it clear he was

on his own. And he's too proud to ask. He's got it in his head that if he can help the people of Earth break the God spell that there will be a sufficient ripple effect across space and time so that even if he's no longer around it will be enough to make a difference to other worlds down the road. Plus . . ." she broke off.

"Plus?"

She sighed impatiently. "He's also got some romantic notion that by offering himself as some sort of sacrifice it will atone for all the shitty things he's done to humans down through the ages."

"Well, that's just stupid," I said flatly.

She arched her feathery eyebrows. "I agree."

We sat glum and silent, the sand beneath us and the sky above still and cold. *What a strange place and scene this is!* But I was no longer interested in trying to understand where I was. Polymnia was showing me that it was enough to simply be here.

"We both love him," I ventured. "Between the two of us would that do some good? Give him energy?"

"Love?" she said. From her tone you would have thought I'd said 'turd.'

"Yeah. Love—you know, the most potent force in the universe?" I said sarcastically.

"What scroll did you read that in?"

*What scroll?* "Everybody knows that," I started defensively.

My beautiful elder sister, woman–I-am-to-be," she said pityingly. "Love is all well and good. But loving him will get him about as far towards Sira as raising our skirts and blowing farts at him." She shook her head.

"You have something better in mind?" I asked, affronted.

Her face lit up. "Yes," she said softly. "As a matter of fact, I do."

⊗⊗⊗⊗⊗⊗⊗⊗

"Sex magic?" I asked. "Seriously?"

"Yes. You know, that inconsequential act that creates life itself?" she mocked.

"But . . ."

She gazed at me, eyes unreadable. "How can a race of people get so smart and so stupid at the same time?"

It was a rhetorical question so I didn't bother answering.

All the same, she softened. "Jehovah has created great ugliness in humans, planet after planet," she said sorrowfully. "He twists all that's lovely and pleasurable and turns it into filth, destroying people's very souls."

She picked at the bodice she had carelessly tried to push back together. "I'm sorry," she said.

"For what?"

"For all the terrible things I said to you earlier."

"Why?"

"Because you have been . . . I will be . . ." She sighed. "You cannot help being the way you are

because your world has been poisoned with shame."
She moaned sorrowfully, "I wish with all my soul we
could have stopped it."

A part of me wanted to weep as well, although
for what I wasn't sure.

"So," I said, briskly, "sex magic it is. But I hope
you're not trying to say that me making love to
Apollo is going to be so fantastic that it blows his ass
all the way to another planet?"

I laughed and continued laughing semi-
hysterically until I helplessly collapsed on the sand.
"Oh, God," I wiped my eyes, sitting back up. "What
a thought."

"You're right," she giggled. "No, you can't do it
on your own. You can't even do it if I join you. Not
even with all my people."

My mind flashed to the fleeting seconds spent
merged with Polymnia while she and Apollo made
love on Mt. Parnassus. She nodded. "That's how I
became aware of you," she said. "I felt your presence.
And as you joined us, I joined you."

She moved a little away, enough to straighten
her skirts and smooth them over her knees. "I've
been able to tap into your life stream ever since. And,
of course, I can always . . ." she shrugged. "Apollo is
part of me. It was easy to discover what he was up
to."

"You've been spying on us?"

"Enough to understand what's going on. And
once I knew I couldn't let him throw his life away."

"But he wants to get this information out to

people, Polymnia. I can't thwart his wishes. It's important."

"But he doesn't have to be around for you to write about what he tells you. Does he?" she asked, eyes pleading.

"No," I admitted. "Probably not."

"So that's it."

"That's what?"

"Let him say what he has to say then you convince him to participate in the ritual of the Triune Goddess."

"The what?"

She looked at me strangely. "Don't you know *anything?*"

I stared back at her silently. Sighing, she went on. "We invoke the three sacred faces of the Goddess—maiden, mother and crone—and all three of us engage in the ritual with Apollo simultaneously across time and dimensions and send him on his way."

She made it sound easy. Like, "We write a grocery list and go to the store and then make dinner." But before I could even ask who the third woman in that "us" was, a sudden blast of cold wind shook the air and her red hair whipped about her.

"Ah no!" she cried, looking wildly up to the gunmetal sky. "Not yet!" she screamed. "We need more time! Goddess, give us more time!"

*What was happening?* "Time for what?" I cried.

"Come!" she called in a panic. "We must find the mother! You have to find her. She's too far ahead in time for me to be able to reach without the circle!"

*Huh?*

She ripped a small amulet from around her neck and shoved it into my hands. Whatever was in the smooth hide bag it was hard and oddly shaped. "Hold onto it and don't let go!" Polymnia yelled. Then she threw herself on the sand in front of me, spread her legs wide and raised her skirts, exposing her genitalia.

*A true redhead* was my only thought as I stared at her in shock.

"You've got to find her!" she screamed above the roaring wind and sudden pounding of the sea. "It takes three of us to do the ritual. I'm the maiden. I've never borne children. You're the crone. You have to find the mother—the future self who will be with Apollo and join him as we have—the fertile third who will bear fruit as neither of us can! Go!" she wailed as she pried her vulva apart with her fingers, the wind spiking, the stars shimmering in a melting sky. "We might never have this time again!"

"What do I do?" I screamed back.

Her eyes bulged at the enormity of my question and the towering mountain of her primal knowledge compared to my empty panicked modern mind, but she forced herself to calmness. "Focus on the entrance to my womb. Focus with all of your might and *will* yourself into the darkness to the cave of the Great Cosmic Mother! Call Her! Ask Her to guide you for I cannot!" She was weeping and trembling but kept her legs resolutely open, her gaping labia spread wide, the darkness of the unknown void of all creation beckoning.

GO!!!!!

The word came on a mighty gust of wind and blowing sand and I gritted my teeth and wiped my eyes while my insane mind bellowed its discomfort at kneeling in front of a woman staring at her vagina, insisting this was impossible and disgusting and ridiculous and . . .

*SHUT UP!!!!*

I don't know whether she screamed or I did as I focused hard, ignoring my terror and the wind and the bite of cold and the dissolving sea. I moved closer to Polymnia who was now lying prone, praying in a strange language to all the gods for time and strength and a miracle to occur as I stared at her exposed sex.

*Don't look at it you fool! Let go! Walk through the gate!*

I remembered Apollo's copper eyes pulling me into him that day on the mountain and forced my gaze to the blackness between Polymnia's legs . . . the elliptical cave beckoning . . . the warm slit, moist and smelling of Earth and everything fecund and new and old, birthing and dying . . . blood and water and magic . . . and I felt the tug—my own belly heaving in response and heard a roaring in my ears—and then the world was dissolving, the white cliffs falling as I entered the cave, slipping through the entrance as it narrowed and narrowed, squeezing.

I fell from half-light into darkness, screaming in terror and exultation in the pitch black void and suddenly there was another light—a pinprick in the vast distance—a pulsing throbbing light that exploded into my vision with colors beyond colors any human eye could see. And within that revolving spiral of color and Light there was Darkness—a Dark Intelligence that probed my frightened soul like the tongue of a lover exploring my essence, tasting, sipping nectar, spitting out the pips, probing womb and brain and guts and mind. And suddenly there was laughter, a great rolling thunder of amusement that was kind and terrible, loving and indifferent, gentle and eviscerating, ripping the formless truth of my Being to shreds, looking into, through and beyond me.

*What is it you seek child?*

*I seek the mother!*

*I am the Mother.*

*I seek the mother I will become and a future with Apollo whose seed I will receive to finally bear the fruit of life for the hope and love of all life to come!*

No answer . . . just a massive shrug of energy and I was falling once again, tumbling and flailing, filled with the despair of failure until the terrible weight and squeezing began.

Pinched and rolled, shoved and pinned, I screamed in fear with a mouth that was full of water and could make no sound. The squeezing went on and on, contractions that threatened to break my bones. And then there was another light, a pinprick through a slit in the dark tunnel of forever night. And I struggled for the light and the opening grew wider and wider and I tumbled slickly out of the cave that held me and great harsh hands lifted me up and the light around me was harsh and cold and I trembled and cried hearing a voice say, "It's a girl."

And another voice, exhausted and soft, whispered, "Desma, my little dove. Give her to me." And then darkness and I knew nothing more.

⊗⊗⊗⊗⊗⊗⊗⊗

## CHAPTER THIRTEEN

Disoriented, I awoke to the streaming light of a late morning sun and the uncomfortable feeling that I was being watched.

My eyelids were heavy as millstones and my body felt like it had run a marathon. Groaning, I rolled over and looked around. Apollo was sitting across the room in the straight-backed chair perched in front of the dressing table, staring at me, eyes hard and intent.

He looked completely out of place in the small feminine space. And my first confused thought was *He spent the night watching me?* Which seemed odd and mildly creepy. Then the nighttime journey came rushing back in a kaleidoscopic torrent of images and emotions. "Polymnia!" I gasped, sitting bolt upright, looking around wildly.

"What have you done?" he asked softly. Not moving a muscle, he didn't smile. Nothing. Just sat, watching me like a hawk.

Inexplicably, I felt a twinge of guilt. "Me?" I said. "Nothing." The words came out thickly, as if there was something wrong with my mouth. Gingerly I raised my hand to explore my sore jaw and found myself clutching something. A small blue leather bag hung from a length of cordage twisted in an oddly knotted design. *Where? What?*

Oh my God. It really happened.

I forgot about my mouth and opened the bag with trembling fingers. A tiny clay figurine of an ancient faceless goddess tumbled into my hands, worn and darkly polished by thousands of years of handling, bulbous breasts sagging onto an enormous pregnant belly, her legs and feet joined as one atrophied appendage tapering down to a spiked point at the bottom, designed to be set anywhere in the earth to sit upright.

Across the room, Apollo gasped. Instantly, he was beside the bed, snatching the little goddess from my hands. "Where did you get this?" he cried, face ashen, staring at the figurine.

"Polymnia gave it to me," I said.

He didn't say a word. Just cradled it tenderly, bringing it to his lips, closing his eyes as if trying to communicate with its long-dead and yet very much alive owner. Feeling like an interloper, I fled to the bathroom, closing the door.

*Oh my God, it really happened.*

I staggered to the mirror, uncertain what I would see. The tumultuous dark night engaging my wild self under three moons hanging in the sky, the shock and the overweening strangeness and terror, then tumbling through the void into the uncomfortable bosom of the Great Cosmic Mother. Surely all this had seared my very soul and must show?

Hm. Maybe not. My hair looked unusually wild and spikey. Dark circles rimmed my eyes and a large purple-black splotch looking suspiciously like a handprint stood out against the tan on the left side of my face. How could I explain that?

*Oh, it's nothing. I was just sitting on an alien planet last night with a former self from the good ol' Druid days and I didn't like something I said. How was your night?* I got past the bruise, gazing intently at my image, searching for some inner mark and didn't find one. Amazing.

Carefully, I splashed cold water on my face and brushed my teeth, unable to open my mouth very far, uncertain whether Polymnia had loosened some teeth. Holy Moses, that woman packed a punch! Talk about a force of nature! I'd never met anyone like her and wasn't sure I wanted to again. But by God she was alive and powerful . . . for a dead woman.

No wonder she'd given Apollo a run for his money.

Turning on the shower I let it run then stepped in, groaning with pleasure as the hot water melted the knots and tension in my body. In the meantime, my mind, of course, wanted to pull apart the night's events.

I might not understand the process, but clearly I'd been magically summoned by her and it had taken the energy and focus of an entire Druid clan to hijack me in some form or other and land me on that planet? Dreamscape? Back lot sound stage at Universal Studios? Damned if I knew where we'd been. What had she called it, so filled with impatience at my curiosity? Ah yes, "The place where we could meet."

Nothing but the no-frills obvious for Polymnia.

And speaking of obvious, whatever form the engagement had taken, it absolutely had affected my physical body. For God's sake, I'd brought her amulet back with me. And bruises!

I washed my hair, enjoying the sensuous scent of the shampoo and the softness of the lather, contemplating the terrifying astral ride I'd been sent on looking for the Cosmic Mother. There was no way I could possibly have imagined *that*. I shuddered under the hot water, mind spinning.

And my birth . . . or rebirth as Desma.

Where and when was that? How would Polymnia and I hook up with her? Polymnia hadn't even been certain she and I would ever connect again. And why had she given me her totem of the Goddess? To speed me on my way? As a talisman to bring back— or rather forward—to Apollo?

I felt a sudden pang of jealousy over what they'd had together.

How close they must have been, not only sexually, but spiritually, plotting together to shift people away from the destructive "kill the pagan goddess" trend that Jehovah and others of his ilk were so focused upon fostering. What a task! And then I suddenly wondered how much of Polymnia's anger and impatience with me had been driven by jealousy as well?

In her shoes I wouldn't have been disposed towards pleasantness. Gently, I lathered my sore jaw, holding it under the stream of steaming water and sighed. *All things considered, I'd say we managed rather well.*

The water ran and ran, and reluctantly I turned to the task at hand. How the devil was I going to convince Apollo that what we had in mind was a good thing? It's not like I could force his cooperation. *Please darling, participate in the Triune Goddess sex ritual with me and my alternate selves across time. I promise we have nothing in mind but a good roll in the hay.*

Yeah, right.

Nope. Somehow, I was going to have to get him to change his plans midstream. How was just one more question mark in a series of question marks. Whether I was up to the task I didn't even stop to consider.

The water felt wonderful, but I was stalling for time. Apollo hadn't looked happy with my night's outing—as if I'd had any choice in the matter. And seeing Polymnia's totem had genuinely shaken him. Delaying confrontation was not going to help. Reluctantly I turned off the shower and dried myself off. Maybe if I pranced out naked it would take his mind off things? *I wish.*

I stalked back into the bedroom with the towel around me and found it empty. The little goddess was back in her bag and carefully placed upon my plumped-up pillow. I stared at it, uncertain, then slipped it over my head. It was tight, but I got it over my ears and the soft leather-covered weight felt right hanging between my breasts—like she'd always been there.

Taking a deep breath, I pulled on my caftan, brushed my wet hair and headed for the stairs.

⊗⊗⊗⊗⊗⊗⊗⊗

Apollo was nowhere to be seen, the coffee pot was empty and my heart sank.

The tangible reminder of his ex-lover must have been too much for him. Or something. Who knew? The clock read almost noon, which was shocking. I hadn't slept this late in decades—if sleeping is what I'd been doing. Despite the shower I still felt muzzy-headed and off-balance. *Coffee . . . need coffee.*

The pot was just ready when I heard the sound of a car coming up to the house. Now what? I definitely remembered Apollo closing the gate the night before. I looked out the window to see Chris wearing a bright blue beach dress getting out of her car and sighed.

I beat her to the door, flinging it wide. "Come in," I called in false pleased greeting. "I just made coffee." I turned back to the kitchen and hauled two mugs out of the cupboard. The sound of rustling paper bags and footsteps grew closer.

"I called and called to see if you wanted to go to the beach early but you didn't answer," she said as she walked in, eyes darting around, obviously seeking signs of male presence. "I stopped at the bakery on the way back and thought you might want some croissants. They're still warm."

*You, my transparent friend, are on a fishing expedition,* I thought. But I only said. "Yum. I haven't eaten yet this morning. I just got up."

Giggling happily at the implications, Chris sailed around the kitchen counter. "Holy Mary Mother of God!" she cried, dropping the croissants on the floor. "What happened to your face! That bastard hit you! Are you okay? Oh, Jesus! I'm so sorry!" Her eyes were huge behind her glasses and before I knew it I was being smothered in a motherly embrace.

What to say? No way could I play the "walked into the bathroom door" card. The outline of a hand was clearly stamped on my cheek. Gently I extricated myself from her grip. "He didn't hit me, Chris."

She pulled away and looked at me searchingly.

"Honest."

"Look, I know he's gorgeous and that it's great having a guy like that want a woman our age. But nothing is worth *that*." She waved at my face.

Chris, cross my heart and hope to die, he didn't do it." An idea suddenly dawned. *God, I hate lying.*

"His girlfriend did it."

"His girlfriend?" She looked dubious.

I nodded. "She's Greek," I rolled my eyes as if that explained everything. "And young. She followed us and confronted us after dinner. Frankly, I'm not sure why she hit me and not him. Either way I'm not happy about it."

She looked at me long and hard. "First he has a boyfriend and now he's got a jealous girlfriend? Sweetie, I don't think this guy is worth all the trouble."

*If you only knew.* "I know it sounds terrible and looks worse, but there's something about this guy

that's important to me, Chris. Really important."
She started to interrupt but I headed her off. "We
haven't done anything more than kiss a couple
times. It's just not about what you think it's about,"
I finished lamely.

"Really." She was clearly not convinced. "Then
what's it about?"

"I can't tell you."

"Why not?" she asked, not giving up.

"I can't explain that either." I looked at her
beseechingly. "I'm sorry. If I could I would. But I
can't! Please . . . just don't worry. I'll be all right.
Honest."

Her eyes hardened and I could tell I was pushing
the limits of our friendship. Then she shrugged. "If
you won't say, you won't say. But be careful." She
picked the croissants off the floor and placed the bag
on the counter. "I've got to get going."

With that she turned and stalked out the door.

Her car raced out of the yard with a decisive
spitting of gravel that told me exactly what she
thought of my non-explanation. *Rats.* I sighed,
heartily wishing I could talk about my situation with
her. But I knew I couldn't. And even if I could there
was nothing she could possibly do to help. I poured
coffee, sincerely contemplating whether or not to
add a shot of brandy.

It had not been a good start to the day.

◇◇◇◇◇◇◇◇◇

Despite, or perhaps because of, my blurriness and whirling non-stop thoughts about Polymnia, sex magic and the missing god Apollo—I opened my laptop and tried to get some work done. Checking my calendar, I saw I had an Internet radio talk show to do with a British host at six o'clock that evening. *Ack!* Missing that would not have pleased my hard-working publicist or the show host or his producer.

Thankfully, the interview was about one of my first books on the divine feminine. I'd done at least a hundred shows on the topic and wouldn't have to do any preparation. I scrolled down the long line of unread email messages, plowed in, and before I knew it two hours had passed.

Still no Apollo.

I got up and stretched. There was just enough time to run to the store for groceries and then get to the beach for a quick swim before the show. Maybe that would clear the remaining fog out of my brain?

After doing my best to cover the rapidly discoloring bruise on my face with makeup, I drove into the village. The thought of eating didn't interest me and I ended up buying more booze than food. Who knew how many long nights it would be before Apollo came back? But then I remembered *He has nowhere to go*. Horrified, I almost dropped the case of red wine I was carrying in the middle of the street.

Apollo wasn't at the house and he wasn't at the beach and my mind was filled to overflowing with a thousand concerns, all of them circling back, over and over to one question: *How can he be dying? Fading away to nothing after millions of years!* Had Polymnia seen things aright? And if so, how could he be so stupid as to sacrifice himself like that? What good could possibly come of it?

I swam as far out in the bay as my tired body would let me, then turned around and swam back, almost breaking into tears as I did my crab walk out of the sea, remembering Apollo's outstretched hand, his casual nakedness, laughing at me as he dragged me ashore.

Dried off and dressed, I climbed the cliff and trudged back to the empty house. How could a being take up so much space in my life in such a short period of time? And after Apollo, would anything ever be the same again?

I knew it would not.

Desultorily, I stuffed some feta cheese, pitted olives, and tomatoes in a sliced croissant, drizzled it with olive oil and ate it standing at the kitchen counter. Then I mounted the stairs and, avoiding looking at the bed where I had oh-so-briefly slept in Apollo's arms, headed to the bathroom for my second shower of the day.

◎◎◎◎◎◎◎◎

"You say, and I quote, 'Western women are not truly liberated and modern society is missing the key element to sexual equality.' That's quite a statement. Could you please tell me and our audience what you mean?"

So far, most the questions I'd been asked were straight from my press kit—a sure sign the show host hadn't read the book itself and was winging it as best he could. Which wasn't unusual. Radio and podcast show hosts are notoriously overworked. Reading a book a week then prepping for an hour interview on top of whatever regular work they do is no small feat. Which is why hosts depend on press kits and prepared questions from the authors they interview. It makes for a less spicy show. But at least the questions are relevant.

"I'm so glad you brought that up, Tim." I said, ploughing into the topic. "A hundred years ago when women first began entering the work force, it was a man's world we were entering." I rattled on, building up a head of steam on the oh-so familiar subject matter and the time flew past. Before I knew it my host had pitched to his last commercial break, music swelled in my headsets and I heard the first words, "Do you suffer from migraines and period pain?" and turned down my headset volume.

I took a sip of water and looked at the clock. Twelve minutes to the end of the show.

"Kathryn?"

It was Tim, talking on a side channel while the commercial for some sort of pain medication rattled in the background.

"Yes?"

"Is there anything you'd like me to ask before we wrap up?"

"I'd like to pick up where we left off and then

finish with some encouragement about how things are changing and some things people can do. That work for you?"

"Perfect. Thirty seconds."

The channel went dead and I was taking another sip of water when a sudden movement outside caught my eye. It was Apollo, slowly strolling along the cliffs, headed for the gate. My heart slammed into gear and I almost choked.

"Fifteen seconds," I heard in my left ear.

*Shit! What was I talking about?*

"Five, four, three . . ."

"Annnnnd we're back, talking with Kathryn Adams, author of the book *Feminine Divinity.* Kathryn, you really left us hanging there with that last comment about women having to be like men both in bed and out. Would you like to expand on that for us?"

I blessed my host for the pickup line, forced a laugh and focused for all I was worth.

"Absolutely Tim. But you know it really is like that. The male perspective and male values are all that really matter in this world. I call them Penis Values. For example . . ."

"Penis values? Can we say that on air?"

I laughed again. "Think about it. Our whole world is about profit, possessions, and power. Actually, most masculine values seem to start with the letter "P"—which is how I got inspired to call them Penis Values—things like property, progress, pride and prowess.

"Women coming into a man's world had to adopt these values as their own. I'm not saying that women aren't interested in profit and possessions or power. It's just that for women other things are at least equally important—more feminine values like love and compassion, cooperation, harmony and connection."

The remaining minutes of the show whipped past and soon my host was talking about where to find my books and then the music swelled again. We made our friendly goodbyes and I was off the air.

In seconds I'd dumped my headset on the desk and was running out the door and down the stairs to the kitchen. And there he was, in a grey t-shirt and jeans this time, snacking on olives. The whole scene looked so normal I wanted to cry and I started to hurl myself into his arms. But then I remembered, *It's Polymnia he wants, not me.* The look on his face seeing her totem was all the proof I needed to realize I was just an older New Age substitute. While Polymnia. Ahhh, Polymnia. She was the real deal. Wild and fierce, undomesticated and unbroken. Whereas I . . .

Hitting the brakes, I skidded awkwardly to a stop, just managing to keep the kitchen island between us, a tiny safety zone of polished concrete.

"You are doing it again," he said, popping another olive in his mouth.

"Doing what?"

"Selling yourself short."

"I don't know what you mean," I lied.

He placed his hands on the counter and leaned

towards me, muscles rippling, copper eyes intent. "You never would have met Polymnia had you not been capable of getting there yourself. She could only put out the call and spin the meeting place into existence. You had to answer and follow the energy trail to her."

Energy trail? All I'd done was fall asleep, get tossed around in a golden cosmic washing machine and spit out onto a beach.

He rolled his eyes. "Not everything is accomplished through conscious volition, you know. In fact, most of what humans do is unconscious."

*That* was certainly true. "So, I guess you know all about it?" I said.

He shrugged. "I only know that you met her." His eyes clouded with something I couldn't put my finger on. "Which is more than I have done in the last two thousand years."

His voice was even, but I could clearly hear what I'd missed in his eyes . . . longing. And my heart sank even lower.

"Dammit!" he slapped his hand on the counter. "Of course, I long to see her again! What man would not? And yes, I miss her, even after all this time. And yes, I wish she would put out a call for *me*. But I know she never will because our time is done and that is not how these things work. Magic is never done for personal gain and pleasure. When it is, there is always a terrible price to pay.

"She is too wise." He shook his head. "*You* are too wise, to do such a thing. But I would be lying if I said I did not wish she would. And I would be lying if I said that if she did I would not be tempted to go to her. But Ekateríni, you *are* her. How can you fail to see this?"

He threw his hands up in exasperation. "You have had countless lives and experiences since that lifetime. You are more than she ever could be. Do you crawl backwards across this illusion called time and become a baby again? No! You move forward. Which you have done. All that Polymnia is and knows is inside you. And so much more besides.

"Gods, woman! When will you get it?"

He slapped both hands back against the counter-top, willing me to let go my fragile female ego and stop wallowing in comparisons and self-judgment. But it was so hard! It was as if the sense of less-ness . . . the unending lack of self-esteem was hard-wired into me, body and soul.

"And *that* is the truth," he snapped. "It is."

He walked around the counter, grabbed me by my upper arms and pulled me close, fixing my eyes with his. "Self-hatred *is* wired into you. The sense of worthlessness has been passed down through your female genetic line for over three-thousand years."

He gave me a shake. "I would give the soul I never had to have spared you that. But I could not. And I want nothing more right now than to take you in my arms and carry you up those stairs and make love to you so long and so hard that all the doubt and fearful thoughts that you are not good enough are wiped away forever. But I will not."

He shook me again. "And do you know why?"

My knees had gone so weak it was only Apollo's grip that kept me upright. I stared up at him, transfixed by his words and the emotions behind them.

He repeated his question. "Do you know why?"

I shook my head.

"Because if I make love to you now you will wake up in the morning and think that I did so to make you feel better, not because I desire you and want nothing more than to join with you. You will believe that I made love to you wishing you were *her*. And until you get it straight that I love you for you I cannot touch you."

He let me go with such force, flinging his hands away, that I staggered and grabbed the counter for support.

"It is you keeping us apart, Ekateríni. Only you."

The words rang like a bell in my heart and mind, shocking and clear. "So, my dear," he continued. "What are we going to do to fix this situation that is driving us both slowly mad, eh?"

He looked at me for a long time, eyes stormy yet calculating. Then he walked around the island to the tiny pantry, reached inside and pulled out one, then two, then three bottles of red wine, lifting them high. "We are going to drink. And we are going to talk . . . something you dearly love to do. And you are going to understand this demon inside you that keeps you from being everything you long to be and yet already are."

He set the bottles on the counter and walked to the sink, gathering wine glasses. "We are going to get drunk and be sad and lighthearted and angry and passionate and whatever else it takes. And then we will see what happens from there. Deal?"

Wide-eyed and breathless, all I could do was nod.

"Good. At least we have a place to start. Now, where is the cork screw?"

I pointed silently to the proper drawer. "Go get your shawl," he commanded, starting in on the first bottle. "Or whatever else you might need for warmth. Turn off your phone and join me in the living room. It is going to be a long night."

"But you need to save your strength!" The words fell out of my mouth before I could stop them.

He looked at me strangely. "What did you say?"

Oh, my God! There it was. No preparation. No subtle feminine manipulation. Just wham! Concern for his wellbeing right out there in the open. Which meant there was nothing to do but dive right in.

I squared my shoulders and said in a rush, "Polymnia told me that you're staying here to sacrifice yourself and we both think it's stupid and it's my task to talk you out of it and get you to participate in the Triune Goddess ritual so we can get you back to Sira and the whole thing freaks me out but I'm willing to do anything it takes to save your life and I've just totally blown the whole thing by telling you."

I looked at him mutely, all my love and two women's worry plain in my eyes.

"I see," he said.

"Do you?" I shot back, stepping up to him. "I doubt it. In my experience once a man has his mind set on something, not changing his mind becomes a matter of pride. Are you telling me you're suddenly smarter than that?"

We glared at each other and it was Apollo who broke the silence first. "I do have a vastly larger view than you. And I think that bears some consideration in this matter," he said stiffly.

"Oh, really?" I chided. "Sounds like you think you can tell the future. Either that or you're playing the 'I'm a god and you're a lowly human and can't be expected to know as much as me' card."

"You know that is not what I mean!"

"Yeah? Then what exactly do you mean?" I challenged.

He was stumped. We both knew it and it was Apollo who lowered his gaze. He turned, picked up the wine bottle, poured two glasses and shoved my glass towards me, wine slopping crazily over the rim onto the concrete. "Touché" He raised his glass to his lips and drank, eyes hard.

I didn't touch mine.

"Apollo," I said softly and waited. Finally, he looked at me. "This isn't a contest. I don't want to be right. I want to talk about this. I want to figure this out with you. I want to live and thrive. I want *you* to live and thrive. I want the world to live and thrive. And many worlds to come. Surely, my love," I reached out and touched his hand, "there has to be a better way to help humanity than the Bringer of Light doing himself in at this late stage in his career."

It was a statement, not a question. For a long moment we stood there. And when I felt a slight give in the hardness of his body, I let go his hand and reached for my glass. "To finding a better way," I said, and drank.

"It is already too late," he said, quietly.

"I know that," I said, equally calm. "At least I know it's too late for you to leave this planet under your own steam. And I think you're a totally glorious, amazing, dumb idiot for doing what you've done. And I love you. And Polymnia loves you. And . . ." I paused, not knowing whether to say anything more, then deciding *what the hell*. "And there's a beautiful young woman in your future who will also love you and bear your child and her name is Desma . . . and she is also me."

I heard Apollo's sharp intake of breath, saw his eyes take on a sudden extra brilliance and I reached for his hand once again. "She is my pledge, *our* pledge for a better future. But my love, that will never happen . . . you'll never meet her unless you get your head out of your ass and start thinking about life instead of a sacrificial death on some scruffy little planet on the outer rim of the Milky Way."

I raised his hand to my lips and kissed it. "In case you hadn't heard, that act has already played here." I teased. "Trying to beat Jesus at his own game?"

He sighed deeply and clung to my hand. "No matter what the future might contain, you have to know that what matters most to me is being here with you," he said, his voice rough-edged and thick. "And carrying out the mission Polymnia and I failed to accomplish all those centuries ago."

"Of course, I know," I semi-lied, trying to soften the heaviness in my own heart. And then, in a flash, I realized what I needed to say and the truth of it. "Apollo, you have to know that I can accomplish our task without you staying here with me."

"What?" he asked, startled.

I laughed gently. "Not to diminish your importance or anything, love, but unless you're willing to reconsider doing party tricks to wow the crowds, the book and everything about marketing it and getting it out to the world—that's on me. And I already know how I'm going to do it."

He looked stunned, shaking his head, his red-gold curls dancing. And it occurred to me now was my chance to sink my fingers into that enticing head of hair like I'd been wanting to for so long. My right hand crept upwards of its own accord and *ahhh*, his hair was silky and thick and felt like the fine mane of an Arabian stallion slipping through my fingers.

"Care to share?"

"Huh?" Mind in my fingertips, I'd almost forgotten what we were talking about.

His chest rumbled with laughter. "You are easily distracted."

I shrugged, grinning like a loon, my fingers continuing their gentle combing. "Legs are your weakness. Hair is mine."

"Shall I start calling you Delilah?"

"Have no fear, Samson. The scissors are upstairs." With deep reluctance, I ceased caressing him, dropping my hand to pick up my wine glass. Eyes sparkling over the rim, I said, "It's going to be a romance."

"Excuse me?"

I snorted. "The book silly. It's going to be a romance novel."

He frowned. "Are not those particular kinds of books, uh . . ."

"Frivolous entertainment?"

He nodded, eyes troubled.

"Frivolous entertainment read by millions upon millions of women hungry for love and affection, starved for deeper meaning and information, lusting after an intimate yet powerful connection with their mate, eager to improve themselves and their lives, dreaming of ways to uplift the world to make it a better place for their families and their children's children to come."

"Ahhhh." His eyes cleared and he nodded.

"I know what I'm doing, Apollo. At least with this." I touched his cheek with gentle fingers. "I am the audience for this book. What you tell me, I need to hear both as a human being and as a woman. What you tell me, you tell all women *through* me, and through them all humanity whether a book is ever even written or not."

He looked at me questioningly and I laughed.

"Have you not affirmed we are all One?" I

chided, gently. "If I fully receive your message hasn't all of womankind?"

His eyes widened and then he smiled, acknowledging the truth of what I'd just said. "And the student teaches the teacher," he said gravely, bowing gracefully from the waist, one hand on his breast. "This is a fine moment indeed."

ΟΟΟΟΟΟΟΟΟ

## CHAPTER FOURTEEN

It was dark outside and Apollo started a fire as I sat cross-legged on the sofa watching him contentedly. I was deeply relieved I'd told him about Polymnia's plan. We hadn't yet come to a spoken agreement about his participation in the ritual. But at least the cards were on the table, he wasn't freaking out, and I wasn't trying to plot some weird seduction aimed towards performing a magical sex rite I didn't know a thing about.

He came and sat next to me, stretching his long legs across the top of the coffee table, and for a while we sat, companionably silent, watching the crackling flames, sipping our wine. And yet as the minutes ticked past I felt a growing unease. What "demons" had Apollo been referring to that needed to be gotten rid of? And how was he planning on doing it? Finally I could stand it no longer and broke the silence, asking a question that had been burning in my mind. "Tell me more about Polymnia—about you and Polymnia and what you were planning together."

"What did she say?" he asked.

I shrugged. "Nothing much. There wasn't time. But I got the impression the two of you were working together for some purpose and that it related to you know who." I giggled. I'd almost invoked the famous Harry Potter line, *He who shall not be named.*

Apollo didn't smile. Instead he gazed at the fire for a long time. Finally he spoke."To answer that I've got to give you some background."

"Of course you do," I said indulgently. If nothing else I'd certainly realized that with Apollo answers to my questions were rarely short or direct.

"The coming of the Christos—what you call the Christ—is a huge event on every planet signifying the great shift in consciousness away from the illusion of separation and the worship of false exterior gods to the recognition of Source, or God, within self and all other beings. The Christos, also known as the Redeemer, is not a person at all. It is the birthing of a higher level of consciousness within every woman and man that spells the end of pain and suffering caused by ignorance of the divine nature of humanity.

"But here on Earth this awakening was thwarted because the one who came to teach the world of unity and love and God within, Yeshua, the man you call Jesus, was betrayed and killed and his message twisted and coopted."

"By Jehovah," I whispered.

He nodded.

*And so the plot thickens.*

"You have no idea." Apollo thought for a moment. "To give you the proper perspective on Yeshua and his mission, we need to go way back to the heyday of the Goddess religions."

He sipped his wine and laughed. "Source Intelligence is neither male nor female. But the idea of creation being born out of a male god is especially absurd," he said bluntly. "I cannot fathom how anybody comes to believe such nonsense."

"It's jealousy," I said, smugly. "And male insecurity."

He snorted. "Indeed! But seriously Ekateríni, the Goddess comes first on every planet that has ever birthed a sentient species, and rightfully so. It is the females who are responsible for carrying life. And not just in the reproductive sense. Women are psychically sensitive and open to receiving information from the spiritual realm of the Ideals. Thus, it is usually women who first receive and birth the art of fire, becoming the tribe's fire guardians— with a few prompts from me whispering in their dreams, of course," he added modestly.

"You won't find this in your anthropology texts, but women are always the first physicians, learning the art of herbs and healing from their wild food gathering. Your modern medicine is based upon hundreds of thousands of years of knowledge women have gleaned and developed. And while historically you see pictures in books of the brave Neanderthal men out on the hunt and most believe it is they who sustained the primitive clans, it was actually the women who provided the majority of the food the clan ate.

"Women are always the first farmers, reseeding medicinal plants and seed grains in their regular foraging pathways, refining their knowledge of seed propagation and planting. Of necessity, they are the first pottery makers and weavers, developing everyday household implements and clothing. They also developed the first dyes and inks for decorations by which they honored life's processes and forces."

"But what about the early cave paintings of animals and the hunt in places like Lascaux in France?" I said. "I thought painting was man's secret rite and art."

"Most of your anthropology texts say that, yes. But Ekateríni, modern life is based upon a writing of history by men as told through the masculine lens. Why do you think it is called his-story?

"And yet the paintings in the caves you mention are usually accompanied by the handprint of the artist stenciled onto the cave wall. Anthropologists are now discovering that the majority of those handprints belonged to women." He held up his hand. "See my fingers? Men have shorter index fingers than ring fingers whereas women's index and ring fingers are close to equal in length. That is how they can now tell."

I studied my hands. He was right!

"Being a writer you will love this. Guess who develops language?"

Women?" I whispered, eyes wide.

"The men are certainly in on it. But complex language first arises out of the need of Neolithic women to communicate all the information they have gathered about herbs, medicines, food sources and preparation techniques they have developed in cooking and tanning, pot making and the arts."

He rubbed his chin.

"At a certain point in human development, left-brain function kicks in and that is *always* signaled by the introduction of the written word, which is the cognitive domain of the masculine. Writing is a left-brain process that triggers even more left-brain development. Then mathematics, which is also a left-brain process, swiftly develops. Once men develop writing and mathematics, they begin to record and then slowly coopt and expand the information and skills the women have developed."

"And because they have greater physical strength they get away with it," I observed sourly.

He laughed outright. "Not always. The Goddess never goes quietly into the night of obscurity the gods desire for Her. There have been fierce women warriors here on Earth, as your legends of the Amazon women attest." He smiled. "There are whole worlds, Ekateríni, where the Goddess is never unseated and women rule."

Wow. *Who knew?* With a start, I realized Apollo was giving me his version of the whole masculine enculturation thing I'd been talking about earlier on the radio. I raised my wine glass to my lips only to realize it was empty. Gravely, Apollo refilled my glass, tipping out the last contents of the first bottle he'd pulled from the pantry.

"But what does all this have to do with you and Polymnia and Jesus and Jehovah?" I asked.

"Patience, my dear, I am getting there."

He got up and carried the empty bottle to the kitchen, opened both remaining bottles and brought them back to the table. I topped up our glasses while he added a couple small logs to the fire, giving it a few prods. Then he proceeded to stand there, one bare foot planted on the plaster hearth, wine glass in one hand, the other resting on the mantlepiece, looking for all the world like the lord of the household in t-shirt and jeans.

"As we've discussed, the physical world is made up of opposing forces, starting with positive and negative, protons and electrons—a duality that reveals itself at a higher level as masculine and feminine genders. The battle of the sexes, as you call it, is a very real dynamic. And it always shows up in the primitive stages of civilization when humans put down roots, abandoning the nomadic lifestyle.

"Eventually, the coming of the Christos marks the beginning of the end of that kind of conflict as man and woman are gradually anointed into the understanding that there is a higher force of unity underpinning the world."

Like quantum physics points out," I interjected.

"Precisely. Once the essential oneness of all life is grasped, eventually all the wars and conflict, including sexual conflict, cease, because the universal equality of all beings is finally understood and the scales of fear have fallen from everyone's eyes."

*What a heavenly vision*! I thought.

"Indeed, it is, Apollo agreed. "The time when

heaven and earth meet is the great turning point."

"So how did Jehovah manage to screw this evolution up on Earth?" I asked.

Apollo stared into the fire for a moment, then prodded a log a little further into the flames. "There is a lot more to it than what I want to get into tonight. But basically, he stirred up trouble in the Sanhedrin against Yeshua's teachings. He was the dark angel visiting the priests' dreams at night, whispering how Yeshua's teachings about the equality of man and woman were blasphemous."

"Jesus taught sexual equality?" I asked, shocked.

Apollo nodded. "Although you would never know it today. All his teachings about women being the equal to men were struck from the scriptures. Of course, he also accepted women as disciples, an historical fact even two thousand years of scriptural rewriting hasn't been able to disguise."

"Mary Magdalene."

"And other female disciples who are less well known—Mary Salome, Miriam, Martha, Joanna and Arsinoe, and even his own mother." He smiled fondly. "Yeshua was a powerful yet gentle teacher much loved and appreciated by women. His message of compassion and love was something they could understand and practice, while for most men it was a teaching of weakness that they despised.

"The priests deliberately stirred up misunderstandings of Yeshua's claim that the One God—then known as Yahweh—was his father and that he and his father were one."

He snorted. "Yeshua never claimed to be the only son of God. That was the lie that was perpetrated because nobody understood the concept of oneness he was trying to teach." Apollo shook his head. "Everybody took his words literally . . . except, of course, the Magdalene."

He sighed. "Herod and Pilot both tried to get him off the hook. He was no threat to them. But the priests, inspired by Jehovah, had been inciting the people with rumors about the Messiah and the coming of the King of the Jews and the need to throw off the yoke of the Romans for over a hundred years.

"The whole situation was primed. So, when Yeshua came back to Israel from his years of study in India, it was an easy matter for Jehovah to channel the fear, hatred and hope he'd already inspired amongst the Jews onto him and his teachings. He even managed to infiltrate Yeshua's inner circle of disciples."

"Judas." I said, making the obvious leap.

He shook his head. "Peter. The tulpa's deep hatred of women and the whole lie he spreads about their sinfulness and their corruption of man was an easy sell to men like him and Paul."

"Let the woman learn in silence and with all subjection," I said, remembering the Apostle Paul's words.

"And let us not forget Peter's protests about the Magdalene's presence amongst the disciples. 'Let Mary leave us, for women are not worthy of life'," Apollo quoted.

I shuddered. But then a question that had long plagued me popped into my head. "Were Jesus and Mary Magdalene married?" I asked, curious. "There've been so many books about that—even stories that they practiced tantric sex and that part of the reason Jesus managed to resurrect his body was because of her spiritual support and added energies."

He nodded. "The ascension of Yeshua is a tremendously complex subject which I will not go into tonight. But yes, they were indeed husband and wife. And it was a fiercely guarded secret."

"Why?" I asked.

"Because of the whole headship of the husband tradition Jehovah had inspired in the masses over the centuries. If they had been publicly seen as married, Mary would have automatically been placed beneath him in people's eyes no matter what Yeshua said or did to change it. And since a large part of his teaching was the equality of women and men, they both decided it would weaken his position to come out with the truth too soon.

"You see, he was intending to elevate Mary as his chief disciple. Few of the rest understand what he was saying and stood for, especially Paul and Peter who were outright bigots and misogynists.

"Mary, on the other hand, was a tremendously evolved being. Had their plans not been sabotaged by Yeshua's betrayal and death, they would have traveled and taught together for decades to come. The example of their love and respect for one another and the eventual recognition of their marriage *and* their equality would have changed everything."

He sighed. "If their plans had worked, Jehovah would have had to leave Earth to peddle his agenda of misery and guilt somewhere else. But he managed to destroy Yeshua. Worse, he then had the unmitigated gall to usurp his role as the most holy Redeemer and Christos by spreading the belief that he, Jehovah, had come to Earth in the form of Yeshua to sacrifice himself for the sins of the world.

"Eventually he even managed to smear the Magdalene, turning her from the Apostola Apostolorum into a repentant whore."

"The Apostla whatla?"

"The Apostle of the Apostles. That is how highly regarded the Magdalene really was. Hippolytus, the bishop of Rome himself, called her that."

"So, what happened to her?" I asked. "Did she go to France like some of the legends say?"

"She did. She wanted to continue teaching in Israel after Yeshua was killed, but there was too much enmity from some of the disciples and the Sanhedrin and she was forced to flee. First, she went to Egypt and then to southern France where she ended up raising their daughter and teaching for the rest of her life. Her faithful followers of the Rose Cross, the Knights Templar, took up her banner for many centuries to come."

"And she's remained a thorn in Jehovah's side ever since," I joked.

"Not enough of one to make much difference,

unfortunately." He lifted his wine glass and drank, motioning from across the room for me to do the same. I complied and he walked back to the table and topped up both our glasses.

*I guess he wasn't kidding about getting drunk tonight!*

Apollo didn't respond to the thought. Instead he started pacing. "Real power comes when the masculine and feminine join forces. Working together, teaching that redemption is in each and every man and woman, teaching that feminine values of love and compassion should be respected and cultivated alongside masculine values of power and control, that sensitivity and intuition are just as important and useful as intellect, they would have been unstoppable. Which is why Jehovah had to act so quickly once Yeshua came back to start his ministry in Israel."

He stopped to stare moodily at the floor.

"You still haven't explained what Polymnia has to do with all this. She . . . I . . . came along, what, about three hundred years before Jesus' time?"

"A little less," he said, sighing heavily. "We planned to set the stage for the coming of the Christos—the new archetype."

I gasped. "The Christos is an archetype? *Oh, my God!* Are you telling me Jesus was a tulpa too?"

He shook his head violently. "No. No. The Christos is the birthing of divine wisdom within man and woman. It is indeed an archetype, but the whole point is that it marks the end of the supremacy of exterior ideals and forces." He grinned. "And the first Christos that comes is not always a man either."

Before I could digest that startling thought, he continued.

"Polymnia and I planned to help pave the way. You see, the tide was already turning away from the Goddess by the time I purportedly vanquished Ge's Python."

"Ge's python?" I asked.

"Ge or Gaea is the Earth goddess, 'The Mother of Everything Beautiful in the world, the ever-sure foundation of all the deathless ones who hold the peaks of snowy Olympus'." Apollo shook his head, smiling. "Ge is one of the very first principles of all Creation and the legends proclaimed her to be my great-grandmother."

"What?"

"Legends, Ekateríni. Ge and Uranus mated and produced the Titans who produced offspring, among them Zeus, my dear father." His mouth twisted sardonically. "The battle with Ge's python was a symbolic battle that never actually took place. But it was a singularly important historical marker, signifying the beginning of the switch from a Goddess-centric culture to the solar masculine principle that occurred when Delphi turned from worship of the Earth Goddess to me.

"You have to remember, Delphi was the navel of the world and a center of religious power long before my time. The policies of the temple affected the entire known world. When I overthrew the Goddess, I knew what the rise of patriarchy meant and this time I was determined not to play so easily into Jehovah's hands by opposing the Goddess. My goal was to keep her viable and visible. Which is why I placed women in the roles of power in my temples and gave the role of prophecy to mature married women.

"And it worked. For over a thousand years the prophesies and what became known as the Delphic Maxims of the Pythia were incredibly popular: Φιλοσοφος γινου – be a seeker of wisdom, Οσια κρινε – choose what is divine, Εστιαν τιμα – honor the hearth and woman, Υφορω μηδενα – down-look no one.

"But by the third century BC the power and importance of Delphi was waning. The masculine was coming to full potency in the arts and science, politics and philosophy. The Gallic invasions of the Balkan region were about to begin. Women were losing status and in some places their legal rights. And it was at this point that Polymnia came to the temple.

"I was immediately struck by her beauty, talent and sheer raw female power."

"No kidding about the raw power," I muttered, tenderly rubbing my swollen jaw.

He was silent for a moment, remembering, then sighed, "Unfortunately, if you look at the chronicles of the Olympian gods, you will find that on planet Earth pretty much every relationship I had with human females came to a bad end," he mused. "And Polymnia was no exception."

*Great*, I thought. *That bodes well.*

"I tried to keep her at a distance. But in the end that only managed to bring her closer. As a Druid, she was hugely dismayed by the diminishing status of the Goddess. She begged me to unmask myself, to step forward and openly teach the importance of sexual equality, justice and balance, not just through veiled prophesies from a priestess in a trance in the mountains, but as actual teachings coming from the mouths of a masculine god and a human woman, walking side-by-side in the world as equals."

Again he started to pace. "The rest of the Olympians thought I was mad to even consider it. The days of us directly meddling in the affairs of humanity were long over. Some people already believed we were only myths. At best, we were absent overlords. But there was a window while the mythic mind was still in play where such a display would have been acceptable. And the Druids in the Misty Isles gave us their support."

His face was animated and his eyes sparkled. "By the gods it was a bold idea!" he said admiringly.

"So, what happened? Did Jehovah get wind of it?" I asked tentatively, hating to quench the happy moment. And indeed, his jaw tightened and the sparkle died.

"Yes," he said, grimly. And for a while I thought he would say nothing more. But he ploughed on. "You know the gist of it. Jehovah used his influence to poison the mind of the aging Pythia, convincing Tanis that Polymnia was after her power.

"Such a waste," he cried, balling his hands into fists. "And so unnecessary! In those days, it was common for more than one Pythia to reside at the temple. Polymnia and I would have left Delphi to Tanis while we traveled the city states." He shook his head.

"Tanis was easy prey. She knew me as a divine presence in her mind, not as a god in her bed. And certainly not as an equal and friend. Jehovah's whispers played on her fears and her own natural jealousy." He walked back to his wineglass sitting on the table, downing the contents in one gulp. "You know the rest."

He came back to the sofa and sat down, refilling his glass with the remains of bottle number two. "Last bottle, eh?" He looked over at my glass. "No lagging behind, Ekateríni. It is not polite."

Not to be outdone I sank the remaining wine in my glass.

"Good girl," he said, giving me a refill. "Now another."

"You're trying to get me drunk!" I accused.

"I'll drink with you. Come. You will need it for the rest of the story." He chugged his full glass, urging me with his eyes to do the same.

I am not proud of the fact that at this advanced point in my life I could still rise to a drinking challenge. My darling, sweet-tempered mother had gifted me with the genetics of not one, but two hollow legs. Over the years, I'd taken enormous satisfaction in drinking many a man who thought he could take advantage of me this way under the table. Not to be outdone by a mere god, I looked Apollo in the eye and drank the next full glass down.

The contents hit my empty stomach with a heated *whump!* Wiping my lips with the back of my hand, I pushed aside my empty glass which Apollo promptly refilled. It was getting late and the little room was warm and cozy—if not a little fuzzy around the edges. I rearranged my position, ignoring the buzz in my brain, burrowing more deeply into the pillows, ready for whatever might come next.

For a long moment Apollo sat silently, staring off into the distance. Then he took a deep breath and slowly turned his gaze upon me. The moment stretched puzzlingly as his eyes searched mine. What was he doing? Assessing my sobriety level and ability to continue?

Smugly, I assured him I was fine. "Please, go on," I said, with a slightly dizzy wave of my fingers.

I caught a fleeting glimpse of oddly conflicting emotions . . . determination and . . . sorrow? in his eyes. But before I could puzzle the reason for it, abruptly he stood back up, wine sloshing dangerously in his glass.

"The impact of the death of Yeshua cannot be overstated," he said, pacing the room once more. "The core of what he had come to teach, the glorious divinity and equality of man and woman, was railroaded into a saga of sin and redemption through pain and blood sacrifice."

He shook his head in disgust. "In the aftermath

of the crucifixion, Jehovah played upon the egos and guilt of Yeshua's remaining disciples, pushing the ridiculous idea upon them in their sleep and every waking hour that Source itself had manifested solely through the body of one man, and that Yeshua was the only son of God.

"Αχθος αρούρης!" he spat the curse words with a sudden violence as his fingers clamped down on his glass, shattering it, wine spilling over his hand and onto the rug.

I must have been drunk or mesmerized for I didn't even flinch. Nor did it occur to me to get up and clean the mess of splintered glass and red liquid off the floor. Instead I sat, riveted and slack jawed, watching Apollo's powerful form in the firelight, listening to his words, imagining the beautiful future for the world Jesus and Mary Magdalene had planned and given their lives to set in motion, the compassionate loving world Apollo and Polymnia had wanted to help them create, where every future man, woman and child born across the fullness of time would flourish and flower together, all to the infinite glory of Source itself.

*Ohhh! What a dream that was!*

As usual, Apollo tracked my thoughts. "After the crucifixion, instead of being elevated into their divinity, man and woman were reduced to cheap stick figures of clay, sinful creatures put on Earth for one purpose only—to worship and adore a power-mad *tulpa* in the guise of the Christos." His tone turned the word into its own curse.

"By turning the Redeemer from a shining example of what a human being really is into a suffering sacrificial victim, the Western world was successfully plunged into the Dark Ages. Humanity was now responsible for the death and suffering of God himself in the form of the Son. And guilt ruled the day."

Apollo sat back down on the sofa next to me, angry, the jagged stem of his wineglass still clutched, unnoticed, in his right hand. When he turned to me his eyes had gone black as night

"The sins of humanity were responsible for the terrible suffering of the Son. And, of course, for over a thousand years, the Chosen Ones of Israel had been taught by Jehovah to believe that the source of all sin and evil is . . .?" He leaned into me, his beautiful face suddenly strangely foreign. I shook my head, my brain befuddled by wine and words and too much information.

"Huh?"

"Surely you can remember that much?" He pressed. "Your brain isn't that small." His voice was harsh and seemed to come from far away. He was almost on top of me, one hand still clutching jagged glass, and I gasped, shrinking away from him on the sofa. *What the . . . ?*

"Answer me, Ekateríni! The source of all sin and evil is . . . ?"

Mind spinning, room whirling, the words refused to come.

"You were taught the answer before you were

born! Now tell me!" Voice lashing like a whip, he slammed the base of the glass on the table next to me. "Who is responsible for all sin and evil?"

"Woman," I whispered.

"Ha!" He laughed an ugly laugh. "Finally, we have arrived at the truth."

What was happening? The room faded from view as Apollo's body suddenly covered mine, his legs straddling my hips, until all I could see was his face above me twisted into a ghastly leer. His hand briefly caressed my face, lingering on my lips. "You understand the only thing you're good for, don't you?"

Shockingly he thrust his fingers inside my mouth, then trailed the moisture down my throat to my breast.

I flinched away, crying out in shock, but his hands grabbed my shoulders, pinning me down, hips thrusting, face dark, his breath hot on my face. "You know you want it," he growled. "You've wanted it since the beginning." He sniffed the air around me. "My little bitch dog in heat." Then he lowered his mouth on mine, forcing his tongue to the back of my throat, gagging me, pushing his hardness into my belly.

Jerking my head to get away from that lascivious thrusting tongue, I wrestled him, panicked and confused, trying to get a purchase against his chest to push him off me. But he was enormous and heavy and everywhere I tried to move he blocked me, relentlessly pressing me down and down until all I could feel was his weight upon me and his heat . . . roaring red flames above and beneath me.

The room rocked and a harsh buzzing filled my ears. The heat and burning sensation increased, igniting my nerve endings and I twisted and writhed trying to escape. Swiftly sitting upright astride my hips, Apollo looked down at me, black eyes filled with loathing.

"Fucking whore! Devil's spawn! Witch!" he cried, violently thrusting the palm of his right hand against my forehead.

With a mighty *CRACK!* the bottom dropped out and I fell screaming into a lake of fire that consumed me even as I fought the bonds securing me to the stake, flesh and fat melting in the flames, my hair crackling like a living torch, my eyeballs sizzling and bursting, my throat crisped beyond any possible shriek of agony and then I fell again . . . past a living sea of jeering men's faces dancing in the firelight as I burned . . . down and down until there was only one man's face above mine.

"Confess child, that's all you have to do and it will stop. I promise." The priest smoothed my sweat and tear-soaked hair with his greasy palm, his pendulous face close above my glazing eyes, the silver crucifix around his neck kissing my own. "No?" he cooed. "Tsk tsk."

He nodded and another man pulled the glowing iron from the fire, approaching my slick spread and trembling thighs and I felt the sizzling heat nearing my tenderest parts. Grinning, the man thrust the searing rod up through my vagina and into my womb and I shrieked, body arcing, bones breaking against their bonds and I fell . . .

Onto a bed . . . a child's bed with moonlight streaming in through the open window, the thatched ceiling above and my father's face over mine as he thrust himself into my tiny slit, cursing all the while, hitting me, crying "Bitch slut! You make me do this, vile harlot!" The words slammed my ears as he rutted away, his balls slapping my thin widespread legs and I felt a terrible internal tearing and screamed, tears running like rain down my cheeks and I fell . . .

Into cold freezing damp, bound by chains, iron chains in the dark pulling me down down down past the chittering rats and their fire-like nibbling kisses as they gnawed my legs and naked toes and I fell . . .

Into torchlight and the yowling of beastlike men taking turns thrusting their filthy organs into my vagina and mouth, laughing as they ripped and thrust and the sky rained blood and semen and filth and I fell, screaming . . .

Into water where cutting bonds held me to the dunking stool and I felt the sickening drop and lift, drop and lift, as I was plunged under water, the heavy bar holding me under as I choked and struggled. *Only a witch floats and we shall not suffer a witch to live!* And I fell . . .

Into the hands of women holding me down as someone roughly sawed through the flesh of my clitoris and labia with a dirty knife, mutilating me against all future pleasure and I fell screaming . . .

Into firelight and Apollo holding me, cradling me in his arms as I shrieked and fought like an animal, kicking, clawing his face, the rage and torment of a thousand deaths giving my limbs strength while my soul moaned, *You deserve to die.* And I threw back my head and howled, hating life, hating myself, hating him, filled with the living horror of what it meant to be a woman.

"Ἀγαπητός ἀγαπητός . . . shush, shush my darling, my little one, shushhhh. I am here, you are safe. I am here, you are loved. Shhh, you are safe."

Apollo cradled and rocked me and slowly, slowly my animal terror subsided and I recognized where I was and I remembered who I was and who I was with and with an even more despairing wail I ceased struggling and threw my arms around Apollo's neck and sobbed my heart out. Great wrenching lamentations that went on and on . . . sounds to curdle brain and bone. And then suddenly my stomach heaved and I leaned over and threw up red wine that looked like blood all over the carpet and coffee table. And then the chills and shudders began.

Without a word, he picked me up and carried me up the stairs to the bathroom. Depositing me on the toilet, limbs shaking, teeth chattering, he quickly opened the taps and ran the water. "Can you stand?" he asked.

I shook my head. "I d-d-don't th-th-think s-so."

Swiftly he kicked off his shoes and skinned out of his jeans and t-shirt. Then he gently lifted me, supporting me with one hand, deftly divesting me of my clothes with the other. "Several million years of practice," he joked.

"H-h-ha h-haaaaahhhh," my sorry attempt at laugher turned into another wail and uncontrollable tears streamed down my face.

"Ahhh, little one . . ." He guided me into the enormous marble shower and got in with me, holding me steady on my trembling pins of legs under the hot, soothing stream. And slowly, ever so slowly, the shaking stopped while the cleansing water soaked my hair and lathed my skin, washing away the tears and snot and stink of wine and vomit. And all the while he held me tenderly, steady as a granite boulder.

We ran the solar geezer dry. Only then did he shut off the taps and leave me leaning against the warm slick marble while he grabbed a towel. Gently he rubbed me dry. And then without asking if I could walk, he picked me up and carried me into the bedroom, depositing me beside the bed like precious cargo, whipping back the duvet and easing me under the covers. Then he got in beside me, pulled the down coverlet up to my chin and snuggled me into his arms against his shower-warm chest.

"Go to sleep little one," he stroked my wet hair with one hand. "Go to sleep. I am here. You are safe. You are loved. Go to sleep."

Despite the images of fire and flame beating at the corners of my mind, I obeyed.

۞۞۞۞۞۞۞۞۞

## CHAPTER FIFTEEN

Mercifully I did not dream.

When I awoke to the predawn sound of a rooster crowing, at first I didn't know where I was. The room was dark and rocking in that terrible alcohol-induced way and I realized, groggily, that there was a warmly naked male presence beside me in bed.

*Apollo!*

Instantly, the image of his leering face over mine, the terrifying words and accusations he'd screamed at me the night before filled my mind and I began to fight against the covers. And then Apollo was holding me, rocking me once more, whispering, "It was just a dream. Go back to sleep. It was just a dream. Go back to sleep, shhhhhh. " And relaxing I did just that, gratefully sliding back into oblivion.

The next time my eyes opened the room was filled with early dawn light. Apollo was sleeping at my side, one golden arm slung across the bed under my neck, the other draped casually over my belly on top of the duvet. And I was glad of his warm presence and pressed my naked body closer to his under the covers.

It was only the slightest movement, but it was a major effort and I was stunned by how much everything hurt. Was there a square inch of my body that didn't feel like it had been hammered by Hephaestus himself on an anvil in the bowels of hell?

I turned my head, suppressing a groan, and gazed at Apollo's sleeping profile, his lips slightly parted, a soft not-quite-snore ruffling the air, and smiled. *Ouch!* Even my face hurt—at least the side where Polymnia had hit me . . . what, just two nights before? *It feels like a million years ago.* I rolled my head carefully back into its original position and stared up through the mosquito netting hung above the bed.

Mercifully my brain was already wrapping the horror of the previous night's experiences in the gauzy veils of memory and much of the shock had faded. The details were available to me . . . my mind touched a few grisly details and skittered away like a fawn frightened by a hunter. But there was a steadily growing sense of distance to the whole nightmare that gave me refuge—at least temporarily.

I lay there in the aftermath realizing, among other things, that I didn't want to review what had happened. But I knew I had to. Apollo hadn't done what he'd done for me to gloss over it.

*Sweet Jesus, what a horror!*

Answering Polymnia's call and then falling into Apollo's trap designed to force me into experiencing the layers of soul memory and epigenetic programming of terrible sexual abuse trapped in my DNA had been a fiercely down and dirty process. Nothing sanitary or pretty about it.

I shuddered, remembering his face and the terrible words and actions that had triggered a full-scale . . . what? Download? Meltdown? Psychotic break? And were those memories and experiences even all mine? Or had I tapped into the Akashic Record of life and been given first-hand knowledge of the monstrosities that had been inflicted upon women—monstrosities that were *still* being perpetrated against women all around the world to this day?

And did it matter where the information came from? This is what woman—*all women* at some point in time or other—had experienced. The universal abominations were trapped in us like a frozen scream, unmentioned, unexpressed, unacknowledged, and definitely unhealed. The realization made me want to weep a river of tears that would never run dry.

I moaned softly, recalling all the times I'd done a spiritual process or meditation and tapped into the marrow-deep self-hatred inside me and shied away from the abyss, cried a few tears, did a little breath work or some primal screaming, pounded a few pillows and walked away thinking it was all done with and neatly handled.

*Oh, my God. I've been spitting on a forest fire.*

No wonder so much rage had boiled up in me and in so many other women around the United States when Dr. Christine Blasey Ford had been skewered during the Congressional Hearings over the Supreme Court appointment of Brett Kavenaugh. A raging cesspool of pain lay just beneath the surface of the female psyche.

With infinite sorrow I recalled retreats I'd

attended where women had wailed and bawled and how many times I'd judged them, lying on the floor in their midst after some emotional release process, congratulating myself on how "together" I was, thinking there was something wrong with them.

Polymnia's voice flashed in my mind. "All you've got is a grip! A grip on your emotions and mind, a grip on your vagina . . . a grip so tight no juice can flow and nothing can get through!"

Including the pain—*especially* the pain.

Shared wounds bound us all. But at least the women I'd judged so harshly had been willing to get into the pain pool and swim whereas I . . . I'd stuck with doing the manly thing, keeping a stiff upper lip, feeling superior, pretending there was nothing wrong inside me at all. No wonder no matter how many books I read or how many books I wrote or how many seminars and retreats I went to or gave there was still this roiling sea of self-despise and guilt inside me!

How could I have been so blind? It was all so clear now where my endless insecurity and sexual uncertainty originated, where the relentless striving inside me to be "good" came from. The need to be perfect. To be nice. To not make waves.

I groaned out loud under the sheer weight of the realization of my former ignorance and denial and the even greater crushing weight of my current enlightenment. Instantly, Apollo was awake, bending over me. "You are okay?" he asked, gently tipping my chin up to meet his eyes.

*Ohhhh, I'm so not okay!*

And instead of trying to hide it, I let the tears well up and spill down my cheeks and I threw my arms around his neck and buried my face in his chest and cried in suffering and sorrow for myself and all the women in the world who carried this burden and for the men who shared in it through what they had been taught to believe about us and had done to us and continued to do.

I cried for what women accepted and kept silent about and thus perpetuated.

I wept for our guilt and shame and unworthiness and all the crazy things we did and thought in our efforts to escape from the deep sorrow buried within us. And I wept over how men and women hated each other and loved each other and feared and misunderstood each other in a huge ongoing mess of ancient guilt and ignorance.

Apollo sat up, bedclothes falling away, pulling me into his arms, letting me cry myself out, soaking his chest and my breasts with salty tears. It was nothing like the storm the night before. Thank God. Just an endless fountain of grief pumping from a well that seemed like it could never be emptied.

But tear ducts can only handle so much. Eventually the torrent slowed, then stopped, and I hiccupped and wiped my streaming nose with my hand. *God, I must look a wreck,* I thought, imagining my swollen eyes, red nose and black and blue face.

Apollo chuckled. "Indeed, you have looked better, love."

But instead of feeling embarrassed and wishing I hadn't been so self-indulgent, running off to go clean up in the bathroom, I laughed and slumped exhausted in his arms and let him stroke my undoubtedly messy hair, relishing being with a man—well, at least a male of some sort—who finally totally understood.

*Ahhh God! If men and women could just do this simple thing for one another! If we could just stop trying to dodge the shadows and stop shrinking from taking responsibility for the ghastly things we've done to each other and face it and accept it and apologize and look into each other's eyes without guile or guilt or blame. If we could weep enough, all the pain would be washed away and we could start over, whole and healed, and find new and healthier ways to be together!*

"It is my fondest dream and desire that that should happen here on Earth," Apollo said quietly into my hair.

For a long while we simply sat, entwined, as the sun ascended, presenting us with the rosy dawn of a new day. And then, despite the growing light, exhaustion tugged once more at my eyelids and I relaxed again into slumber.

⊗⊗⊗⊗⊗⊗⊗⊗

I dreamed of bathrooms—of finding them and peeing gratefully, over and over again. Finally, I wakened. Late afternoon sun was streaming into the room from the open doors to the balcony. Apollo was nowhere to be seen.

Groggy and stiff, I staggered out of bed into the real physical bathroom. *Thank you!* Finally!

The cool marble felt good on my bare feet. And I thought about brushing my teeth. But somehow it seemed like too much effort to drag my heavy limbs over to the sink. Maybe I'd just sneak back to bed for a little while?

I did.

∞∞∞∞∞∞∞

When I wakened, it was night.

Apollo sat beside me, bare chested, blue jean-encased legs stretched out on top of the duvet, staring out the open French doors to the sea. There was no wind and the sound of the waves was faint. The only light in the room came through the lace-curtained windows from the half-moon floating above the hills to the west.

"What time is it?" I croaked, mouth furry, tongue thick.

"Almost dawn," he said. "Can I get you anything?"

"Water."

He reached over to the side table and produced a glass, holding it for me as I thirstily drank, still half reclining. I drained the glass and struggled to sit up. "More."

The glass didn't magically refill itself. Instead, Apollo got up and padded to the bathroom sink to get me some. I polished it off as he sat beside me on the bed, stroking my tangled hair out of my face.

"Thank you," I said quietly.

He didn't have to ask what for.

"I am so very sorry for the terrible things I said and did to you," he replied.

"I know."

Was there any way I could have come to my present understanding and the sweet sense of peace that now filled me without consciously going through the hell I had endured the night before? No, wait, two nights ago? *Probably not.*

We could have talked about the abuse of women until the cows came home and I would have been left with nothing but an academic understanding that got me precisely nowhere when it came to healing my own deep-seated wounds.

He sighed, gently disentangling the sheets wadded around my waist, then took the empty glass from me, setting it on the table. "If there had been any possible way to spare you that I would have done so. You know that?"

I nodded and leaned against him, unconcerned with my nakedness. Would I ever worry about such a petty thing again?

"The time for sparing ourselves is over, Apollo. Sparing ourselves from facing our insanity just means the demons will continue to drive us to more of the same. Truth is the only thing that can break the cycle." My stomach rumbled emptily. "Nothing is more painful than ignorance. Not even what I went through."

My stomach growled again, insistent, and I laughed. "Truth is, I think I'm hungry."

He helped me out of bed and I stumbled off to take a hot shower while Apollo headed to the kitchen to make coffee and breakfast. By the time I got out, I actually felt like a human being—although the mirror showed me a jaw that was now turning an interesting mixture of green and purple.

By the time I'd dried my hair and gotten dressed it was getting light. As I headed down the stairs, I shuddered to think what the living room rug and furniture must look and smell like by now. But everything was neat and clean as if nothing had happened.

"I see there are some advantages to living with a god," I observed as I walked into the kitchen sniffing the heavenly smell of fresh coffee.

"What? Cleaning up the mess we are responsible for?" Apollo was slicing fresh bread at the counter. "Actually, we are not particularly known for that. Usually we stir up trouble then bugger off."

I couldn't fail to notice he hadn't bothered putting on a shirt or shoes and I walked around behind him, slipping my arms around his waist, pressing my breasts into his back, kissing his delicious sculpted shoulders. I heard the *clank!* of the knife swiftly being dropped on the concrete counter and he turned in my arms.

"You are okay with this?" he asked, eyes scanning my face.

"If what you mean by 'this' is *this*," I stroked his

bare chest, following my fingers with a trail of light kisses. "Then yes, I am."

"Well, in that case." He tipped my face upwards, leaned down and kissed me.

It was a leisurely, exploratory kiss with none of the violence of two nights before. His mouth tasted like fresh coffee and cream and his tongue wandered happily around inside my mouth seeking every crack and crevice. Then he dropped his lips to my neck, nibbling his way over to my right ear. Chills washed my body and I felt a delicious thrill of energy and pushed my groin into his.

Slipping one hand down my backside, he pressed me closer to him and I could feel his hardness. Then his mouth was back on mine and I gave myself up to his lips and tongue. We came up for air and Apollo smiled at me, delighted. "My, we are hungry this morning."

"My, we are indeed," I murmured back.

"Breakfast first." He lightly kissed me once more then turned back to his kitchen work.

"That sounds promising," I said. "I poured a cup of coffee. "What can I do?"

Apollo put me to work grating cheese to put in the omelets that he stuffed with sautéed spinach, capers, tomatoes and onions—although I had to grate more because by the time the chef was ready I'd already eaten the first batch.

By the time we'd finished the simple meal and had more coffee, the sun was well up. We both pushed back from the table, replete.

*Now what?* I wondered, uncertain whether the sudden butterflies in my stomach were from nervousness or excitement. Apollo eyed me lazily. "I was going to suggest some sort of physical activity."

The butterflies increased.

"How about catching the early ferry to Antiparos and exploring the island?"

"How about exploring something else?" I asked pointedly.

"How about letting your body assimilate everything that's happened the last few days?"

"How about making me forget what's happened the last few days?"

His eyes sparkled looking like pure gold in the morning light. "Really, Ekateríni. Hasn't anybody ever told you that anticipation is the spice of life?"

"I thought variety was the spice of life." I pouted. "So far all we've done is eat and talk and drink." I shuddered, revolted by the very thought of red wine.

"And now we shall go exploring." He got up and came around the table and stood behind me sliding his hands sensuously down my arms then cupped both my breasts, his thumbs lightly massaging my nipples. "Lovemaking takes many forms, Ekateríni," he said huskily. "Did you know in many South American countries lovemaking can last all day and long into the night?"

I closed my eyes as sparks flew through my body and let my head fall back against his naked stomach, mouth suddenly dry, tension mounting.

He chuckled and kissed my neck, sliding his

tongue upwards, briefly dipping into my left ear, lathing it with his tongue and I gasped. Then he stopped.

Grabbing my hand, he pulled me to my feet, almost tipping my chair over backwards. "Get up and get ready to go."

"But I thought you said . . ."

He touched my face gently then bent down and kissed me again, first softly, then with an increasing sense of urgency, his lips kindling mine. Again, he stopped and I leaned into him, demanding more. Obliging, he briefly cupped my mound with one hand, massaging lightly. Then, with a squeeze, he let me go. "Enough wench," he commanded. "Go change if you need to, but we are going to Antiparos."

I sighed and let him go.

"But first." He reached out and touched my swollen cheek. I felt a light tingling and a flash of heat, then a coolness. Instantly, the soreness was gone from my jaw. "We cannot have people thinking I have been beating you, now can we?" he said lightly.

"Only psychically," I joked, then gasped, seeing the quick pain in his eyes. "Oh, God, I'm sorry!"

He hugged me to him. "Do not dare say that to me," he chided. "It is I who am sorry."

I hushed him with a kiss. "It was necessary and we both know it." And before he could respond, I turned and dashed up the stairs to go change, a smile on my lips and delight in my heart as I anticipated the many forms lovemaking might take over the course of a day.

◊◊◊◊◊◊◊◊◊

It was only a 15-minute ferry ride to the small island
hugging the west side of Paros. Apollo and I hung
over the rail like two teenagers staring down into the
unfathomably blue waters speculating how deep the
channel was and how long it would take the captain
of the ferry to stop in case one of us fell in.

Landing in the town of Antiparos was like
stepping back in time 30 years or more. Gone
was the bustle of Naoussa and the main port of
Paraikia. Here the pace was slow and deliberate.
The colorful streets were wider with fewer shops, the
main shopping district small and distinctly local. We
wandered the streets, hand in hand, bumping hips,
jostling and touching, checking out the shops as they
opened, finally coming to a small family-run curtain
shop that also displayed handmade lace blouses.

"Oh, look at that!" I let go Apollo's hand and
skipped up the steps, noting that my body was feeling
much better and that the aches and pains were
almost gone. A lovely white blouse fluttered on its
hanger in the slightly fish-smelling breeze wafting up
the street from the harbor. I took it down, examining
the craftsmanship. An elderly woman came out on
the green cement porch smiling broadly and said
something in Greek.

"Χαιρετισμούς μητέρα," replied Apollo. Her
gapped-toothed smile broadened and she giggled
like a girl, shyly responding.

"Try it on, "Apollo suggested

I didn't need prompting. There was no fitting room, just a little alcove with a curtain behind the sewing machines where the old woman, her daughter and daughter-in-law worked—details I found out later from Apollo. I was wearing a white silk chemise under a long-sleeved shirt, and the blouse with its open network of lace filigree went with it perfectly.

I walked back outside and Apollo interrupted his conversation with the old lady, beaming his approval. "You should wear it." he suggested. "That way I can be teased by glimpses of what is underneath all day."

"You're just bad to the bone," I said happily, feeling extremely feminine and blessedly a lot cooler than I had in my previous outfit. The proprietress bundled my old shirt into a bag and I paid, then we sauntered across the cobbled streets for another coffee.

Noon found us far up in the hills at a tiny taverna eating the best goat stew I'd ever tasted—although Apollo insisted his was as good, if not better. We laughed and flirted and talked about nothing serious and after lunch continued to poke along the back roads, exploring. Finally, we headed back towards the harbor town and the ferry.

Reaching the top of the island's tallest hill, the view was breathtaking and I pulled into the overlook. Getting out of the car we stood on the low rock wall at the edge of the sheer drop, the wind whipping our hair and clothes, soaking in the sunshine and the glory of the day.

Antiparos is not a highly populated island and the high rolling desert hills held only a scattering of homes. Sailboats and sleek powerboats pulling water skiers plied the strait between Paros and Anti-Paros, the sister islands. Windsurfers skittered across the water like bright butterflies. Across the narrow stretch of water the central mountains of Paros, crowned with cellphone and microwave towers, looked exactly like the view from my house, just from the opposite direction. To the south a wide swath of the Aegean Sea stretched towards the volcanic island of Santorini. To the north, although we couldn't see it, lay Delos.

I watched Apollo's face as his eyes swept the vista. He was curiously intent and I realized he was committing the moment and the scene to memory. I didn't interrupt. But everything in me wanted to grab him and shake him and tell him he didn't have to remember the view. He didn't have to fade away clinging to memories. There was physical life ahead of him as well as behind. There was a pathway back to Sira.

At least I thought there was.

The path was far from tested. In fact, I didn't even know what the path entailed. But so what? I reached out and took his hand, twining my fingers through his and pulled him around to face me, willing him to see what I saw—the gate standing wide open waiting for him to walk through—willing him to accept the love and hope being offered.

He glanced down at me. "I do not want to leave

you," he admitted. "And I do not want to leave this." He looked across the islands and the sea. "Three-thousand years is still not enough time here, Ekateríni. Earth is a jewel in creation's crown. And by far one of the most beautiful."

My fingers tightened on his of their own accord. "You will leave me and leave this planet one way or another, my love," I said. "But at least Polymnia's path offers some sort of future in another time and place with a future me." I shrugged and rushed on. "And it offers a future with the current me here." I laughed, "As long as this body lasts."

He started to speak but I shushed him. "We'll never know unless you agree to try, Apollo. Don't you see?" I stared up at him beseeching, committing my own strange act of memorization, watching the wind tousle his thick red-brown curls, seeing how his tanned face looked like carved bronze in the sun, soft yet cleanly etched against the blue Aegean sky, his mouth so sweet and full and quick to smile. His eyes . . . oh, those green-flecked copper eyes.

"What have we got to lose by trying?"

He gave no answer, just swiftly bent and lowered his lips to mine, lips warm from the sun and their own aliveness, tender yet demanding, yielding yet compelling. A slow dance of give and take conducted by our caressing tongues began, breath mingling, breathing quickening, our bodies begging for more.

"Let's go home," I whispered.

As one we turned and headed back to the car.

∞∞∞∞∞∞∞

We kissed and cuddled at the rail of the returning ferry. Apollo caressed my hand on the shift knob as I drove home. He possessed my legs, necessarily apart as I drove with both gas pedal and clutch, fingers snaking up the interior of my thighs under my skirt, lightly stroking, drifting farther north, teasing and tantalizing.

By the time we got home I was shaking like an aspen leaf.

Apollo closed and locked the gate while I fumbled my way into the house, taking three tries to get the key in the front door lock. I crossed to the kitchen, dropped my purse on the counter and took out my cellphone, pressing the power-off switch, turning as I heard him walk in the door.

He closed it, never taking his eyes off me, turned the lock and slowly withdrew the interior key, deliberately letting it fall to the floor. It was a breathtakingly sensual message and I pressed my body back against the counter as he advanced across the living room, copper eyes smoldering and intent. And suddenly I knew what a gazelle must feel like being stalked by a great cat.

Just the sight of him was enough to take the strength from my knees. Sleek chest and muscular arms clearly showed through his open shirt. Slender hips and straight long legs molded into his blue jeans, the bulge at the zipper extremely apparent.

Locking eyes with mine he stopped only when our loins met. Then he pressed hard, grinding into me, not touching me with hands or lips, just a groin level thrusting clearly meant to communicate shades of things to come.

He dropped his eyes and briefly touched me through the lacey holes in my blouse, a caressing touch on the shoulder, my collarbone, above my left breast, my right nipple. And all the while the heated pressure and the hard bulge pushed into me.

I groaned and closed my eyes. It was clearly to be a one-way seduction.

Slowly he bent me backwards over the counter, his strong hands on my upper arms, his lips at my throat, then my breast and I could feel the heat of his breath soaking through the lace and silk. Sliding his hands down my waist to my hips, he slowly pressed lower, curling his fingers around to grasp my buttocks.

I reached up and dug my fingers into his curls, briefly savoring their glossy feel and dragged his head up from my breast. His eyes, his eyes, I had to see his eyes. Just inches from mine, they were hot and glowing. And yet, as I looked deep, I saw that behind the heat lay love, clear as a bell ringing through the fire of our mutual passion. He was with me. He hadn't gone away, mind overtaken by lust. He was almost frighteningly present.

He slid his hands back up to my arms, easing the pressure on my body, then gathered me to him, folding me into a firm embrace, kissing me softly, seductively, tongue penetrating, dancing with mine, then withdrawing as lips caressed lips. Then his mouth became more insistent and his tongue probed again. Finally, he withdrew, dropping to my neck, nibbling and snacking, sucking and kissing all the way down to my breast.

Finally, he straightened and leaned back, keeping us locked at the groin, looking straight at me.

"I am with you, Ekateríni. All the way to paradise."

At which point he lifted me into his arms with as much ease as it would take to lift a basket of flowers and headed for the stairs.

∞∞∞∞∞∞∞∞

Our disrobing was a blur of kisses and touch, languorous exploration and fierce urgency.

If ever there had been worried moments when I wondered if my aging body could keep up—and there had been many—if ever I'd worried about such things as fewer hormones, less lubrication and duller responses—and I had—it swiftly became obvious it had all been a waste of time.

My body still knew exactly what to do. By the time Apollo lowered me onto the still unmade bed I was sopping wet and my trembling womb was consumed with the need to be filled. I wanted him inside me now!

But no.

Apollo continued to torment me, kissing and

caressing my nipples until they ached, slipping his hand down my belly, lower and lower, a finger touch into my slickness then away, then back and away, penetrating deeper each time until my body arched and I moaned uncontrollably as he flicked his thumb against the aching button of my clit, then slid his fingers back in until his palm pressed hard against my mound.

"Oh, God, please!!"

"Yes?" Grinning fiendishly, he withdrew his fingers, looming over me, hands on both sides of my face, his boldly engorged manhood touching my belly, the glistening tip oozing fluid, pushing past the foreskin. He laughed, taunting me, tracing little circles of moisture on my skin. I reached for it but he eased away.

"Tsk tsk, Ekateríni. No touching."

"No touching?" I gasped, wiggling underneath him, desperate for penetration.

"I am completely selfish." He reared back on his knees, his beautiful large hand encircling his erect organ. "I know what I want this to touch first." He slid his hand easily on his manhood pulling the foreskin back to reveal the glistening fluted glans.

I practically fainted from lust. "Then do it!" I cried.

Slowly he massaged his penis in front of me, teasing. "You are sure?"

Frustrated beyond measure, I reached for it like a kid trying to grab a toy and he pounced, grabbing both my wrists, then transferred his grip to one hand, pinning my hands neatly above my head. "Well, my dear. Since you insist."

He leaned over me, eyes locked on mine and slowly guided the head of his penis past folds of my throbbing vulva and gently but thoroughly entered me.

Filled at last, I cried out and arched against him, seeking even more and he paused, embedded to the hilt. Releasing my hands, he leaned down and caressed my face and hair, then kissed me deeply, hungrily, tongue probing, lips pressing my mouth ever more widely open, relentlessly seeking.

Finally, he lifted his lips and gazed deeply into my eyes, shoving his hardness even deeper to the very opening of my womb. "Hello, my love," he whispered.

I gasped and moaned, pinned, managing a whispered return "Hello," tears of pleasure and the joy of communion welling in my eyes.

Slowly he withdrew . . . and it was the sea departing forever from the shore. I followed his flesh with my mind and whimpered for the kiss of its return and the sea obliged, plunging back into the depths of me over and over and over. And all the while those copper eyes held mine, gathering me heart and soul as his body rode mine, deeper and deeper, until there was a total merging and I knew not where his flesh left off and mine began, until finally a great storm gathered in my belly, surging up from the depths as pleasure rose and built towards a final outpouring.

"Stay with me!"

I heard his call as if from a great distance and with an effort I opened my eyes and reached out for him as the seas within me crested higher, finally exploding as my womb convulsed and I cried out, body arcing like an archer's bow, fiercely willing all the energy of my orgasm out through my body and into Apollo's flesh piercing mine.

He rocked and cried out in turn as the wave hit him and for a frozen moment in time we were one, bound in love and passion across centuries, joined in the flesh, tossed on a seething ocean of energy. And I rode the darkness and light in my womb, consciously gathering the life energies, directing them all one way. *My gift back to you my love* . . . and in one long heartbeat I watched the coffers of his strength gently replenish as he received the energy. And I knew I had given him, if nothing else, a little more time.

☉☉☉☉☉☉☉☉

It wasn't the candlelight or my imagination. To my utter satisfaction, Apollo fairly glowed with the added energy given back through our couplings.

"How did you know to send the light back like that?" Apollo asked.

It was somewhere far late in the night—the time when the world is hushed and slumbering, neither still tired from the day nor yet ready to rouse to greet a new dawn, the time when, if you are alone, you lie in the silent dark, looking for answers. And if you are with a lover, you drift on a life raft called a bed, floating in an ocean of intimacy so strong it could keep whole navies at bay.

We'd slept and then made love in the evening, then raided the kitchen, gathering cheese and olives, wine and bread, making a small feast on the duvet as dusk turned to dark. Then we'd made love again and slept some more.

I popped an olive from the evening's feast into my mouth, biting off the flesh. "It just seemed the right thing to do," I replied, shrugging. "Maybe Polymnia's rubbing off on me."

"Not a bleed through?"

"Nope. Just me darlin'." I shook my head. "Besides, we both would have sensed it if she'd joined us."

He nodded assent then picked up the knife to slice what remained of the cheese. I watched him, marveling at his form in the candlelight. The dexterity of those elegant hands—the hands of a surgeon that had been so skillfully employed in a completely different occupation shortly before, his dark red-brown curls with a touch of gold tumbling across his face, curls I had finally managed to endlessly tangle around my fingers during our extensive lovemaking.

As for me, I hardly recognized myself sitting bare-breasted, covers tucked below my waist, brazen, unashamed, thoughtless of wrinkles and creases and tummy fat. I was too full of life, too full of *him*, to think of such things. What did they matter? They didn't get in the way of communicating love and other good things through the extraordinary bodies we'd been blessed with. They didn't get in the way of the pleasure to be had. It was the thoughts *about* wrinkles and lumps, bumps and creases that destroyed all the fun. Languorously, I leaned back against the plumped-up pillows mounded against the headboard, sated on every level.

"If woman can be shamed the whole world can be controlled."

Apollo's words startled me out of my reverie. "Hm?"

"If women can be convinced they have no worth except for what their bodies can provide and then be shamed about it—if they can be manipulated into thinking the only way of living is the masculine way, this world will meet the same fiery end as other planets where gender balance has been destroyed."

Well, *that* sure punctured the idyllic moment.

"But," I protested. "If the world is destroyed, who reaps the benefit?"

"It is not about the end but the process getting there. The more chaotic things become, the more disempowered people become, the more society turns to past masculine solutions and ever-greater methods of control."

"Like religion."

"Exactly."

"This is hardly the normal three a.m. lover's conversation, you know," I mused.

Apollo leaned over and kissed me on the nose. "No, it is not. But, then, this is not what you would call a normal love affair either. Eh?"

He was trying to be light-hearted, but I could tell there was much on his mind.

"What?" I asked. Not really wanting to know.

He sighed. "Nothing. I just wish we had time to visit with your friends and have picnics on the beach and make love with no concerns." He eased his body closer to mine. "I would like to go to America with you. We could walk the streets of New York and eat hot dogs. Travel to the wonderful world of Disney and go on all the rides."

"You've never been on an amusement ride? No roller coasters?"

"Is not life a big enough roller coaster for you, my love?" He slid lower on the bed, mouth level with my left breast. "Speaking of rides . . ." and started nibbling.

I ran my fingers through his curls as he suckled, the heat rising between my legs. Lazily the fingers of his left hand wove their way down my belly until he dipped, yet again, between the folds of my labia, still wet from our last passionate embrace. Plunging his fingers deep inside me, he bit my nipple, sending a cascade of deliciously painful sparks through my body. I gasped in instantaneous response, pushing up into his hand, legs parting, seeking deeper fulfillment.

We were done talking for the night.

◊◊◊◊◊◊◊◊◊

## CHAPTER SIXTEEN

For the next week Apollo and I did exactly what we wanted to do when we wanted to do it. We swam and walked, slept and made love, cooked and ate, wrapping ourselves in a cocoon that held nothing but us. Shopping trips were fleeting runs to Naoussa, timed so we would see no one we knew. And all the while Apollo talked and talked, pouring his knowledge into me.

Knowing that I might not have him around in the future to make clarifications and corrections, I cracked out the digital recorder I used for magazine interviews and carried it with me everywhere. *At least his voice will always be with me.*

I recorded everything, from what I called his "lectures," schooling me in ancient Greco-Roman history and politics, religion, and esoteric cosmology, to our late-night post-coital conversations where he revealed the more intimate details of his extraordinary existence as an archangel and then a hybrid tulpa. The only thing he refused to talk about was Polymnia's plan, putting me off again and again with an enigmatic, "Now is not the right time to discuss it."

The bruises on my body healed, my tan deepened and, except for the Cheshire Cat smile and glow of a thoroughly-loved woman, physiologically I felt my normal self again. My interior landscape, however, was a different matter. So much had happened so fast. So many devastating revelations had been dropped, so many astounding experiences had occurred in so short a time, I wondered at my equanimity. I *looked* okay. And I felt wonderful. How not with Apollo at my side all day and in my bed at night? And I was pleased to note that as my knowledge grew about Jehovah and all the gods and their dynamics with humans over the course of millions of years, my questions became sharper and more evocative.

But it was the things I learned about myself that rocked my world the most.

I'd seen other lifetimes and been to other worlds. I'd faced the suppression of my sexual abuse and ripped open the great feminine wound that had crippled me. And I'd come face to face with the superficiality of my sexual identity as a woman. My God! How many decades had I spent worrying about tight abs, perky tits and the ability to orgasm, thinking such things defined me as female?

Being with Apollo and meeting Polymnia I was appalled at the narrowness of my former view of the feminine domain and deeply saddened realizing the lack of intensity and true intimacy in my sexual relationships with men and with life itself.

I was also shocked at the predominance of masculine points of view in my thinking and interacting with the world. I began to wake up to how deeply programmed I was to depend upon

my intellect and logic, and how my lack of trust in
life and my finer intuitive capacities and sensitivity
revealed a profound disconnect between my spiritual
identity and who I'd thought I was and reality.

Through Apollo's eyes, I saw my whole world
and society in a new way. Saw how the endless
distractions and noise kept the scariness of self-
reflection at bay, how the relentless focus on material
goods and sexuality kept me and everyone else busy
and empty and dissatisfied, trying to fill ourselves up
with the pleasures and false security money and sex
could buy.

"Humans pursue pleasure so avidly because
there is so little joy in their lives, Ekateríni."

It was a harsh commentary on modern Western
civilization but a true one. It wasn't until I traveled
to second-world nations like Greece and some third-
world countries like Ecuador, Peru and Costa Rica
that I found a genuine light-hearted joyousness in
people. There was true poverty in those nations, but
also a simplicity and a love of life and nature, family
and friends, that positively radiated from people, old
and young alike.

I watched as men walked up to old women
bent over their canes and flirted with them in the
streets, giving them flowers, calling them "mother,"
honoring their womanly presence. I watched as
people embraced and walked, singing, down the
streets together at all hours of the day and night.
I watched how children ran free, laughing in the
streets and fields and forests, swimming in mountain

streams and diving from the tops of waterfalls, unafraid of molestation by strangers. And I wept when I came back to the States and saw the grey, unhappy, stressed faces of adults with their whining, over-pressured, over-controlled children trapped in the realm of smart phones and video games as their main source of joy.

Everywhere I traveled I saw how the masses of ordinary people, including Americans, just wanted peaceful lives—a pleasant safe place to live, fulfilling work, love and family, education for their children and the company of friends. Simple simple things. Nobody I knew or had ever met wanted to conquer the world and other people, wanting to lord it over them. People just wanted to be left alone to do their own thing.

But if everyone was content and happy, where would the negative emotion come from for entities like Jehovah to feed upon? No wonder the global media kept pumping out violence and terror twenty-four seven. No wonder people were kept stirred up and at each other's throats while commercialism kept us frantic with envy and competition. No wonder religion continued to be pushed as the answer.

How was it possible I hadn't seen what was going on? And how on God's green Earth had I not fully realized the devastating impact destroying all respect for woman and feminine qualities had had upon the world?

"The Goddess is life itself," Apollo said. "To worship her is to love the mystery that all this exists and to open yourself to it." We were sitting alone in the bow of a small excursion boat bobbing atop the clear blue waters, watching the molten sun go down to port. As the last golden rays sank into the sea we immediately turned to face east, watching a full lavender moon lift over the rocks, floating upwards into the dusky violet-velvet sky.

All the other passengers, eight in total, had quickly retired to the stern. Maybe it was the salt-spray kicked up during our short passage from Alyki to the low-slung deserted islands several kilometers away. Or maybe it was the blatant June-October sex vibe Apollo and I were emitting that had chased them away. Either way, we were happily left alone, sitting close, fingers entwined, as the silent reflective symbol of the Goddess slowly rose, turning from lavender to orange to gold. In the stern, the laughter and talk revved up as the advertised goal of the full-moon trip was successfully achieved and people turned to the more serious pursuit of drinking and eating.

Apollo leaned in close, his breath tickling my ear. "The Goddess is the face of God itself, Ekateríni."

I looked around appreciatively. The glistening waters, the islands, the moon and darkening sky, the boat with her laughing occupants, every puff of wind, every glowing light in the distance, every molecule of air, every hair on my head was the face of God . . . the physical mirror of an invisible mind of such limitless immensity, complexity and beauty it was impossible to fathom.

The captain came forward along the rail, wine

jar in hand. "Isn't that something?" He waved in the general direction of the softly glowing moon. "Second blue moon this year. Wind was too bad to take her out last time. More wine?" he offered. But we waved him away with a smile, assuring him we had plenty thanks, and he left us.

◌◌◌◌◌◌◌◌◌

We got home late to a message on my cellphone from Chris reminding me of the Sunday hike. The previous week's excursion had been cancelled because nobody showed up. I smiled, remembering where Apollo and I had been and what we'd been doing that particular morning.

"We're on for Lefkes tomorrow, meeting at ten sharp. Hope to see you both there!"

I glanced at Apollo, questioningly. "Still want to go?"

"Do you?"

"No fair. I asked first."

He closed the few feet between us, bent and kissed me, at first tenderly then with increasing passion.

"If I make love to you the rest of this night will you still be up for it?" he asked, breath hot on my face. I met his eyes. He wasn't kidding.

"Well," I sighed voluptuously. "Why don't we find out?"

∞∞∞∞∞∞∞

I was in the car at 9:45 a.m. the next day purely as an exercise to prove it to myself that I still had it in me. Apollo, as usual, looked bright and cheery. Or did he? I looked at him more carefully as soon as I got out onto the main road. Were those shadows underneath those copper eyes? Or just a trick of the morning sun?

Pulling into the small parking lot near the start of the ancient trail between the sea and the inland marble quarries beyond the mountain village of Lefkes, I saw the tribe was already there—Chris and George and Gita, Doris and Francine. As we got out of the car, Doris immediately fixed her gaze upon my companion. "Hello Apollo," she said, turning his name into a caress.

The normal melee ensued as everybody with dogs let their four-legged friends reacquaint themselves while their owners fished around for daypacks, water bottles and leashes. But eventually we started out with George, as usual, in the lead. Doris and Francine immediately flanked Apollo and, out-gunned, I joined Chris and Gita.

"I don't know what he's trying to prove," Gita puffed, watching her husband rapidly disappear with their dog up the hill.

"It's those long legs of his," Chris volunteered. "He's got the equipment for it."

We jostled for position on the trail which started

off at a mean incline. The ancient granite and quartzite paving stones laid out by the Romans two thousand years before were tilted and overgrown with thistles, wildflowers and grasses. But for the most part it was easy enough for two people to walk abreast. Chris and I paired off and I resisted glancing behind me to see whether Doris or Francine had managed to secure Apollo at her side. But my bets were on Doris.

"Your face looks better," Chris commented.

*Here we go!* "Thankfully, yes." No way was I going to volunteer more.

"And you guys are still seeing each other." Another obvious comment.

"We are." I kept my voice neutral. Then I had to laugh. "Although if Doris has anything to do with it we won't last long."

"Do you see yourself with him long term?"

I paused then said honestly, "Sadly, no."

"Why not?"

"It's complicated."

"You said that already."

"I know. I'm sorry."

She sighed. "I gather he's worth it?"

I looked at her and grinned. "He is indeed. And what's on the inside is just as glorious as what's on the outside."

"Really?" She looked behind us, disbelieving.

"Oh, yeah." And to distract her I said, "Come on, let's see if we can catch up with George."

⊗⊗⊗⊗⊗⊗⊗⊗

By the time we'd reached the olive groves and the old Roman bridge at the base of the last rise to the town, we were all ready for a break. Between the rapidly-increasing heat, the uneven footing and hills, even George had slowed down. I looked back at Apollo, but he seemed okay and I caught snatches of conversation as he entertained Doris with the ancient Greek meaning of her name and naughty tales of various ladies who had borne the moniker. Francine pulled up the rear with Gita, looking put out.

The olive trees were ancient, some over a thousand years old, gnarled and twisted but still gamely bearing fruit. A large herd of goats grazed the hillside, each one a different color—brown, black, cream, piebald, brown and white—each one sporting a collar with a bell of a different size, shape and tone. As the goats grazed and leaped about a veritable tinkling symphony of bells was ours.

I stopped to listen and watch with delight, telling Chris to go ahead. Which meant Apollo and Doris, Gita and Francine finally caught up with me.

"Oh, Apollo, listen. Isn't it beautiful?"

"It is indeed, my love."

Despite the fact that we were both hot and sweaty, he stepped up behind me and put his arms around me, pulling me tight, resting his chin on top of my head. We stood transfixed, ignoring everybody else. Gita and Francine politely moved on, but Doris was stubborn, shuffling uncomfortably from one foot to the other, waiting for us to break the embrace. When we didn't and Apollo started gently nibbling my salty neck she finally stamped off to catch up with the others rapidly disappearing up the hill.

I laughed. "Sorry to mess up the tête-a-tête."

"I am sure you are."

I leaned against him, radiantly content in a moment filled with goats and bells, companionship, sweaty bodies and laughter, remembering our lovemaking the night before. Apollo had been unusually tender and passionate all at the same time—which was saying something for him—and the result had been one shattering union after another until the agonizing pleasure of linked bodies, minds and hearts had vaulted us out of our Earthly shells and we had tumbled, coupled, out into the universe, sharing our passion with the planets, stars, nebulas and unnamed dust clouds around us.

In my wildest dreams, I'd never imaged such a union between man and woman, heaven and Earth was possible. Afterwards Apollo had chuckled, saying, "I told you I'd take you into me again sometime and show you creation."

To which I'd lazily replied, "If I recall correctly you were inside me this time." Then I'd drifted off to sleep.

Standing with Apollo on the road amongst the olive trees, I couldn't fail but realize what a glorious privilege it was to be alive. Ecstatic, I lifted my face to the blue Aegean skies in humble gratitude, knowing it was nothing less than a miracle that such a union had happened through me, and that there was no conscious path that had been adopted to bring me to this place with Apollo.

Life itself was responsible.

My prayer of thanks issued forth on wings and my entire life seemed poised upon a peak of light and love. And then, in the very next moment, all of it came crashing down.

"Would you mind very much if we took a break for a while, my love?"

Only one thing would have made Apollo speak those words, and my heart lurched as I whirled to face him.

He'd long since told me it was becoming increasingly difficult for him to manifest and hold his physical body. And even though I'd pushed the energy of our lovemaking back into him every time, I could not keep the ebbing tide at bay. I'd even told him to go away and save his energy. But he'd only laughed and ignored me, saying my love was enough to sustain him and just try to keep him away.

And now he stood before me, smiling crookedly, acknowledging that it was not true. That love was not enough—just as Polymnia had said.

"I confess I am beginning to feel tired, Ekateríni. A new and not entirely pleasant sensation. I think it might be best if I took some time off from the body."

*Oh God oh God oh God!* I wanted to hurl myself into his arms, weeping at his words, but I didn't. I simply nodded, all my love and heartbreak in my eyes.

"Do not worry and do not fear. I will be back." He kissed me gently on the lips and then my eyes and then my forehead and then my lips again. And then he was gone.

∞∞∞∞∞∞∞

I turned around and started back the way we'd come.

Chris called on my cell, asking where were we and was everything all right? I made up some cockamamie excuse about Apollo getting a text and needing to work, telling her we'd turned around and that I'd call her later. After that it was simply a matter of placing one numb foot in front of the other all the way back to my car.

Somehow the tears, pain, fatigue and heat didn't do me in right there on the trail from Lefkes. Somehow, I got home. Somehow I got to the doorway of my bedroom, *our* bedroom, looking at the rumpled bedclothes where we'd so recently lain entwined in love.

I wanted to cry, but no more tears would come. Not believing I could lie there again without him, I considered going to my office to sleep on the spare bed. But I tottered to our bed instead and lay down fully clothed, burying my head in his pillow, falling to sleep to the lingering scent of him on the sheets.

∞∞∞∞∞∞∞

The great sucking golden whirlpool tugged and

pulled at my exhausted body and mind until nothing but the sound of cresting waves beat in my ears.

I found myself tumbling down and down, heard chanting voices and saw pale sand churned by dancing, circling feet next to the black obsidian sea—feet that finally resolved into a single leather-wrapped pair of boots firmly planted at eye level. Stiffly, I sat up.

Polymnia stood over me, hands on hips, red hair wild, face outraged, lips moving.

"How could you waste his energy like that, constantly humping like rabbits, when you knew perfectly well it was the last thing he needed to be doing and it totally kept you distracted and I couldn't reach you and what in the name of all the gods were you thinking!?"

"Hello to you too," I said, covering my instant sense of guilt with sarcasm.

"Are you insane?" she screeched.

"Not yet." I replied mildly.

But she kept at me and I finally lost it. "Back off and give me a goddamn minute, would you?" The world inside me—or was it the world outside?—was still rocking sickeningly.

Ignoring my outburst, she stamped around, waving her arms. "How could you ? I can't believe . . ."

"Hey!" I yelled. "Shut up!"

Resolutely, I stood up on wobbly legs for a face-off. "Have you ever tried to change Apollo's mind or talk him out of something he was determined to do?"

She had the grace to look abashed.

"Yeah. So there. Done is done and screaming at me isn't going to help him any." I took a deep breath, ignoring the deathly-still landscape, the towering chalk-white cliffs and the question of how the hell we were speaking the same language and grimly focused on what mattered. "So, I'm here. Now, what are we going to do?"

Her face fell. "Gods, I don't know."

I was shocked. "What do you mean you don't know? What about the three goddess ritual thing? I met Desma. I was her. I know her vibration. Did you tap in when I became her? Was born as her? What happened here after I left?"

My questions fell all over each other and for a moment Polymnia and I locked eyes—twin sets of despairing eyes—and suddenly compassion for both of us overwhelmed me. "Come on," I said sitting back down. "We can figure this out."

"I don't know how," she said, dully, plopping on the sand next to me. "The whole plan hinged on Apollo having enough life force to perform the ritual *and* direct his energies to Sira. But now . . ." she shook her head, hair dropping forlornly over her face. "Did he even say he would do it?"

"The ritual?" I shook my head. "Every time I brought it up he said it wasn't the right time to talk about it. He never said 'yes'," I said wanly. "But then he never said 'no' either."

She sighed. "It wouldn't make any difference. There's no way he can cast a circle."

"A circle?" I asked.

"It's how we get you here. The whole group of us calls you. We build a group energy in a chant-dance ritual then spin a gateway through space and time." She shrugged again, "You and I connect through aligned energy and mutual intention and then here you are."

A wormhole in space-time. That must be what she was talking about. "Are you sure he hasn't got the power?" I asked, dismayed.

She nodded. "His etheric body is about finished." Was the catch in her voice a sob?

"Does Desma need a circle on her end too?" I asked, wondering just how complex this whole operation really was.

"No."

"Why not?"

She sighed. "Remember when you joined Apollo and me that time?"

I swiftly recalled the scene in my living room: me saying incredibly stupid things about remaining independent and "spiritual" and Apollo showing me my former self in his embrace in the meadow on Mount Parnassus.

I nodded.

"No circle or ritual was needed because you and I share the same essence—we're the same being—and Apollo wasn't trying to bring you bodily into the picture, just your awareness. Same thing with Desma. We simply need to tap into her consciousness to complete the triad of sexual energy feeding him once he's cast the circle on your end and linked to our circle."

I got the gist of it. But the overall design of the plan still puzzled me. "So why do we need to cast any circles at all?" I asked.

Polymnia looked at me as if she couldn't believe how stupid the question was. But she answered me evenly enough. "Because sexual energy alone won't do the job. We need the additional energy of a group-created vortex pulsing between two grounded circles to create enough energy for Apollo to use to get to Sira."

Scientific words like *scalar energy waves* and *beat frequencies* danced in the back of my mind. Polymnia shrugged despondently. "Talking about it is pointless. Without a circle on your end the whole thing is impossible."

I thought hard. "Does it have to be a circle? Can we use a different source of energy?" The image of the white-haired professor in the movie *Back to The Future* running around, tearing his hair, crying "One point two one gigawatts! Impossible!" floated through my mind.

"Um, what about a lightning bolt?" I asked, feeling stupid but desperate enough to suggest anything. "Maybe Zeus could . . . ?"

"Different problem. Too much energy and no circle to direct it. You'd be fried. Even if Zeus could be talked into providing it."

"One piddling little lightning bolt. How much could that cost him?"

Again, Polymnia shook her head. "It's the whole father-son thing. Apollo always comes along and steals his thunder. Zeus will be glad to see the last of him."

"Pretty small-minded for a god, isn't it?"

"Didn't he fill you in on the Olympians?"

"Yeah."

Glumly we sat on the sand.

"So, what if I had a circle? Would it work then?"

"If they were trained and knew what they were doing, yes. But you don't."

Something was niggling at the back of my brain . . . a conversation I'd had with Chris over a year ago. It was a long shot, a really, really long shot. But then something was better than absolutely nothing.

Excited, I turned to Polymnia and told her what I had in mind.

⊗⊗⊗⊗⊗⊗⊗⊗⊗

As soon as I woke up the next morning, I called Chris and invited her to dinner.

"Aren't you and Apollo busy?" she asked sullenly.

"No," I replied, abruptly. "But if you're still interested in knowing the truth about him, I'm ready to spill the beans."

"What time?" she asked breathlessly.

"Let's make a social statement and try to be unfashionably early. How about 6:30?"

"I'll be there!" she cried, not bothering to suppress her excitement. And indeed, at 6:15 she was getting out of her car at the front door, a bottle of good red wine in hand.

We fiddled around in the kitchen opening the wine and putting out appetizers. Knowing she was finally going to get the dirt on Apollo, she had the grace not to pounce immediately. For myself, I was filled with doubt. How could I possibly convince her about who and what Apollo was? I had zero proof and no Apollo around to do magic tricks. Would she believe me? If she didn't there was no chance in hell of her providing the information and connections I needed.

"So . . ." my voice trailed off and I stared at her across the patio table. "Um. To the gods and goddesses and to the mystery of life." I raised my wine glass in a toast.

Chris looked surprised, then smiled oddly. "To the gods and goddesses and to the mystery of life," she repeated softly. We both drank and she settled into her chair, squirming with excitement. "So, tell me tell me," she said.

*Goddess guide me,* I muttered to myself.

"Okay, here's the scoop. First off, I can tell you right now that you're not going to believe a word I have to say. Okay? But I have to tell you what I'm about to tell you because if I don't then—*Apollo will die* my mind wailed—because if I don't then something terrible will happen and I have to try. So here goes."

I looked her straight in the eye. "The Apollo you met is the original god Apollo, the Bringer of

Light, god of knowledge, healing, music, dance, the works." I swallowed hard, knowing not to bother with explanations about tulpas and such things. *Keep it simple.* "I met him when I was in Delphi—or rather he appeared to me up on Mount Parnassus the morning after I'd been to the temples and he sat down beside me and said we needed to talk and that was how the whole thing started."

She hadn't moved or laughed, so I barged on.

"Then he showed up in Athens. And I mean like *POOF!* showed up while I was walking through the botanical gardens. Scared the crap out of me, I have to tell you. Anyway," I took a deep breath and rushed on. "He told me he had a message for humanity and that he and I had been, um, lovers back in the day when Delphi was the power center of the ancient world and that I'd been poisoned in that lifetime before he and I could do the things he wanted to get done back then and that he'd been waiting lifetimes for me to be ready to meet him again and for the world to be ready to hear what he has to say. And he kept showing up and we kept talking and I fell in love with him and he told me he loves me too and then he and I . . . um, became lovers again and then he had to leave yesterday because his energy is failing and he can't keep showing up in corporeal form anymore and . . . and, oh God, he's gone and I miss him so much!"

I burst into tears. "I-I know it's ridiculous, but it's what ha-happened and . . ."

"Kathryn," she said.

"I know if I were you I'd think I was absolutely crazy and I wouldn't blame you if you left right now and I know it's a lot to ask you to believe me but . . ."

"I believe you," she said.

"You do? Wha . . .? Why?"

"Because Apollo came to me early this morning in my dreams and told me exactly what you just told me. In his own way, of course."

"He did?"

She nodded. "I thought it was just a dream. A wild one and, oh, wow, so very real! But then I've been so intrigued by him and what's been going with you two that I figured, well, you know. He was on my mind so I thought that's why I dreamt about him. But now . . ."

"Oh, Chris." The relief getting it all out in the open and being believed was amazing. "Now you know why I couldn't say anything! Why I had to keep you in the dark." I swiped at the tears on my face. "You would have thought I was nuts."

Her brown eyes were wide behind her glasses, her face flushed. "When you toasted to the gods and mystery, I was like . . ." She shook her head and I watched it hit her. "Wow, Kathryn! Wow!"

"Yeah. Wow."

We sat and stared at each other and drank wine. For a moment there was nothing else to say. She needed a few minutes for the whole thing to really sink in. And when it finally did and she stopped shaking her head in amazement, I sensed the shift in her and easily tracked where her mind went next.

Predictably it went to our relationships and sex. But she was far too polite to ask. So, I volunteered.

"Being with him is . . . imagine the most sensitive, intelligent, wise, funny, fierce, terrifying, passionate, unpredictable, gentle man you've ever dreamed of who's had half a million lovers to practice on and then package it in a body that looks like that, then give him a blind eye to age and cellulite, then toss him into your life and your bed."

She was doing her best to imagine it.

"I actually had an orgasm that blew me out of my body and then we tripped through the universe together."

"No!" she cried, incredulous.

"Yes." I said. "And on top of everything else, he's the most unbelievable cook."

"I totally hate you," she said, not joking. And for a few minutes we indulged in girl talk complete with details that would make a seasoned sailor blush. Finally, the giggles and laughter died down. And then, of course, it hit me why Chris was sitting there across the patio table and not Apollo. And it occurred to her at the same time.

"So, what's the deal with him not being able to show up anymore? What's the problem?"

Which is when our conversation turned serious.

∞∞∞∞∞∞∞

By the time I'd gotten to Polymnia's plan and tripping into the future to meet Desma, it was almost a decent dinner hour in Greece. Chris and I were in the dining room chomping our way through a vast pile of pasta with loads of fresh garlic, olive oil, tomatoes and capers.

Heartsickness not being an appetite stimulant, I'd only had a piece of toast for breakfast and nothing else all day. But sharing my story made me hungry. And the flicker of hope that there might be something I could do to help Apollo gave me an interest in keeping my strength up.

And it was pasta after all.

"Sex magic . . ." Chris choked and it took a minute before the coughing died down. Eyes watering, she got up and poured a glass of water at the sink. "Jesus, what have you gotten yourself into?"

"To be honest, I don't know. But I can't just sit around and let Apollo die can I?"

"No, of course not. But sex magic? That, that's just evil!"

"That's a strong word, girlfriend. What's evil about it?" *My how a few weeks have changed my tune!*

She blushed. "It's just wrong!"

"Sex with a man who's been my lover across multiple lifetimes across thousands of years—a man whose life I'm desperate to save—is wrong?"

"You know what I mean. It's *magic!*" The way she strangled the word made it sound even worse.

"What's magic, Chris? Huh?" She stood by the sink, face shuttered. "I'll tell you what it is. It's the science of working with life forces—a science modern people don't understand because for two thousand years the Church has gone ape shit calling it satanic, killing women left and right, burning them as witches, while the guy who made up all the sick rules about what's right and wrong is laughing his ass off manipulating us six ways from Sunday."

"Huh? What are you talking about?"

*Shit.* I hadn't had time to fill her in on the whole Jehovah thing. "Uh, that's another part of the story I'll tell you about later." I took a couple deep breaths, forcing myself to calm down. No sense jumping all over Chris for reacting from the very same programming I'd been struggling with—the same programming almost every woman on the planet had been indoctrinated into for God knows how many lifetimes.

"Try looking at it this way. We want to scientifically use the power of sex and orgasm, the very thing God gave us that creates life—beautiful innocent babies . . . little boys and little girls—to save someone's life. And not just any old someone's life, but the life of a god who's spent thousands of years trying to make life better for humans who also just happens to be willing to *die* to save this whole planet!"

"What on Earth are you talking about?"

"I told you Apollo has a mission. And it's to save the Earth and everything and everyone on it from Armageddon!"

Her eyes flew wide. "Seriously? You weren't just saying that for effect?"

"I'm being totally straight, Chris. Armageddon. That's what Apollo told me we're heading towards unless people start to understand who they really are and what the gods like him really are, and well, other things I'll get into later." I took a breath. "I'm not shitting you Chris. It's that serious!"

She dropped her eyes and set her water glass on the counter. "I don't know," she shook her head.

"You think sex magic is shameful and wicked. I get it. But Chris, that's two-thousand years of Christian programming talking, not you."

She stared at me mutely and I backed off. "Sorry," I muttered.

I pushed my rapidly congealing pasta around my plate, at a loss what to say. So, I got up, walked over to her, put my dish in the sink and hugged her. She hugged me back and for a moment we just stood there holding each other. Then I stepped back a bit. "It's not my job to try to convince you of anything, Chris. And I'm sorry if I'm pushing you too hard."

I laughed. "Trust me, it's not like I'm looking forward to doing . . . whatever needs doing. But I've already had the experience of sharing Apollo when I accidentally joined him and Polymnia on Mount Parnassus while they were making love. It's me after all . . . just me and him no matter what the bodies look like or how many of them there are." *Or how many people are watching* I trailed off, uncertain.

She grabbed my hand, imploring. "I don't mean to sound prudish. I really don't. It's just that you've really struck a nerve with this."

I knew I had and I knew why. "Because of Spiros," I said quietly.

She gasped. "You remember?"

"Of course, I remember. When a friend calls from across the world in the middle of the night, sobbing and frightened that she's been dating one of the Devil's disciples, it kinda sticks in your memory."

Her soft brown eyes filled with tears. "I never wanted to talk about it because I was so freaked out. And now this whole thing with Apollo and Poly . . . whatever her name is, is pretty much the same thing and . . ." she gasped as she connected the dots. "Oh, my God, you want me to introduce you to Spiros!"

I nodded. "Come on, let's go sit in the living room." I grabbed the wine bottle and my glass and lead the way, wishing for a fire, feeling how dead and empty the cozy little space felt without Apollo lighting it up. *Don't go there!*

Ruthlessly I pushed my sorrow aside and we settled on the sofa. "When I was with Polymnia last night, I had a sudden flash and remembered you telling me about Spiros and how you broke up with him when you found out he was a Wiccan."

Her hand flew to her mouth and a little "oh" escaped her lips.

"Apollo's too weak to perform the ritual tasks Polymnia says have to be done to get him back to Sira. The only possibility—and I mean the *only* possibility—is if there's a circle of people on this end to help provide the power for him to get back where he needs to be."

There. That was it. I'd said it.

"So, you want me to talk to Spiros and see if he

will work with you in performing this ritual?" Her voice was a bare whisper.

"Yes." There was a long silence while I drank some wine and so did she. But I couldn't keep my mouth shut for very long.

"Chris, up until a month ago, I felt exactly the same way you do about magic. But since meeting Apollo I no longer think the way I used to think. I've seen through all the bullshit and lies that have been told about women and a lot of other things, including the use of white magic."

Before she could start to object, I rushed on. "I don't know anyone in the Wiccan community. But I've heard that, by necessity, they're a careful lot. Spiros sure as hell wouldn't respond to some wacked-out American showing up on his doorstep asking him to perform sex magic as if it were a hat trick. But darling, you almost married the leader of the Athens circle! The only circle in all of Greece! I had to ask you. Can't you see?"

Chris didn't say a word and I sat there, dumb, not knowing what to do. Keep cajoling? Keep quiet? Drink more wine? I opted for door number four. "I'm going to the bathroom," I muttered, heading for the stairs. "Be right back."

Once upstairs I fiddled around looking for a sweater. Then I brushed my hair, trying to give her some space. When I got back downstairs, Chris was in the kitchen, washing the dishes. She looked up as I came in.

"I don't know if he's still at his old number," she

said, quietly, setting a clean plate in the drying rack. "It's been over a year. But I'll call him first thing tomorrow morning. I promise."

The sudden rush of gratitude was enormous. I went to her and threw my arms around her neck. "Thank you, thank you, a thousand times, thank you," I gushed, starting to cry.

She hugged me back. "You really do love him, don't you?" she asked shyly.

I nodded, my tears overflowing. "Yes, darling. I really, really do."

∞∞∞∞∞∞∞

## CHAPTER SEVENTEEN

One day passed. Then two.

Sleep? Impossible. Emails? Who cared. Work? Forget it. The only positive thing about my anxious waiting process was that by the time I saw Apollo again—if I saw him again—I'd probably be down at least ten pounds.

And then, on the third morning, Chris called. "I'm sorry it took so long. But it took me a while to reach him," she said.

"And?"

"It was pretty weird," she said.

"And?"

"He said he was willing to meet you."

*Yes!* I could have done an end-zone dance.

"On one condition."

"And that is?" I asked, heart thumping.

"That I come with you."

It had never occurred to me that Chris wouldn't be there. But now I realized that had been quite an assumption on my part. After all, she'd gone through a lot of pain and turmoil over their breakup. And it hadn't been all that long ago. Maybe she didn't want to see him? "Is that a problem?" I asked, cautiously.

There was a pause, then she said, "No."

*Thank God!* "So, when can he meet us?"

"Day after tomorrow on Saturday. We can catch the morning ferry then take a cab to his place."

"Did you tell him anything?"

"No, not really. I did say that it was a matter of life and death, though."

If it hadn't been so tragically true, I would have laughed. After all, how often does a writer get the opportunity to play that line? We talked ferry schedules, ending up agreeing to come back to Paros the same day if Spiros turned out to be a bust. If not—*fingers crossed!*—we'd catch the 7 a.m. ferry back the next morning.

"You sure you don't want to stay longer in Athens?" I asked her. "It's on me."

"No," she said quickly. "Thanks. But Athens and I don't agree much lately."

Was it Spiros, I wondered? Probably. She'd never been reluctant to hang out in the city before. I told her if she changed her mind to let me know. "Darling, I just want you to know that I know this is all way above and beyond the call of duty on your part and how much I appreciate it. Thank you."

"I know Apollo a little and I want to help," she said. "And don't worry about me and Spiros. It's not a bad thing seeing him again. Nothing ever happens by accident." She laughed shakily. "All this must have come into my life for some reason. You know?"

I knew. And I hoped for her sake that the trip would prove healing rather than more upsetting. We hung up, promising to touch base the next day. But my mind was already miles down the road by the time the line went dead. One more hurdle successfully crossed!

How I was going to convince Spiros that my story was true, I had no idea. How I could get him to work circle magic with a complete stranger, I had no idea. Was his circle large enough and experienced enough to handle the task? Was Spiros even still involved in Wicca? I had no idea. Would Apollo be able to make an appearance even if I could set the ritual up? Would I ever even see him again?

The list of all the things I didn't know and couldn't control was depressingly long and increasing by the minute.

∞∞∞∞∞∞

The rest of Thursday and then Friday crawled past. Finally, Saturday morning arrived. I drove to Chris's house and picked her up. Then we headed to Paraikia and the 10:30 ferry.

As we stood at the gate amidst the throng of tourists and workers headed to Athens, I couldn't help but recall my arrival with Apollo at my side a little over a month before. How excited and thrilled I'd been!

*How abysmally ignorant and uptight.*

We found good chairs on the upper deck out of the wind, then fetched coffee. At first, we didn't talk much. Then Chris hesitantly opened up about her past relationship with Spiros. It was an eerily similar tale to my experience with Rick, my fundamentalist

Christian almost-lover, except in reverse. It had been Chris's conservative religious background that had kept Spiros from confessing his pagan orientation for the two years they dated while she was teaching creative writing at an American school in Athens.

As had happened to me, when it came down to talking marriage, Spiros finally admitted that he was not only part of the only Wiccan coven in Greece, but its leader. And for Chris, that was a show stopper.

"I was raised in a fairly fundamentlist Southern Baptist church in Montgomery, Alabama by radically conservative parents," she explained. "I was weaned on hellfire and damnation and the wily ways of the Devil. Spiros knew it, which is why he hid the truth from me for so long. When he told me I packed my bags and left that very day." Her eyes clearly revealed her ongoing torment. "I couldn't bear to be in the same room with him! I felt totally betrayed. Plus, I was terrified. I thought he was in league with the Devil. And I couldn't imagine how he'd kept such a thing from me."

I rocked back in my deck chair. Southern Baptist! Well. That explained a lot. No wonder she'd been frightened. My first husband had been a Southern Baptist minister's son and one screwed up, uptight dude.

"Oh darling," I cried in sympathy, reaching over and squeezing her hand. "I so get it. Duncan, my first husband, was Southern Baptist and the whole sex thing with him was just awful. It's why we finally got divorced."

That broke the ice and we started sharing religious war stories, talking about the conservative purity ethic, the double moral standards for women, the shaming, the hypocrisy, the guilt.

"The first time I touched a boy's penis I thought I was going straight to hell," she laughed, finally beginning to sound more like the Chris I knew. "I spent the whole night crying and praying in my bedroom afterwards and was so sick I couldn't go to school the next day!"

"Ha!" I said. "I didn't think I'd go to hell for touching a penis. My biggest fear was when I started questioning the Christian church and what I'd been taught." I shook my head, remembering. "I was living in Atlanta working the evening shift at a TV station. And every night when I got off after the eleven o'clock news I'd drive up Peachtree Road and for about a mile all I could see was this big illuminated cross on top of the Episcopal Cathedral. I was terrified it was a sign from God that Satan was tempting me to read books about other religions."

We sipped our rapidly cooling espressos. "So, have you ever investigated Wicca?" I asked, curious.

She sighed. "Sort of. About six months after Spiros and I broke up I finally Googled it a few times."

"And?"

"It didn't seem so bad, really. Just about loving nature and honoring the Goddess and women and the Earth." She looked at me, eyes welling with tears. "It made me wonder if I hadn't made a terrible mistake. I never even let him explain what he believed. And then I felt so guilty and confused I figured it was too late to go back." She wiped her eyes, voice dropping to a whisper. "I never talked to him again . . . up until the other day."

It was such a human story, so filled with ignorance and fear, hope and despair, differences and missed opportunities. The rest of the trip we said little, both of us deep in our own thoughts, battling increasing nervousness for totally different reasons. And then suddenly there was the blaring announcement of our arrival in Piraeus and the mayhem of disembarkation and the melee of people, cabs and cars and trucks on the docks.

Soon we were in a cab tearing through the busy streets of downtown Athens towards Spiros' address in the Mets district and my next encounter with the unknown.

◊◊◊◊◊◊◊◊

It was definitely a strained start.

From the moment Spiros opened the door to his lovely 18th century house near the old stadium (old as in 330 BC), he and Chris had barely taken their eyes off one another. At the same time, they were painfully shy about even speaking to each other.

Tall and lanky for a Greek, Spiros was somewhere in his early sixties with grey-streaked dark hair caught back in a ponytail, serious brown eyes and a thin, hawk-like nose. Barefoot with long sinuous toes sticking out from beneath the cuffs of his faded jeans, I watched him make coffee in his galley kitchen and saw he had the thin bony fingers to match.

"You're a writer, like Chris?" he asked, not looking at her, setting our coffee cups on the wooden table in front of a tall old-fashioned set of sash windows. Then he returned to the kitchen for his own coffee.

"Yes," I replied. "My genre is non-fiction though, mostly spirituality and psychology, that sort of thing."

"I see. Sugar?" He set the little pot of brown crystalized sugar on the table within easy reach.

"No thanks. Cream if you have it."

"I'm sorry. I have only milk. Will that do?"

"Of course, yes, thank you."

With the three of us sufficiently prepared with caffeine, he got down to business. "Chris," he said, and this time he looked at her, "says you desire to speak with me about a matter of life and death and that there may be something I can do for you?" His tone was polite while at the same time mildly disbelieving.

I had thought long and hard about how to start this conversation and had come up with one decent opener. It had nothing directly to do with life and death and everything to do with obscure spiritual esoterica. But given his Wiccan roots it seemed like the best approach.

"Spiros," I said, catching his eye, "do you know what a tulpa is?"

No doubt about it, he knew. His eyebrows rose to his hairline and his pupils dilated sharply.

*Ahhh . . . good.* I plunged ahead. "For the last five weeks, I've been in touch with a tulpa that can also revert to etheric form—a tulpa that calls himself Apollo, as in *the* Apollo of Greek myth." I paused. "Although I'm hardly an expert in these kinds of things—I mean, who would be?—I've been given enough proof, I think, that this being is who he says he is."

"What kind of proof, may I ask?" Spiros managed, eyes veiled.

"Instantaneous apparition and dis-apparition in full daylight out in the open as well as various magical feats that indicate full control over the elements, such as the manifestation of physical objects . . . coins, paper money, coffee cups, whatever is physically needed, at will." I rushed on before he could ask another question. "I've witnessed these things in daylight and at night in full control of my senses. No drugs, although," I rolled my eyes and couldn't help smiling, "We do tend to drink quite a bit of red wine when we get together in the evenings."

He opened his mouth but nothing came out, so I pressed on.

"He has also spontaneously extracted my etheric body and sent me on various journeys through time. More than just visions, Spiros. Full-on, controlled, out-of-body experiences with total consciousness."

Spiros cleared his throat. "And what has made you believe this . . . tulpa is who he says he is?"

Here we entered even shakier ground and I knew it. But hey, he was still sitting there, asking questions. The fact that he hadn't laughed in my face and asked me to leave was hopeful. "Consistency of historical information, appropriateness of message and attitude, but, unfortunately, nothing concrete. I've had visions of him and our relationship during the early third century BC. And yes," I hastened to add, "I know it's possible these visions have been manipulated and contrived or I might have been drugged or hypnotized. For that matter, I could be completely insane." I shrugged. "But I don't think so."

"Why not?"

"I can't prove my sanity. But I've always been highly mentally and emotionally stable, and there's no history of mental illness in my family. Plus, I have a background in psychology. Which brings me to the hypnosis theory. Frankly, hypnosis just doesn't work like that. I also have a thirty-year experiential background in meditation, plant medicines and altered states of consciousness. These are not hallucinations, Spiros. Although some of the things I've seen and done have been plenty crazy, like encounters with myself in other incarnations, specifically a Druid temple priestess named Polymnia, also from the third century BC."

I rushed on. "She and her Druid circle cast what I believe to be a wormhole in space-time. Through this energetic portal she's been attempting to instruct me at night in various magical rituals to enable me to work with Apollo and help him in the tasks he has come to this time period to accomplish—tasks he is unfortunately currently unable to complete because . . . because the source of energy he depends on to be able to stay in manifested form . . . well, lets just say he's been cut off from that source."

It was as good an opening gambit as I could produce and I stopped talking to let him engage. And if ever I've watched another human being's mind grinding away, turning information this way and that, I was watching it now.

"And why, pray tell, have you come to me?"

"Because you are the only person who might be able to help me get Apollo back to the place of his energetic food source before he . . . before he . . . well . . . dies." My voice trailed off thinly.

For a solid awkward minute he didn't say a thing. Then, instead of responding to me, he turned to Chris. "Do you believe what she has said?"

Her eyes flew wide and her chin trembled but she didn't look away. She nodded. "Y-yes, I do." She rushed on. "I've met Apollo several times and I think he is what she says he is." She swallowed hard. "I-I had a vision of him recently. Well, a dream or something. And he told me everything she just said. A little different approach to the story. But . . ."

She paused, then added with devastating simplicity, "I like him."

Spiros rocked back in his chair. Then he asked her softly, "And does all of this frighten you?"

She hesitated. "No," she finally said, and her answer clearly surprised both of them "It did at first. But I know Kathryn and I've been getting to know Apollo. She shrugged, "They're just like normal people."

*Goes to show how little anyone should trust appearances,* I couldn't help thinking. But Chris was still talking to Spiros, answering his question, and I kept my mouth firmly shut.

"I'm learning to trust my own intuition. And I've realized . . ." her voice caught, but she soldiered on. "All this has made me realize that I've been taught to be frightened of things that are natural. Well, maybe not natural as in everyday occurrences," she giggled nervously. "But certainly not anything to be frightened about either."

Looking pleadingly at Spiros, hands knotted in her lap, eyes welling with tears, she whispered, "I'm sorry, Spiros. I am so, so sorry. I n-never even gave you a chance to explain." Abruptly she stood up. "Excuse me," she sniffed, then rushed out of the room, wiping her eyes.

Spiros' chair scraped as he leapt up. For a moment he stood rooted to the spot, hands helplessly clenching and unclenching at his sides. Then, echoing her words, with a brusque, "Please, excuse me," he rushed from the room after her.

∞∞∞∞∞∞∞

It was far easier convincing Spiros than I had thought it would be. And I owed it all to Chris. As the story unfolded in more detail, his initial skepticism turned to amazement which then quickly turned to fascination and then finally to excitement. And it was incredibly touching watching the two of them begin to tentatively reengage.

Evening came and we ordered pizza in—quite the treat after living on a small island with only fish on its mind for a month.

"Do you know how large her circle is?" he asked, mouth full of the vegetarian deluxe with extra garlic.

I shook my head. "Every time I've landed where I've landed it's been a blur of dancing men and women and then Polymnia and I are left alone together."

"Any symbols, music, chants, fire?"

"The first time I remember them calling my name and dancing. But that's all. Oh, and drums. Definitely drums."

"And the rite she wants you to perform if the circles can be cast and the wormhole established?"

Swallowing a bite of pizza, I said, "Something she calls the Triune Goddess ritual."

"Hm."

"You know it?"

He grimaced. "I know of it. It's ancient."

"She also mentioned Apollo has to appear in the ritual as the Great Stag."

"The Horned One," he said, nodding. "Yes."

"The horned one?" repeated Chris, looking suddenly apprehensive.

"The proud stag with its great antlers was the most ancient symbol of male virility," Spiros explained gently. "The horns represent the pathway of wisdom from the heavens above—forked lightning translating knowledge, strength, and potency down to Earth and into the body of the stag . . . or rather the man who wears its horns."

"That's it?" she asked, astonished. "Horns are the way the wisdom of heaven connects to Earth?"

"That's the symbolism, yes."

"But . . ." she started.

"Chris," I interrupted. "The Church took every symbol of the Goddess religions and deliberately gave them an evil interpretation in order to frighten people enough so they'd worship Jesus and Jehovah. It was pure scare tactics."

"Oh, my God," her lower lip quivered.

"Don't feel rained on," I added kindly. "Hundreds of millions of people still believe the whole Satan story we've been given. You're hardly alone."

"But it's just so awful having such beautiful imagery turned into something evil."

*Never mind twisting the story so that we end up thinking the bad guy is the good guy and worshipping him . . . it.*

We were sitting at the little kitchen table and Spiros reached over to cover her hand with his. "I can't tell you how good it is to hear you say that, Chris."

She blushed, but she didn't look away and she didn't remove her hand, either. And suddenly I had the feeling I was definitely the third wheel in the room. I'd thoroughly scanned Spiros' bathroom and seen no sign of feminine presence. I was sure Chris had made a similar superficial investigation. The doorway was obviously open for a reconciliation, and a quick one at that.

I cleared my throat, interrupting the moment. "So, where does that leave us?"

Spiros made a typical Greek moue of shoulders and mouth. "Not very far, I'm afraid. I'm willing to talk to my circle about your request for them to participate in a casting. But without a detailed description of the ritual . . ." Again, the shrug.

I slumped in my chair, pizza forgotten.

Then suddenly, lightning, of a sort, struck. "What a minute," I cried. "Here." I tugged at the leather cord around my neck securing Polymnia's totem. "What about this?" Carefully, I opened the bag and took out the little goddess, hearing Spiros' sharp intake of breath as she tumbled into my hand.

"Where did you get that?" he whispered.

"From Polymnia," I said. "I brought it back from my first meeting with her." I handed it to him, open palmed.

He took the little goddess with the greatest possible reverence. For a long time he gazed at the rotund little figure, turning her gently, examining. Then he closed his hand over her and closed his eyes.

Nobody said a word. Outside the house, modern Athens bustled, a good twelve to fifteen thousand years distant from all the things the little icon stood for.

I waited.

Finally, Spiros opened his eyes. "May I keep her for a little while?" he asked,

I nodded. "That was my thought. Perhaps she will guide you to Polymnia." I laughed. "God knows, stranger things have happened lately. And Polymnia is the only source I know for learning what we need to do."

Spiros gently slipped the little goddess back in her blue hide bag, appreciatively fingering the softness of the leatherwork. We talked desultorily of minor things for a few minutes more. But I increasingly felt the urge to give them some alone time.

I stood up. "Spiros, thanks so much. Chris? Do you want to come with me or . . . ?" I left the question hanging.

Chris ducked her head shyly then looked at Spiros through her lashes. I didn't see the look that passed between them, but her answer left no room for doubt. "I think I'll stay here for a while, if you don't mind."

"Not at all. Great. Well, um, I'll see you soon."

Spiros started as if poked by a cattle prod, tearing his eyes away from Chris. "Please, let me call for a taxi."

"Don't bother," I said, picking up the small backpack I'd stuffed with overnight things. "I know where I am. I can catch a cab at the bottom of the hill and get to the hotel. I could walk it, for that matter. No problem."

And then, after a few more polite words and hugs, I found myself out the door at last, standing in the lamplight and cool night air.

*Now that*, I thought with satisfaction, *was a good meeting.*

〇〇〇〇〇〇〇〇〇

Chris called the next morning at 6:30 as I was riding to Piraeus. "I'm staying in Athens for a couple days," she said breathlessly. "I just wanted to let you know so you didn't bother trying to find me at the ferry."

I chuckled. "Good for you. I'm so glad you and Spiros are catching up."

"Oh, God, me too," she paused. "Thank you, Kathryn."

"Hey, I didn't do anything. If you hadn't been there I don't think he would have given me the time of day."

"I don't know about that," she laughed. "He's pretty blown away. Listen, I'll be back on the morning ferry on Monday. Can you pick me up?"

I assured her I would.

"Spiros is going to talk to his group. And if they go for it, which he's pretty sure they will, he was wondering if you could come back next weekend to meet them?"

"Sounds like a plan. Give him my best, would you?"

We rang off. And I was left facing yet another ferry ride and another long lonely week to fill.

〇〇〇〇〇〇〇〇〇

When I picked Chris up on Monday she was a changed woman.

It was as if the light that had kindled me so fiercely for the last month had been transferred to her. I was thrilled for her and touched by her vulnerability and excitement. But listening to her gush about how it was like they'd never been apart and how stupid she'd been to run away in the first place and how Spiros hadn't had any significant relationships since they'd broken up and how wonderful their lovemaking had been . . . it made me want to pull the car over and scream until the windows cracked.

How was it possible to be so filled one moment and so empty the next? For life to be so bright and blazing and then turn so swiftly bleak and meaningless? I felt like a burnt cinder of a woman, a husk with no purpose or direction except for the desperate hope of seeing Apollo again. And then to what purpose? So I could say goodbye one more time and then lose him again, possibly forever, in a strange ancient ritual I didn't even know would work, surrounded by strangers in the cold and dark of night?

And yet as the hours and days crawled past I prayed for the opportunity. Prayed to Source to extend more energy and life to the one I had loved across time and space and through so many endings. *No matter what the cost . . . please, please, whatever powers there may be, please let there be one more parting.*

And then early Thursday morning my cell phone rang and my prayers were answered. The next doorway opened.

"Kathryn, this is Spiros."

Instantly, I knew something was up. "What? What happened?" I cried.

"She called me—her circle called me and I met them . . . met them all."

*Oh, my God!* "You met Polymnia?"

"Yes! The whole circle. It was . . . it was . . . I understand what we need to do. And Kathryn, prepare yourself. We need to do the ritual Sunday night."

∞∞∞∞∞∞∞∞

The rest of the day was a blur.

I packed and repacked, emptying everything out of my bag and starting over. What to wear for the ritual? Just my skin? I wanted to look pretty for him. Maybe the lace blouse I had bought that day on Antiparos with the long black skirt?

Chris took me to the 10:30 ferry Friday morning, face anxious, eyes worried, hugging me close, wishing me luck, saying as I walked away, "Give my love to Apollo." Which just about dissolved me on the spot.

There was never a question of her coming. I'd asked her the day before and she'd been clear and firm. "You and Spiros need to focus on getting this thing done for Apollo," she said. "I'd just be in the way, never mind a nervous wreck!"

When I finally got to his apartment Spiros was revved. Pacing his living room wearing a long ratty beige t-shirt, jeans and bare feet, he talked a blue streak about his encounter with Polymnia, sharing how much he'd learned, how powerful her circle was, how amazed he'd been to find himself in Druidic times in England.

"You were in England?" I cried. "How could you tell?"

He looked at me like I was crazy. "Who in the world doesn't know what Stonehenge looks like?" he asked. "Although it was very different, it was clearly the henge."

"Oh," I said, nonplussed. "Polymnia and I didn't meet there. We met—*where the hell did we meet?*—someplace else. On a planet with three moons."

"Wow!" he said, looking impressed. "Another planet!"

"Or something. It could have been an astral dimension or a freaking mirage for all I know."

We stared at each other, two 21$^{st}$ century humans very much out of our depth, doing our best to cope with an exceedingly bizarre situation. But I had to admit, it felt really good having most of my experiences with Polymnia validated by a fellow Earthling.

"Oh," he started. "Least I forget." He reached into one of his pockets, pulling out the blue leather bag. With obvious reluctance, he handed it to me. For a moment, the bag dangled from his fingers, oscillating on the leather thong like a pendulum. I took it gladly, slipping the cord over my head. The little goddess was a comforting presence, nestled back between my breasts.

Spiros and I talked late into the night, going over

and over the details of the ritual, which, for my part, included things I was still nervous about . . . magic, nakedness, and sex in front of strangers. But such was my determination to help save Apollo that I didn't flinch. And it helped tremendously that Spiros was unperturbed and clinical about the whole thing. He actually seemed to find it natural. And I thanked him for his attitude.

He looked surprised. "But it *is* natural, Kathryn. How can exercising our God-given abilities and one of our greatest powers be unnatural?" He cocked his head, wonderingly.

"Well, when you put it that way."

"How else can I put it? You don't hesitate to use your intelligence do you? Your ability to communicate with words? Why would you shy away from using your intuitive capacities, your sexuality and your passion to help the one you love create a better world?" His eyes were genuinely puzzled. "It is beautiful what we are trying to do."

"I know, I know. At least a part of me knows. But that doesn't mean there's not still a part of me that was raised to think very differently about such things. And that part of me still has a voice in my head." I paused. "Chris and I are much alike in that. But we're doing our best to get over it!"

He smiled warmly. "Don't worry. The Goddess will guide you. She's there inside of you, waiting to come out."

The conversation shifted and we began sharing our hopes and dreams for what might yet unfold for our planet. Everything the little goddess hanging between my breasts stood for was in play. Would she ever be consciously welcomed back into our world? Could humanity regain the wisdom it'd lost? Was there a healthy way for man and woman to go forward at peace with one another at last?

We talked about how miraculous it was that Apollo had brought him and Chris back together. About how weird it was to be able to understand Polymnia and her circle. Were they speaking modern English and Greek? Were we speaking ancient Greek? Or was there some sort of psychic translation field that enabled us to effortlessly communicate with one another? And wasn't it lucky that Spiros had the requisite minimum of thirteen for our circle? And oh! How convenient it was that one of the members of the group had a large minibus that could take us all to Delphi.

Spiros sang the chants Polymnia had taught him, haunting sounds that raised the hair on the nape of my neck. He talked about how excited he was to meet Apollo, how everyone in the circle was waiting with bated breath to meet the great god of Light himself.

"If he shows up. If he *can* show up." There. I'd said it. I'd voiced my greatest unspoken fear and my voice hadn't even trembled. Never mind the very thought sent my heart into a tailspin.

Spiros didn't bat an eye. "Have faith Kathryn," he said, gently patting my hand. "Have faith."

By the time we wound down it was two in the

morning and I tottered off to Spiros' spare bedroom
grateful for and at the same time vaguely jealous of
his excitement. For him it was all a grand adventure—
no doubt the most thrilling thing that would
ever happen in his entire life. But he had no deep
emotional investment in the proceedings beyond
the validation applying the fruits of a lifetime spent
following the philosophy of Wicca. How thrilling to
put his years of dedication to such use!

As for me, there was nothing but personal
investment. Despite my fatigue, it took a long time to
finally get to sleep.

∞∞∞∞∞∞∞

Saturday dawned a clear, blue-sky day in May. Spiros
hummed around his house preparing for the meeting.
Would I like breakfast?

I wasn't hungry and declined, then deliberately
changed my mind and forced myself to eat eggs, toast
and bacon. It wouldn't do having me pass out from
hunger during the meeting or the ritual. Then I went
out for a walk.

The botanical gardens where Apollo and I had
strolled during our second meeting lay at the foot of
the hill below Spiros' house about a five-minute walk
away. And I couldn't help but marvel at the circular
perfection of being there again on this of all mornings.

For at least two hours I walked, trying to get a
handle on my frayed emotions. My excitement at
possibly seeing Apollo again would rise, only to be

cancelled out by the fear that he wouldn't be able to show up. And then there was the depressing fact that even if I did see him again it would be for such a brief time. And then only to perform a terrifying ceremony the whole point of which was to separate us again.

I wandered back to the house, and at noon people started arriving. Alexis. Georgios. Dimitrios. Alexa. Stephanos. Phoebe. Men and women whose names I would never remember. Either that or their names would be engraved in my mind for the rest of my life. Hard to tell which.

I smiled, shook hands and remained on edge.

Gradually, the room filled up. And then it was time and Spiros started to speak—in Greek of course. He'd already prepared everyone with the background details of the whole story, plus the timetable we were on, plus information about the trip to Delphi the next day.

Quickly, he dove into the story of his meeting with Polymnia, which was the really big news because therein lay the validation for this whole enterprise and, of course, the instruction manual. Everyone's face was rapt with attention as he described the meeting and the ritual and what had to take place. Then he started teaching them the chants.

It took hours for Spiros to explain the details and respond to all the questions, hours in which I alternated sitting on the edge of my seat in the living room, letting the foreign words wash over me, and wandering bored and distracted into the kitchen to stand and stare out the window at the street below.

I could contribute nothing to the conversation and no one paid any attention to me. And then suddenly, just as I was about to head back to the kitchen for the umpteenth time, the vibe of the room changed. The air hummed and crackled as if all the window shades had suddenly snapped open to receive the energy of the very sun itself. And then, in the middle of the room, Apollo appeared.

Even though his presence had been anticipated and very much hoped for, his abrupt arrival out of thin air still drew screams from the women and yelps of shock from the men, and several chairs tipped over as people lunged to their feet. Spiros looked carved from stone, mouth open between one syllable and the next. As for me . . .

With a high-pitched cry, I hurtled across the room and into his arms. And for a timeless moment we simply stood, locked in each other's embrace, heedless of the people and their shocked faces and excited voices. He kissed me gently and everything sad and blue melted away and it was spring in my heart and body once more.

"Ekateríni," he said softly. Making a hymn of it.

"Apollo." How could there ever have been a time in my life when my lips didn't exist to shape that name?

And then all hell broke loose.

⊙⊙⊙⊙⊙⊙⊙⊙

# CHAPTER EIGHTEEN

People crowded around him, touching and talking, trying to convince themselves that what they'd just seen happen had really happened. They pressed closer and closer and I kept asking for "a little breathing room please" over and over as they basically ignored me. One woman produced a pair of nail scissors and tried to clip a lock of his hair.

Gravely he thanked each person for being there and for being willing to help. Photo ops took at least half an hour—although what anybody thought they could do with the photos aside from look at them later and pinch themselves, I had no idea. He looked like any other handsome Greek guy in modern clothes. Nobody would believe it if they told them who it was in a million years.

Then there was a whole next round of questions about the ceremony with Apollo answering what Spiros could not, translating into English for my sake. Eventually, the questions started wandering off track, at which point Spiros started herding the two of us towards his bedroom—a maneuver that took another 15 minutes. But he got us there, closing the door in his circle's eager faces, giving us some privacy.

"What do you want to do now?" he asked quietly.

"Get us out of here!" I insisted, loudly. Every minute that passed was one less minute Apollo and I had together and it was all I cared about.

Apollo and Spiros exchanged a look—a very male look. "You are comfortable with the ritual?" Apollo asked.

Spiros nodded. "Between you and Polymnia? Very clear." He shrugged. "She and her circle are doing most of the heavy lifting. All we have to do is tune in, hook up and anchor the gateway on our end. Then it's all up to you," his glance included both of us, "to do your thing."

If I'd been less haunted by the pressure of time, I would have blushed. As it was, if somebody had told me it would buy us an extra hour together, I would have stripped and run naked through Syntagma Square.

"What time do we meet at the temple?"

For some reason Spiros glanced at his watch. "The precise moment of the new moon is 12:53 am. Polymnia said to time the . . . uh, climax of the ritual as close to that as possible."

Apollo nodded easily as if this was all in a day's work, which for him it was. "So, we should start creating the gateway no later than eleven-thirty."

"Good. Yes." Spiros sighed heavily. "It will be difficult not having a fire. Frankly, I can't imagine doing this ceremony without one. But there's just no way we can risk it."

"Do not be concerned about being seen," Apollo said.

"Excuse me?"

"Just as I said. Do not worry. There are those who still serve Apollo in this world, especially at Delphi. There will be wood there. And a guardian. He will help you prepare as big a fire as you want."

Spiros eyebrows escalated towards his receding hairline and his eyes widened.

Apollo smiled. "What happens at the temple will not be seen tomorrow night. From any direction by anyone." Again, the amused look.

Spiros started to argue then suddenly remembered who and what he was dealing with and backed off, although he couldn't quite resist a shy, "As big as we want?"

Apollo nodded.

He let it go, shifting his gaze to me. "I'll bring a robe for you."

"A bathrobe?" I croaked. It wasn't exactly what I'd had in mind and it showed.

"A ceremonial robe," he amended.

"Oh. Um . . . thanks."

"Okay. So we'll start prepping the temple of Athena around ten. That means leaving Athens no later than seven." He hesitated. "You're coming with us?"

I cast a despairing look at Apollo who slipped his arm around me, hugging me close. Surely it didn't take a mind reader to know the last thing I wanted was to spend my last hours with him crammed in a bus with fourteen other people?

"Thank you, but Ekateríni and I need time alone

and a place near the temple is being prepared as we speak."

*Thank God!* My mind had refused to imagine the two of us holed up in Spiros' house with its cramped spare bedroom and pullout sofa bed. Likewise, I'd been unable to picture us at a hotel—even something as grand as The Grande Bretagne. The prospect of room service and cable TV our last night together felt like some sort of strange blasphemy. But for the life of me I hadn't been able to figure out any other options in case Apollo did show.

"I knew I should have brought my car. Should I rent another one?" I asked Spiros, heart sinking. *There goes another two hours farting around at Hertz.*

"Take mine," he said. "Can you drive a shift?"

"Yes." I paused. "Although finding my way out of the city is going to be interesting."

Spiros waved his hand dismissively. "I'll drive you out of the city. Dimitrios can follow us then bring me back here."

The last hurdle neatly handled we all looked at each other, searching our minds for loose ends. As big an undertaking as this was, we couldn't seem to find any.

"I guess that's it," Spiros said, uncertainly.

I was fairly jumping up and down with impatience. "I'll go grab my stuff."

"Change your shoes, Ekateríni," advised Apollo, looking down at my feet. "Be prepared for a hike."

∞∞∞∞∞∞

An hour later the driver's side door slammed shut on Spiros' retreating back and such was the relief of being alone at last all we could do was burst out laughing.

"Apollo Aureleous Tavoularis, that was one hell of an entrance you pulled back there. You should have seen people's faces."

"I did see people's faces," he replied. "I am glad I could give them the show they desired."

"It made their whole day. Hell, it made their whole lives." I shifted rapidly through the gears as I got onto the main E75 highway north of Athens. "God knows it made mine."

"I told you I would come back," he said.

"I know. But even if you came back I didn't know if you would do the ritual!"

"I am sorry I left you . . . how do you say? In the lurch?"

"Yes, in the lurch. Exactly."

He was silent for a while, watching the scenery scroll past. "To be honest, Ekateríni, I did not realize how quickly the life force was leaving until the candle was almost out."

What could I say to that? Nothing. But I definitely wanted to know why he'd refused to tell me whether or not he would go through with the ritual. "So why did you keep putting me off about the ceremony?" I asked. "Why keep me in the dark?"

"It did not feel right to tell you."

"What?"

"You are learning deeper, more profound ways to communicate being with me, are you not? About the language of silence and intuition. Yes?"

"I guess so. Yes."

"Feeling is a large part of the language of intuition, Ekateríni. It did not feel right to tell you. So I did not."

I drove on, digesting what he'd just said. "So, if you had told me . . . "

"If I had told you and decided to save my strength for the ceremony, then some other path would have unfolded and not the one we are currently on."

*Hm.* "And this is the path that feels right?"

"Does it feel right to you?" he challenged, turning the tables on me.

I thought about all the things that had transpired because Apollo had not committed verbally to the path Polymnia originally plotted out for us. Keeping his cards close to the vest and his choice to stay in the body the entirety of our last extraordinary week together had sent Polymnia over the edge into despair while at the same time kicking me into gear to become proactive in finding a solution, subtly shifting the energy dynamic between us. It had brought Chris and Spiros back together. It had already altered the lives of thirteen other people. And who knows how many others in the future would be affected because of that? And none of this would have happened if . . .

"Exactly," he said. "Now do you understand?"

I nodded, impressed and slightly overwhelmed by the subtlety of the dance Apollo had been conducting.

"It is brilliant, by the way, the solution you came up with."

"Spiros? It was a wild card for sure. But so far so good." The tenuousness of the whole plan still unnerved me. And yet now that I'd been clued into the larger picture, suddenly the wisdom of our endeávor didn't seem quite so dubious after all.

My heart lightened and I changed the subject. "I have a question."

"When do you not, my love?"

"Did you pull that name of yours out of a hat back in the wine shop that day or does it actually mean something?"

He chuckled. "Meaning is highly overrated, Ekateríni. But in this case, you are right, I chose it deliberately."

"And?"

"Aureleous means golden. Which definitely fits," he said modestly. "And Tavoularis refers to someone who is a literary assistant."

*Apollo: Golden Literary Assistant.* "Ha! But isn't literary assistant my role?"

"It depends upon how you look at it, does it not?"

"I suppose. Very clever for a last-minute cover."

"Thank you."

There was so much to talk about and so many things I wanted to avoid talking about, I didn't know what to say. Finally, I circled back to the strange thing he'd just said. "What do you mean 'meaning is highly overrated'? "

"Inquisitive to the end," he mused and my gut twisted hearing the word 'end.' "Speaking of which," he continued, unperturbed, "I highly advise you to adopt that attitude at the end of this lifetime."

"What?"

"Greet death with curiosity and wonder, Ekateríni. Not fear. If you greet death with the fear that naturally arises if you see death as *the* end rather than just an ending of one particular phase of life, a less than pleasant experience unfolds. If you spend your last moments on this Earth curious about death and where you are headed next, it opens you up to wondrous vistas."

"You don't think you're coming back!" I gasped. Why else was he giving me last-minute advice? And about my death of all things!

"Ever the optimist," he said dryly.

"But . . ."

He reached over and grabbed my hand resting on the shift knob, holding it tight. "Let us put this fear of yours to bed once and for all, shall we?" He raised my hand and brushed it with his lips. "I am merely being cautious, my love. I have great faith in Polymnia and great faith in the science of life you call magic. I also believe Spiros and his circle will do a credible job with the ceremony."

*And me?* I couldn't stop the question from forming.

"You, my dear, I never doubt."

"So?"

"So what?" he asked.

"So, please finish putting my fears to bed!"

He chuckled. "If I survive this gambit and make it back to Sira, I can assure you there is nothing in this universe capable of stopping me from coming back to you."

My heart did an instant happy dance and tears stung my eyes.

"Reassured?"

I nodded, squeezing his hand, and for a while I drove in silence, all thoughts of any possible failure with the upcoming ceremony banished firmly from my mind. And then another thought hit me. Never once through this whole drama had Apollo seemed in the least bit perturbed over the thought of his own possible demise.

"Before this body I am and after this body I am," he said quietly. "Death does not frighten me, Ekateríni. Unfortunately it terrifies most people who want a continuation of the familiar. Which is why Jehovah and other gods like him get such a hold on their followers." Apollo sighed. "He promises life will continue just as it is with the same body and the same family and friends—an endless holiday in a nicer house in the sky with no mortgage . . . which is most people's idea of heaven."

"Or hell," I laughed, "depending on your family."

"Indeed," he said. "My point is, the terror people have of death keeps them in a box. Which is why I urge you to leap forward gladly into the unknown when your time comes."

Being ever so human, my mind skittered away from thoughts of my demise, leaving room for an even stranger question. "Were you looking forward to a new adventure?"

He shrugged. "What is, is, my love. There is so much focus and determination from so many quarters insisting on my keeping this present embodiment, it would seem that life itself intends me to keep it for a while. We shall see."

He was quiet as I cautiously navigated the twisty streets and roundabouts in the town of Livadia, hoping to catch a recognizable road sign for highway 48 to Δελφοί. One more roundabout and *ah!* there it was. Soon we were traveling the narrow, twisting two-lane highway heading north into the mountains.

*Pity it's not earlier in the day. This is such a beautiful drive.*

"It was once a mere goat track," Apollo mused. "You could barely get a chariot up into these hills. Which is one reason Delphi remained untouched for so many hundreds of years. That and the mystique was too great and my good graces too valuable to those in power seeking prophesy and fortune in their constant warmongering."

He snorted. "Even the Persian kings Darius and Xerxes spared Delphi. Both were canny strategists and wary of the gods. After the fall of Athens they controlled the temple gold anyway without even setting foot in the temple precinct."

My American mind, schooled to think 300 years was an immense period of time, marveled at the antiquity of the countryside we were passing through. Amazing to think of all the lives, the battles, the joys and dreams, the plots and counterplots these mountains had witnessed. A thousand stories were to be had from every bend in the road.

"So, what does it all mean, Ekateríni?"

His question caught me off guard. *Mean?* I shot him a startled glance. He looked so relaxed, so beloved and familiar, dark blue shirt and jeans molded to his body, casually leaning against the passenger door, drawing me deeper into his world and mind.

"You asked me about meaning."

*Ah, right.* I downshifted around a corner and came upon a small herd of brown and white goats crossing the road, a tired-looking farmer behind them desultorily waving a stick, his moustache and shoulders drooping.

As I patiently waited for the last spotted nanny to cross the road, I thought about it. *What does this all mean?* The dying sun behind the hills, the dusky sky, the momma goats, kids cavorting at their sides, kicking up their heels, the disinterested farmer—a scene played millions of times across this land. Apollo, the returning lord of the domain, driven up into the mountains in a horseless metal chariot by a lover who had returned after two thousand years to be his companion and accomplice once more.

I had no idea what it all meant.

He laughed aloud, delighted. "My point exactly, Ekateríni. "Meaning is a will-o'-wisp. It changes moment to moment depending upon your emotions and point of view. It therefore means nothing."

"What?"

"Meaning is inconsequential. It only gets in the way of the most important thing of all."

That got my attention. "What? What's the most important thing of all?"

"Living, my love. Simply living." He laughed again and soon his whole body was shaking with mirth.

"What's so funny?" I asked.

"Oh, Ekateríni," he wiped his eyes, grinning broadly. "If you were not so damned busy searching for meaning you would not even have to ask." He watched the passing scenery for a moment then added, almost to himself, "Life is far too important to be taken seriously."

Where had I heard that quote before? *Ah yes.* Oscar Wilde.

"Perhaps this Oscar Wilde of yours has been quoting me?" he said, even more amused.

"You take things seriously," I shot back. "Or you wouldn't be doing what you're doing trying to make a difference in this world."

"Really?" he said. "Is that so?"

"Of course."

"My dear, do not project your perspective and mistake it for mine," he scolded mildly. "Just because I desire to ease people's suffering by waking them up to the lies they've been sold does not mean I take all this seriously." He smiled. "I am the servant of Source, going where life leads, doing the best I can. But serious? I think not."

And for that I had no answer.

⊙⊙⊙⊙⊙⊙⊙⊙⊙

It was dark by the time we reached Delphi. We slowly drove through the village with its gaily-lit tavernas, hotels, and populated main street. Just outside of town Apollo had me turn right onto an almost invisible dirt track heading up the mountain. "Where are we going?" I asked as I slowly navigated the narrow rutted road.

"You will see."

I couldn't see anything, but continued to wind uphill, higher and ever higher. Entering thick woods, eventually we came to the boundary line fence far above the backside of the temple precinct. The track turned left and straight uphill away from the fence line, so steep in parts I wondered if Spiros' little car would make the grade. But it did. And after another ten minutes we came to a tall, rusting chain link gate across what was rapidly becoming little more than a trail.

"Pull over here."

I parked in the tall weeds and shrubs to the right of the gate, hauled my backpack out of the back seat and locked the doors. *Now what?* I wondered, wishing I'd brought a flashlight.

Instantly light blossomed in the direction of the gate as if in direct answer to my desire and I gasped, shading my eyes, unable to see a thing in the sudden glare. A dark shambling figure holding a flashlight loomed close and I shrank back against the car.

"Γεια Petros," said Apollo.

"Χαιρετισμούς κύριε," rasped a male voice, rough with disuse and decades of tobacco use. An old man dressed in ancient khakis and a greasy-looking jacket loomed out of the darkness. Without a word, he picked up my pack and walked to the gate which was open just far enough to let us pass through.

"I have used this place on and off for a very long time," Apollo explained. "Petros and his wife are its guardians." The old man shoved the gate closed behind us, rusty hinges complaining loudly.

I started. "What about the guards?" I whispered nervously. "Won't they hear us?"

"Nothing is seen or heard here that I do not wish seen and heard," he stated flatly, reiterating his comment to Spiros. "Come." He pointed to a narrow footpath and headed off at a rapid pace, climbing up the hill, disappearing into darkness. I moved forward more cautiously, the path illuminated by the old man's bobbing light behind me.

We climbed for about 20 minutes, Apollo so far in the lead I couldn't even hear him. Apparently, he could see in the dark. Or perhaps, after three thousand years, his feet simply knew the way. And the old man behind me made not a sound. Which is more than I could say for myself. Despite Apollo's assurances I nervously reacted to every noisy misplaced footfall and crackle as I fought through the brush and overhanging branches. Suddenly we turned a sharp corner and the path abruptly ended in what looked like a huge jumble of impenetrable rock.

"Come." It was Apollo's voice above me and the torch revealed what looked like a goat track heading steeply upwards through the rocks. Despite the cool night air, by the time another 10 minutes of climbing had passed, I was breathing hard and sweating beneath my light jacket. But then the path abruptly flattened as it reached the base of a boulder as big as a house, turning sharply left to follow the rock face. The light, however, shone to the right. I hesitated and the old man jiggled the light impatiently, again indicating right and . . . no path and . . . nothing.

Well, okay, there was enough earth for a bare foothold around the boulder. I side-stepped along, pressing my face into the rock, nerves jangling, grateful I couldn't see what the emptiness behind me contained. Abruptly the trail reappeared and I almost fell face forward into a narrow cleft between the boulder and another set of rocks. I moved into a quickly narrowing fissure until it was so tight I had to turn sideways to get through. *Thank God, I'm only a B cup,* I thought as my breasts scraped uncomfortably against the stones. Ahead of me I caught the rumble of laughter in the dark. Then I was out the other side and Apollo took my hand.

We stood in a small yard ringed by vertical cliffs, twin lights of a tiny cabin shining like square amber eyes in the dark straight ahead. Then a door opened between the windows and the warm glow of firelight backlit a short squat figure in a headscarf and long skirts. Apollo tugged me forward towards the light.

I followed him into the cabin, ducking through the rough-hewn entry, then straightened and looked around. The room was small, constructed entirely from squared logs, with a low-beamed ceiling and wooden plank floor. Pegs on either side of the door held jackets. A pair of well-worn Nike's were on the floor on one side next to a narrow wooden clothes chest running beneath the window.

A massive rough-hewn granite hearth dominated the space, seemingly carved out of the cliffs themselves. Some sort of wrought-iron armature held an ancient cast-iron pot over the flames. A rough camp kitchen flanked the left-hand wall, shelves holding food supplies, kerosene lantern, a large basin and pitcher and cooking utensils. In front of the fire stood a small wooden table set for two with plates and glasses and two chairs—the only furniture in the room aside from the bed which was tucked away into an alcove on the right. The place was immaculate, warm and cozy, and whatever was simmering in the pot smelled delicious.

A huge grin split the face of the ancient Greek woman dressed in black as Apollo entered the room. "Καιρός ήταν," she said in mock scolding tones, waving her massive wooden spoon at him. Apollo laughed, saying something in reply. Her grin widened revealing mostly missing teeth. Then she turned her sharp black eyes on me, stripping me to the bone in the most thorough three-second assessment I'd ever received.

Turning to her cooking, she spoke with her back turned to the old man delivering my bag. "Δίπλα στο κρεβάτι," she said in a crackly voice, stirring the cauldron.

Obediently the man dropped my bag at the foot of the double bed which was covered with cream-colored, soft-looking woven blankets and a very large goatskin. He exited without a word.

"Welcome to my humble hideout and sum total of all my worldly goods," Apollo said, smiling radiantly, arms held wide.

My stomach growled in answer.

"I am hungry too." He turned and spoke to the woman and she nodded, the long grey braid of her hair bouncing down her back beneath her colorful headscarf.

I took off my jacket, hanging it on a peg beside the door. Apollo held a chair out for me and I sat down. Joining me he picked up the pale blue earthenware pitcher on the table and poured red wine into our glasses. Wordlessly we saluted each other and drank as the old woman ladled hot stew into two matching blue bowls, setting them on the table, serving Apollo first.

A large loaf of crispy bread followed on a wooden plate.

Ravenous, I grabbed my spoon and dipped into the stew filled with chunks of meat, vegetables and potato. It was as fabulous as it smelled.

"My famous goat stew recipe," Apollo translated the taste for me. "Bread?"

I nodded and he tore off a large chunk, handing it to me.

"How do you say 'delicious' in Greek?" I asked.

"Νόστιμο."

I smiled at the woman, holding up a spoonful of the stew, repeating the syllables. "Nóstimo. Efkaristo."

Her black eyes, almost hidden beneath the seams and wrinkles of her face, didn't flicker. Sniffing, she turned away and began scrubbing the already spotless boards passing for a kitchen counter.

"You must excuse Kalista," shrugged Apollo. "She has served me well for nearly a century. But she is not known for friendliness."

*A century?* I looked at her curiously, but with her back to me there was really nothing to see. Unsettled, nonetheless I applied myself to the meal with the kind of attention Apollo always gave his food. But I also kept an eye on the old woman as I ate.

Her gnarled hands were busy, her face resolutely turned away. But as indifferent as she appeared, it was apparent she was hyper-vigilant to every move Apollo made. It was as if she had eyes in the back of her head or antenna tuned specifically to him, ready to instantly respond to his every need. Indeed, before he even spoke, she was already turning towards him.

"Παρακαλώ, αφήστε μας," he said, quietly.

Clutching her rag tightly, she bent her head in response to his words, then flashed a black look at me. "Δεν είναι έτοιμη," she said, disapprovingly.

Apollo didn't even look her way. "Δεν είναι η θέση σας να πω."

"Αυτό είναι αλήθεια," she said, voice harsh. "Αλλά ξέρω τι βλέπω." Turning away, she dropped the rag on the counter and stalked out of the cabin, closing the door, not softly, behind her.

"What was that about?" I asked.

"Nothing important. More stew?"

Apollo got up and served us both a second bowl while I repressed my curiosity. Beyond a shadow of a doubt I knew whatever she'd said to Apollo was about me and that it had not been complimentary. *Oh well.* Finally, we were full and Apollo poured more wine, leaning back in his chair, staring into the ruby contents of his glass as if it were a great liquid heart pulsing in the fire's glow.

My own heart felt full as I watched him, committing every detail of his face, body and the cabin to memory. Unbidden, my mind swept to the sunny day we'd spent on Antiparos and the moment standing on top of the windswept hills overlooking the straits. *The day we first made love.* Could it have been only two weeks ago? Memories spilled over . . . the love and tenderness, the excitement and mystery, the passion and pleasure, the laughter, the pain and the tears.

Apollo didn't move throughout the entire mental

recital. Was he sharing those moments again with me in his own mind's eye? Or was I already alone? I sighed. *I wish I could read his mind as easily as he does mine!*

He smiled gently but didn't respond in any other way. And as the silence between us extended the fullness grew uncomfortable.

It was like a million words were dammed up inside me demanding to get out while there was still time . . . human sentiment fighting to get past the conflicting realization that there was absolutely no need to say anything—a vast emotional logjam of personal need pitted against the totally impersonal assurance of the eternal nature of our connection.

"I cannot resolve that for you, my love," he said softly, his copper eyes dark with compassion.

"I know."

The logs gave way in the fireplace, sending a shower of sparks up the stone chimney and Apollo got up to add more wood, prodding the fire back into a cheery blaze. For a time, he stood there, ruminating, back to me. Then he gently leaned the iron poker against the stones and turned to look a question.

*What now?*

What now indeed? Milk every last moment, clinging and desperate? Or gracefully surrender? I made my choice and the bottleneck within me shattered.

"Let's go to bed," I said.

Leaving the bowls and glasses on the table we

separately disrobed. His body in the firelight in the small primitive space was like a gold-bronze statue, carved and hard and impervious to trials and time, yet at the same time soft, malleable and vulnerable.

I placed the goatskin on the floor beside the bed, turned back the creamy blankets and lay down. He looked enormous standing over me, primal, almost fearsome, face and body in deep shadow limned in firelight, his dark red-gold curls glowing like a halo.

A passionate yearning arose in me and I wanted nothing more than to feel his body throbbing deep inside me once more, filling me to overflowing . . . womb, heart, and mind intoxicated and burning, lost in him . . . traveling with him.

But the time for that kind of memory-making was past.

"Come my love." I reached a gentle hand up to him. "Lie with me."

He slid in beside me and our bodies warmly nested together. Quietly we watched the firelight cavort about the room, setting every molecule of our tiny world alight with a crackling golden glow while the illusion of the larger world outside the door and windows pressed back at us with black cold indifference.

And it was enough.

Finally, as the fire sank to embers, we slept.

❀❀❀❀❀❀❀❀

# CHAPTER NINETEEN

I could tell by both the brightness of the sun through the tiny windows and the disapproval on Kalista's face as she banged about cleaning up the meal from the night before that it was already late when I woke.

Apollo's side of the bed had long since turned cold and I stretched under the blankets, playing for time, wishing the old woman would leave, wishing I had a nightgown—anything to place between me and those judgmental black eyes. But there was nothing for it.

Flinging the covers off, I stepped onto the cold floorboards, skinning into my jeans, not bothering with underwear, throwing on my t-shirt from the day before.

"Kalimera," I said, determined to be polite despite my intimidation. And I was shocked when she nodded in reply.

It was probably too much to expect coffee, but again I was surprised when she pulled a small pot off the restarted fire and poured viscous black liquid into an earthenware mug and offered it to me.

"Krema?" I asked hopefully.

Without a word she turned and grabbed a small pitcher off the counter and added milk—hopefully not goat's milk—and handed it back to me.

"Efkaristo."

Again, there was no reply. *At least she didn't chuck it at my head.* Taking that as a morning blessing, I scooped my hiking sandals off the floor next to the door and escaped barefoot out into the sunshine.

A small area of grass and wild flowers lay between the cabin and the huge boulders I'd passed through the night before—boulders the size of two houses. The cabin itself was built directly beneath a towering cliff that jutted out and over the roof. It would be impossible to spot the structure even if one were standing directly on the cliffs above. The hearth and chimney had indeed been carved out of solid rock.

No wonder Apollo hadn't been concerned about being seen, at least at the cabin. The only thing capable of spying on this place was birds.

I set my steaming cup on the small wood bench beside the door and quickly visited the old-fashioned outhouse I'd been introduced to the night before. Then I sat in the morning sun, gratefully drinking my coffee—typical thick Greek coffee with an inch of grounds adding texture towards the bottom and good fresh cow's milk. Finishing, I put my sandals on, contemplating whether to ask Kalista where Apollo had gone. Was it worth going back inside and facing the old woman?

*Definitely not.*

I ran my fingers through my hair, taming it into some semblance of order, resolutely turned my back on the empty bench and mug, and headed out of

the yard. Scraping between the rocks I was shocked
to see how steeply the ground fell away on the other
side of the fissure. An almost vertical drop strewn
with boulders and bushes lay at my feet. A swath of
forest lay far below, most likely hiding the boundary
line fence from view. To my right lay the narrow ledge
around the boulder I'd traversed the night before.

I turned and pressed my body into the rock,
repeating the cautious two-step shuffle until there
was an actual path under my feet again and I found
myself standing on a well-defined goat track running
uphill into more rocks and downhill back towards
the car. *Clever.* Nobody of sane mind would chose to
go right at that point.

I stepped onto the goat track and climbed.

It was another blue-sky day, still cool with a light
breeze. Swallows swooped around the cliffs to my
right, calling and darting, catching bugs. Somewhere
nearby crows called and I stopped and searched
the sky. *Ah!* There they were, up and to the right,
stooping at several layers of jagged cliffs facing east.

A half-hour's hard trekking brought me to
the top of the cliffs, gasping and perspiring. Here
the mountain leveled off and the goat track ran
straight across a scrubby tree-dotted plateau before
it disappeared into the rocks and the climb began
again. To my right several paths branched off to
various viewpoints amongst scattered boulders,
facing the Pleistos river valley below.

Again, I watched for the crows and saw several
doing aerial acrobatics, black wings slicing the air in

front of one particular ledge. With nothing else better to go on, I set off in that direction. At worst, I would enjoy a spectacular morning view of the temples and valley before slinking off to get directions from Kalista—if I could even understand them.

My feet crunched lightly across the sandy soil and, as I rounded a large rock, I saw Apollo sitting near the edge of the cliff, knees bent, brown arms clasped around his legs, facing the open sky and sun.

My heart leapt at the sight of him and I stopped and watched for a moment. He was utterly still, rapt, in fact. And I wondered whether I would be intruding. Surely, he had much on his mind, this of all mornings.

But before I could start dithering about it he turned and smiled a golden welcoming smile and I unglued my feet from the stone and joined him on the ledge.

"Excellent," he said. "You came right to me."

"Huh? Oh. I watched the crows," I confessed as one flipped past with a saucy cry.

"Only a fool does not use every signpost to find what they are looking for, Ekateríni." He turned and faced the valley again and I sat down beside him, not quite touching. Two more crows screamed past, ripping the air like paper.

"We will find each other again," he said, reading my mind. "Never fear."

*If the ceremony works,* I thought.

"Even if it does not work," he said, face resolutely turned towards the sun. "Forever is a very long time, my love. It has to be to allow everything to happen."

His voice was even and matter of fact, like he was talking about whether the morning paper would be delivered on time. But me . . . I didn't have anywhere near his perspective and thus his assurance eluded me.

"I wish I could remember this us next lifetime. I want to remember! It would make finding you so much easier!" I cried, frustrated.

"Not necessarily."

"Why not?"

"You think it would be easier, remembering. But trust me, ignorance will allow life to pull our streams together much more easily than memories. Memories just get in the way."

"But, if the ritual doesn't work and you . . ." I gulped. "You will remember?"

"I believe so, yes."

"But you don't know."

He shrugged and I marveled at his equanimity.

Far below several shiny tourist buses pulled up to the temple gates disgorging passengers and we caught the sounds of occasional voices, the slamming of a car door, a bus motor revving up the hill. But mostly it was just the wind soughing past the cliffs, the cawing of the crows and the beating of our hearts.

Finally, Apollo turned to me. "Kalista will prepare you for the ritual."

"What?"

"She will do all the things that must be done

physically to make sure you are ready and at your most receptive in order to deal with the energies we will be working with tonight."

"Such as?" I asked warily.

"The ritual involves tremendous focus and total surrender to the powers that need to be harnessed. There are herbs that must be drunk that have been used for thousands of years at this temple just for this purpose."

"What herbs?" I interrupted. I was certainly no stranger to substances. But it had been years since I'd engaged any plant medicines.

"Herbs to enhance perception and make you relaxed and more receptive, that is all. The temple priestesses have always used them. Kalista . . . I know you do not like her. But she comes from a long line of priestesses who know and practice the Old Ways still."

I crossed my arms in unconscious resistance. "It's not that I don't like her," I muttered. *It's more that she doesn't like me.*

He turned and looked at me sternly. "Do not be small-minded, Ekateríni. Like, dislike, such things are unimportant. She simply knows what is at stake and does not trust you to perform the ritual. She would prefer I used her in your place," he said abruptly.

My jaw dropped. "B-but she's like a million years old!" I gasped, horrified and more than a little repulsed. "You've got to be kidding. You'd . . . you'd *do it* with her?"

He sighed. "This is not about lovemaking and

getting turned on. This is about using the science of life and precisely applying it to accomplish a very specific task. Kalista is incredibly old but exceedingly powerful. She is the living archetype of the Crone herself. I cannot think of anyone on this planet more capable than she of performing the ritual."

Stung, I felt suddenly humiliated and, of all things, jealous. And I didn't care how stupid it made me look. "Then why don't you get her to do it?" I cried. "Why use me at all?"

"Because," he said, "this is a very odd practicing of the Triune Goddess ritual. A ritual reaching across time and space with one priestess representing all three faces of the Goddess . . . literally the Three-In-One." He shook his head. "I do not believe it has ever been attempted before."

He paused, looking past me into the distance. "That is one of the reasons I have not resisted this path."

"What do you mean?"

"It is hard to explain," his eyes focused back on my face. "I have no idea what the ripple effect of this working will be on the time-space continuum. I believe . . . I sense it will be powerful and fortuitous for many." He lifted his hands palms up in a gesture of surrender.

"And it will either be a raving success or a complete disaster depending upon how well each one of us does our job," I said.

His eyebrows quirked upwards. "As usual, my dear, you have grasped the essential point quite well."

*Great. No pressure.* For a moment we looked at each other and then I burst out laughing like I always do when things get tense. "Well then," I said, practically weeping with mirth at the bizarreness of my situation, "We'll just have to get it right the first time, won't we?"

Apollo laughed as well. "I daresay we must."

I wiped my watering eyes. "So, what else besides the herbs?"

∞∞∞∞∞∞∞

It was almost noon by the time Apollo finished the recital of all the things that needed to be done for proper preparation. "Christ," I said, "No wonder the Pythia only prophesized once a month. It took that long to get her ready."

"And even longer for her to recover," Apollo added a warning.

I looked at him curiously. "So, are there any weird gases steaming up from the depths of the earth in the temple that made the Pythia prophesy like so many archaeologists suggest?"

Apollo looked amused. "As you will shortly discover, there are indeed gasses that enter the waters of the springs that the Pythia drank that affect psychic processes. Everyone assumes that if it was the water then it must have come from the Castalian Spring at the bottom of the temple complex and those waters have been tested hundreds of times. Of course, they find nothing. What people don't know is that the gases are found in high concentrations in only one very specific location deep within the mountain—a place that has never been discovered."

"No being strapped to a tripod and hung over a pit to inhale the fumes?"

"Hardly," said Apollo. "Although the Pythia did sit upon a tripod to prophesy because the tripod is a symbol of the wise use of the mind, body, and spirit as the foundational base of all action."

*Interesting!* And suddenly the extent of the loss I was about to suffer when Apollo left hit me full bore. And it wasn't just the personal stuff. There was so much I wanted to know! So much *to* know! I looked at him mournfully.

Scooting closer on the rocks, he put his arm around me and I leaned my head against his shoulder, grateful for his understanding, battling the emotions that threatened to overwhelm me. "Have you been able to tell me all the things you wanted to say?" I whispered.

"Mostly," he replied.

*Good.*

He squeezed me tight then straightened. "Time to get some nourishment into these bodies." He rose effortlessly, hauling me to my feet, and for a moment we rocked together in a tight embrace as we stood upon the cliffs overlooking the great vista of Delphi. I rested my head against his chest and listened to his heart beat beneath the thin cotton t-shirt against my cheek, knowing well it would be our last private embrace.

"I will miss you so much," I whispered, clinging to him. Six pathetic words trying to capture a universe of feeling.

"As I will miss you, my love," he answered. Then he put me a little away from him and said with absolute certainty, "We will see each other again, Ekateríni. The ritual will work. And I will send a talisman to show that all is well." He reached out a gentle hand and touched my cheek.

"I promise."

◎◎◎◎◎◎◎◎

The table was set in the cabin when we arrived. Kalista looked up at our entry and, again, there was the swift assessment. Then she grunted and nodded towards the table. Obligingly we sat.

The broth she served was rich and delicious although unseasoned. "Bone broth," said Apollo. "High in nutrients."

"No bread?" I asked, surprised.

He shook his head. "Nothing solid until after the ritual."

*After the ritual!* My stomach knotted with sudden nerves and I looked at the remaining liquid in my bowl with mild nausea. Then I deliberately relaxed my stomach and breathed deep, consciously releasing the building tension.

Apollo looked up from his broth and winked approvingly.

We finished the sparse meal in silence. Then he

set his spoon down neatly beside his bowl and rose, the sound of his chair a shocking rasp across the floor. Immediately Kalista was at his side, wiping her hands on her skirts, face attentive beneath her black scarf. Briefly they exchanged words, once or twice glancing my way. "Ne, ne," the old woman growled.

I rose uncertainly, reminding myself that "ne" in Greek means 'yes.'

Apollo turned to me. "You must do everything she tells you to do," he said firmly. "No questions asked."

I nodded. "I will." *Not that I could ask anyway.* I looked at Kalista and met her black impenetrable eyes, giving her my non-verbal assent as well.

"Good."

"You're going?" It was obvious, but I didn't want to believe the moment had finally come.

"I have my own preparations to make," he said, gravely.

"Of course."

*Of course . . .* how natural I sounded. How casual.

"It is life, Ekateríni. It will have its way with us." He reached for my hands and lifted them to his lips, bowing. And then, with a final gentle squeeze and a loving look, he let them go, turned, and walked out the door.

As usual it was as if the only light in the room had been switched off and I felt my knees go weak. Briefly I gripped the table's edge drawing an unsteady breath. Then I lifted my chin and looked at Kalista. Was that a tiny flicker of compassion I saw in those black eyes? Hard to tell. But it didn't matter. Whatever she thought, I was in her hands now.

Walking over to my backpack she gestured, plainly indicating that I was to empty the contents, which I did on the now remade bed. I watched her paw through the sparse items . . . hairbrush, toothbrush and toothpaste, a clean t-shirt and a pair of underpants, socks, cell phone, Spiros' car keys. Nothing interested her and she turned away, grabbing my hand, pulling me over to one of the windows.

Her grip was powerful, her fingers dry and callused. Quietly she studied my palms and fingers in the light, turning my hands this way and that for several minutes. With a grunt of surprise, she dropped them and looked up into my face, clearly recalculating.

"Έλα μαζί μου," she said, opening the door. Then she pointed to my jacket hanging on a peg, gesturing for me to bring it.

I looked back at my things strewn on the bed.

She shook her head. "Αφήστε τους."

I followed her outside, quickly glancing around. Apollo was long gone from sight. I sighed at my heart's foolishness and followed the black-swathed figure around the left-hand corner of the cabin. The short stretch along the kitchen side was smooth logs with no openings. But around the next corner at the backside of the cabin there was a narrow, padlocked door leading into some sort of storage shed squeezed between the cabin and the cliff.

Kalista paused, fumbling in her skirts and drew out a small ring of keys. Finding the right one, she unlocked the padlock and opened the door, gesturing me inside.

The small space was jammed. A few tins of food, canned tomatoes, beans and meat were stacked on a shallow set of shelves on my right. A couple old jackets hung from nails against the left-hand wall. At the back were some tools, a pick and shovel, an axe and a small stack of kindling. Kalista squeezed past me and rummaged behind the kindling, feeling for something, and I heard a soft *click!*

To my very great surprise the section of wall to my left swung noiselessly aside revealing a narrow entrance into darkness.

"Εισάγετε," she gestured.

Right.

Hoping a herd of poisonous snakes wasn't waiting for me on the other side, I put my jacket on and slipped through the door into a damp cool space carved out of the rock. Kalista closed and bolted the shed door, which had the immediate effect of plunging us into semi-darkness.

Kalista entered the space where I stood uncertainly. I heard another soft click! and the last rays of light were obliterated as the inside door slid shut. The sudden blackness was absolute and all my senses went on high alert. Then I heard rustling and a flashlight clicked on.

We were standing in what looked to be a small roundish room carved out of solid stone. On a shallow ledge next to Kalista were several flashlights and a dry storage jar full of batteries. In another jar were matches. Secured by pitons driven into the wall were several old-fashioned kerosene lanterns, clearly full by the stink of petroleum in the confined space.

But where did we go from here?

Silently she handed me an extra flashlight and batteries which I dropped into my jacket pockets. Then, bending down with a grunt, she shoved her gnarled fingers into an almost invisible fissure in the wall close to the ground. Nothing happened that I could see or hear. But she straightened up and confidently pressed against bare stone and a section of rock revolved, creating an opening.

*Really??* A rush of cooler air moved past me and I shuddered, hair prickling on my arms. She stepped through and, feeling very much like I was in some sort of Indiana Jones movie, I followed.

We were standing in a narrow granite passageway that was not quite as tall as I was. Stooping to avoid scraping my head against the curved ceiling, I helped Kalista shove the well-balanced pivot stone silently back into place. Once shut, even though I knew where the closure was, I could barely discern a seam.

Without a word, she turned and started down the passage, light bouncing off the grey-gold walls, setting millions of tiny flecks of quartz in the stone to sparkling. I dogged her footsteps, tested my flashlight and then switched it off again, grateful knowing there was some sort of reserve system available in case of emergency.

The footing was smooth from the passage of time and many feet, almost slick. And when the passage started to angle downwards I had to balance carefully as I walked, head bent, perforce looking at the ground and my feet. The walls were surprisingly dry.

Down, down, down we went, then the passage angled sharply right and a series of shallow steps, deeply worn in the centers from time and use, swam into view. Another ledge carved out of the rock at the top of the steps held more flashlights and matches and several more kerosene lamps. Reassured by the redundancy, I switched on my light as Kalista led the way down the stairs.

The ceiling rose as the floor fell away and I no longer had to crouch to get through. After about twenty or thirty steps I paused, flashing my torch upwards. Blackness swallowed the light long before any solid surface could be touched. Kalista didn't pause, and I hastily followed her descent into the heart of the mountain. The stairs were carved into a natural vertically-slanting fissure in the rock and I counted over four-hundred steps before I finally gave up. I'm not claustrophobic or anything. But something whispered to me that it was better not to know just how deep into the bowels of Mount Parnassus we were heading.

After what seemed forever, we reached the bottom. Somewhere in the impervious darkness I heard the distant sound of falling water. I shone my pathetic light in that direction and a vast stretch of wet blackness glistened, massive calcified stalagmites rising from the water like jagged orange-white mismatched teeth.

The floor was relatively even as the path skirted the abyssal lake and we walked for another good half mile in the dripping silence before we came to a tangential wall of rock. Kalista stopped, flicking her light downwards towards the floor. I tracked the beam, stepped forward and saw it—a crotch-height fissure in the stone to my left.

Another brief flick of her light and I got the message. *Get down and crawl.*

My nearly empty stomach gave a sideways lurch and the general level of my apprehension rose. But I got down on my hands and knees and obediently prepared to enter the slit. Before I could proceed, however, Kalista reached down and snatched the light from my hands, switching it off before handing it back to me. *You gotta be kidding.*

She wasn't. I put the flashlight back in my pocket and, as I entered the passage, she turned off her own torch and my world was plunged into an endless pit of blackness so oppressive the only thing that kept me from screaming in terror was pride. I would be damned if I was going to confirm whatever low opinion the old woman had of me. So, I did the only thing I could do . . . kept my mouth shut and crawled.

It was excruciating on the knees and utterly horrifying sensing the weight of solid rock pressing against me. To make matters worse the little tunnel became increasingly smaller and warmer, the walls damper as I moved along. How far had we come? A hundred feet? Two hundred? I was totally disoriented and the heat was becoming oppressive as I inched along, getting more and more grossed out as the stone grew slimy under my hands and knees and an odd mineral odor assaulted my nose. Only the reassurance of Kalista's breathing behind me gave me the heart to keep going.

Finally, the tiny passage opened abruptly. I was amazed how much my body had become sensitized. I felt the space open around me as obviously as if there'd been a neon sign. I stood up eagerly—too eagerly—and cracked my head sharply against the ceiling. I yelped and Kalista spit out a phrase in Greek somewhere down by my knees. Groaning with the effort, she hauled herself to her feet. Or I assumed she stood up. There was no way to tell except by the sound of her rustling clothes. I marveled at her strength and resilience. Most women my age couldn't have made it this far let alone a woman who, if Apollo was to be believed, was well over a hundred.

She gripped my arm—no fumbling and not for support—a quick, precise grab of my upper arm and a downward yank that clearly said "stay put." Then she let go and moved away.

*Don't worry sister, I ain't budging.*

I heard her footfalls as she moved away, muttering a breathy chant in the thick dark. And I heard something else I couldn't quite define. A sibilant hissing? Then she stopped. I heard more rustling and she struck something, flint against stone, and a spark jumped, shockingly bright and beautiful—an arc of white, orange and blue catching the wick of a small clay oil lamp—shattering the blackness. I gasped, shielding my eyes, then gasped again as shock bolted through my body setting my heart hammering. We weren't alone!

Strange wispy white figures were undulating in the darkness. And just as I was about to let out a strangled scream, I realized what the lamplight was illuminating: steam from a sullenly bubbling hot sulfur spring.

I swallowed hard watching Kalista move counterclockwise around the steaming spring, locating and lighting the ancient lamps set into the stone, chanting, deftly creating a spark with one strike until five lamps had been lit and the little chamber was sparkling with light.

It was beautifully done and more than anything I was reminded of Apollo and the deliberateness with which he did simple things, like eat, making a ceremony out of the daily moments of life. Watching the old woman, I promised myself that I would never take the tiniest spark of light for granted ever again. If, that is, I ever got out of this disorienting place in one piece.

Kalista indicated that I should disrobe. I un-velcroed my hiking sandals and kicked them off, my feet making contact with warm, moist stone. My jacket and t-shirt followed. After placing them on top of my shoes, I tugged my jeans down and stepped out of them, folding them and dropping them onto the pile.

Again, Kalista gestured. *Get into the pool.*

I walked to the edge and peered down. It was impossible to see anything with the light dancing across the bubbling surface, but I trusted she hadn't brought me this far to boil me alive and stepped gingerly into the water close to the edge.

It was hot, but not unbearably so, and there was a ledge about a foot below the surface. I stepped in, then felt for another step. It was there and soon I found myself up to my waist in a bubbling cauldron. I sank down with a grateful groan and let the waters wash over me.

It was unbelievably sensual and relaxing after the cold uncertain passage through the cave and hard stone tunnel and I closed my eyes, letting my head tip back into the water until finally I was floating, breasts bobbing above the surface, arms outstretched.

For a long time, I soaked. And as the tension in my body slowly melted away, my mind began to relax. The whirling unanswerable questions, the anxiety about the ceremony and Apollo's fate, the fear of my strange surroundings—all of it slowly drifted away. What could I do about any of these things? Nothing. What good did worrying do? Nothing. Gratefully I let the burden of my thoughts drop away.

About the time I began to wonder if I was turning into a prune, Kalista appeared holding a large cloth. Reluctantly, I left the water and reached for it. But she shook her head and instead of letting me do it, vigorously dried me off herself, sparing not one centimeter of flesh, including my nipples and between my legs. Then, dropping the cloth on the cave floor next to my neatly piled clothes, she jerked her chin in what I now recognized as her "come hither" gesture and walked to the slit in the wall we'd arrived through, pointing down.

I started to retrieve my clothes but she made a swift cutting motion with her hands. So, I got back on my hands and knees, buck naked, and reversed the passage. Or at least I thought I was reversing. The tunnel wasn't as low and narrow as I remembered—my bare shoulders weren't even touching the walls. And there was a spark of golden light far ahead of me.

The place I emerged was not by the black lake. It was another room, already lit by six . . . no seven lamps. And this room, too, contained another pool of water.

As soon as she was through the passage, Kalista pointed to the pool, and, with greater confidence than I'd approached the last, I walked to the edge and got in, barely suppressing my shock at the bite of freezing cold greeting my feet. *Yikes!* I gritted my teeth, determined to show no weakness, stepping straight into the depths of the pool, flesh cringing in protest.

Three times she made me duck my head under. By the time she indicated *enough* my teeth were chattering and my vagina ached with cold. Again, she thoroughly toweled me dry at the edge. And again, she showed me the way to yet another dark passage.

The third room was also lit, this time with six lamps—yes, I confess that for some strange reason I am an automatic counter of such things. It also contained a pool and what looked to be a sheepskin-covered table which, upon closer examination, turned out to be a massive sawed-off stalagmite growing up from the floor. By now I had the hang of the routine and stepped into the third pool, grateful to discover it was satisfyingly warm and sulfur-free.

⊗⊗⊗⊗⊗⊗⊗⊗

Between the walking and crawling, the paths and pools, the stairs and tunnels, the light and dark, the heat and cold, the fear and relaxation . . . somewhere along the way my mind stops and so does time.

Kalista gets me out of the third pool and dries me off, gesturing for me lie face down on the soft sheepskin. Her hands, when she begins touching me, are strong and covered in scented oil. And for a long time she massages my body, eventually turning me over, making sure everything, and I mean *everything*, is deeply oiled.

Then she beckons me to rise.

*I have to get up?* I wonder, groggy with sensual pleasure.

An impatient waving of the hands urges me on and I get up, rolling off the fur-covered stone table, carefully stepping forward on well-oiled feet.

The next passage I barely have to stoop. Where am I? How many rooms so far? Does it matter? I stand on warm sand and Kalista is rubbing my skin with handfuls of grit, scrubbing everywhere. I flinch, covering my breasts with my hands, protesting, but she ignores me, shoving them aside, continuing the rough abrasion. Then she scrapes the sand and oil off with an ancient stone strigil and leads me to yet another passage.

I don't count the number of lamps illuminating the next room. An unidentifiable scent fills the space, neither sweet nor pungent, and the pool, when I step into it, is pleasantly cool and delightfully fizzy against my enlivened skin. The bubbles frothing to the surface tickle and I giggle as Kalista dips a stone cup into the pool and holds it to my lips.

I drink. The bubbles pop all the way down.

I lie upon another stone altar, this one bare, smooth with time and bodies and oil. And again, Kalista's gnarled hands work my flesh, kneading herbs and unguents into every pore over and over, saturating my very being.

"Σήκω."

The word comes as from a great distance. Does she speak aloud? I have no idea. Somehow, I know what the word means. Unquestioningly, I sit up on the oil-slicked stone, legs dangling over the side, feet not quite touching the cave floor, aware of every cell singing in my body.

"Ποτό."

I take the small silver goblet from her hands.

Moonstones softly glitter around the base in the lamplight and two elaborately carved snakes twine around the stem, arching away then kissing the bowl, serving as handles. It is ancient and beautiful and as my lips touch the rim I feel the tug of other presences, see the vague flicker of women's faces in other times . . . women called to serve life and the Goddess.

"Ποτό."

I drink.

Again, Kalista prompts me and I stand on legs as tall and sturdy as tree trunks. With each stride across the lamp-lit cave I cover a thousand miles, each step upon the Earth a planting of roots, an outreach of limbs and senses reaching down and down into the stone.

Again, I enter darkness. No sparks of light. Total obliteration.

"Κάτσε κάτω."

I sink to the cold floor, oiled thighs, buttocks and genitals touching stone, legs crossed beneath me, body and soul connecting to the flesh and soul of the Mother. And then there is no me and no Mother, no flesh and no stone, just the Dark One, vibrant, impenetrable yet utterly pliable, formidably complete, voicelessly challenging, "Who dares enter my domain?"

There is no answer.

No one is entering.

I laugh.

There is no me laughing.

"Σήκω."

An epoch for each vowel, an eon for each consonant, an eternity for a word. There is no going out and no coming in and no longer a Kathryn. Yet "I" get up and move again in the endless dark that may as well be light, for darkness and light are one and the same and the way is clear and obvious. I crawl through another tunnel, forced to my belly, writhing like a well-oiled snake, swimming like an infant through rock into a space of boundless scintillating crystals refracting innumerable lives and worlds and galaxies—each facet a gateway within the vastness of forever, revealing every living atom in every universe, intelligent, aware, unique and yet One.

I lie in the crystal cave and Eternity is my Being.

"Είναι ώρα."

I stand . . . a sweeping fluid movement like the sea and walk an eternity of walking, each step a foaming curling wave breaking upon the shore, a flood of majestic movement through long passages until a doorway opens out of the earth into the lighter darkness of night and I see before me a faithful dog of a man, a slave, a general, a peasant, an Emperor, each lifetime clearly stamped upon his features.

He bows and hurls a cape red as blood around me, leading the way across gravel and macadam still warm from the sun long gone from the sky, down a winding treed path, leaves whispering their millions of individual greetings, right then left. And all the while the drums call and the flames of a great fire pulse in the middle of the stone floor of the crumbling circular temple below, beckoning.

A Great Calling into the void has begun.

Men and women—individual soul sparks— weave and stamp around the flames and ancient broken columns, bodies writhing across the steps through the weeds and grasses, sinuously coiling and unfurling, life breathing in and out through their skins—all One.

I throw my head back, ululating a primal sound, laughing at the illusion of individual male and female forms, and the dancing figures pick up the call, sending it back to me, heads tossing, manes of hair glistening with sweat as the rhythm of the drums increases.

Moving against their clockwise flow the great mountain that is "I" dances counter-clockwise, and now there are two circles, counter-rhythmic energies, sending throbbing bands of etheric light corkscrewing down into the stones of the ancient temple securing a base and more bands of light emanating outwards into the heavens, both bands resonating beat frequencies hooked to my vibration, throbbing, pulsing, singing a message into the earth and out across the stars and dimensions . . . *I Am Here!* . . . commanding a joining of that which has never been parted.

In a far distant land and time I dance, proud and strong, naked limbs flashing whitely between the stones, my red hair like a banner streaming in the wind, small feet stamping in timeless rhythm.

Polymmmmnnniaaaa . . .

Spiros' circle calling.

Polymmmmnnniaaaa . . .

Spiros?

Who is Spiros? I should know. Somehow it is important . . .

*I should know!*

*I?*

*Who is I?*

With a soundless *CRASH!* the infinite tidal wave of the Boundless Presence collapses into a small riffle of awareness called . . . ? . . . Ekateríni? . . . Kathryn?

The swift change in perception from goddess to human is staggering and I fall to my knees, suddenly drained, the red silk ceremonial cape spilling around me. The drums stutter . . . the corkscrew of light dims and flickers, the universe groans . . . and then a mighty force—the Great Earth Mother herself, the Mighty Ge whose presence hasn't trod the surface stones of Parnassus in almost 3000 years—crashes up through the temple floor, exploding through my flesh, obliterating mind and body and any tiny fleeting spark of individual awareness once more. And now there is only the power of life itself—the Great Mystery of the One and the Many—the paradox of creation playing out through the insignificant panting bodies twirling like fireflies in the night.

With a great shout, I hurl aside the silken garment, leaping into the center of the circle near the flames scorching the crumbling inner columns of the temple. The drums increase, the dancing figures howl, and a bolt of lightning sears the sky. Stamping and pounding in a circle around the fire, the massive telluric forces ride through me like a great storm and I throw back my head, screaming, commanding, one arm outstretched to the sky, the other to the earth, dividing the forces from the circle as they pass through me, sending pulsing energies down into the ground and out into the heavens with exponentially increasing power until an answering call thunders back through the dimensions—a great vortex of energy roaring into and through me, hurling my body to the ground.

*CRACK!*

I tumble, hurtling through the blackness of space towards a fast-approaching face wreathed in crackling red hair. With the force of two stars colliding, Polymnia and I merge—memories, emotions, needs and victories, weaknesses and strengths, smashing and fusing as one. Whirling and dancing in the void to the pounding rhythm of the drums, laughing ecstatically, hands clapping, we celebrate our oneness while at the same time calling, reaching out for an essence so known and loved, calling a sound, a name into the void.

*Des-Ma.*

Lightyears apart in space-time, the two circles struggle to hold and anchor the vast moiling energies of the vortexes, hooking them together, as Kathryn/ Polymnia whirls as one being between the two poles. And suddenly there is Desma standing beside a becalmed sea, all stillness and grace, brown hair collected in long braids, face tilted upwards filled with longing and wonder. And in one giant surge the tidal wave Kathryn/Polymnia reaches her and pulls her in, green eyes flashing an instant's welcome before they disappear with a great foaming hiss as Desma essence merges into the energetic embrace and flood of union.

Laughing at the ridiculous beauty of names and flesh and time, death and distances, we descend through the wormhole back into the star fields of Earth until our feet stamp as one upon the ancient stones of the crumbling temple of Delphi while the drums thunder on.

And suddenly, with a violent *WHOOSH!* the fire explodes upwards, singeing the moonless sky, and into the pulsing life-singing circle leaps the Great Stag.

It is Apollo, the Sun God himself, come to do battle with the Goddess, and the dancers stagger under the tide of surging energies, desperately holding the gateway—the great vortex spinning through space/time—dancing closer, intense, sweaty, weaving the gathering forces, feeding them into the circle, into Apollo, shouting and wailing, exhorting the Horned One to do his best.

The Great Stag looks around, fierce eyes searching, finding mine.

I laugh. I am the Maiden. Hands on my hips, breasts glistening in the firelight, red hair wild, I boldly taunt him to "Catch me!" With a howl, he lowers his head and horns, charging across the fire-lit stones and I let him get close, almost touching me, before I twirl lightly away.

He skids to a stop near the edge of the circle, turns and, powerful legs churning, lunges towards me once more. I skip away, laughing as his fingertips graze my heated thigh. On and on the dance rages, Apollo, the powerful stag and I, the teasing Maiden, strong in my young flesh, my warrior spirit unassailable. Again and again he charges and again and again I dance away. The stag's slick sides are heaving now, his breath coming in stabbing gasps. And it seems the Maiden will best him at the game.

And then the Mother rises.

Curling my fingers enticingly, I softly coo, inviting him in. And this time as the Stag approaches, I do not move away, but let him touch my soaking flesh and breathe in the scent of my willingness.

He stands before me, head thrown back, bellowing his victory, and I sink to the hot stones, leaning back into the pool of my long silken brown hair, knees bent, opening my legs, spreading wide the lips of my slick cave, fingers and panting body shaking with desire.

For a long moment the Horned One towers over me, phallus erect in the firelight, straddling my form, eyes glowing, knowing he has won.

He sinks to his knees between my legs, grabbing my hips with powerful hands, pulling me across the stones towards his glistening shaft and in one merciless thrust, embeds himself to the hilt. I cry

out, body arcing, gasping, eyes blind to the firelight
and stars and twirling figures as he pulls out and then
thrusts back into me, the tip of his penis cresting
against my cervix, commanding total surrender.
Flesh melting under his relentless probes, I feel an
explosion deep inside . . . a thundering current of
energy building as the Great Stag continues to move
in and out, in and out to the rhythm of the drums in
the most ancient dance of all.

I moan and writhe, his hardness piercing me, my
womb quivering under the brunt of his last desperate
shoves. And as he spills his seed my world convulses
and a thunderous *CLAP!* echoes through me and
across the temples and valley as God and Goddess,
Man and Woman, Masculine and Feminine, Sky
and Earth, Sun and Moon unite . . . the great
primal mating of the opposing forces of life itself
consummated before the fire.

And as the bow wave of our blended orgasm
rides outwards to impregnate the void, the Crone
rises with a great roaring cackle and I stand, hurling
the Great Stag across the stones like a rag.

Short, spikey, witchy hair, mouth stretched in a
ferocious grin, eyes burning with the wisdom of life
and death, an eternity of beginnings and endings, I
reach out my hands and gather the seething energies
released from the joining, entwining them with
the power thundering through the vortex pumped
towards me by the circle, holding it all within my
being as it builds into an intolerable crescendo and I
can hold it no longer. Then, with a mighty sweep of

my arms, I point gnarled fingers at the panting Stag, focusing the colossal forces, hurling them at him, shouting in a thunderous voice *BE GONE!*

And in a blinding *flash!* the Great Stag and Apollo, God of Light, vanishes.

෴෴෴෴෴෴

## CHAPTER TWENTY

I awoke to filtered light, birdsong, and the sensation of someone sawing the top of my head off with a breadknife.

With a groan, I turned away from the light and all too quickly reaped the consequences, throwing up violently into a deep bowl held by steady weathered hands. Someone gently wiped my lips and then a cool damp cloth was laid over my eyes, blotting out the horrible light driving splinters into my brain. And I descended, sickeningly, back into darkness.

I awoke and the dance repeated itself. Violent pain and retching followed by soothing cloths and the sensation of someone stroking my hair. Then I fell off the edge of the world back into the abyss.

The next time the light was . . . tolerable. A dark shadow swam into view and I was gently lifted. Then a cup was pressed to my lips.

I drank. Whatever it was tasted awful and my head spun, feeling like it was going to fall off. Then I was eased back onto soft pillows, and this time I slept and dreamed—dreamed of grey clouds and storm-tossed seas and crows, black crows dancing across the sky calling to each other across the waves.

The next time my eyes opened it was to a grey pearlescent dawn.

The light was soft and my head felt like something I wouldn't mind keeping around. Tentatively I looked to my right. Kalista was asleep in one of the little wooden chairs in Apollo's cabin, sitting before a long-dead fire, hands folded in her lap, chin to her chest, snoring.

I tried to sit up but my arms seemed made of cotton batten, useless fuzzy things that lay on the blankets incapable of doing anything but twitching occasionally. My mouth tasted unimaginably foul, pasty and dry. *Water!* Water suddenly seemed the most tempting substance on the planet.

The black-clad figure started and Kalista looked straight into my eyes. Instantly she got up and poured a cup of water from the pitcher and came over to the bed, lifting me with one strong arm, placing the cup to my lips. *My God, what's wrong with my body?* I wondered as I drank, the cool liquid softening the tissues of my mouth and parched raw throat.

Nothing had ever tasted so good and I looked my thanks to my nurse as she lay me back down. And before I knew it I slept again.

⊗⊗⊗⊗⊗⊗⊗⊗

It was five days before I could finally sit up without wanting to puke or pass out. Another day before I could actually lift my arm and hold a cup without dropping it. And the morning I could actually make it out of bed to use the chamber pot Kalista had produced for me was a major victory.

Details of the ritual swam in and out of focus. But I didn't think much about it. It was too much effort. The doings and concerns of my former life seemed equally vague and unimportant.

My entire world centered around relearning how to use my body—just me, nobody else. And each new thing I accomplished, walking to the door and sitting on the bench outside, seeing a bird soar against the blue sky, hearing the frogs chirping in the valley below the cabin at night, feeling the sun warm on my face, was unbearably important and precious.

How was it possible I'd taken such things for granted before?

Time passed. And then, nine days after the ritual, Kalista brought me my backpack. I sat in the sun on the bench outside, pawing through the contents like a monkey examining a hotel bill. What were these things and why were they important? It wasn't until I discovered Spiros' car keys that a bell rang . . . my summons back to Earth.

Or perhaps my summons away.

I looked at the little pieces of pressed metal in my hand, suddenly grasping their significance. Spiros knew nothing of where I was or where his car was. I hauled out my cell phone and tried turning it on. Nothing.

Kalista came and stood in the doorway, watching me. I looked up at her, useless phone in one hand, keys in the other, all the questions I hadn't remembered until now to ask, questions I couldn't ask her because of the language barrier, bubbling to the surface.

Making soft clucking noises, shaking her head, she plucked the phone out of my hand, dropping it disdainfully back in the pack, her action and thoughts as clear as day. *What use are these dead things when you know so much of LIFE now, eh, little one?*

And suddenly the two realities—my regular life and my life with Apollo and the staggering forces I'd worked with in the circle—collided with a shock that sent me reeling as I fully grasped the profane shallowness of my previous modern existence. And with the realization came a sudden overwhelming sense of loss.

Not the loss of Apollo . . . never Apollo. He was with me and in me . . . now and forever as much as breath filled my lungs and water filled the seas. No, it was the terrible loss of my ignorance that suddenly arose like a foul specter before me. I shrank away, physically squirming against the rough log wall, feeling a splinter drive into my shoulder blade. And I welcomed the small sharp pain because it was real and feeling it meant I was gloriously alive. The metal points of the car keys bit into my flesh as well.

How could I possibly go back? What was there to go back to? I lived in a harsh grey world filled with— what had Polymnia called us?—*dead machine-people* mucking around in self-important lives, thinking we knew what life was about when all the while we knew absolutely nothing.

Oh sure, science was giving us a powerful lens into the mysteries of existence. But almost no one was paying any attention. I groaned and closed my eyes, willing the whole mess to *go away!* Wishing the great Earth Mother would rise up and take me back home into Her bosom where I could dwell in the full light of darkness and never have to deal with anything in my old world ever again.

Wilting against the front wall of the cabin, I turned to Kalista's black form and wept into the solidness of her hip, clinging to her skirts, wailing in sorrow for myself and all the people living out their tired, uninspired lives—women, men and little children who would never be given the slightest chance to glimpse the raw, shattering power of existence they really embodied.

And as I wept in that moment of terrible understanding I finally grasped why Apollo had been so willing to sacrifice himself. What difference could it possibly make to a Deathless One to die, knowing the difference their actions might make?

I laughed and sobbed and shook until Kalista bodily plucked me off the bench, ushering me back inside, closing the cabin door, leaving my backpack on the ground outside in the sun.

∞∞∞∞∞∞∞

It was a long, slow hour's walk, but the next morning found me sitting on the hill above the temple outside the archaeological site boundary fence where Apollo and I first met, enjoying an unobstructed view of the stadium and tourist-packed precinct below.

Steady warm breezes blew in off the Sea

of Corinth, combing the early summer grasses. Somewhere close by a cuckoo was doing its famous song. And I lay back in the grass and warm sun, watching the seed heads wave in the wind overhead, feeling life come full circle.

As much as I wanted to stay at the cabin and live out the rest of my days as Kalista had lived hers, holding onto the torch of her knowledge, I knew I couldn't do it. I knew too much and cared too much about my world to not do everything I could to help it waken from its slumber.

Apollo had worked against the forces of time itself to jolt me from sleep. I couldn't pass the buck. Who was it said, "With great knowledge comes great responsibility?" Surely someone?

Swallows darted through the air, swooping hapless bugs and mosquitos into their beaks, glad for the nourishment they could take back to their babies squawking at home in their tiny feathered nests. Life feeding life. And suddenly the soundtrack from the movie *The Lion King* swelled dramatically in my head and I laughed. What was that line Apollo had quoted?

"Life is far too important to be taken seriously."

I could hear his voice now and I chuckled, eyes closed, imagining he was sitting next to me on the hillside, his brown fingers stripping the fuzzy layer off a stalk of grass, telling me some astounding thing or other.

When all of sudden I had a thought.

What if I simply told Apollo's story like it

happened?

I sat up abruptly.

What if I described how he bounded over the rocks towards me wearing those stylishly ripped jeans of his and that earth-shattering smile? How he sat down next to me, invading my space, poised to blow my world apart?

I closed my eyes again for a moment, feeling him sit down beside me. Watched him reach into his pocket for a piece of gum. Then I opened my eyes on the empty meadow and the sweeping valley view. Who cared if nobody believed it? The point was in the telling. That was my promise. No more.

Sitting in the sun, remembering the story as it had unfolded, a smile touched my heart and my lips. When out of seeming nowhere a crow suddenly tore the skies apart, landing on a rock not two feet away with a thunderous triumphant *CAW!!*

My spirits rose as the bird cocked its head from side to side, bright beady eyes gazing intently into mine. *CAW!!!!* And I laughed, remembering Apollo's promise to send me a sign if all was well.

I leaned close to Apollo's messenger and whispered, "Tell him to travel well. And that I can wait as long as it takes to see him again."

And watched as the bird turned and flew away.

֎֎֎֎֎֎֎֎